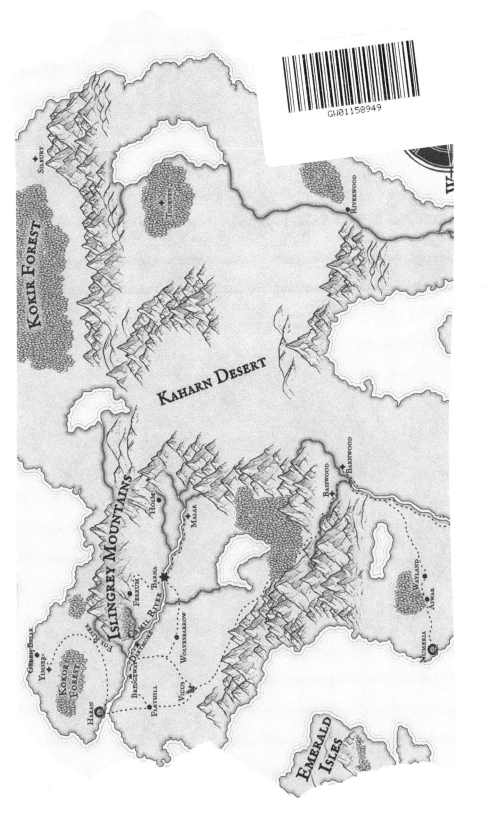

TALES & TREASURE

ROB MORTELL

For Lindsey
Here's to the stories we've shared and the stories yet to come

A NEW STORY

Vatis

Vatis stepped over the corpse of a man he didn't think could die. He was almost sad. There were only a handful of stories he knew that didn't end with death, and those unfortunate people usually begged for release at some point.

Maybe that's how all stories should end.

Vatis sat between the inviting roots of a willow tree and retrieved his diligently wrapped journal from his tattered pack. It was swathed in thin but pliable canvas held together by an emerald bow. He placed the covered journal on his lap and closed his bag. Its frayed drawstring hung limply over a hole that wasn't supposed to be there but had persisted in its development from unnoticeable to coin-size.

What's his story?

Vatis carefully pulled his quill and ink from a compartment sewn to the front of his pack. The bright blue quill had lost most of its downy barbs from constant rubbing against a troublesome wart on his right middle finger, leaving a feather that looked more like a sparse pine tree than part of a blue jay's wing. He closed the compartment, tightened the silver latch, then pressed the buckle's tongue into another hole that wasn't there when he bought it. But as the thread in the extra compartment loosened, the strap was no longer tight enough with its original punch holes. So, Vatis improvised. He punched a new hole, a jagged thing that was more of a slit than a hole, but it did its job.

Vatis dipped his quill into his nearly depleted bottle of ink. *I'll need to replenish this soon. Where's the next town? Basswood or Barnwood. I can never remember which one is west of the river.*

He pressed a small dot onto his palm. It joined dozens of faintly washed dots marking the inside of his left hand. He hated wasting paper.

Where do I begin?

Gunnar had been everything a hero was supposed to be: loyal, brave, strong, and even intelligent. Well, more astute than most of the so-called heroes Vatis had encountered lately. His hands wanted to write, but his mind didn't have the same desire.

It's been two days. What am I missing? Vatis stood, scratched his head, and walked back to the corpse. He checked Gunnar's pockets for the third time. The back of his hand rubbed against the cold, tough skin. It felt almost like armor; unfortunately, Gunnar's actual armor hadn't been able to stop the arrow, whose broken shaft still stuck a few inches out of his chest. *This wasn't how his story was supposed to end.*

Vatis didn't want to interfere with the outcome of any story. He was an impartial observer, recording the deeds of Emre's finest heroes as well as a few villains. *But sometimes the protagonist needs a little nudge in the right direction,* he thought as he returned to his journal. The dark leather cover was now blacker than its original hazel color. He flipped to the first page. It read:

Stories of Emre

Vatis cringed as he saw a faint black line in the bottom right-hand corner of the page. One too many cups of ale had led to a careless night of writing, tarnishing his beautiful, flowing script. He took pride in his penmanship. His fellow bards were always envious of his handwriting, but it had been a long time since he was active in the guild. He wasn't sure if they'd be envious of him now, not anymore.

Squirming, Vatis moved past his mistake and flipped through the book. He loved the way the paper felt against his thumb. He stopped skimming his notes of Gunnar when he came to a page detailing their encounter with a bear outside Numeria. *Heroic, yes, but story-worthy, no.*

The next page recounted Gunnar saving a drowning boy in the Camil River. *Now, that might be a start – a good introduction.* Vatis continued his recollection of Gunnar, flipped to a blank page, and wrote:

Gunnar-The-Good
Killed by an errant arrow near Wayland. A decent man with a good heart.

That was all he could come up with. The rest would have to wait for another day. Vatis had followed Gunnar for half a year, and all he had was one line. *Waste of time,* he thought as he lifted his pen from the page, biting the end of his quill.

The problem with Gunnar's story is the stakes. He was a city guard without a city to guard. If only we made it to Barna, if he could have entered the King's service. He could have been something. I have no idea what that something is, but more than a single sentence in the Stories.

Vatis blew on the wet line of script, packed his writing supplies away, and like he did so often, he waited for ink to dry. A thin cloud shaped remarkably like a snake, open jaw and all, drifted through a pink sky. Two wired-tail swallows flew in intricate circles around the lone willow tree at the pond's edge. Now that Vatis had backed away from Gunnar, the birds swooped down to feast on an assortment of insects that often gathered near dead things. The larger swallow's unique wire-like tail drifted behind his blue body. It landed on a branch amongst the cascading leaves of the willow. The smaller swallow did not have its wired tail yet, but its brown head gave it away as a juvenile, not a female.

He dabbed the text with his finger – *dry. Good.* He carefully closed his journal, wrapped it like a mother swaddling a newborn baby, tied a perfect bow, and gently placed it in his pack. The sun was setting, and he did not like to be far from the road at night. *I can persuade a thief to spare my life; bears and wolves aren't as gullible.* Not that he had much luck with thieves, but he was still alive, and that had to count for something.

It was a three-day walk to Basswood or Barnwood; Vatis was pretty sure it was Basswood. He hadn't been there in decades. He hadn't been to a town in weeks. Gunnar had been trying to track down a missing girl in the marshlands northeast of Wayland. So, of course, this meant Vatis had also been wandering around marshes and bogs for the better half of a fortnight. They never found the girl. Though they might have, if that hunter had not thought they were bandits. He was still impressed that Gunnar was able to dodge the next arrow, kill the hunter, and walk almost five miles with a broken arrow in his chest. *He certainly was stubborn,* Vatis thought, scratching the itchy stubble on his cheek as he remembered their final moments together.

"Is there really nothing when it ends? Just darkness?" Gunnar asked.

Vatis clutched Gunnar's shaking, blood-stained hand. "I don't know,"
he said honestly. "I certainly hope not."

Gunnar's teeth chattered. "Me too."

4

"It's just another adventure," Vatis said, leaning closer. A smile crept through shivers and convulsions onto Gunnar's cracked lips. His dirty blond hair covered his cloudy eyes. "Vatis," Gunnar coughed. The words came slower. "I know..."

And then Gunnar died.

What did you know?

Vatis closed his fingers into a fist, kissed the back of his hand, and gently tapped Gunnar's forehead – a ceremonial gesture they used in Gunnar's hometown. Gunnar deserved a better death; he deserved to be remembered; he deserved to be buried, but Vatis didn't have anything to bury him with. His body would provide the ecosystem of the small pond with essential nutrients. There are worse ways to be put to rest.

"Goodbye, Gunnar. Good luck on your next adventure." Vatis said, hiking back to the road. He put the fading orange sun on his left shoulder and walked until he couldn't anymore.

Time to find a new story.

Embers smoldered in his makeshift campfire, thrown together seconds before exhaustion overcame him. Exhaustion was Vatis's only constant companion, the one thing he could count on as the sun set on Emre each night. He didn't know where he would sleep. He didn't know what he would eat. He didn't know whose story he would chase, but Vatis knew when the bitter dark of night arrived – he would be exhausted. As far as company went, exhaustion wasn't that bad. It was undoubtedly better than boredom.

It had been three full days of hard walking, no rest, no writing, and no stories. A deep, sharp pain suddenly accompanied his exhaustion as he rolled onto his back. He grasped at the pain unsuccessfully. His hand was unable to provide the slightest relief as his fingertips teased at a reprieve. He stretched further, almost providing the necessary counter-pressure, but before he could, a sharper pain coursed through his shoulder, sending him back onto his stomach. Perhaps it was a stroke of luck. At least the pain in his shoulder was consolable. His arms trembled as he pushed himself upright.

Vatis stretched gingerly, careful not to extend too far. He rubbed his aching shoulder and brushed the dust from his once-white shirt—somewhere birds sang their morning song. Vatis whistled back, echoing their tune flawlessly. He could identify birds by their sweet, chirping melodies. The high-pitched, bouncy song surrounding him, like a cheerful laugh mocking his pain, could be none other than the common wren. Their songs could be heard throughout Emre and woke him pleasantly on many occasions.

An hour later, the road transitioned from barely recognizable, trampled-down grass to a remarkably well-kept dirt path, which meant only one thing: he was getting close to civilization and opportunity. It was time to act. It was time to become Vatis-of-the-Road, the jovial, carefree bard whose antics teetered dangerously close to annoyance on many occasions. Of the characters he played, Vatis-of-the-Road was his favorite. For a day, he could forget about his troubles and simply meet new people and tell stories. What else would a traveling bard want?

An arrow-shaped sign reading Basswood was affixed crookedly to a rotting lamppost. One of the wrens landed atop the swaying lantern that looked about one bird away from falling. Vatis kicked dirt into the air and forced himself to smile. He pushed thoughts of Gunnar's death to the back of his mind like an experienced executioner. The journey had taken its toll on him, and he had difficulty getting into character. *Come on*, Vatis thought, rubbing his temples. He could feel the oil on his hair and skin. *I need a bath.* Vatis continued various tricks he had to get in character. He slapped his right cheek three times; that didn't work. He opened his eyes wide like his eyelids would burn his retinas if he allowed them to close; that didn't work. Finally, when everything else failed, Vatis sang:

Running through the garden
Skipping by the trees
Where is she hiding?
Where could she be?
Is she in the window?
Is she in the hall?
Ah! There!
In a bright blue dress
Coming for us all

Hopping in the castle
Twirling through the hall
Where is she hiding?
Where could she be?
Is she in the kitchen?
Is she in the wall?
Ah! There!
In a dark red dress
Hunting for us all

Running through the stable
Hiding in a stall
Where is she hiding?
Where could she be?
Where could she be?
Where could she be?
Ah!

Vatis danced in coordination with the silly melody children sang while playing hide-and-seek. It worked. He was Vatis-of-the-Road. His thighs and calves burned as he crested a long hill, but when he reached the top, he continued his jig in rhythm with the tune.

"Basswood," Vatis said to himself, changing his voice slightly to test the pitch before he met anyone. "The city of broken promises." No one called Basswood the city of broken promises, but Vatis thought it had a nice ring to it. Vatis-of-the-Road loved to add these types of details to towns, cities, landmarks, and people – they added flavor to the world in his head.

An immense bridge adorned with stone bears spanned a quick-moving river before turning into the main road where Basswood's shops were located. Two guards in polished green armor vetted a short line of travelers seeking entrance. Vatis skipped into the line of what looked like two merchants, a husband and wife, and a hunter carrying various pelts over his shoulder.

"Basswood, the city of broken promises," Vatis repeated as he stepped into the line.

The tall, muscular hunter scowled at Vatis, stepped forward, and let out an exaggerated sigh. He was huge, larger than Gunnar, and carried the longest bow Vatis had seen; its thick dark wood looked almost like steel.

"What a lovely day. Hello. I'm Vatis, Vatis-of-the-Road. What's the story behind those pelts and that bow?" Vatis asked with a graceful gesture toward the hunter. "You see, I'm a traveling bard."

The hunter turned with speed that Vatis did not think possible for a man of his size. "None of your business," he said, reaching for a dagger sheathed on his hip. His hard, scarred face issued one of the most frightening threats Vatis had ever received, and he'd been threatened a lot.

"Understood," Vatis said, holding up his hands and cowering into the chest of an elderly woman who had filed in behind him. *Now, this man might have a story worth telling.* "Ah, sorry, ma'am."

The hunter huffed and stepped forward as the guards ushered up the next travelers. Vatis followed but kept his distance, listening to the guards question the couple in front of the hunter.

"What brings you to Basswood?" one of the guards asked the husband and wife.

"We are passing through on our way to Barna. We were hoping to stay at the inn," the man said with his arm around the woman.

On your way to Barna, you're a long way off, Vatis thought.

"Where are you coming from?" the guard said.

"Numeria, sir," the man answered.

"And what business would a couple from Numeria have in Barna?"

"Ah, well, that's a matter of some discretion, sir. We … we have business with the King. I assure you we will be no trouble. No trouble at all. We only plan to stay the night."

Business with the King, that could be interesting. Vatis desperately wanted to go to Barna. He dreamed of performing at the King's Tourney, but he couldn't even muster the courage to perform in one of the qualifying events. For now, his stories would have to live in his mind and small uncrowded taverns. Vatis rubbed his eyes to release himself from his daydream.

"What is the blacksmith's name in Numeria?" the other guard asked.

"The blacksmith," the man said, scratching his chin. "I don't have many needs for a blacksmith, but I believe his name is Alvor."

The guards nodded at each other. "Welcome to Basswood. Over there with the lantern hanging in the doorway, that's the Rau Tavern. There should be room for you."

"Thank you, sir, thank you," the man said as they gathered their belongings and walked across the bridge.

"Next," the guard said.

The hunter stepped forward. "What brings you to Basswood? Oh, it's you," the guard said.

The hunter pointed at the pelts on his shoulder. "You want to sell those, Elbert?" The hunter nodded fiercely.

"That's all?" the guard asked.

Elbert. There's a start. He must be from nearby, Vatis thought.

The hunter nodded sideways as if he was saying yes and no simultaneously. "Fine, just stay away from Ember. She wants nothing to do with you," the guard said as his voice cracked on the empty threat. "Next."

The hunter marched across the bridge, and Vatis stepped forward.

"What brings you to…"

Vatis cut off the guard's initial question. "Ah, Basswood, the city of broken promises."

"What? This is not the city of broken promises. No one calls it that," the shorter guard said.

Vatis pointed at the hunter halfway across the bridge. "Well, I'm sure that fellow will do more than sell his pelts, so there is one broken promise already."

The guard ignored Vatis's observation. "What brings you to Basswood?" he said. He glared through the narrow slit in his faded emerald armor.

"I'm but a simple bard seeking an audience and shelter," Vatis said, puffing out his chest before punctuating his statement with a perfectly executed, ball-worthy bow.

The guards looked at each other. Vatis could almost hear their brows furrow in confusion inside their helms. Then, they each nodded, trying to guess what the other was thinking. The shorter guards spoke first. "How long do you plan on staying?"

"Only the night, my friends. If you are off duty, you should come by the inn. I've got quite the story to tell."

"Where are you coming from?" the shorter guard asked.

Vatis smiled. "The road."

The guard grunted. "Where did you last perform?"

"Wayland."

"Aye, what inn?" The tall guard said, stepping forward.

Vatis thought for a moment. *What was that inn called? Red something. Ah, yes.* "The Red Fox," Vatis said confidently.

The guards shrugged, looked at each other again, and tilted their heads like a scale balancing. 'You may enter. Welcome to Basswood," the taller guard said reluctantly. "Stay out of trouble," he added.

"I promise."

Vatis skipped across the bridge, humming his song. The guards on the opposite end of the bridge gave him the same unsure look as the two who let him into the city, but they allowed him to carry on. Tall wooden buildings lined a well-kept stone road. A shop with a strange triangular sign caught his eye–Trivial Distractions. He curiously approached the building; a worn piece of parchment was nailed to the front:

The bird is
NOT FOR SALE

"Interesting," Vatis said as he danced into the shop. There must be a story there.

The musty scent of old books immediately brought a smile to Vatis's face. He didn't have to act. It was his favorite scent in the world. One day he would have a library of his own with well-kept books that earned an intoxicating scent after years on a bookshelf. A shopkeeper wore thick, black-rimmed eyeglasses, so thick that Vatis doubted the man could even see. He looked up from behind a neatly organized desk containing various jars, books, and two stacks of parchment. A glass jar containing two dragonflies sat on top of a book called "The Lost Forest."

"What do you want?" the shopkeeper said, returning to his document review.

"The Lost Forest, that's one of my favorites," Vatis said.

The shopkeeper looked up from his documents; his long eyelashes flickered against the murky lens of his glasses as if he were seeing the customer for the first time. His bushy grey eyebrows furrowed then rose as the corners of his dry, blistered lips turned slightly upwards. "You know 'The Lost Forest'?" he asked.

There we are, a warmer greeting. I bet he doesn't get many customers who can read in Basswood. "Know it. Ha. I've read it a dozen times," Vatis said. "Some believe it's a true story; that somewhere in the far northeast, there's a forest with magical creatures. I don't know if I believe it, but maybe someday I will try to find it. Don't mind me. I'm just an old man with childish dreams."

"You don't look that old," the shopkeeper said, adjusting his glasses.

Vatis forced himself to laugh. "It's not how you look. It's how you feel."

"Aye, so they say. 'The Lost Forest' is a children's tale, but I enjoy reading it now and again," the shopkeeper said.

"There's a lot of truth in children's tales."

"Aye. So, what brings you into my shop?"

"I want to see the bird," Vatis said, looking around the cozy, candle-lit shop.

"She's not for sale," the shopkeeper said quickly. His interest in Vatis seemed to dwindle, and he scanned his documents slowly, marking an "x" in the bottom right corner before moving them to the neighboring pile.

"I don't want to buy the bird. I just want to see her. A bird must be something special for you to nail that sign to the front of your door. Why else would people continually ask to buy a bird?" Vatis said.

"She is something special for a wren." The shopkeeper bent down and brought up a black birdcage. Perched on a wooden bar inside was a common wren. It looked almost identical to the dozens of birds that he whistled along with this morning, unremarkable brown feathers over a tan underbelly, except its beak was gold, not a pale yellow, but gold like a king's crown. Vatis whistled its morning song, and the bird cocked its head back and forth, listening. It flapped its wings excitedly when Vatis finished and echoed the tune.

"Where did you learn to whistle like that?" the shopkeeper asked.

"It's just something I picked up on the road. I have spent many mornings in the company of wren; their song is one of my favorites. She certainly has an interesting beak. I have never seen one like that. Is it natural?"

"It is," the shopkeeper said. "I found her outside my bedroom window one morning. She has been something of a good luck charm since, but the beak isn't even the most impressive part." He whistled sharply to get the bird's attention. "Heppni, say good morning."

"Good morning," the wren squawked; morning sounded like marning.

Vatis's eyebrows raised as he bent closer to the cage. "That is impressive. Does she say anything else?"

"A few other phrases, but she is best at saying good morning."

"Good marning," Heppni repeated. "Good marning."

"Ha, that's terrific. I can see why people would want to buy her," Vatis said. He reached for his belt and pulled out a worn leather coin purse.

"She's not for sale," the shopkeeper said defensively as he pulled the cage behind the desk.

"I understand," Vatis said, holding out an affirming hand. "I want to buy your copy of 'The Lost Forest.' It has been a long time since I read it, and I feel nostalgic today. How much?"

"Ah," the shopkeeper paused. "It's not really for sale either, but I could part with it for ten Kan."

"Seven."

"Ten."

"Will you go to nine? I need enough coin to stay at the Rau tonight," Vatis said.

"Aye, I can do nine," the shopkeeper said as he pulled the book out from under the jar of dragonflies. The glittering azure bugs fluttered around as their container jostled back and forth.

Vatis counted out nine Kan. His purse was nearly empty, well, the purse he carried on his belt. Only a few coins rattled as he reattached it. He picked up the book and opened it to the first page. A large drawing of a tree surrounded by a circle of perfectly round stones sat above the title: "The Lost Forest." He smiled and tucked the book into his bag.

"Thank you. It was a pleasure meeting you and Heppni. When I am back in town, I expect to be able to have a conversation with her." The shopkeeper laughed, and Vatis bowed as he walked backward out the door. It was time to go to the tavern, where Vatis-of-the-Road shined brightest.

A STROKE OF LUCK

Vidmar

"Why did I take this job?" Vidmar said, wading waist-high in sewage on the outskirts of Basswood.

The smooth, slimy floor of the man-made pond slid underneath his bare feet as he shuffled along, searching for a ring he knew he would never find. The clothespin pinching his nose shut hardly helped contain the acrid stench of urine and fecal matter, but it was better than nothing. Yesterday, he didn't bring anything to cover his nose and nearly passed out before he even stepped into the thick, green-brown water. Today, he arrived prepared and continued his course, systematically shuffling back and forth to cover every inch of the small pond. He rounded the corner on his third pass when he kicked something hard.

"Please," Vidmar said, bending down.

He carefully lowered himself deeper into the water, stretching his neck like a turtle coming up for air as he searched the floor with his hand. The thick slime made it nearly impossible to grab the object. Finally, after several unsuccessful attempts and a great deal of cursing, Vidmar brought his prize to the surface. A smooth, ultra common, not-at-all-rare rock. He screamed. Birds scattered out of a nearby pine tree, and he threw the stone at them, but as he threw, he lost his footing on the pond floor and fell backward into the waste.

He scrambled to get out, gasping for air as he resurfaced. After he regained his breath, he yelled again. Waste dripped from his nose into his open mouth. He spat before slamming his fist into the water, splashing slimy liquid high into the air. He dropped to his knees. His right knee landed on something sharp. Pain reverberated through his thigh into his hip, but he didn't dare move. "Please, please, please." He said as he bent down to search again.

This time, he emerged holding a silver ring with a large topaz stone. "Fucking Darkness. I found it."

Vidmar laughed as he slid his feet timidly along the pond floor, careful not to fall into the waste and lose his prize. He waded to the shore where his clothes sat and placed the ring next to his leather jacket. His pack lay open on its side, with a few of his limited possessions spilling out near the edge of the pond. A small stone with intricate gold markings teetered on the edge. That was too close. Vidmar could feel his heart in his throat. He put the stone in the bag, pushed it further away from the pond, took several steps sideways, and pulled himself out of the water. He did not want any of the waste getting onto his only set of clothes, so he laid on the shore, naked and exhausted.

Ember's home was a short walk from the pond, just far enough that the smell only reached her home when the wind was blowing southwest, which, fortunately for Ember, rarely happened in Basswood.

She sat on a rocking chair on her porch, knitting what looked like socks or a small hat. "Oh my," she said as she saw Vidmar approach. "Oh my, you look horrible, oh, and you smell even worse." She had a glum expression on her face. Yesterday, she hugged him despite the mess, hoping that he had her ring. Vidmar had thought about her look of disappointment all night. It was the only reason he was back today. I would have made it much farther in this world if it wasn't for my damned conscience.

Vidmar rolled his eyes. The waste still dripped from his hair onto his shoulders, leaving faint streaks as the liquid cascaded down the length of his torso. He was naked but covered himself by carrying his clothes in front of him, the clothespin still attached to his nose. "It's like I went diving in a pond full of shit for some old women's ring," Vidmar said, wiping sewage off his shoulder.

"Did you find it?" Ember said eagerly.

"I'm back at your house, midday, covered in shit because I didn't find it," Vidmar said, tossing the ring towards Ember.

She jumped up in nervous excitement, dropping her carefully knitted garment. The ring bounced off her palms and ricocheted towards her feet. "Are you trying to lose it again? This ring is more valuable than your life," she said as she picked the ring up off the ground.

"Pa used to say, 'If it hits you in the hands, you should catch it,'" Vidmar said with a smile. "But there you go, one family heirloom returned safe and sound, although it might never smell the same again." Vidmar unplugged his nose and gagged. "Same goes for me. If you draw me a bath, I'll take five Kan off the price." Vidmar hated these bounty-board jobs, but he needed the money. He was completely broke and wouldn't make it back to Haran without money. Haran. Vidmar shivered at the thought of returning empty-handed. Not again.

"Cold?" Ember asked, smiling. Her tongue poked out of the hole in her teeth. "There is no chance I'm letting you in my home.

Take off three, and I'll give you a few buckets of warm water. You can rinse off back there," Ember said.

"Two and a bar of soap with the buckets," Vidmar said, replugging his nose with the clothespin. He winced as the wood pinched his sore skin.

"Deal," Ember said, looking at her recovered ring. "I'll be honest. I would have let you rinse off for free after bringing my ring home, but a deal's a deal."

"Damnit," Vidmar laughed.

After seven buckets of warm water and nearly a whole bar of soap, Vidmar's skin was raw and pink, but he no longer smelt like a cow's ass. He dressed and collected his payment from Ember, forty-eight Kan; his usual rate of forty Kan for finding lost objects, a negotiated ten extra for swimming through a pond of shit, and minus two to smell slightly better than a farmhand after a hard day's work.

With his purse as full as it had been in months and a storm rolling in, Vidmar walked into town towards the Rau Tavern, one of his most frequent stops when he passed through Basswood, but an impulse sent him to Trivial Distractions first. A gust of wind slammed the thick wooden door closed behind Vidmar; glass jars rattled on the desk, nearly falling onto the floor.

"Gil, Heppni, it's been too long," he said.

"Would you believe it, Hep, the treasure hunter is back? We heard you were in town yesterday, thought you forgot about us," the shopkeeper said, pulling the birdcage onto his desk.

"How could I forget about you?" Vidmar said, leaning close to Heppni's cage. He scratched underneath Heppni's beak and began searching the shelves of herbs, jars, and miscellaneous trinkets. The wren gently cooed as if urging Vidmar to come back and continue.

"Most people do."

Vidmar smiled. "You two are the most interesting things in a hundred miles—a talking bird and Gil, the merchant or shopkeeper. I'm not exactly sure I know what you are."

"Just Gil. Are you looking for anything in particular?" Gil said, joining the search.

"Got any new books?" Vidmar asked.

"Actually," Gil said excitedly. "I just happened to save one for you. I don't get a lot of folks in here asking about books, except for this strange, gangly-looking bard who came in a few hours ago—took my only copy of The Lost Forest, but he paid double. Let's see. Where did I put it?" Gil rifled through drawers in his desk, flinging loose papers into the air as he searched. "Where is it?" He continued his frantic search like he was digging up a buried treasure. "Ah, here it is." He blew some dust off the worn cover and handed it to Vidmar.

"The Secrets of the Kaharn Desert," Vidmar read aloud as he examined the book. "Very interesting. I've never seen this book before—quite the find, Gil. How did you come by it?"

"A woman traded it to me for a new shirt, three balls of yarn, a knife, and a single Kan," Gil said, sticking his chest out high, obviously proud of the deal he made. "Can you believe it?"

"What did this woman look like?" Vidmar asked.

"I couldn't see her face. She wore a long black cloak and kept the hood over her face. She was in and out faster than Heppni can say good morning."

"Good marning," the wren repeated.

Gil smiled and scratched the back of the bird's head through the cage before dropping in a handful of seeds. The bird fluttered off its post and happily gobbled up its reward.

It can't be her. Vidmar raised his eyebrows. "Let me know if this cloaked woman ever comes by again," Vidmar said, watching Heppni peck at the seeds. Then, he turned his attention back to the book in his hand. "How much?"

"For anyone else, I'd charge twenty, but for you, I could part with it for fifteen," the shopkeeper said.

"Thirteen and a ball of the same yarn that woman bought," Vidmar said.

"You're lucky. I've only got one spool left, but I can't part with the book for less than fifteen. Although, I am willing to throw the yarn in, free of charge," Gil said, placing the yarn on top of his desk.

"Deal," Vidmar said, carefully setting the yarn and book into his ragged traveling sack. "It's always good to see you, Gil. I don't know when I will be back in town."

Gil cut him off. "We know. Take care, Vidmar, and stay out of trouble."

Vidmar nodded and walked out of the shop.

Rain poured on the muddy street—ankle-deep puddles formed in wagon tracks and old footprints. Vidmar weaved across the road jumping over the expanding puddles. A bright flash of light illuminated the dark path. The thunderous boom that followed nearly startled Vidmar into the water behind him, but he was done swimming for the day, maybe for the rest of his life. All he wanted was a warm fire and a strong drink, and the Rau Tavern had plenty of the latter. He shook the excess water off like a dog after a bath and entered the tavern.

The smell of roast chicken and ale floated between dark wood beams and small circular tables. A hazy fog of pipeweed wafted over the mantel and around the bar, hanging like a cloud above the patrons, who crowded around a thin man with unmistakably road-worn clothing. A bard or a peddler? In Basswood? Vidmar thought. The man was clean-shaven, his long brown hair tucked behind his ears. Numerous lines around his hazel eyes hinted that he was older than he appeared; dark bags revealed his exhaustion.

Whatever he was, he captivated the audience so much that no one besides Rane, the bartender, noticed Vidmar. A table with a collection of empty mugs and two missing stools stood close enough to the fire to keep warm but far enough from the group to remain unnoticed. Vidmar motioned Rane with two fingers, a practiced gesture of tavern frequenters that could mean anything from "hello" to "ale" to "goodbye." In this instance, it meant both "hello" and "ale." Rane translated it perfectly. He brought a large mug over, sliding it onto the table. The bartender let go too early and the ale nearly toppled over if not for Vidmar's reaction.

"Sorry," Rane whispered as he absently wiped the table with a rag tucked into his apron. He gathered the empty mugs and retreated behind the bar, never taking his eyes off the mystery man. Vidmar sipped his ale and listened as the man began telling a story.

"Montalvo was like any other man, indistinguishable from commoners and the wealthy alike. Place him in a crowd of beggars, and he'd fit in, give him elegant clothing, and he could attend the finest ball in Barna," the apparent bard said.

Vidmar raised his eyebrows at the mention of Montalvo. Not many people know that name anymore. Who is this bard? He could be useful. What other stories do you know? He thought, fidgeting with the gold-marked stone in his pocket. Vidmar drank his ale, observed the eager crowd, listened to the story, and waited for his chance.

MONTALVO-THE-KIND

Vatis

Vatis felt years younger, which made his job easier; the characters and performances were always better when well-manicured. Well, other than the beggar he played in Numeria, he was not desperate to play Gron again, not after the dungeon incident. Vatis shivered, trying to shake those thoughts out of his head. A long bath and a shave rejuvenated his aching muscles and gnarly appearance, but the prospect of performing tonight genuinely excited and terrified him. He hadn't been in front of a crowd in months.

What story shall I tell? Vatis thought as he changed into his only clean shirt – an azure-colored garment with a raven embroidered over his heart. It was his last performance-worthy shirt. He brushed his hair behind his ears, fighting through several knots. *What would the people of Basswood want to hear?* Vatis rarely took suggestions from his audiences. He knew which stories to tell.

He pulled his trousers up over his waist, nearly to his navel, cringing as the cloth passed over his protruding hip bones. The pant legs rose to the middle of his shins, their frayed ends hanging like half-broken branches. He tightened his belt as far as possible, but his pants were still loose. *Perhaps The Merchant of Dartmore. It's a classic tale.* Vatis thought for a moment while tying his boots. *No. That doesn't feel right. How about one of Mia-The-Maiden's heroic tales?* He continued his debate as he tried to smooth out the wrinkles in his clothes.

Vatis straightened his collar, checked his buttons, and adjusted his sleeves; his performance preparations were nearly finished. *I could tell them the story of The Lost Forest,* he thought, looking at the book on his bed. *But, no, that doesn't feel right either.* He rubbed his fingertip on a piece of charcoal, applying a thin layer to his eyelids. Vatis thought the makeup added a subtle layer to his performance. It was easier for a man of his slender frame to be frightening with his unnaturally dark eyes. He brushed his wiry mustache with his fingers; the charcoal also helped to hide a few of the white hairs that poked through. There was no mirror to check his work, but years of the same preparations had made him an expert. He knew how he looked.

The door creaked on its rusty hinges; floorboards whined beneath his feet. As he made his way down the stairs, the loose railing jiggled in his shaking hand. Vatis exhaled thrice, slowly, his breath joining the wind, whistling rhythmically through a slight crack in a window. *Montalvo,* he thought, humming the tune to a nearly forgotten song. He knew what he would perform tonight.

The pleasant murmur of conversation brought a smile to his face as Vatis-of-the-Road reemerged into the tavern's common room. Rain drummed on the roof, creating a pleasing melody with the whispered conversations. He walked past the low burning fire, the flames warming his exposed shins momentarily. Shadows cast from the stone hearth danced on the wall to his right. Vatis found a stool, pushing a half-empty glass toward the bartender. No one saw him, so he hummed–rather loudly at that. Still, no one noticed him, so he hummed louder.

"Would you quit that humming?" a patron from the opposite end of the bar called.

Vatis hummed more dramatically.

"I'm warning you," the bearded man yelled.

"Hmm, hmm, hmm," Vatis hummed in a deeper tone.

The stool screeched across the wood floor and toppled over with a loud thump. Thunder crashed outside the tavern echoing the room-silencing thud.

"All right, men enough," a commanding voice from behind the bar said. "Sit down, Graham. And you quit that damn humming."

"Montalvo, Montalvo, where did you go?" Vatis sang.

"Montalvo," the bartender said. "Why do I know that name?"

"Ah, most of us have heard the name. Montalvo-The-Kind. Montalvo-The-Lucky. Montalvo-The-Terrible. He was known by many. His name still carries weight even centuries later," Vatis said.

"Who was he?" Graham asked.

"Oh, you're interested in my song now that it has words," Vatis said.

"He sounds familiar, that's all."

"As he should. There was a time when every man, woman, and child in Emre knew his name."

Light burst into the tavern, briefly giving the shadows more dancing partners; a vicious boom followed, rattling the neatly arranged glasses by the bar. Graham picked his stool up off the floor, nodding his apology to the bartender. "Excuse me," he said as he set the stool closer to Vatis. "It sounds like you've got a story, and since we are stuck here," he gestured to the window, "how about you tell us about this Montalvo-The-Nice."

"Montalvo-The-Kind, and yes, he has a tragic story," Vatis said. "I could tell you … for an ale … or two." *A bard gets thirsty, after all.*

"Ha, fine, Rane get this would-be-bard an ale," Graham said. "For what it's worth, I'm sorry, long day at the forge."

"And I apologize for the humming. I was simply trying to get someone's attention." *And I've got them,* Vatis thought as his audience began to build.

Graham slapped Vatis on the shoulder. "Well, it worked."

Rane set a frothy, golden ale in front of Vatis. "Ah, you can't tell a story without a good ale," Vatis said, wiping foam out of his mustache with the back of his hand. Vatis's hand trembled as he raised the mug to his lips again. He slurped a long drink, his tense shoulders relaxing with each gulp. Nerves always fought a battle between his stomach and mouth before he performed in front of a crowd. Alcohol helped calm those nerves, or so he thought.

"Well, you got your ale. Now tell us about Montalvo," Rane said.

"We don't get many bards in Basswood these days," Graham added.

A few eavesdropping patrons pleaded for a performance from a nearby table.

"The audience grows," Vatis said. He took another drink. Sweat dripped from his brow despite the frigid night. "All right, I will tell you the story of Montalvo. Keep in mind, it is tragic, so don't get angry with me if you don't like how it ends."

Another flash of light, followed by an even louder bang, shook the tavern. "I guess the gods want you to start the story, too," Graham said.

"Well, I wouldn't want to anger the gods," Vatis said.

"Mon… Montalvo," Vatis said. He stumbled over the words. His lips quivered as he raised his mug for another drink. He wiped his mouth clean with the back of his hand and began again.

"Montalvo was like any other man, indistinguishable from commoners and the wealthy alike. Place him in a crowd of beggars, and he'd fit in, give him elegant clothing, and he could attend the finest ball in Barna. Wherever Montalvo went, good things followed. He passed through Vicus, and withered crops came back to life. He stayed a night in Haran, and the fishermen caught record hauls. He peddled wares in Yimser, and a dry well was suddenly refilled. Similar events followed Montalvo everywhere he went earning him his first nickname Montalvo-The-Lucky."

Vatis paused to take another drink, but his mug was empty. "Rane, was it? Can I have another?" Vatis asked.

The young, brown-haired bartender refilled the cup with a practiced efficiency that usually comes from work in a much busier tavern. "Thank you." Vatis diligently cracked the knuckles on each hand before taking a drink. A man sitting in the back of the crowd watched Vatis with an eagle eye. His hard, angular face set him apart from the other bystanders in the Rau Tavern. *Who are you?* Vatis took another drink and continued his story, pushing thoughts of the mysterious man aside.

"Montalvo-The-Lucky began to gain quite the reputation; however, one thing confused people. He never stayed in the same place for more than a day. Once, he visited a small mining town outside of Numeria. Within the first hour of his visit, a miner found a vein of iron ore so large it could have sustained the village for months if not years. The townspeople begged and pleaded with him to stay one more day.

'I wish I could,' he said. 'But there are more villages that could use my luck.'

Still, they continued to beg. 'Fine," he relented. 'One night.'

The townsfolk rejoiced. They danced and drank into the early hours of the morning, but Montalvo's demeanor grew grimmer with each passing hour. Finally, the sun rose, the miners returned to work, and tragedy struck. The long-standing mine collapsed, killing the men working inside and burying their recently found treasure."

Vatis paused, taking a moment to let the sudden turn take its toll. He sipped from his mug as the anticipation built amongst his audience.

"What happened next?" voices called from the growing crowd. "Come on, don't keep us waiting." *An eager crowd tonight*, Vatis thought, scanning the room. The man in the back showed no excitement, but his gaze never wavered. Vatis licked his lips, tasting the bitter combination of charcoal and ale. He continued.

"Devastation. The people could not comprehend how quickly their fortunes had turned.

'I must go before more tragedy strikes,' Montalvo cried.

'You mean this was your fault,' a newly made widow asked.

'I told you that I shouldn't stay,' Montalvo replied. 'Whenever I stay in one place too long, tragedy follows. Maybe if I return in a few years, I can bring another stroke of luck.'

The townsfolk cried. 'A few years. Our town will be lost by then. We lost our mine and most of our men; we have nothing. There must be something you can do,' they pleaded.

'I am no mage. The longer I stay, the more likely another tragedy will occur,' Montalvo said. 'I have to leave.'

The elderly man wept as he walked away from the town, vowing never to stay in the same place longer than one day again, but the damage was done, and this was how he first earned the name Montalvo-The-Terrible."

The patrons sat silently, awaiting more of the story. Vatis took another drink. The warmth of the ale flowed through his body, giving his limbs a pleasant tingling sensation. He took a deep breath and began again.

"In the years that followed, Montalvo stuck to his word. He passed through town after town delivering small miracles and selling miscellaneous trinkets. The people seemed to forget the mining incident, even dubbing him Montalvo-The-Kind as he never had a bad thing to say about anyone.

Before I continue, I should say something about this time in Emre. A terrible, bloody war led to a terrible, bloody king sitting on the throne, Geils Dallain. He was known for his harsh temper and even harsher punishments. When he sentenced a man to die, he did not send them to the gallows or the headsman. No, he had an iron dragon built upon a gigantic pyre in the square. This dragon was not a simple statue. It was hollow. A thick black door just big enough for a man to fit through faced the crowd. In as plain of terms as I can put it, the convicted man was thrown inside and was cooked alive. But that's not the worst part. The King had this monstrosity so well engineered that it sounded like a dragon roaring when the victim cried and screamed. King Dallain loved it. I will let you put together your conclusions as to what kind of a man can relish that gruesome of a punishment."

Vatis looked at the horrified faces before him. "I told you this was a dark story. Do you want me to continue?"

Graham looked at Rane, then downed his entire mug. "I'm going to need another before you continue," he said. "Same here," a few voices called from the back of the crowd.

Vatis sipped his ale while waiting for his audience to refill their cups. Rane smiled as he left a table of two young couples. They picked up their benches, moving closer to Vatis. A lopsided stack of bowls teetered in the center of their now-vacant table. The man in the back was gone. *Where did you go?* Vatis thought. He appeared at a new table with the same unrelenting stare a moment later. The tower of bowls must have obstructed his view. Vatis exhaled. He relaxed, knowing where the mystery man was sitting.

"Is everyone ready?" he said once it seemed like the crowd had settled into their chairs. "Good. Where was I? Ah yes, King Dallain had put fear into the people of Barna."

"In all his years of traveling, Montalvo never visited the capital city. He feared that the King would try to abuse his luck. But word of Montalvo's miracles had reached the King, and Geils Dallain was not a patient man. One morning, as he pushed his cart down the road a few miles outside Haran, a rider wearing polished steel armor branded with the King's dragon sigil approached him.

'Montalvo?' he asked.

'Indeed, I am,' Montalvo answered in his usual cheery fashion. 'How are you doing this fine day? Can I interest you in a candied apple? They're fresh.'

The strong guard grabbed the back of Montalvo's shirt and lifted him onto the back of the horse. 'The King has summoned you,' he said as they galloped away toward Barna.

As they approached the palace, people stopped and stared. 'Is that Montalvo-The-Kind?' they whispered as they rode by.

King Dallain welcomed Montalvo with open arms and unaccustomed enthusiasm.

'Is this the Montalvo I've heard so much about? Come, come. I've had a feast prepared in your honor,' the King said.

Montalvo was overwhelmed by the extravagance of the feast. The long wooden table was filled with more food than Montalvo had seen in months: an entire roast pig, whole chickens, dozens of varieties of bread and preserved meats, and bowls of fruits and nuts.

'This is too much, your Grace,' he said. 'I cannot guarantee miracles, but I appreciate your unrivaled kindness.'

The King dismissed the notion. 'Nothing is too much for Montalvo-The-Lucky,' the King replied.

As Montalvo guiltily ate a whole chicken, a midwife burst into the dining hall.

'Sir,' she said.

The King sprang to his feet.

'The Queen has given birth. It's a boy.'

You see, the King and Queen had been struggling to sire a boy. Four, well five, princesses were born. The last died shortly after birth.

'A boy,' the King yelled. 'I finally have a boy. I knew you would be the luck that I needed, Montalvo.'

The King departed with the midwife to see his firstborn son. While he was gone, Montalvo snuck handfuls of the preserved meats to the servants.

'Come. Eat this food. I fear it will go to waste,' he said as he invited them to the table. 'But be quick. I would not want the King to find you at his table when he returns.'

That meal with the castle's servants was the last time Montalvo would be truly happy. He told stories of his travels, all the miracles, and all the tragedies. 'Thank you for sharing this meal with me. Now return to your posts as I fear the King will return soon,' he said.

The King returned in a marvelous mood. Who could blame him? He had been desperate to secure his lineage for years."

Thunder crashed outside the Tavern. Vatis jumped in his seat, as did most of the audience, which had now grown to ten patrons. Even the man in the back jumped, though not as noticeable as the rest of the crowd. "God, that's a way to make a dramatic point," Vatis said. The crowd chuckled. He emptied his mug before continuing; Rane anticipated the refill this time.

"On the house," the bartender said.

"Why, thank you, Rane," Vatis said. "Let's continue, shall we?"

"The King returned to his dining hall, almost dancing with excitement.

'How's the prince, your Grace?' Montalvo asked.

30

'He is wonderful. He has my chin but my wife's eyes. He will make a fine king one day,' Dallain said.

He beamed with joy. At that moment, he seemed human, not like the monster many thought.

'I can't help but think this has something to do with your arrival,' the King said.

'Well, I don't know about that,' Montalvo said.

'Don't be so modest. I could use a source of good luck. Therefore, I am appointing you as a royal advisor. You will have lavish rooms in the palace with whatever amenities you desire,' the King proclaimed.

Montalvo bit his lip nervously. He had anticipated this kind of offer. It was an offer that you don't dare turn down. It was why he avoided the capital city. 'Your Grace, that is a tremendously generous offer,' Montalvo said before the King cut him off.

'Then you accept, wonderful.'

'Well, your Grace, I must decline. You see, I cannot stay in one place for too long, or my luck sours.'

The King looked puzzled. He wasn't used to denial. 'Nonsense, I'm sure that is a simple coincidence,' he said as the excitement from earlier teetered on the edge of anger.

'It's true, your Grace. I'm sure you've heard the story of Randall, the mining town outside Numeria,' Montalvo said.

'A true tragedy,' the King said. All happiness vanished from his expression leaving only a deathly cold stare. 'There are other, less comfortable rooms you could stay in.'

Montalvo knew he had no choice. 'I hope you are right, your Grace. I accept.'"

Vatis stretched his arms straight into the air turning slightly to crack his sore back. His audience was as attentive as ever. *Now, the climax.*

"For two days, news of no miracle or tragedy reached Montalvo. He began to think that maybe the King was right;

perhaps he wasn't cursed. But of course, Montalvo was correct; on the third day, fever tore through the city, afflicting many innocent civilians. Late that morning, the King burst into Montalvo's room.

'What witchcraft is this? Half of the city is infected. Undo this spell or suffer the consequences,' the King demanded.

Montalvo wept. 'Your Grace, I am no wizard. I am no mage. I am cursed, as I have told you. If you let me go, no more tragedies will befall your city.'

The King ran at the old man, grabbing him by the neck. He threw him against the cold stone wall. 'Liar. If this plague is not cured, no amount of magic will contain my wrath.'

Before the King stormed out of the room, he ordered three guards to ensure Montalvo didn't escape. There was nothing Montalvo-The-Kind or Montalvo-The-Lucky could do. It was Montalvo-The-Terrible's turn.

That night an ancient bridge over the Camil River collapsed, killing dozens and cutting off one of Barna's most important supply routes. At midnight King Dallain and his guards broke down the door to Montalvo's chamber.

'Now, you cut off our supply of medicine. What kind of warlock are you? Montalvo-The-Kind more like Montalvo-The-Killer. Guards bind him and take him to the dungeons,' the King commanded.

Montalvo pleaded. 'Let me go, Your Grace. Let me go, and no more tragedies will destroy your city.'

'Gag him. I don't want him to be able to utter another spell or lie,' the King said as he punched Montalvo in the gut."

A fit of coughing from a feeble-looking man beside the hearth interrupted Vatis momentarily. "Sorry," he grumbled. Vatis smiled as he watched the crowd eagerly awaiting his story. He felt euphoric, a warmth far superior to anything alcohol could provide. He took a moment to enjoy the silent expectancy.

"Montalvo was thrown into a dark, damp cellar with a ridged stone floor. His only light came from a tiny gap underneath a triple-locked iron door. There was no escape. He could only sit and wait for the next terrible event. He sat in darkness for what seemed like days, but he could not be sure how much time had passed. Finally, the heavy door opened, bringing forth a blinding light. In the doorway stood the silhouette of a tall man.

'Are you happy?' It took a moment for Montalvo to recognize the voice. It was the King. 'My son has caught your sickness.'

'I've told you, your Grace, I cannot stop these tragedies from happening. I can only provide solace if I leave the city and get as far away from here as possible.'

King brooded in silence as if contemplating Montalvo's release. 'I will not stomach any more of your lies. Cure my son by tomorrow morning, or it's the dragon for you.'

Montalvo dropped to his knees at the King's feet. 'Your Grace, I beg you do not kill me. The curse upon me will find another, and I do not wish this fate on anyone else. Let me go, and your son may live,' he cried.

'I told you, I have had enough of your lies. Cure my son, wizard, or die,' the King said as he slammed the heavy door shut. Montalvo clawed at the door's lock until his fingers bled. In the morning, he knew he would die, but worse yet, he knew dozens, if not hundreds, would die as well. Worse still, he knew someone was about to be invaded by one of Emre's worst curses."

The crowd shifted in their seats. The only sound in the tavern was the crackling fire in the hearth and rain drumming on the roof. The story consumed them.

"The king returned with the prince in his arms the following day.

'Look what you have done—my son. My only son has died because of you. Bring him back to life. Now,' the King wept.

Montalvo cried along with the King. 'I cannot, your Grace. I am no mage; I am cursed.'

The King was utterly helpless for the first time in his life. He stared at his cold son swaddled in a blue blanket hugging the tiny corpse like he was rocking him back to sleep. 'So be it. Guards bring Montalvo-The-Killer to the square and announce his execution.'

The guards roughly grabbed Montalvo's underarms and yanked him to his feet. 'Your Grace, I beg you do not do this. I'm profoundly sorry for the loss of your son, but I do not wish the curse upon anyone. Let me go. No one else needs to die.' Montalvo cried.

The King looked at the ragged old man with murderous eyes before turning to the guards. 'Remove his clothes.' The King said as he walked out of the dungeon.

'Please, no,' Montalvo pleaded one last time. The King didn't acknowledge the plea; he only searched his son's stiffening face for a sign of life. The guards stripped Montalvo of his already torn clothing and marched him, naked, toward his death. People stared, pointed, laughed, and even threw stones at him as the guards dragged him through the most public route to the square. The King, Queen, and Prince were waiting for Montalvo along with a starving crowd. The King held up his son for the people to see.

'This demon is who caused this plague rampaging through our city. He killed my son. Now he will suffer the consequences. I'm deeply saddened that I did not do this sooner. Perhaps I could have saved some of your family and friends or even my son.' The King gave the baby to the Queen and continued. 'Montalvo-The-Killer, you are sentenced to die. Do you have any last words?'

Tears ran down Montalvo's dirt-covered cheeks, splashing onto his bare chest. 'I'm sorry to you all, especially to one of you,' Montalvo's words were cut short as he was shoved into the menacing dragon-shaped oven. Friends, I will spare you the details of Montalvo's last moments. I only add that some as far as Haran say they could hear the dragon's roar that day, and with that, the story of Montalvo-The-Kind comes to an end. A tragically kind, cursed man whose life was ended by the greed and stubbornness of a mad, vengeful king."

Vatis finished his ale and awaited the reaction of the crowd. There was no applause, but his audience was satisfied. He could see it in their faces, how they slid closer to their loved ones, and how their eyes widened when they looked at Vatis.

Graham was the first to speak up. "That is a sad story. Thank you for telling it," He said, draining his cup.

"Thank you," the room echoed.

A few patrons offered to buy Vatis another drink, and a couple came up and shook his hand. Still, most of the room sat silently contemplating the story's finer details or drinking their somberness away until the rain subsided. The man in the back of the room disappeared in the commotion.

Damnit, Vatis thought. *That man has a story.* He looked around the room for a while but eventually gave up. The crowd passed a bowl around for coins. Vatis would have told stories for free; the money was a bonus and a means to get to the next tavern. He collected twenty-two Kan in total. *Not a bad night.* He put the coins in his purse and placed two on the bar for Rane before heading to his room.

With one foot on the stairs, Graham called, "What's your name? I know bards can use all the help you can get. I want to be able to spread the word."

"Vatis-of-the-Road," the bard said with a flourishing bow. He smiled and retreated to his room.

MORE QUESTIONS

Vidmar

Vidmar's hands trembled as he returned to the Rau Tavern. The bard had noticed him earlier, it was clear. Even when he moved tables, the storyteller still found him in the crowd. *I'm getting careless.*

Five years ago, no one in the bar would have known he was there. Somehow, the bard had captivated him, pulled him close, and lowered his guard. Vidmar escaped to the stables to calm his nerves.

The tavern was quiet. An elderly man was sprawled out on the end of the bar, a half-full mug still in his hand. Rane began his nightly cleaning ritual, overturning stools on top of tables. A young man desperately tried to convince the only remaining woman to come up to his room, a scene Vidmar had witnessed in different taverns across Emre a hundred times. It usually ended with a disappointed man, but luck seemed to be on his side; flirting progressed from banter to light touches to passionate kissing before they disappeared upstairs.

Rane struggled to escort the old man to the door. The drunk was well-fed, a rarity this far south of Barna; his bare feet dragged behind like an anchor. Vidmar hurried over, grabbing the man's limp, tree trunk of an arm, helping the bartender bear a bit of the burden.

"Thank you, Vidmar," Rane said.

"Don't mention it," Vidmar said, grinding his teeth. "Where to?"

"There's a bed in the stables. Hugo has had a tough time of late."

"There are worse places to sleep the ale away," Vidmar said.

Rane smirked. "Aye, suppose you're right."

They set Hugo down as gently as possible, but he caromed off the stall, startling the nearby horses.

"It's alright," Vidmar said, petting a brown mare's nose. The horse snorted a few times before calming down and returning to its hay. "Good night," Vidmar said, scratching behind the horse's twitching ears.

Rane waited by an empty stall at the front of the stable. "How about that bard tonight? Gods, I haven't seen a crowd like that in a long time."

"I haven't heard Montalvo's story in a long time, not since I was a kid. What was his name?" Vidmar asked.

"Vatis," Rane said. The name brought a smile to his face. "Vatis-of-the-Road. I hope he'll stay a few more nights."

"I'm surprised I've never heard of him," Vidmar said. "I've traveled across most of Emre, seen many bards, even attended a few tourneys, but I've never heard of Vatis-of-the-Road. I wonder where he's from."

"I had the same thought this afternoon. I asked Vatis when he first entered. He said, 'He's from the road.' He's quite odd when he's not telling a story," Rane said, locking the stable door.

"Most bards are."

Rane laughed. "That's true."

Vidmar kicked mud off his boot as they approached the tavern's backdoor. "Do you mind if I go up to his room? I need to ask him a few questions."

Rane eyed Vidmar carefully before opening the door. "Don't scare him, Vidmar."

"What?" Vidmar said, grinning. "I would never scare anybody."

"What about Elbert?"

"Well, somebody needed to put that oaf of a hunter in his place. Ember said he hasn't bothered her since we had our little chat."

"He hasn't been back to town since your *little chat*. You put quite the scare in him."

"And I would do it again, but I want to ask Vatis a few questions. I won't be long," Vidmar said, leaning toward the stairs.

Rane pulled a cloth from his apron and cleaned spilled ale off a nearby table. "Fine, but be quick."

Vidmar smirked and crept up the stairs. The tavern's second floor consisted of a long, dimly lit hallway with five doors lining the left wall. Two drafty windows with tattered curtains looked out over the stables. The first door wasn't numbered. The other four doors had a brass number at eye level. Three of the rooms showed no sign of an occupant, no light under the door, no noise from within, nothing, but the fourth room, the smallest room in the tavern, let a faint glow of candlelight escape through the cracks. A soft tapping came from inside, like a musician keeping the beat with his foot. Vidmar knocked.

The tapping stopped, the lock clicked, and the door creaked open, revealing the storyteller. He looked much older than he did in the common room; dark lines hung beneath his eyes as if weights were pulling down his eyelids. His skinny frame strained to stand; his right leg shaking from the effort. "Hello there," he said with feigned enthusiasm. "How can I help you?" His voice trailed off. *He recognizes me,* Vidmar thought. The bard closed his eyes; his eyelids struggled to reopen like a child resisting early morning work.

"Forgive me, but I hadn't heard the story of Montalvo-The-Kind in many years, and I hoped you could answer a few questions," Vidmar said, trying his best to act like a fan.

"You know of Montalvo?" Vatis said, his voice regaining strength.

What are you hiding? Vidmar found it odd that the bard's voice shifted in inflection and accent. "Yes. You tell the story better than anyone I've heard."

"Thank you. Why don't you come in?" Vatis said, his powerful voice returning to its performance level.

Satisfied, Vidmar huffed and walked into the room. *Let's see what you know.*

A small bed with a multi-colored quilt sat against the back wall under a window. The room was cramped for one occupant. An oak nightstand with an almost burnt-out candle and a rickety-looking wooden chair filled nearly all the remaining space. Vidmar scooted sideways and sat on the chair; Vatis sat on the edge of the bed with his hands on his knees.

"This is *cozy*," Vidmar said.

"It is plenty for me," Vatis said, bouncing his legs up and down, recreating the rhythmic tapping Vidmar heard from outside the room. "I won't be staying long." The bard shook his head as he peered longingly out the window. "Now, what questions do you have?"

"Rane will be disappointed. He hoped you would stay a few nights," Vidmar said, contemplating which question he should ask first. "Here's what I never understood: when and how did Montalvo find out he was cursed? He always seems to know when the mining disaster happens. So, how did he figure it out before? There must have been a series of awful events leading up to his discovery."

Vatis rubbed his eyes like he was waking from a nap that went a few hours too long before looking at the floor absently. A cockroach scurried out from under the bed, climbing out the window. The lone candle burnt out, leaving the two men alone in the dark, with only faint moonlight left to illuminate the room. Vatis looked like a skeleton in the darkness. His bony cheeks sunk into his jaw; the wrinkled skin pulled tightly as he forced a smile. He stood up slowly. The joints in his knees and hip popped in unison. "I'll find us another candle," he said, rummaging through his pack. He pulled out a few items from the bag, but Vidmar could not tell what they were. "Here we are." Vatis set the candle on the stand, struck a match, and it flickered to life. "Now, what were you asking?"

"Are you alright?" Vidmar asked. The bard looked as though he'd aged a decade since his performance. The bags under his amber eyes were swollen and purple.

"Quite," Vatis answered quickly.

Vidmar furrowed his eyebrows. Rain fell again; the heavy drops were strident on the second floor. A shiver ran down his spine as he forced images of battle out of his mind. Vidmar focused, ignoring the storm, foul memories, and suspicions of Vatis. "How did Montalvo find out he was cursed?"

"That is a tough question to answer," Vatis said. His voice grew more confident as if he were beginning a tale for an audience. "Some say that when the curse invaded his body, it spoke to him. It told him its laws. Some say the curse was a demon feeding off

Montalvo, giving him prolonged life and constantly bickering into Montalvo's ear, begging him to stay in one place so its evil could be distributed further. Others say that he caused the collapse of the East and that it was only when his mother was killed that he realized he was cursed. There are a few other rumors, but none have much credibility."

"Which do you believe?" Vidmar asked.

"Some answers are better left unknown," Vatis said, staring deep into Vidmar's eyes; something about that answer scared him.

Vidmar focused and searched for his next question: "But it's a true story, isn't it?"

"Mostly, yes."

"What's untrue?" Vidmar asked, sitting up straighter in his chair.

"Nothing that I told was untrue. I take great pride in telling true, honest tales. Any bard can spin some web of lies and make it interesting, but a true story has magnitude and consequences," Vatis said.

Water dripped from the ceiling, splashing onto the corner of the nightstand. "What about Montalvo's warning? Did someone else get cursed?" Vidmar asked. *I need to change the subject,* he thought, but was unsure how to make an unsuspicious transition.

"More rumors. No one knows for certain. Some say it was the last effort of Montalvo to save his life. Others say the curse or demon has yet to find a new host."

"What do you think?" Vidmar asked, trying to pry details out of the bard.

"Neither," Vatis stated plainly.

"Understood. Well, can you answer this? Did King Kandrian Ambita bring the dragon back for executions?"

"I haven't been to Barna in some time, but from what I've heard, the answer is yes," Vatis said. He stared at Vidmar without blinking for quite some time. Vidmar was the first to look away.

"So, it's true. He's gone mad."

"As I said, I do not know the details, only rumors, and I won't be spreading more of those," Vatis said. His head sagged heavily, struggling to stay awake.

Vidmar fiddled with the stone in his pocket. *Just ask him.* "Speaking of kings, what do you know about King Slavanes Greco and his lost crown?"

Vatis perked up. Life returned to his face. "I've got a tale or two about him. The people of Barna killed him after a particularly gruesome tournament won by none other than Dinardo himself, the leader of The Pact. His crown was lost that day and never found. Why do you ask?" Vatis finished, eyeing Vidmar as if seeing him for the first time.

Vidmar stared into the bard's eyes. "Ah, just another story I liked as a kid. I hoped you might know a little more." He wanted to show the bard the stone, his only clue, but he didn't trust him; something about his eyes threw Vidmar off.

Vatis relaxed on the bed. His shoulders hung low as he exhaled. "I'm sorry. I don't know much more. That's one of the stories that has eluded bards for centuries. Unfortunately, I'm not sure we will ever find the answer." The bard turned his back and scribbled in a journal that had been resting on the bed behind Vatis.

Another dead end. "Well, I don't want to keep you much longer," Vidmar said. "I do have one more question?"

Vatis nodded.

"Does anyone in your guild know more about Slavanes Greco?" Vidmar asked.

"Well, I … I," Vatis stuttered. The inflection in his voice changed.

"I'm sorry," Vidmar said. "I thought a bard of your skill would be a member of the guild."

A bead of sweat dripped down Vatis's forehead. He cracked each knuckle on his hands before he answered. "No need to be sorry," He paused, tapping his toes rapidly. He grabbed his leg to stop the shaking. "I … I haven't been active in the guild for some time. The guild hall is in Barna now. Perhaps someone there can help you."

Fucking Barna, of course. "Ah," Vidmar said, trying to hide his frustration. "Well, thank you for answering my questions. I'll let you get some sleep."

Vatis's shoulders dropped. He rolled his head around his neck, revealing a jagged scar near his left clavicle. "Goodnight, Vidmar," he said, closing the door.

Vidmar walked back into the empty common room and sat cross-legged in front of the smoldering hearth. Black logs glowed orange on top of a metal grate. He pulled the stone out of his pocket and traced the inscription with his finger. After finding Ember's ring and hearing the story of Montalvo-The-Kind again, Vidmar wished that every day could be that simple. *Today would have been perfect.* He thought as he glared at the dancing orange flames. *But I'll never have a simple life.* People paid for his discretion, for his loyalty, for his services.

Alcin is going to kill me.

AN OPPORTUNITY

Vatis

Frost crystallized on the window in Vatis's room, covering the glass in intricate patterns; labored breath escaped his mouth and condensed in the air. Golden sun rays fought through the frost, warming the tips of his toes. The slight temperature change was all Vatis needed to realize he had slept too late. He wanted to leave before dawn, but he couldn't fall asleep.

All Vatis could think about was Vidmar. At first, he was terrified, that razor-sharp gaze, the hilts of daggers jutting out from his belt, the scar on his lip that cut into his beard. *That man has a story.* Now, he wanted nothing more than to find Vidmar and follow him. He didn't care where Vidmar went; all Vatis knew was that he needed Vidmar's story. *Why would he ask about the lost crown?* That was the question that kept him up all night. *Why?*

The frigid temperature stiffened his rigid joints, making it nearly impossible to get out of bed. Finally, after some effort, he was able to sit up. Vatis recoiled as his bare feet hit the hard, frozen floor. He dressed, relishing the warmth his shoes and socks offered; a brief needle-like pain was a welcomed guest that arrived slightly before a cozy heat enveloped his feet and lazily brought life back to his extremities.

Vatis walked down the stairs into the common room. Rane stood on a chair, mending a leak in the ceiling; a drop escaped through the bartender's fingers into a barrel. "Good morning, Rane," Vatis said with as much enthusiasm as he could muster.

"Ah, good morning, Vatis. How did you sleep?" Rane asked as he briefly looked away from his task.

"Fine, thank you," Vatis said, ignoring his temptations to whine about the room size, the drafty window, and the leaky roof. Vatis-of-the-Road was not much of a complainer. *I need to find Vidmar; maybe Rane knows him.* "Say, do you know a man named Vidmar? Does he live around here?" Vatis asked, acting as casually as possible.

Water squirted through Rane's fingers. His eyes widened as he turned his attention to Vatis. "What did he do? I told him not to scare you. Dammit, Vidmar."

"No, no, he was fine, truly," Vatis said. *He does terrify me.* "He just asked me a few questions. I thought of the answer to one of them this morning. Is he from Basswood?"

Rane returned his gaze to the leak. His tongue poked out of the side of his mouth. "No. He spent some time here, recovering from a gruesome wound–almost died. Said it was a bear attack, though Zawo told me the cut was too clean to come from a claw. After that, we didn't see him for a couple of years. Now he comes through every so often doing odd jobs. I like him, but there are a few in town who would rather he never come back."

Who are you, Vidmar? "Why was he in town this time?"

"Said he was passing through; I think Ember gave him a job," Rane said, stepping off the stool and examining his work.

Unsatisfied, he stepped back up and dabbed the leak with a cloth. "She might know where he is; lives over the bridge on the northern end of town." *Ember,* Vatis thought, committing the name to memory. "Or you could ask after him at the market. It's just across the road," Rane added, water dripping from his hand as he pointed. "He usually picks up a few supplies when he's in town."

"Thank you, Rane," Vatis said, walking toward the door.

"Vatis, would you like to stay another night?" Rane asked. "I'll give you the room for free if you have another story to tell."

"That's awfully kind of you, but I cannot stay. I want to get to Vicus before the pumpkin harvest ends," Vatis lied. He wasn't sure when the pumpkin harvest began, much less when it ended.

Rane exhaled, the disappointment evident on his face. "That's too bad. Next time you're in town, I'll have the same deal, a room for a story," he said, mending the leak with what looked like plaster. A glob of the thick clay-like substance splashed into the barrel. "Vicus, you say, Gods, it's been ages since I've had a pumpkin pie," Rane continued. His focus seemed to shift, causing more plaster to fall into the barrel. "Damnit, I'm sorry, Vatis. I have to fix this so I can get a stew going."

"I'll be on my way. Thank you, Rane. I'll hold you to that deal if I visit Basswood again," Vatis said. *Highly unlikely.*

"May your feet find the road," Rane said, wiping a drop of water off his chin with the back of his hand.

"And yours."

The market was his closest lead. Hopefully, the shopkeeper could point him in the right direction. A tall cart pulled by two enormous horses passed in front of him as he walked out of the tavern. The bright sun surprised him when the shadow of the carriage moved on. Vatis sneezed, trying, unsuccessfully, to shield himself from the sunlight.

"Health to you," a woman nearby said.

"Thank you," Vatis said, blinking to adjust to the light. "Excuse me." He approached the woman as she walked across the road. She carried a woven basket of various fruits and vegetables. "Excuse me," he repeated, closing the distance between them.

"Good morning," she said.

"Good morning. Would you be so kind as to point me in the direction of the market?"

She pointed towards a peculiar-looking shop; it wasn't in line with the main road like the other shops in Basswood, but its front porch hung into the thoroughfare like an overbite. A painted yellow sign read "Basswood Market" above a bowl of various groceries. "Thank you," Vatis said as he bowed and strolled towards the store.

A bell rang as Vatis opened the door. An herbaceous aroma filled the store with a scent that urged customers to stay longer than they intended. The Basswood Market looked like most general stores in central Emre. Tall shelves stocked with fresh produce, dried meat, household items such as thread, and various traveling materials lined the shop's perimeter.

"Welcome," a brown-haired, middle-aged woman said, stocking a shelf with green apples.

"Good morning," Vatis-of-the-Road said cheerily.

"Can I help you find anything?"

"That would be lovely. I need lamp oil, thread, maybe a needle or two, and enough food to last two weeks on the road," Vatis paused. "More importantly, do you know a man named Vidmar? Has he been by the store recently?"

"Yes, the treasure hunter. Ember came by this morning; said he found her ring. He picked up a few supplies the day before yesterday," the woman said, placing the last apple in her basket on the shelf. "But I haven't seen him since. Sorry, love. I can help you with the rest of the list, though. This way." *Damnit.* Vatis wanted to leave and find Vidmar or Ember, but he *did* need a few

47

supplies. *A few more minutes won't hurt.* They walked through the store gathering everything on Vatis's list: two containers of lamp oil, black cotton thread, a single sewing needle, a few apples, a loaf of hard brown bread, and dried venison. She even refilled his ink. As Vatis reached into his coin purse, the shopkeeper said, "Oh, I just received a shipment of juicy, ripe oranges from Numeria. You must take some. They are wonderful on the road."

"I'll take three," Vatis said, pulling out a few more coins.

"What? No? It can't be?" The woman said from across the store.

"What's wrong?"

"The oranges. They've turned, but they should have been good for another week. I don't understand," the shopkeeper said. She held a large wooden basket, nearly overflowing with fist-sized oranges covered in green, fuzzy mold. "I just sold one yesterday to Vidmar, actually, and they were beautiful and sweet."

"There must have been a rotten one at the bottom of the basket," Vatis said.

"Gods, I swear I checked them all when they came in. They seemed fine," she said, examining each orange. "I'm sorry. Is there anything else I can get you?"

"No. I appreciate your help," Vatis said, placing the payment on the counter near the basket of moldy oranges. He added one extra Kan to the pile. "For your trouble."

I need to find Ember. What did Rane say? The northern end of town, over the bridge. Restocked, Vatis started toward Ember's. The small city of Basswood disappeared behind him as he walked. The road was unusually vacant for a sunny day, mid-morning. A single rider trotted past Vatis carrying what looked like deer pelts on the back of his horse. He nodded a polite greeting and continued his course. On the other side of the bridge, a slender man with a traveling pack walked like he was running late. His wavy brown hair flowed over the collar of his leather jacket. *Vidmar. It must be.* Vatis ran to catch up to him, the supplies in his pack clicking rhythmically together. "Vidmar," Vatis said, breathing heavily.

"Vatis," Vidmar said, looking annoyed that someone interrupted his walk. "Are you running from someone?"

"What? No, no," Vatis said. A fire smoldered in his lungs. "Where are you headed?"

"Haran." He didn't elaborate.

Vatis usually traveled alone; it was easier. He could leave when he wanted, walk at whatever pace he wanted, sing whatever song he wanted, and most importantly, be himself; he didn't have to act. It would be nearly impossible to play Vatis-of-the-Road for long. Traveling alone was his preference in almost every way imaginable, but he craved new stories, and Vatis needed Vidmar's story. "I," Vatis paused. Can I join you?"

Vidmar sighed, then tilted his head back and forth like he was weighing his options. He rubbed his eyes. "I don't know."

"We can share stories along the way," Vatis said eagerly. "Maybe I can answer some more of your questions."

Vidmar huffed in agreement. "You need to keep up. It will take more than a week to reach Vicus," Vidmar said.

Vatis whistled, doing his best impression of an excited blue jay. "Vicus? I thought you were going to Haran."

Vidmar took something out of his pocket and carefully placed it in his pack. He turned his back to obstruct Vatis's view. *What's that?* Vatis thought, extending onto his tiptoes. "I am, but I'll need to restock in Vicus," Vidmar said, tightening the bag's straps and waving Vatis forward. "Where are you headed?"

Vatis smiled. "The road is my home. I'm simply looking for some company, and if I got a story along the way, well, that would be fantastic."

Vidmar furrowed his eyebrows. "Fine."

They walked in uncomfortable silence for a while. *Vidmar even walks confidently,* Vatis thought, searching for something, anything to start a conversation. He usually did not have trouble talking. *Should I ask him about his past? Where he's from? No, not yet. He's too guarded. I need something else.* Then, a crisp, citrusy scent filled the air as Vidmar began peeling an orange.

"Did you get that from the market?" Vatis asked.

"Yes."

"When?" Vatis asked, despite knowing the answer. *He can't know I was asking about him.*

"Two days ago."

"And the orange is ripe? No mold?"

"No," Vidmar said, his tone getting sharper with each answer. *Information is going to be hard to come by with this one.*

"I tried to buy some this morning, but they had all turned. They looked as if they were three months past ripe," Vatis said, trying to sound as innocent as possible.

Vidmar threw bits of the peel into the trees. "Must have been a bad one in the bottom of the basket." Vidmar tossed a slice to Vatis.

Vatis bobbled the catch ungracefully. "Thank you."

Conversation became slightly easier after that. Vatis told Vidmar of his adventures with Gunnar and his interaction with Heppni and asked gentle yet prodding questions like: where did you get that dagger? And how did you get that scar? Each question was answered with a short response. Vidmar *did* seem to be interested in Gunnar, though. His eyes gave away more than his words.

They stopped around noon for Vidmar to relieve himself. Vatis took the opportunity to write a note in his journal. He flipped to a blank page, readied his quill, and wrote:

Vidmar Notes and Deeds

He underlined the title on the center of the page and gently blew on the fresh ink.

"What are you writing?" Vidmar said.

Vatis jumped. His book closed prematurely and fell onto the dirt road. "Gods," he said. Vidmar didn't make a sound as he returned from the woods, not that Vatis had been paying close attention to the sounds around him. It seemed like Vidmar could go wherever he wanted without anyone knowing. *A dangerous skill that comes with too much practice.*

A smile snuck onto Vidmar's face. "Jumpy, eh?"

"No… Well, yes, but Gods, don't sneak up on me like that. You almost gave me a heart attack," Vatis said, dusting off his journal. He opened to the page he had been working on, and a thumb-sized smudge took the place of the word deeds. *Damnit.* Vatis clenched his fist, channeling his anger toward his carelessness, not Vidmar.

They walked for a few more hours. Vatis carried most of the conversations ranging from King Kandrian Ambita to the price of ale. Soon, a purple sky emerged over the tops of the tall golden-leafed trees. "We better stop here for the night," Vidmar said.

Vatis nodded. "Seems like a fine spot; plenty of time for a story or two. We might even be able to light a fire."

"We'll see," Vidmar said, walking off the road into the forest. He gestured for Vatis to follow. "Come. We can't sleep on the road."

After some searching, Vidmar found a cozy spot on the other side of a hill nestled between a cluster of sparsely leafed oak trees. Vidmar ran to the top of the slope, examining their surroundings. Only faint rays of sunlight remained, leaving behind long shadows that played on the ground before darkness consumed them.

"What do you see?" Vatis asked.

"Nothing. It gets dark too damn quickly these days. Get a small fire going. I'll circle the camp and make sure no one can see it."

Vatis gathered small branches and kindling; he piled them in the organized, tent-like fashion his father had taught him many years ago. He struck his flint and steel together. Once. Twice. Three times. Three times for luck, his father used to say. One time was almost always enough, but it never hurt to have a bit of extra luck. Sparks sprung into the pile, clinging to the wool-like kindling. Soon a fire sputtered to life. Vatis wanted to call for Vidmar but restrained himself. He grabbed his journal and scribbled some of his thoughts about Vidmar onto the smudged page as he waited.

It seemed like hours had passed before his new companion entered the welcoming circle of firelight. Vidmar sat down and warmed his hands by the fire. "No signs of wolves or bears or bandits, but that's not surprising. We are still close to Basswood," he said.

"You seem like you have a lot of experience on the road?" Vatis said, posing the statement as a question.

"It's where I spend most of my nights," he said, relaxing on the trunk of a fallen tree. He pulled a dagger from his belt, cleaned it with his shirt, and sharpened it with a stone. The rhythmic clink created a charming melody with the crackling fire and chirping crickets. Vatis watched him repeat the same cycle for six other knives, three more than he knew Vidmar had been carrying.

Why does he need seven knives? That was the question Vatis wanted to ask; however, he awkwardly returned to their conversation from earlier. "I've traveled most of my life, and I have never run into much trouble."

"Consider yourself lucky," Vidmar said, tucking the last of his knives away and pulling some dried meat out of his pack. "You have to be extra cautious these days" *What does that mean?*

You need to ask him already. He had been avoiding *the* question all day. "You seem like you have led quite an interesting life, Vidmar," Vatis said, adding a small log to the fire.

"And nothing to show for it," Vidmar said, his tone deathly serious.

"I'd like to know more about it. I want to add your story to my collection," Vatis said, poking the fire with a stick to avoid eye contact with Vidmar.

"Why?" Vidmar asked.

"I collect stories. You're more interesting than anyone I have met in a long time, including Gunnar. You must have a story worth telling. Why else would you carry seven knives, constantly look over your shoulder, and walk silently like an…." Vatis paused when he noticed the fire in Vidmar's eyes, not a reflection from their camp, but a fire burning with either hatred or regret.

"An assassin," Vidmar said through gritted teeth.

Vatis dropped the stick in the fire and held up his hands. "That was not what I was going to say. I…." *I can't lose him now, not when I'm so close.* "I'm sorry." *That's it. Play it apologetically, garner his sympathy.* "Vidmar, I'm truly sorry."

"No, I'm sorry, Vatis," Vidmar said, running a hand through his hair as he looked up at the stars. Vatis followed his gaze, the lights twinkling through the thin canopy. After a long pause, Vidmar continued. "How do you collect a story?"

Vatis tried to contain his excitement, but still, his lips curled into a smile. "I follow you around for a bit and ask questions about your life along the way. You don't have to answer every question, and you can ask me to leave at any time. I won't get in the way. I promise."

Vidmar sighed. "Fine. You can have my story, but it's getting late; we should get some rest. I'll take the first watch."

Vatis screamed inside his head. *Yes.* His fingers tingled; his lips trembled. It took everything in him to act calm. "Splendid. Do you need to take watch? I thought you scouted the area."

Vidmar's eyes narrowed. "Yes."

THE PEDDLER

Vidmar

Whistling woke Vidmar again, not the pleasant soft chirping of birds but a loud, insufferable echo from his new traveling companion. "Do you have to whistle every damn morning?" he said.

"Of course, nothing puts you in the mood for traveling like singing with the birds," Vatis said.

"How about a knife in the leg?"

"Absolutely not. It would be rather difficult to walk with a knife in one's leg."

"Then I suggest you stop, or you'll be walking to Vicus with one of my knives buried in your thigh," Vidmar said, rolling over underneath his ragged, red blanket. The bard did not stop. There was no point in trying to go back to sleep, not while Vatis performed his morning ritual of whistling, singing, and practicing different dialects from western Emre. *His Haranian accent is pretty good*, Vidmar thought as Vatis acted out a conversation between two dock workers.

Vidmar rolled his blanket neatly, fastening it to the top of his pack. He secured all his knives into their various sheathes and hidden compartments. His neck cracked as he put on his jacket. He checked his pocket; it felt empty. *No.* His jaw clenched as he patted himself down. Vidmar could feel his heart in his throat. Then, he remembered he had tucked it into his pack. His hand burrowed into the bottom of his bag like a squirrel searching for a nut in winter. The back of his hand brushed against something hard, cold, and all too familiar. The stone was still there. He exhaled slowly.

"What are you doing?" Vatis asked. He was great at asking questions that Vidmar didn't want to answer.

"Packing," Vidmar said. "I suggest you do the same."

While Vatis packed, Vidmar practiced throwing his knives. He started with a few conventional throws at a dead pine tree twenty paces away. The first knife found its mark on the left side of a coin-sized knot. The second struck the right side of the knot; two smaller knives found the top and bottom. All four blades surrounded the protruding lump. A fifth landed directly in the center. Satisfied, Vidmar retrieved his weapons and looked for another target. A mushroom grew out of the stump of a fallen tree. Vidmar threw the first knife side-armed; it trimmed a tiny piece off the top of the fungus. His next throw was left-handed; it clipped the bottom of the mushroom. His final throw was underhanded, directly from the sheathe on his thigh; it chopped the mushroom off completely.

"Why do you throw like that? Off-balanced and side-armed," Vatis asked.

"It's important to be able to throw at any angle, from any direction. You never know what will happen in a fight," Vidmar said, happy to talk about one of his passions. "So, I practice throws that might be useful someday. The same reason you practice whistling and accents—tools of the trade."

A strange smile snuck across Vatis's face.

"What?" Vidmar asked.

"That's the most you've said in days. I think we might be getting somewhere."

Vidmar huffed as he went to retrieve his knives. He brushed the mud off the one that severed the mushroom. When a steady, *thump, thump, thump* came from the road. Vidmar focused on the sound. A cluster of birds scattered from the tree to his right. Fortunately, they hadn't seen anyone on the road besides a father and son traveling to Basswood to sell wool. Vidmar had hoped to get to Vicus without being noticed.

"Sounds like a peddler's cart," Vatis said, walking towards the road.

Vidmar was tempted to throw a knife at the bard. Luckily, a pinecone landed near his feet; he picked it up and threw it at Vatis instead. It broke as it struck him in the back of the head. "Do you want to get us killed?"

Vatis rubbed his head. "What bandits are up this early in the morning? There is no harm in looking to see who it is."

"Smart bandits, deserters, mercenaries, or worse. I have traveled with you for five days, and you couldn't sneak by a rock. I'll see who it is. You stay here."

"Fine, Vidmar, but I traveled quite a bit without your help. I know the sound of a peddler's cart when I hear it," Vatis said, sitting down and opening the book he was always writing in.

"I don't know how you made it this far," Vidmar said.

"Why, my unmatched charm, that's how," Vatis said without looking up.

"When we run into bandits, let's see how far your charm gets us."

Vatis stood, mimed a sword fight, and then used all his flourish to perform an overly ornate bow. "Aye, the bastards would all give me their purses and thank me for taking them."

"I would like to see that. Now stay here and practice your charm on the birds."

Vidmar walked silently through the trees, inching closer to the road. He dropped to his stomach and then crawled under the low branches of a pine tree. He wormed his way forward until he could see the road. A small wooden cart pulled by a gray mule tottered south towards Basswood. The contents of the cart rattled together in wooden crates. Two burly, well-armored men walked on each side of the carriage, while a scrawny man with a thick black mustache and elaborate purple hat drove the cart with the reins in one hand and a pipe in the other. He blew large smoke rings straight up into the air that floated over his head like clouds.

"Halt," the peddler yelled, yanking the reins hard enough that the slow-moving mule's front legs lifted off the ground in surprise. "Amir, bring the barrel of pipeweed up here. I'm running dangerously low."

"Yes, sir," one of the guards said.

Vidmar turned, preparing to head back to camp, when he heard a gut-wrenchingly cheery voice. "Good morning, gentlemen," Vatis said.

That fucking idiot.

Vidmar slithered closer, careful to remain unseen. The other guard approached Vatis, his hand resting on his ax; the driver turned his attention from preparing his pipe to Vatis. "Good morning," he said with a hint of anger.

"Where are you fine fellows headed?" Vatis asked, unconcerned.

"That's none of your concern," the guards said simultaneously like well-trained dogs.

"Boys, I'm sure this man doesn't mean any harm," the driver said, making an intricate hand gesture to his guards. "My name is Zidane, and we are heading south to sell our," He paused. "Wares."

Vidmar pulled himself into a crouching position behind a thick mulberry bush, quietly snacking on the sweet berries as he watched. Even as the bard tried to get himself killed, Vidmar couldn't pass up mulberries.

The two guards stepped closer to Vatis.

"You wouldn't happen to have any blankets for sale," Vatis said, ignoring the approaching guards. "Mine is so travel-worn. It might as well be a pile of wet leaves."

"Well, that is unfortunate," Zidane said. "But I don't sell blankets."

"Oh well, what do you sell?"

"Specific wares for a specific client, who would be immensely displeased if we sold any before he received the shipment," Zidane said, looking at his guards. The two men took another step towards Vatis.

"Ah, too bad. Well, I wish you all safe travels. May your feet find the road."

Vidmar pulled a knife from his boot. If the situation escalated, he was confident he could take out one of the guards with a well-placed throw and still have time to catch the other by surprise.

"Where are you headed, if you don't mind me asking?" Zidane asked.

"We are headed to Vicus."

"We?"

Damnit, Vatis. He sprang to his feet, brushed the dirt off his clothes, and ran toward the road. "There you are, Vatis. Everyone was worried that you had been kidnapped," he said, hoping that Vatis would catch on. The bard furrowed his eyebrows. Vidmar gave Vatis his best please-cooperate look; either the stern glance or the swift elbow to the ribs was enough for the experienced actor to know to play along. "We have been looking for you all morning."

58

"Well, here I am. I thought these fine gentlemen were peddlers. I hoped to buy a few supplies," Vatis said, pointing at the cart.

"Well, I do have some supplies," Zidane said, emphasizing the last word. "But they are not for sale."

Vidmar put his arm on Vatis's shoulder, pulling the bard close. "Thank you, gentlemen, but I need to bring Vatis back to the camp before they start looking for me too." Vatis opened his mouth to speak before Vidmar interrupted. "Safe travels to you."

"Safe travels to you and your camp," Zidane said, smiling at his guards. "Perhaps we will run into each other again."

"May your feet find the road," Vidmar said dryly.

Zidane cracked the reins. "Come on, boys. We need to be on our way." Vidmar and Vatis waited in the road for the cart to disappear over the hill.

"I told you to wait," Vidmar hissed as loud as he dared but not loud enough for Zidane or his lackeys to hear.

"I apologize. I could have sworn he was a peddler. The jingling glass, the spicy aroma, I'm dreadfully sorry. I'm usually not wrong about these things," Vatis said. Vidmar couldn't tell if the apology was sincere.

"We have to get back to camp."

"Why?"

"Why? Because when they come looking for us, I want it to seem like there are more than two of us."

Vidmar bombarded Vatis with a slew of insults that would have made the sailors in Haran tip their hats as they walked back to their camp.

He frantically rummaged through the camp, rolling over his sleeping area like a pig in mud. This cycle repeated until the beds of twelve heavy-sleeping, non-existent companions emerged from the forest floor. He rushed back and forth all over the camp, running to the eastern edge; then, changing his gate, he ran to the north, south, and west sides. A thoroughly trampled area emerged as he finished his last pass.

"Thanks for your help," Vidmar said, out of breath. He brushed as much of the leaves and dirt off himself as possible.

"Was that necessary?" Vatis asked.

"Yes, and it probably wasn't enough to stop them from following us. We must stay off the road for as long as we can. We are at least a day and a half from Vicus. If those peddlers, as you so gently call them, come looking for us. I want to be hard to find."

"No," Vatis said.

Vidmar turned his head to face the bard, biting the inside of his cheeks to restrain himself. "No, what?"

"I am traveling by road. I will not slog through the thick trees simply to put your mind at ease. Ha, trees and ease, there's an unlikely rhyme. I might have to incorporate that into a poem," Vatis said, gathering his belongings.

Stunned by Vatis's stubbornness, Vidmar said nothing. He sprinkled crumbs of stale bread over a few of his beds. The silence between them lingered uncomfortably. Finally, Vidmar spoke up. "Then best of luck to you. I'm not getting killed because I followed a bard with the commonsense of a rabbit. Wait, I take that back. A rabbit would avoid danger at all costs. You have the common sense of a–of a…mushroom. I don't know. You're an idiot, is what I'm trying to say. Good luck on the road, Vatis."

Vatis scratched his head as he looked back and forth between the road and Vidmar. He whispered something under his breath that Vidmar couldn't hear, grabbed two fistfuls of his hair, and stomped his foot. "Fine. Have it your way, but I think this is completely unnecessary."

"Noted."

They walked silently. Vatis began to hum when Vidmar quickly unsheathed a finger-length knife out of his left jacket sleeve. His aggravation seemed to enhance his reflexes; the blade was waiting for Vatis's thigh before the bard took another step. Vidmar pulled back before the knife found its mark, but not before it made its point. Vatis immediately stopped humming, and they walked for the rest of the day in exacerbated reticence, like a husband and wife fighting for reasons unknown to the husband.

Twilight approached. They searched for a campsite in the same fashion as the previous four nights. "How about here?" Vatis asked, breaking the silence. He pointed towards a nearly identical spot to last night's camp, well-covered with trees and dry at the base of a hill.

Vidmar walked over. "This will have to do." In truth, the spot was perfect, but part of him didn't want to relent to the bard. His instincts overcame his annoyance. Vidmar knew they needed to make camp fast so he could prepare.

"Fantastic, one more night on the road, and tomorrow we can enjoy the unparalleled hospitality of Vicus," Vatis said, placing his pack on the ground.

"Have you been to Vicus?" Vidmar asked.

"Yes, many times. The rolling fields of corn, wheat, and barely are a welcomed sight after these mountains and trees."

"Yeah, there's no better sight than a cornfield," Vidmar said.

"Would you be willing to indulge me with a few more details of your time in Jegon?" Vatis said, pulling his book from his bag and eyeing Vidmar like a puppy begging for a scrap of meat.

"Once we are safe, maybe," Vidmar said, cursing himself for revealing that detail last night. "I'm going to check the perimeter and gather firewood. But, for the love of whichever god you worship, stay here."

"Yes, sir," Vatis said. He straightened and saluted Vidmar.

That arrogant little shit, Vidmar thought as he circled the camp.

He walked purposefully, setting snares and other traps, some for small game, others for larger prey. Vidmar worked in darkness, trusting that his well-practiced fingers could manage the job. He braided long grass together and set his final snare, triggering it once with a long stick. It snapped around the wood perfectly; had it been a rabbit, it would have made a fine dinner. Had it been a bandit, they would only have tripped, but the trap worked regardless of its target. He picked up the firewood and slunk to camp.

Vidmar heard voices as he approached. Either Vatis was practicing accents again, or Zidane had found them. Part of him hoped it was Zidane because he didn't know how much longer he could tolerate the bard's dialect practice.

A small fire burnt in the center of camp, casting quivering shadows on the trees. "Zidane, it's good to see you again," Vatis said, offering his hand as if they were friends reuniting in a tavern.

"Where's the rest of your party?" Zidane said. Four men stepped out of the trees, the two who guarded the cart earlier and two who could almost be considered giants. Each guard stood at least a head taller than Vidmar, although that wasn't saying much as he stood on the wrong side of small his entire life.

"They are out gathering firewood," Vatis said. "Come sit. We can share a meal and swap stories."

Let's see if charm works, Vidmar thought as he crept closer.

"That won't be necessary," Zidane said. "Amir." He nodded at Vatis.

The guard punched Vatis in the gut, knocking him to his knees. Amir followed his punch with a flurry of kicks that left Vatis trembling as the guard searched his pockets. Finally, he ripped Vatis's coin purse from his belt and emptied it into his hand.

"Fifty Kan and change," Amir said, counting the coins. "And this." He held up something, but Vidmar couldn't tell what it was from his vantage point. Every instinct in Vidmar's body told him to leave. Vatis meant nothing to him, but he couldn't leave him alone to be beaten and robbed or worse. *Damnit.*

"Found his pack," Another guard said, dumping the contents into the dirt. Vatis moaned.

Amir kicked him again. "Shut up."

Zidane picked up the other coin pouch and counted in the same fashion as Amir. "Help him to his feet, boys," Zidane said, transferring Vatis's coins to his purse. "It's our lucky day," he said, jingling the coins. "Tell me. What are you doing traveling with so much money? Didn't your mother tell you to travel light?"

Vatis sighed. Amir slapped him. "Answer."

Vatis could barely hold his head up. "I'm a traveling bard. I don't have a home to store it," he said, choking the words out.

"Well, then I almost feel bad for taking everything you own," Zidane chuckled.

Damnit, damnit, damnit. Vatis did not deserve this; no one did. Vidmar needed to act quickly. He couldn't fight all five men conventionally, but Vidmar never characterized his fighting style as conventional. Some called it dirty. He preferred to think of it as stealthy, always inventive, but never conventional.

He took an inventory of the weapons he had at his disposal: eight knives, six good for throwing, a small hatchet, three bandit-sized traps he set around camp, and a pile of sticks that would not be much use.

Zidane stepped closer to Vatis. "Where are your friends?"

"Gathering firewood," Vatis stuttered, spitting out more blood. Vidmar clenched his fists.

"More like setting traps," one of the new guards said, holding a spiked log.

Two traps, then. The guards closed in on Vatis like a pack of wolves. Vidmar needed to act. He whipped one of his throwing knives at the closest guard. They wore thick leather armor, bracers, and boots, but fortunately for Vidmar, no helmets. His knife buried into the back of the guard's neck, slightly above his collar. The big man dropped instantly. *Four left.* The other attackers stood in shock just long enough for Vidmar to relocate.

"Up there," one said in the direction Vidmar had been crouching. Two men rushed up the slope. The third stayed close to Zidane, guarding him like a dog protecting its master. Vidmar quickly climbed a small tree and perched himself on a branch. He threw a stick toward the two guards, and it caught their attention.

"I heard him; over there."

In Vidmar's experience, it usually paid to be the fastest in the group, and he usually was, which made him feel slightly remorseful for the quicker guard that fell on the first of his traps. A well-covered, knee-deep hole with numerous spiked sticks on the floor and walls. The wall spikes pointed downwards to ensure whatever fell in couldn't pull itself out without ripping its legs off. The faster guard fell in with a cringe-inducing squish of wood penetrating flesh. He screamed. The slower guard tried to pull him out. "Come on," he said.

The man in the trap screamed. He fell to the ground with a dull thud as his face bounced off the hard dirt. He had almost certainly passed out from the pain. *Three left.*

The slower guard stepped over his companion. "Where are you? Show yourself," he said, walking with more caution. He waved his sword over the ground as he walked back and forth, searching for traps.

The guard looked up, exposing his neck. Vidmar jumped off the low-hanging branch, turning in midair while slashing a deep gash across the guard's throat. The big man fell to the ground with his hands desperately trying to stop the blood pouring from his wound. Defeated, he rolled onto his stomach, mouth ajar, eyes staring into vast nothingness. *Two.* Vidmar wiped blood from his forehead with the back of his hand.

Zidane and his guard, the biggest of them all, stood, weapons ready, scanning the area for signs of Vidmar. They undoubtedly heard the unluckily fast guard's cries, but they may not have heard the other. Vidmar circled back towards the trap. The guard caught inside twitched. Vidmar plunged his bloody knife into the back of his neck sympathetically. He wouldn't be able to draw Zidane and his guard away from Vatis. He had to strike from afar – his preferred way to attack.

He tested the weight of a knife in his right hand, adjusted his grip, and threw it at the gigantic guard's forehead.

It found its mark. A perfect throw, except the hilt hit first. *How?* The handle never hit first when Vidmar threw knives.

The blade fell to the ground, bouncing in front of Vatis. It was a powerful throw sure to discombobulate most opponents, maybe even knock out smaller men, but this enormous sentinel seemed unfazed, and he now knew where Vidmar was.

He charged. His jagged mace pointed towards Vidmar like he was leading an assaulting army. Vidmar had taken down his share of bigger men but couldn't remember one this large. Most men of substantial girth had one thing in common, especially ones in the mercenary business. They were simple-minded – see the target, kill the target. Rarely did they expect a counterattack, so Vidmar charged back, screaming and waving his knife in the air like a lunatic.

A second of the guard's confusion was all Vidmar needed. The colossal man faltered. Vidmar slid under the mighty mace swinging towards him, through tree-trunk thick legs, and behind his opponent. He slashed the exposed tendons on the guard's right knee. The guard wailed as he toppled to the ground, desperately swinging his mace in Vidmar's direction. Vidmar ducked under the savage attack, slicing upwards at the guard's underarm. The sentry hissed as blood surged from the fresh cut. He dropped the heavy mace. Vidmar somersaulted, springing to his feet in front of the kneeling, bleeding guard, knife ready.

The guard reached under his limp arm. "You motherfuh…" he choked before collapsing.

Zidane stood mouth agape, trying to comprehend the sudden turn of events. He picked up the knife and pulled Vatis to his feet. "Not another step," he said, holding the blade to Vatis's throat. "Drop your knife, or he dies."

Vidmar sighed. "Alright," he said as he dropped to a knee and drove the knife into the back of the guard's skull. He stood, blood-stained palms raised in surrender.

"What? What was that for?" Zidane asked, the knife wobbling in his hands. Sweat dripped down the obnoxious-looking bandit's face.

"I wasn't sure that he was dead," Vidmar said, panting as the adrenaline of battle began to wear off.

"Hand me your purse, and I'll let him live."

"You're still trying to rob us? A man in your position should probably reconsider, but fine, here you go," Vidmar reached into his belt and whipped a throwing knife underhanded right into Zidane's exposed shin. He dropped the knife and crumpled to the ground, agonizing screams echoing through the thick forest. Vatis collapsed, eyes wide. *I can't believe that worked,* Vidmar thought. He had practiced that throw for years but hadn't found a practical application.

"Are you alright?" Vidmar asked, putting a hand on Vatis's shoulder. Zidane continued to wail. Vatis nodded but did not speak. Vidmar understood. Most men were not accustomed to this type of carnage. Vidmar wished he wasn't, but it had been a long time since anything surprised him. He knelt in front of Zidane.

"Hand me your purse," he said, parroting Zidane's shaky threat from seconds ago. "No, no, no. I wouldn't touch that blade, move it the wrong way, and you're likely to cut an artery.

Unfortunately, I don't see any surgeons nearby who would be able to save you. Well, hold on, Vatis, you're a man of many talents. You don't happen to know any field medicine, do you?" Vatis only stared vacantly at the knife in Zidane's leg.

"I thought not," Vidmar said, stepping closer to Zidane. "So, hand me your purse, and we can get this affair over with."

Zidane howled as he reached for the purse on his belt. He tossed it at Vidmar. "Fine, take it. Don't kill me, please don't kill me," he cried.

"Oh, don't worry. I'm not going to kill you. Despite what you have seen tonight, I do not enjoy killing, but when you threaten our lives, well, every man must make exceptions," Vidmar said, grabbing the knife from the ground. He walked backward toward the big guard, put a foot on the back of his neck, and yanked his other knife free, never taking his eyes off the bandit. "You see, Zidane. It is Zidane, correct? The only way I know to stop a wound like that from killing you is to cauterize it." He wiped the knife off on his pant leg, sheathed it, and laid the tip of the guard's mace in the smoldering coals of the campfire. He tossed a log on top, ensuring the flames would be hot enough. Then, smiling wickedly, he approached Zidane.

"Bite this," he said, shoving a stick into Zidane's mouth. "This may hurt worse than when it went in." Tears rolled down Zidane's cheek; his leg trembled. Vidmar placed a hand on the mistaken peddler's knee, grabbing the knife's handle and twisting it slightly. Zidane screeched. A noise that Vidmar would not have thought possible with a stick in one's mouth. "That wasn't even the worst part," Vidmar said. Zidane moaned his fear through his gagged mouth.

"Ready on the count of three. One." He ripped the knife from his leg. Blood sprang out like water from a broken dam. Zidane spit the stick out and screamed. "Oh gods," he cried, grabbing at the now-open wound.

Vidmar took his time grabbing the handle of the scolding mace from the fire. The weapon shimmered in the darkness. Zidane quivered. Vidmar tried to ask the bard for help holding Zidane down; however, Vatis continued to stare, eyes fixated on the blood gushing from Zidane's shin. Vidmar held the mace steady as he approached. "Now, I can tell you from experience that this will hurt most," he said.

"Ready on the count of three. One."

Zidane rushed to put the stick back in his mouth. Then, he jerked his head back as Vidmar counted 'one,' anticipating sudden pain again.

"Oh, come now, that would be a cruel joke to play twice," Vidmar said. "Two." He pressed the mace onto the wound. Zidane's flesh sizzled like bacon in a pan. The acrid smell of burning flesh and hair permeated over the pleasant wood-burning smell from the campfire. Zidane belted out a remarkably high-pitched squeal, a full octave higher than his previous record.

"You know what? It was just as funny the second time," Vidmar said, dropping the sizzling mace dangerously close to Zidane's crotch. The merchant slid back, spitting the stick out of his mouth. Tiny pieces of bark clung to his teeth.

"Enough, enough," Zidane cried gingerly, touching the area around his tender skin.

Vidmar tossed his waterskin at Zidane. "Here, drink. You lost a lot of blood. You'll need some fluids to make the trip."

Zidane took a tentative swallow, followed by a much longer drink. "Trip to where?"

"To the road. Don't worry. It's not far."

"Why are we going back to the road?"

"Because I wouldn't be able to sleep if I just sent you on your way. I'm sure you'd sneak back here and cut our throats. Right, Vatis?" The bard didn't respond. Instead, he rubbed his belly like a woman expecting a child while staring distantly into the forest.

"Ah, right, as I was saying," Vidmar continued. "To put our minds at ease, I'm going to tie you to a tree next to the road and make you the next traveler's problem."

"You'll what? Tie me up all night? What about wolves?"

"That's a risk we'll have to take. But, I mean, it's either that or I can kill you right now. And I don't want to kill anymore tonight," Vidmar said, digging some rope from his pack. *I've killed too many already.* Each kill seemed to add weight, making it hard to move. He bit his tongue and pushed thoughts of his body count aside. "You know, I'm sacrificing my best rope for you. This rope and I have been through a lot together."

Zidane tried to stand. "Fine, fine," he stopped as he fell back into the dirt.

Vidmar tossed another log onto the fire. "Vatis, I'll be back shortly." The bard didn't respond. Vidmar searched Zidane for weapons before he helped him to his feet. "I don't want to get stabbed while we are having a nice stroll."

They began walking east towards the road, Vidmar holding Zidane upright as he limped along. "Wait," Zidane yelled. "Wait. Can you at least leave me my hat?" he pointed to the extravagant violet wide-brimmed hat. Vidmar let Zidane go. The wounded man dipped onto one knee. Vidmar pulled him onto his feet. Zidane hissed as he put weight on his damaged leg.

"Yeah, you can have it. I wouldn't be caught dead in this thing. Plus, it will make you easier for travelers to spot as they pass by, or wolves," he chuckled. He placed the hat on Zidane's head and escorted him to the road.

An hour later, Vidmar returned to camp. Vatis still sat gawking at the embers of a burnt-out fire. "Are you alright?" Vidmar asked as he neatly placed some kindling on the glowing charcoal. A flame sprang to life. Vidmar fed it an arm-thick log; the yellow-orange heat gobbled it up greedily. The bard didn't respond.

"I'm sorry," Vidmar said.

RUNNING FROM THE PAST

Vidmar

The bird's melodious chirping seemed different this morning. It was slightly softer and less enthusiastic, and there was no echo, no annoyingly accurate echo. Vidmar watched Vatis. The bard sat in the dirt, hugging his knees to his chest. The remains of their campfire smoldered a stride away from his face, smoke spiraling upward into the foggy air. His bloodshot eyes seldom blinked. "First skirmish?" Vidmar asked.

Vatis shook his head, avoiding eye contact. He glanced at the red-stained earth where Zidanc's guard died, then back to Vidmar. He opened his mouth slightly. His dry, cracked lips glistened as he licked them. "I," he started, but his voice cracked as if the words were punched back into him. "It was," he continued. "We could have," he rubbed his bruised face. "My fault," he mumbled, looking at the ground. He sat silently for a few moments.

Vidmar waited. He knew what it was like for most people after a battle. Surprisingly, Vatis handled the situation much better than Vidmar anticipated.

After a moment, Vatis found his voice. "Thank you, Vidmar." A tear escaped from his swollen, darkening eye. "Thank you."

"Just listen to me next time," Vidmar said softly, trying to ease the tension.

"I'm sorry," Vatis said, with more strength returning to his voice. "I'm glad you were here." A shy smile emerged from beneath his mustache.

Vidmar helped Vatis to his feet. The bard hissed as he stood. "Let's see the damage."

He gently pressed on Vatis's side. The bard squirmed, hissing as Vidmar examined him. "At least two broken ribs. Lift your shirt. No signs of internal bleeding. Alright, you can put it back down. A few broken ribs, some bruising, a broken nose, and just a little unrepairable trauma. Not too bad. Pa always told me, 'If you come out of a battle with your life and half your wits, consider yourself lucky,' and it sure looks like you passed that test. Not that you had many wits to begin with–a peddler, really?"

"I'm sorry," Vatis repeated softly. His face reddened despite the bruising.

Vidmar handed Vatis his pack. "I think that's everything," he said. "I just stuffed it in there when I woke this morning. You might want to double-check."

Vatis opened the bag, rooting through its contents systematically. "What's this?" Vatis said as he pulled out a black coin purse embroidered with golden symbols.

"Zidane's purse," Vidmar said, gathering his supplies. "I figured you deserved it after that beating you took."

Vatis paused, weighing the purse in his hand. "We should split it," he said.

Vidmar smiled. "I was hoping you would say that."

They stepped out of the dense forest back onto the road where Zidane was tied tightly to a thin birch tree. He perked up as he heard footsteps. "Help, help, please, I beg," he stopped abruptly.

"Good morning, Zidane. How did you sleep?" Vidmar asked.

"Untie me, you... you twisted goat fucker," Zidane shouted.

"Well, I was considering untying you; that is my favorite rope, but that rash vulgarity is precisely why I must leave you here. You're unpredictable."

"Untie me," Zidane cried. "You can't leave me here."

"Oh, I can. Here you go," Vidmar said as he tossed the thief's purse. It fluttered like a feather before falling to the ground in front of Zidane's feet.

"It's empty."

"Of course it is. Did you really think I would leave you any money? After what you did."

"What *I* did? How about what *you* did? You killed four men last night and nearly a fifth. We were just going to rob you."

"Right? Vatis is proof that you were *just* going to rob us," Vidmar said, pointing at the bard. He stood, more like, hunched next to Vidmar. An orange-tinted sun illuminated his bruised, swollen face.

Zidane nodded at his shin. A bubbly black scab foamed out of the narrow wound. "What about this?"

"You're lucky as far as I'm concerned. I'm sorry, Zidane. We must be going. May your feet find the road... before the wolves find you."

"Get back here, you insolent, black-hearted son-of-a-bitch," Zidane's insults faded away as they crested the hill at the north end of the road.

Vidmar winced. "That was probably a mistake," he said once Zidane's cries were no more than murmurs in the wind.

"What?" Vatis asked.

"Leaving Zidane alive. He is a Gar dealer or at least a smuggler."

Vatis perked up. "Gar? What's Gar?"

"Gar. Gentleman's Bane. Midnight Flower. It is a drug made from the Garvasta flower. A white powder that, when mixed with wine, produces euphoric hallucinations, often leading to crippling addiction and crazed withdrawal symptoms. Gar."

"Ah, I have heard of Gentleman's Bane," Vatis said, vague recollection appearing in his widening eyes.

"It's common in Haran, but it is also starting to seep into other parts of the world. Zidane will likely be working for a much more powerful man with many more guards. So, we need to get to Vicus quickly."

Their path to Vicus wound up over hills, through a densely packed forest, and over a slow-moving creek whose bridge had decayed into nothing more than three posts and some frayed rope. A few hours more of steady hiking in damp clothing through acres of farmland led them to the Vicus's market.

The sweet, spicy aroma of cinnamon and nutmeg filled the cobblestone square. A well-maintained wooden structure with three chimneys sat in the middle of the grassy plaza. A round, friendly-looking woman held samples of sweet rolls on a wooden tray to lure in potential customers. Around the square, farmers and merchants sold their wares from stands, some much more elaborate than others. High, competing voices hollered over the bustling street conversation. "Sweetest apples in Emre. Get your corn here, the finest crop of the season. Trinkets, odds and ends."

A clean-shaven elderly man pushed a wobbly cart through a crowd of people. "Whatever you need, ole Jur has it. Lowest prices in all Vicus," he called as he pushed the jingling, rickety cart slowly, without much heed of passersby.

"That is a peddler," Vidmar said, elbowing Vatis in the side.

Vatis's expression changed from amused observation to annoyed quicker than a mother with a disobedient toddler. "I know," the bard said flatly.

"Too soon?" Vidmar asked. *Don't push him, Vidmar. You know how tough it is to recover.*

Vatis didn't respond. He limped to the peddler. "Excuse me, sir. Do you have any blankets for sale?" His voice changed as he approached the cart. It was friendlier, cheery even. *Maybe I underestimated him.*

The peddler stopped abruptly. Jars and small crates slid forward, crashing into the opposite end of the cart. "Of course, ole Jur has everything," he said, straightening his wares. He pulled three blankets out of a drawer on the side of his cart, displaying them in a neat row. "Let's see. This one is made from sheep's wool from a nearby farm." He pointed to a thick, gray-knitted blanket. "Perhaps if you're lookin' for something a little thinner, this excellent silk fella could do the trick, or if you're lookin' to save some coin, this cotton one is good for travelin'."

Vatis examined each blanket. "May I?" he asked for approval to pick up the wool blanket.

"Of course," Jur said, stepping backward.

Vatis rubbed the material between his fingers, then held it up, eclipsing the sun as he examined it further. "This is quite fine."

"As interesting as this conversation is, I'm going to find us somewhere to sleep tonight," Vidmar interrupted.

Vatis focused his attention on the peddler. "Now this one," his words trailed off as Vidmar strode away.

Vidmar explored the market, stopping at various carts. The first sold a vegetable he had never heard of; the farmer called it zucchini. It looked like a cucumber, and Vidmar hated cucumbers. Nevertheless, he offered his thanks and moved on. The next merchant sold homemade medicine and tonics; her wooden stand was painted in a vibrant shade of green. Collapsible shelves folded out to hold dozens of vials and jars containing colorful liquids and powders. A familiar aroma rose from the cart like steam from a cup of tea. "Oh, sir, you look pale. I've got the remedy you need," An attractive dark-haired woman said, pulling down a small, corked vial with a thick brown liquid inside. "Wormwood, not to worry, I've enhanced the flavor with some mint. It's actually quite pleasant." She offered the vial to Vidmar.

"Thank you, but I'm feeling fine."

"Are you sure? You're rather pale?"

"Pale is my natural color, but I'm sure a week on the road with little sleep hasn't helped. I assure you I'm fine," Vidmar said.

"You need something to help you sleep? I have this wonderful lavender powder; you mix it with a little tea."

"How about wine?"

"Oh," the woman paused. "Oh, I wouldn't advise using any of my medicine with wine."

"Damn, that's about all I drink." *This is going nowhere. Where's the inn?*

"I have a tonic that soothes headaches faster than a cat running from a dog," she said, putting her offerings back onto their shelves and pulling out a tall vial with a clear liquid inside.

"You have my attention," Vidmar said. As he reached to examine the concoction, a deep, booming voice yelled from the opposite end of the square. "Vidmar. Vidmar, you fucking bastard." A muscular man with a long gray beard charged across the yard. "Vidmar," he yelled as he lumbered, pushing unsuspecting men and women out of his way.

"It's been lovely chatting with you, but unfortunately, I have an urgent matter that needs addressing," he said calmly with a bow before spinning and sprinting away from his sudden assailant. Vidmar had only been to Vicus a handful of times. He was unfamiliar with the side streets and nooks he could use to hide, but his nearly three decades alive had provided plenty of experience running away.

"Where's my dagger? You shit-eating excuse of a treasure hunter," the voice closed more distance between them. Vidmar darted into the bakery plaza. He nearly knocked over the woman passing out samples. "Hey, watch it," she said. "Sorry," Vidmar yelled, running backward. Seconds later, he heard a high-pitched screech followed by the unmistakable twang of wood falling on stone. Apparently, the poor woman who narrowly dodged Vidmar's wild pass couldn't replicate the maneuver as the bearded man bulled her over like a battering ram. A chorus of surprised shouts chastised the burly man giving Vidmar the opening he needed.

He ran across the street between two buildings, ducking behind a stack of barrels. His breath returned frantically. The commotion from his chase brought almost battle-like chaos to the usually peaceful square.

The woman sobbed loudly. "My arm, my arm." Her painful cries were joined by a mob of "Get back here.", "Where did he go?" and "What were you doing?" Vidmar couldn't tell who the demands were being yelled at or if his attacker had made it through the crowd, and he didn't dare look.

He knew he had to find a better place to hide, or he had to put some serious distance between himself and the crowded market. If he were alone, he would have been long gone, but he felt obligated to Vatis, at least until he overcame the shock from the bandit attack. *Though he seems to be doing better now that we are in town.* He had been wandering through Emre alone for over a year, and Vatis was an entertaining companion, despite the whistling and signing. Crouching, Vidmar inched his way behind the building to find a door slightly ajar. It might as well have been an invitation. He gently pushed the door open further and entered.

Vidmar couldn't tell what kind of building it was, and he didn't care; he needed to hide. He found himself in a kitchen. To his right, a rickety shelf held different vegetables and spices. To his left, a small kettle simmered in a low-burning fireplace; the herbaceous scent of rosemary and thyme bubbled up from the contents of the kettle. A creaky floorboard might have saved his life; minimally, it spared him an awkward conversation. Vidmar sprang into the shadows behind a pair of crates.

A young, blonde woman brushed her hands on a white apron as he walked into the kitchen. "I'll be there shortly, hun," she called to someone in the front room. "These fucking men have no patience, none." The latter, she said under her breath as she stirred. She grabbed a clay bowl from a nearby shelf and ladled in a steamy soup. "I'm coming. I'm coming. Settle down."

When she was back in the front room, Vidmar crept into earshot. The murmur of many conversations made it hard to distinguish any relevant information, but he guessed he was in a tavern. Suddenly a loud crash halted the discussion like an officer's command. He couldn't hear what the voice said at first, but as its frantic pace settled down, he was able to make out the end of the announcement. "Acer just plowed right through her. I don't know. He was chasing someone. We all know about his temper, but this was different. Whoever that man was, Acer was going to kill him. Poor ole Addy, she's got a broken arm for sure."

Acer. Why is that name familiar?

A slew of questions burst forth from the other patrons. "Who was he chasing?", "What happened to Acer?" and "Is she going to be alright?"

"I don't rightly know who he was chasing. But, aye, she'll be alright. Acer ran around the square a few times before he went into the bakery, hopefully, to apologize, but we all know he isn't one for apologies."

"They ought to throw Acer in jail for this," a deep raspy voice bellowed above the commotion. The crowd went silent. Apparently, the owner of the hoarse voice was a man to be respected. "And that's all I'm going to say about it."

Vidmar peeked out, trying to see the speaker. "We all know how you feel about him, Hobb," the woman replied after a lengthy silence.

The soup began to boil over the lip, splashing onto the coals below with a snake-like hiss. "Shit," the woman yelled and ran back into the kitchen. Vidmar deftly ducked behind the crates again just in time to avoid being seen. The kettle was quickly pulled off its hook and onto an awaiting iron trivet on the floor. Thick yellow bubbles exploded; liquid projectiles cascaded onto the tavern keeper's bare forearms. "Ah," she yelled, dropping her ladle onto the ground.

"Everything alright back there," a voice called.

"I'm fine. You ungrateful louts made my soup boil over."

After cleaning the floor and herself, she ladled out five bowls of soup, placed them on a wooden tray, and brought them to the waiting patrons.

An awestruck silence overcame the commotion of the common room when the front door crashed open.

"Has anyone seen a short skinny piece of shit skulking about? I know he is fond of taverns," the harsh voice said. The door slammed shut, punctuating his accusation.

The silence lingered for an uncomfortably long time, even for Vidmar, who knew no one in the tavern. Finally, Hobb spoke. "What are you doing here, Acer?" *Oh, that Acer,* Vidmar thought, touching a dagger sheathed on his belt.

"This doesn't concern you, Hobb."

"You're lucky that you aren't in jail. Did you apologize to Addy? Did you notice you broke her arm in your tirade?"

"Why does that matter?"

"Well, we all like Addy… can't say the same about you."

"I'm in no mood for your bullshit tonight, Hobb. Either you have seen him, or you haven't."

"We haven't seen anyone out of the ordinary," the tavern keeper said. She was joined by resounding support for the other guests.

With Acer in the tavern, Vidmar used his opportunity to escape to the safety of the street.

The faint purple-orange glow of a fading sunset provided no aid in the unfamiliar surroundings. Vidmar slowly retraced his steps. A few moments later, he found himself in the dimly lit square once again. The farmers and merchants had all but disappeared. Only a few remained. Luckily, he found Vatis talking to a farmer packing up his cart. He approached cautiously.

"No, there's not much work for a traveling bard these days. Not in the South, anyway. I can find work in Barna, Haran, Dartmore, and maybe Yimser, but they aren't fond of foreigners, from what I hear. Hopefully, I can entertain at a few taverns along the way," Vatis said. His cheery disposition seemed to recover from its state of temporary shock. *That's a quick recovery.* Vidmar eyed the bard thoughtfully.

"Well, Kat runs the only tavern in Vicus, but most of the men there would rather play dice than listen to a story," the farmer said, packing the last of his produce into compartments in his cart.

"They have never heard my stories."

"Good luck. It's right there. The Barnyard Cat."

"Thank you, sir."

Vatis started towards The Barnyard Cat, but Vidmar yanked him wrist-first into an adjacent alley. "Don't go in there," he said.

"What? Why? Where have you been? What did you do?" Vatis replied after he recognized his kidnapper.

"We have to go. It's a long story."

"Did you knock over that poor woman earlier?"

"No, but I led a raging bull dangerously close to her. I don't have time to explain. We need to get out of here. But, first, I need you to run back to that farmer and ask him if he knows where a man named Hobb lives."

"What?"

"Go," Vidmar urged Vatis forward with a less-than-gentle shove. "Hobb, ask him if he knows Hobb."

Vatis nearly fell over. "I'm going. I'm going. Hab?"

"Hobb, you dim-witted turd. Where does Hobb live?"

Vatis smiled and jogged uncoordinatedly to the slow-traveling farmer.

A few moments later, Vatis returned out of breath.

"Well," Vidmar said, looking around the square for signs of Acer.

"He told me, but I was hoping to tell a story or two at the tavern. It's how I make my living, after all," Vatis said, scratching the back of his neck.

Vidmar exhaled through his nose. "I can't go in there, but if you want to tell a story, go ahead. Just tell me where Hobb lives, and we can go our separate ways."

Vatis appeared to think like a merchant debating a trade. "Fine, follow me."

A long walk down a dirt path led them to a massive farm. Acres of unrecognizable crops grew on both sides of the road; a well-kept stone house stood at the center of the property. Sharp, threatening barking shocked Vidmar as a black dog ran from the porch. The bard sprang behind Vidmar, using him as a shield.

"What is it, boy," a soft, high voice called.

Vidmar put his hands in the air. "We don't mean any harm." Vatis followed Vidmar's lead but remained silent; he felt Vatis shaking behind him.

The dog growled, baring its teeth. "Easy, Igni. Easy." A young boy with brown shoulder-length hair said, petting the back of the dog's head. "Who are you?"

Vidmar kept his hands in the air. "I'm Vidmar, this is Vatis. Does Hobb live here?"

The boy examined the men before speaking. "Why are you looking for him?"

"I had hoped he could help me," Vidmar said softly.

"Help you how?"

A deep voice calmly thrummed from behind Vatis. "It's fine, Taldor. Go back to the house." The storyteller nearly jumped into the field.

"But Pa," the boy whined.

"Go."

Taldor's shoulders slunk as he turned on his heels. "Come, Igni." The dog's tail wagged happily as he trailed his owner into the house.

Hobb waited until the door closed to speak. "What can I do for you?" The old man said. He snorted as he observed Vidmar, but he eyed Vatis with a suspicious glare usually reserved for criminals facing trial.

"Well, it's a delicate matter. First, let me introduce myself. I am Vidmar, and this is Vatis. He is a traveling bard."

"Vidmar," Hobb said like he was tasting the name. "Vidmar," he repeated. "Why do I know that name?"

"Ah, well, I may have inadvertently caused a bit of a disturbance in the square this afternoon," Vidmar said, rubbing his right thumb into his left palm.

"Are you the fella that Acer was after?" Hobb said. His bushy gray eyebrows nearly jumped off his forehead.

Vidmar cracked the knuckles on each hand. "Yes, I'm afraid so. It's all a big misunderstanding."

Hobb held up a hand. "Not here. Anyone who can get that pile of manure with eyes that riled up can have a seat at my table. Come."

INTERLUDE

Zidane

"Get back here, you insolent, black-hearted son-of-a-bitch," Zidane screamed as his attacker walked away. "You pig-licking, mother-fucking prick, you get back here now."

The only answer came from the rustling of the orange-brown leaves in the wind and the soft song of nearby birds. Zidane's leg throbbed. He could feel warm pulses like a heart beating on top of his shin. "Vidmar, Vidmar, Vidmar," Zidane said, committing the name to memory. "I'm going to kill you, Vidmar." The rope stung the chafed skin on his wrist as he struggled to free himself. He knew his efforts were useless; he tried all night.

Several hours passed, and no one had come down the road. It wasn't exactly a busy thoroughfare, which is why Zidane chose this route in the first place. His limbs were numb, his fingers were purple, and his mouth was drier than the Kaharn Desert. The only benefit to his predicament was that he could no longer feel the excruciating pain in his leg. *I'm going to kill you, Vidmar. You have no idea what I am capable of.*

Time seemed to move slower than usual. The irritatingly peaceful sounds of the forest were suddenly interrupted by the rhythmic thunk, thunk, thunk of wagon wheels. *Please.* Zidane took a deep breath as he waited for the wagon to come around the bend.

He could hear the hoofbeats of whatever animal pulled the wagon, most likely a mule in this area. A tall, brown snout peeked into view—a *horse, a large horse, a merchant perhaps.*

"Help, help," Zidane yelled as an elaborate, green-painted wagon approached.

"Steady," a gray-haired man dressed in obviously foreign clothing said as he pulled on the reins.

"Oh, kind sir, please, you must help me. They took everything and left me tied here for the wolves. Sir, I beg you, please cut me free."

"Steady," the man repeated as the horse stopped in front of Zidane. "Master, this gentleman requests our aid. Shall I cut him down?"

The carriage door slid open. A black-skinned man with a well-manicured beard peaked his head out, a gold etching visible on the collar of his silk doublet. "What is it, Otto? Why are we stopping?" he asked.

"I'm dreadfully sorry to bring your travels to a sudden stop, but it was bandits. They stole everything from me and tied me to this tree in hopes that wolves would find me before a kind traveler like yourself," Zidane said.

"What's your name?" the young man asked.

"Zidane, sir."

"Well, Zidane, how can I be sure this isn't a trap? These woods are known to be the home of many bandit camps. Aren't they, Otto?" He phrased the last sentence as more of a threat than a question. He examined Zidane more thoroughly. "Why that is wonderful," he said, pointing at Zidane's hat on the ground near his feet and empty coin purse.

"Ah, yes, it's one of a kind, but sir, I beg you. Please cut me down. If this were a trap, it would have been sprung as soon as you stopped," Zidane pleaded.

"Possibly, but I haven't made it this far without caution," the young man said, leaning further out of the carriage. "Otto, what do you think?"

"Well, Master, I think he speaks true," Otto said, leaning over the railing to see his master.

"I swear by all the gods. Please, I can't feel my arms and legs." *You ignorant pricks just cut me down already.*

"Fine, Otto cut him down."

"Ah, thank you, thank you. You are a true gentleman," Zidane said, bowing as well as he could while still restrained.

Otto jumped down from the wagon with the dexterity of a much younger man. He pulled a neatly polished dagger from his waist and approached Zidane cautiously, checking the forest for any sign of movement. He quickly sawed through the ropes, and Zidane crashed into the dirt. "I'm sorry, sir," Otto said.

"Don't be sorry. My legs gave out, that's all. I've been tied up there for quite some time," Zidane said, pushing himself up and rubbing the raw red flesh on his wrists. "How can I repay you?"

"Well, it appears your coin purse is empty," the young man said, pointing at the flat purse on the ground. "But that hat might suffice."

Zidane paused. *Is this fucker trying to take my hat?* "Ah, well, ah," Zidane struggled to find any words to say, let alone the right words. "You see that hat."

The young man laughed and threw something at Zidane. "It was only a jest. You can keep your hat. Here are a few coins to help you in your travels."

"Why, sir. That's incredibly generous of you. What's your name so I can spread word of your kindness throughout the taverns of Emre?" Zidane asked.

"Tarver, Tarver Bulago of Numeria. It has been a pleasure, Zidane, but we are already behind schedule. Otto, to Haran. Good day, my friend."

What luck. "You're going to Haran?"

"Ah, yes, a matter of some urgent business."

"Have you been there before?"

"No, sadly, this is the first time Father has trusted me enough to handle business this far north."

Inexperienced too. Perfect. "Well, it sounds to me like you could use a guide. The path the Haran gets a little tricky once you get through Vicus," Zidane said, smiling.

"This is either the most elaborate bandit heist in history or you're simply a kind fellow looking to return a favor," Tarver said, weighing his options. "Why should I trust the navigation capabilities of a man we just untied from a tree?"

Zidane continued to brush the dust off his clothes. He picked up his hat, carefully blowing dirt off its rim. "That is a good question," he paused, searching for an answer. "This forest is a little new to me, but I grew up in Haran; no one knows how the city better. I can find you safe passage once we arrive since it is also where I'm headed."

"Otto?" Tarver said.

"I've been to Haran many times, sir, but Zidane seems trustworthy, and we are going the same way. If his navigation abilities are suspect, he could at least provide some conversation on the road," Otto said, returning to his seat on top of the carriage.

"Good point, Otto. We are still a few days out. No doubt the story of how you ended up in that tree is entertaining," Tarver said.

"Oh, it's a tale fit for taverns," Zidane said, smiling.

"Come in, come in. You can start by telling me where you got that hat."

STORIES BY THE FIRE

Vatis

They gathered around a worn wooden table; Vatis sat with his back to the door while Taldor buttered bread in the seat across from him. Vidmar sat next to the boy, chewing his thumbnail, and Hobb drifted from the table to the stone hearth.

Vatis tried to focus, but his thoughts returned to the previous night's attack. He tried to play a simple traveler earlier in the square. He called the character Jon. *A plain name for an ordinary traveler,* he thought. He wandered through the square as Jon, trying to talk to merchants and avoiding the carts that looked like Zidane's. *I can't believe I was so naive. They almost killed me.* A loud pop in the fire snapped Vatis out of his reverie.

"What did you do to get under Acer's skin?" Hobb asked, returning to the table.

Vidmar shifted in his chair. "Well, see, that's a long story."

"I'm not going anywhere."

"Me either," Taldor said excitedly.

Vidmar ran his finger around the rim of a mug. "I don't know where to start."

"The beginning usually works best," Vatis said, trying to sort through the wave of emotions in his body. *A story will distract me, and I'll learn more about Vidmar too.* If his brain and gut weren't reenacting the fight in the woods, Vatis would have been ecstatic. But, instead, he settled for interested and pulled out his writing supplies.

"What's that for?" Vidmar said, glaring at Vatis.

"Notes," Vatis said.

Vidmar huffed but didn't object, so Vatis readied his quill for a story.

"Why are you taking notes?" Taldor asked.

"I'm collecting Vidmar's story. He's quite interesting," Vatis said, testing the quill on his hand.

The answer seemed to satisfy the boy, but Hobb looked at Vatis with uncomfortable scrutiny. Vatis avoided the old man's gaze by examining his surroundings: wood burnt orange in the fireplace. A steady thump bounced off the wood floor as the dog over aggressively scratched one ear. The smell of sweat, dirt, and pine hung in the small room like a fog.

Vatis watched Vidmar take a long drink of a strong juniper spirit, the only alcohol Hobb had. The farmer said it was typically used to sterilize wounds. Vidmar's eyes glistened as he swallowed loudly. "I know I'm not up to your story-telling standards, but I will try my best. Damn, this stuff is strong," Vidmar said, coughing. "So, I was born in a burrow of Haran. My Pa raised..."

Good information, but unnecessary. Vatis interrupted. "Maybe skip ahead a few years to your involvement with this Acer fellow."

"You said start at the beginning, but very well, I met Acer in," Vidmar paused. "Well, how old are you, Taldor?"

"I'm twelve. Why?" The boy looked every bit of twelve. Acne sprouted haphazardly up his neck onto his cheeks. Dirt clung to his wavy brown hair, and his voice cracked each time he got excited.

"Now see, this might cast a poor light on me," Vidmar started.

"I know about whore houses…' Taldor said as his voice cracked again while his cheeks developed a bright pink hue. "Ev told me about them."

Vidmar laughed. "No, no, nothing like that. I met Acer in a… *tavern* in Haran. I was playing King, Calvary, and Army and doing well; when Acer approached our table," he paused and scratched his chin.

"What's King, Calvary, and Army?" Taldor asked.

"Don't interrupt, boy," Hobb said. He dismissed the boy and glared at Vatis while he took notes.

Vidmar smirked; he seemed more relaxed than usual. "I suppose you will need a little more of a backstory," Vidmar said. "See, I've never been good at much except scouting, and since I'm not in the army, there aren't many ways to use my skills. So, I'd pick up odd jobs posted in town halls and bounty boards. I got pretty good at tracking down lost or stolen objects. Around Haran, I became known as a treasure hunter, though I never found anything truly valuable." Vidmar's hands disappear beneath the table. *He's playing with that stone again.*

Vidmar continued. "Anyway, Acer approached our table. He said, 'Are you Vidmar?' I said, 'Who's asking?' That back and forth went on for longer than it should have, but I am cautious with new customers, especially customers who approach me on a hot streak. Eventually, he got around to asking, 'My dagger. Bandits stole it on my way to Haran. They stole my coin purse and just about everything else, but the dagger is the only irreplaceable thing. Can you find it? It's a family heirloom.' I sat there silently for a few moments. It's always best to keep new customers on their toes. Finally, I said, 'I can find it, but my fees double when bandits are involved.' He said he would be happy to pay double if I brought back the dagger. He went on to describe this knife as a young boy describes his first love, in every *single* detail."

Vidmar's attempt at a story was interrupted as a log crashed onto the loose coals, sending Hobb to the hearth to tend the fire. The floor creaked as Hobb stood up. A black iron rod hung on a hook near the fireplace. He picked it up and adjusted the kindling, groaning as one particularly stubborn log refused to stay in place. Vatis chewed on a stringy piece of peppery meat. He washed it down with a swig of the juniper spirits, coughing as it burned his already sore throat.

Vidmar strummed his fingers on the table rhythmically. "Ready?"

"Of course," Vatis wheezed as if he had just evaded the city watch on a long, tumultuous chase.

"Right," Vidmar began. "In my line of work, I became familiar with most of the bandit camps near Haran; if you kill a few of them, they start to take you seriously."

Everyone around the table nodded. Vatis closed his eyes momentarily; his recent experience had given him unwelcome insight into Vidmar's ability with bandits.

Vidmar sat up. "Anyway, I had a good idea as to who stole his dagger. All I had to do was a little negotiating, issue a few threats, pass a few Kan into the right pockets, and I had it. It was one of my easier finds. I contacted Acer. Keep in mind that I had all intentions of returning the dagger. I mean, one hundred Kan is nothing to scoff at, but this dagger, it had to be worth double that, at least."

Vidmar reached behind his back like he was scratching an itch. "But honestly, part of me wanted to keep it," he said as he pulled a forearm's length dagger out of a hidden sleeve in his jacket. He stabbed the knife into the table, a golden-hilted, intricately carved, well-polished black blade set with a large red stone. Plates and glasses rattled; Hobb rose to his feet.

"What are you doing?" Hobb yelled.

"Oh, shit, I'm sorry," Vidmar said, quickly pulling the dagger out of the table and examining the damage with his thumb. "I got a little carried away." Vidmar licked his thumb like his saliva was somehow going to mend the gap in the wood. "I'm sorry."

"I've seen your knife work. One of your spinning tricks would have had the same effect with less damage," Vatis said.

Hobb grumbled something under his breath. The silence grew uncomfortable as Vidmar rubbed at the table's narrow gash. Vatis chomped on the salted meat and smiled. Taldor stared, wide-eyed, at the dagger absently spinning in Vidmar's hand.

"If you drop that onto my floor. I'm going to feed you to the dog," Hobb said slowly, pulling a well-used knife out of his belt without flair but somehow more dramatically than Vidmar.

Vidmar slowly laid the dagger on its side. "Again. I'm sorry, Hobb." Vidmar seemed surprisingly threatened by the old man. Vatis didn't know if Vidmar was being overly courteous or genuinely scared. *There is something odd about Hobb,* Vatis thought as he watched the farmer expertly sheathe his blade.

The corners of Hobb's lips twitched like he was fighting back a smile. "Don't make me regret inviting you into my home," he said flatly without a hint of sarcasm or empathy.

Let's stay on the right road. "So, what did you tell Acer?" Vatis said, winking at Taldor.

Vidmar cleared his throat. Hobb gestured for him to continue. "Right, a week later, we met at The Ashway, one of the more *violent* inns in Haran. I arrived an hour earlier than we agreed, as I always do, except Acer was already there and drunk. He asked me if I had found the dagger, and I told him I had a few leads, but it didn't look promising. Then he got angry, really angry, like a bear defending her cubs. I told him to calm down, which might be the worst thing to say to a man with a hot temper. He tried to flip the table, except all the tables at The Ashway are nailed to the floor. His face went as red as an apple. He lunged at me. I, uh, *reacted*."

Vatis took notes in his personalized shorthand. He waited for Vidmar to continue.

"What happened next?" Taldor asked eagerly.

Vidmar smiled. "Acer is a large man; I wouldn't have had a chance in a fistfight. In my experience, the only way to catch a big man off guard is to charge him. So, as I bolted toward him, he stepped backward, and I ducked under his arm and slipped behind him. Then, I landed a blow to one of his kidneys and spun to the other side. I stabbed him just above the knee as I spun. He toppled over like a dead tree in a storm and screamed. The Ashway went silent. The first and only time I've heard the sea from inside the bar."

"So that's why he was walking around with a cane last spring," Taldor said. "Ev and I thought he was mocking Pa."

"Who's Ev?" Vatis asked. That was the second time Taldor had mentioned him.

"Evanor. He's my brother. He's in Barna now, but he should be back soon," the boy said.

"So, it's just the three of you working the farm?" Vatis asked.

"Yes," Hobb said. "That's all we need." The farmer stared at Vatis. His gaze was powerful, unrelenting; Vatis hated it. He looked away, trying to focus his attention on the chirping crickets outside. *Why does he look at me like that? I've done nothing wrong.*

Vidmar seemed to pick up on the tension and started his story again, twirling the dagger while he talked. "Right, as I was saying. I bolted out of there. Well, before I ran, I flaunted his dagger in front of him and said, 'You know I found your dagger, but I think I'm going to keep it. A blade of this quality needs to be in more capable hands.' He yelled some nonsense at me that I won't repeat here, and I left town. I've been avoiding Haran for six months, but I'm broke, and let's just say I left some other unfinished business there, so I'm heading back now. If I knew that Acer lived in Vicus, I would have avoided your town and slept in the woods."

"You don't want to sleep in these woods," Hobb said.

"Why?" Vidmar asked as if they had not escaped bandits just last night. Chills ran down Vatis's spine.

"You don't want to sleep in these woods, and that's all I'm going to say about that," Hobb said, crossing his arms.

Vatis glanced at Vidmar with narrow eyes. "I'll take you at your word, Hobb," Vidmar said. "But that's why Acer hates me. I mean, he has as much of a right as any man that I've pissed off over the years; I stabbed him and stole his dagger, but damn, he runs remarkably well for someone with a serious leg less than a year ago."

"He complains about that leg more than Pa complains about the weather," Taldor laughed. "For what it's worth, I'm glad you stuck the bastard…."

"Language, boy," Hobb said. He turned to Vidmar. "You are welcome to stay as long as you like. There is a loft in the barn, though it's not much better than dirt, but it will keep you dry."

"Thank you, Hobb," Vidmar said. "Again, sorry about your table."

"I nearly forgot. Forget what I said. Go as far north as you can tonight before you make camp," Hobb said. Vatis's eyes widened as he looked at Vidmar. His mouth opened as if he were about to speak, but no sound came out.

"Pa, they think you're serious," Taldor said after an unnervingly long time. "He's joking."

I'm not sure that he's joking, Vatis thought. Vidmar laughed or at least played along. "You'd make a damn good card player," he said.

"Who says I'm not a damn good card player?"

Another uncomfortable silence followed that retort. Hobb smirked. He stood up and put another log on the fire. "I'll let you stay, but it will cost you. Vatis? Am I saying that right?"

Vatis nodded. His name sounded different when Hobb said it, causing Vatis to shutter.

"Vidmar said you're a traveling bard," Hobb emphasized the word bard like he was interrogating him. "Do you have a better tale than Vidmar? Some quality entertainment will go a long way towards forgiving the damage he caused to my property."

Vatis was not in the mood to tell a story. He had nothing rehearsed, and his mind still couldn't focus. A second later, Vidmar kicked him under the table. "Will you help me out? Or should we risk the woods?"

I'd rather be in a hot bath in a tavern.

Hobb's scowl cut through the room like a knife. Vatis looked backward out the window. To his left, he could see a tall watchtower in the moonlight; he felt drawn to it like a moth to a flame. *Focus.* "What would you like to hear?" he finally said after pinching the bridge of his nose and mustering as much energy as he could for a performance.

"Do you know the story about Dabin and the draugr?" Taldor asked, scooting to the edge of his chair.

"One of my more popular requests. Dabin is perhaps the greatest hero Emre has ever had," Vatis said. Hobb snorted like he disagreed, but he didn't voice his opinion. Vatis smirked. "Aye, if that's what you would like to hear, I would be more than happy to tell his tale or the part of his tale that earned him fame." Vatis closed his eyes, trying to get in character.

"You've heard that story dozens of times, boy," Hobb said.

"Well, yeah, but I've never heard it from a *real* bard," Taldor said.

"I haven't heard the story of Dabin since I was a boy," Vidmar added.

"I tell true stories," Vatis said seriously. "I do not embellish the details. I can't promise anything you haven't heard before."

"Wait. You mean Dabin was real? I thought he was just some made-up hero like Mia the Maiden," Taldor asked, almost jumping out of his chair.

"Yes, an age ago, when heroes were," Vatis paused. "When heroes were…easier to find." He stumbled over the last words like a cat flailing in the air before it inevitably lands on its feet. "When heroes were more than fictional. Mia was real too." Vatis took a deep breath, rolled his head around his shoulders, and reentered as Vatis-of-the-Road.

"Don't be putting falsehoods in his head, Vatis," Hobb said sharply but looked away at the fire.

"I would never," Vatis said; his voice felt strong, ready for a performance. "There are many fictional stories in Emre. Stories of magic, gods living among men, and monsters, but many of the stories we think are false are true. My predecessors loved straddling the line between truth and fiction, but I think true stories have a more meaningful impact."

Taldor sat silently for a moment before he asked another question. "How do you know what's true and what's false?"

Vatis grinned, letting his expression fade into resolute determination as his gaze shifted from Taldor to Hobb. "A secret of the trade." Smiling again, he looked back at Taldor.

"That means he's full of shit," Vidmar laughed.

Taldor smirked but didn't seem to share Vidmar's skepticism.

"Call me a coward, call me weak, but never call me a liar. I swear by the gods that the stories I tell are accurate down to the clothing," Vatis said. The threat caught the others off guard; even the dog popped its head off the floor. His reactionary defense almost forced him to break his character.

"Sorry, Vatis," Vidmar said. "I meant no offense."

"I'm sorry, too," Taldor added. Hobb remained silent, examining Vatis like a blacksmith inspecting a newly forged sword.

Vatis relaxed his shoulders. "All is forgiven. Shall I get started?" Taldor and Vidmar nodded eagerly in unison.

Hobb nodded once; his eyes narrowed. Vatis quickly averted his gaze and focused on the story.

"Right, Dabin and the Draugr," Vatis started. "Since we are familiar with our hero, I will skip over some of his backstory. An age ago, Dabin, a celebrated military general, was perhaps the greatest fighter in Emre. When the war ended, he roamed the land on the King's orders bringing peace to the dysfunctional towns east of Numeria. Word reached him that livestock, farmers, and even a few children had gone missing in a small, forgotten town. After speaking to a few locals, he headed toward the mysterious area. Dusk approached."

Vidmar, Taldor, and Hobb proved to be a great audience. They listened intently as Vatis performed, even gasping with surprise when the draugr nearly killed Dabin. Riding the waves of euphoria, he told another story of Dabin. His audience remained engaged. He thought about telling a third, but Hobb began to nod off towards the end. Vatis took a deep breath as he finished the second story. "Now, if you don't mind, I'd like to get some rest."

Hobb snapped out of a light sleep, shaking himself awake. "The barn is on the other side of the well."

Vatis looked at Vidmar. "Ready?"

Vidmar slapped Taldor on the back gently. "Thank you, Hobb. See you in the morning."

Taldor sat silently. Vatis and Vidmar gathered their belongings, walking out the door towards the barn. As if coming out of a trance, Taldor jumped up. "Vatis," he said.

"Yes, Taldor."

"I just wanted to say thank you." The boy looked slightly embarrassed as he circled his foot on the floor

Vatis smiled. "You're welcome, Taldor."

SIGNS OF LIFE

Vatis

Vatis wandered through a field of carrots, kicking dirt into the air as he dragged his feet between the neatly planted rows. The sun rose over the eastern horizon. Small, jagged shadows swayed back and forth with the cool morning breeze. Leafy carrot tops created fairy-like shadows. Vatis imagined small creatures diligently working to help the vegetables grow. The self-created distraction temporarily soothed his never-resting mind.

Images of Vidmar's massacre two days prior still plagued him whenever he closed his eyes. His mind wandered like his feet, dragging through the dirty memories until he returned to the Raue Tavern, an entire inn captivated by his stories, each member of the audience waiting with bated breath for the conclusion. He pictured that simple tavern and the carefree folk of Basswood, and his thoughts, as they often did, created poetry. He sat in the dirt, pulled out his journal, and wrote.

A single lantern sways outside the Tavern
To locals, it's relief of pain
for soldiers, it's free rein
A simple lantern shines outside the Tavern
Lustful whispers from a jar

Vatis bit the end of his quill. *What's next? Gluttonous patrons from afar? Ah, that's no good. The pacing is all wrong.*

"What are you writing?" an innocent yet curious voice asked. Vatis jumped. "Sorry. I didn't mean to sneak up on you," Taldor finished, coming into view over Vatis's shoulder. *Damnit, boy.*

Vatis forced a laugh as he tried to compose himself. "It's fine," he said, breathing deeply.

"Don't mind me," Taldor said as he pulled carrots from the ground. "Are you writing a story?"

Vatis put his writing supplies away. "A poem, actually."

"Can I hear it?"

"No," Vatis answered in a colder-than-intended tone. "Sometimes it's better not to know," Vatis finished trying to sound empathetic while picking a caterpillar off a leaf.

"I don't know about that," Taldor said. "I can't stand it when I don't know something. Pa says I'm too curious."

Vatis further examined the tiny greenish insect on his fingers. "I used to be the same," he paused. "So curious, so inquisitive, but when story after story and question after question yields terrifying results, you begin to think of the world differently." The caterpillar crawled between Vatis's thumb and forefinger. Vatis gently stroked the thin white hairs of the squirming creature. "There are very few happy endings, Taldor," he added as he squished the insect, green liquid dripping down the length of his thumb.

Vatis brushed the remaining bits of the insect off his hand. He heard the boy dropping carrots into his basket but nothing else until Taldor spoke. "Do you know any happy endings?" he said after a long silence.

"Huh," Vatis said as if he snapped out of a trance. He thought for a moment. *What is a happy ending? All the stories end the same.* "Perhaps Mia-The-Maiden or Dinardo. They both disappeared and, by all accounts, were generally happy."

"Who's Dinardo?" Taldor asked, his voice cracking.

Vatis didn't answer. He cleaned his thumb on his pant leg.

"Are you alright, Vatis?"

"Hmm," Vatis said, staring vacantly at the dirt.

"Are you alright?" Taldor repeated.

"What? Yes, I'm fine," Vatis answered after another long silence. "I apologize, Taldor. I didn't sleep last night; too many thoughts ran around my head. It certainly doesn't help that Vidmar snored like an ox." His practiced, cheery disposition returned slowly like a carrot emerging from the ground. "I'm sorry, Taldor. I meant no offense."

"When I can't sleep, I like to sneak out and explore the woods but don't tell Pa. He doesn't like me going into the forest, especially at night, but he's a worrier by nature. Anyway, thank you for telling those stories last night." *So young, so full of optimism. Maybe you'll have a happy ending, Taldor.* He thought as the boy rambled about his favorite parts of the stories. "You should enter a bard's tourney. Have you tried?"

"No, I'm afraid not," Vatis said, forcing a smile.

"Why not?"

"There's something about being on a stage that frightens me."

Taldor stood and picked up his basket full of carrots. "You tell stories in taverns. What's the difference?" *Damn, you're persistent, boy.*

"The crowd, fewer drinks, the formality, the competition. At a tavern, I can relax, have a drink, and be a part of the crowd. It's more intimate, but I can't muster enough confidence to perform my tales in front of a large crowd," Vatis said.

Taldor bent down and ripped a weed out, placing it in the canvas satchel on his hip. "Well, you're the best storyteller I've ever heard, and I think you could win. Pa, Ev, and I went to the tourney a few years back, and you're miles better than anyone I heard then. We've only had a few tournaments in town, but I think they have them every year in Yimser."

Vatis's smile felt more natural. "Thank you, Taldor. I will consider it."

Taldor smiled and gently slapped Vatis's shoulder. "Well, I better get my chores done before Pa breaks out the belt."

"The belt?" Vatis asked.

"Oh, he's never hit me, but that doesn't keep him from threatening it," Taldor laughed as he ran off. *There's something strange about Hobb,* Vatis thought as he remembered the intensity of Hobb's glares last night. *I should ask Vidmar about him.*

Vatis roamed the farm for a while; he didn't know how long. He listened to the cows munching grass. He watched Hobb harvest grain. He ate delicious red apples in the shade of a large oak tree. But his thoughts always diverted to the watchtower at the edge of the property. Something about that tower was strange yet familiar. It beckoned him, but at the same time, something inside Vatis warned him to stay away. It was another internal conflict he battled, another skirmish in the war for his sanity. He walked toward the watchtower, no longer capable of resisting its pull. He needed to know what was inside. *Vatis.* A haunting voice echoed in his head. Not a voice he practiced but an unfamiliar, terrible, low voice that seemed to come from the tower.

He heard the metallic scraping of stone on metal as he walked. The sound brought hastily buried memories to life. Images of swords clashing and men dying enveloped Vatis in yet another nightmare.

"You were up early," Vidmar said, distracting Vatis. Battle-like images shattered like glass as he was pulled into reality. "Was I snoring again?"

Vatis stopped walking. "What? I'm sorry?"

"Was I snoring?"

"Huh, no. Well, I mean, yes, but that's not why I was up."

"Thoughts of Zidane again?" Vidmar asked, placing a small knife in a leather sheath. Vatis nodded. "I thought so. You've been distracted since we ran into the *peddler* and his friends. The images fade with time, but it's crazy what reminds you of battle. After my first, whenever it rained, my mind was flooded with images of men dying around me. What's weird is that it didn't rain during the battle, but the sound of water hitting the ground was eerily similar to boots marching over a field. I still get a little jittery when a heavy storm passes through."

Vatis tried to smile, but his lips wouldn't cooperate like they were anchored into a melancholy frown. "Thank you," Vatis said. It was all he could think to say. *Thank you for the comfort. Thank you for the nightmares.* "Taldor thinks I should enter the Bard's Tourney," Vatis said, changing the subject.

"I've attended a few, not in a couple of years, mind you, but from what I remember, you'd have a shot."

"I'd need to go to Yimser to qualify," Vatis said.

"Yimser," Vidmar added. "I do need to see an old friend up there. We've come this far together. What's a few more months on the road? Though, I need to go to Haran first." Vatis felt a wave of relief wash over him; he wasn't ready to part with Vidmar yet. *I still need your story.*

Vatis was about to speak when Hobb approached. "Good morning," he said. He turned and looked for the sun. "Almost good afternoon. Are you planning on staying another night? I'll prepare enough supper if you are."

"No," Vidmar answered before Vatis could speak up. "I need to get to Haran. *We* need to get to Haran." Vidmar gestured toward Vatis.

Hobb smirked. "Understood." The farmer sauntered off toward the house, taking systematic steps with his cane.

"Why don't you want to stay a few more nights? It might be nice to relax for a couple of days," Vatis asked, advocating for a stay he didn't want, but he didn't want to appear too eager to leave.

"I don't want to overstay our welcome," Vidmar answered plainly. "And I *need* to get to Haran." Vidmar looked afraid for the first time since Vatis had met him. *What's in Haran?* He thought but didn't ask.

"I suppose I could be ready to leave in an hour or two," Vatis said, scratching his chin.

Vidmar furrowed his brow. "How would it take you two hours to pack? You have one bag." He smirked.

Vatis scratched his chin, forcing a smirk onto his face. "Well, there are certain aspects of my daily routine that have not happened yet."

Vidmar smiled and opened his mouth to retort, but Taldor appeared yelling and running. "Pa! Pa!" he shouted. He halted when he reached Vatis and Vidmar. He bent over, clutching his calves and panting before he spoke again.

"What's wrong, Taldor?" Vidmar asked, patting the boy's back.

Taldor shook his head, trying to catch his breath. "Nothing," he said through deep gasps. "Nothing." His breathing slowed, and he stood up, interlacing his fingers and placing them on top of his sweaty head. "The cherries are back." He pulled a maroon cherry out of the sack draped across his back. "See. Where's Pa? I can't believe it. The trees are full of them. Yesterday, I didn't see any blooms. Today there are hundreds of ripe cherries. I don't know. I don't know how this is possible. I have to tell Pa. Where is he?"

"He's in the house," Vidmar answered, looking at Vatis. Taldor ran toward the house, screaming his news. "We should follow him," Vidmar added as they watched the boy joyously sprint home. Vatis nodded.

Vatis and Vidmar jogged behind the boy as he ran through the fields. Vidmar pulled ahead. Vatis watched him nimbly jump over a knee-high fence that separated the carrot and potato fields. He moved effortlessly. Meanwhile, Vatis struggled to jog; his head felt light, and air burnt his lungs each time he breathed. Hobb stepped onto the porch; the dog trailed behind. Taldor said something, but Vatis couldn't understand until he limped closer.

"What do you mean?" Hobb said sternly. Vatis joined the others on the porch in time to hear the end of the conversation.

"The cherries are back," Taldor almost screamed. "Look."

Hobb mumbled something and glared at Vidmar. The old man's examination continued onto Vatis. *What?* Vatis felt a warmth in his stomach that could have been from the short run, but it seemed to burn hotter as Hobb's gaze persisted. Vatis turned away, looking at the dog. "Show me," Hobb said. Taldor sprinted again toward the grove, stopping to make sure they followed.

"Vidmar, Vatis, come, you have to see this," Taldor said.

Hobb didn't acknowledge his two guests. Instead, he proceeded on his path, annoyed that something had altered the order of his daily tasks.

"Come on, Vatis. Let's see ourselves a miracle," Vidmar said, joining Taldor.

"I've seen several cherry trees in my life. I'm going to pack," Vatis said, sitting on the steps.

"Suit yourself," Vidmar said.

Vatis watched the group disappear into a thick grove of trees at the northern edge of Hobb's property. He hummed an ominous tune of his creation and rubbed his heavy eyes, struggling to reopen them. Now was his chance, his chance to see the watchtower. Its pull was undeniable.

After a short yet challenging walk, a decaying silver-gray tower stood before him. Loose stones sat on the ground near the entrance; dark green vines crawled up the sides. There was nothing remarkable about it. He had seen dozens of more interesting towers traveling throughout Emre, but there was something strange about this one, like a familiar voice calling his name. *Vatis, Vatis, Vatis.* He could hear the voice in his head. He was unsure if his mind was playing tricks on him or if there was a voice from the tower calling to him. He walked in.

The air felt heavy inside the tower, like walking through a mist. To his left lay a pile of rubble, and to his right, a staircase. Part of him felt that the stones were hiding something, but the voice in his head urged him to climb the stairs. The staircase wound up through the tower; narrow holes looked like footprints of broken stones. Vatis ran his hand along the wall as he climbed, stopping when he stumbled across a strange triangular symbol carved into the face of a stone that, at closer inspection, looked more silver than the rest of the gray bricks. *This is no natural decay. What is it?* He continued his examination, pressing every inch of the stone for additional clues. When his search proved trivial, he continued up the stairs.

As he neared the top, the voice returned. *Vatis.*

"Who are you?" he said, feeling foolish for speaking. *What are you?*

No reply came, but Vatis continued his climb. He was four steps away from the top. He could see the sun reflecting at the tower's peak. The voice called again. Not in its soft, ominous tone as before, but as a loud warning. *Vatis.* It yelled. The sudden change in tone startled Vatis. His ankle slipped and twisted. Vatis desperately searched for something to grab, a handrail, a jagged stone, a strong breeze, anything that would steady him. His nails scratched the wall on his way down. He twisted as he fell, landing squarely on his elbow. Pain shot through his forearm like an arrow. He somersaulted backward; his leg scraped on a loose stone, and his head cracked on the hard floor.

A STRANGE PACK

Vidmar

Vidmar sat cross-legged outside the barn. It had been a long night, and he wasn't sure if Vatis would wake up. He had cleaned and sharpened his knives, laying them in the dirt outside the barn as he tossed the stone, his only clue, up and down, then rolled it around his palms, over the back of his hand, and through his fingers like a street performer doing a coin trick. He desperately tried to distract himself. *Why do you care?* He heard footsteps. He quickly tucked the stone into the inside pocket of his jacket.

"How is he?" Vidmar asked as Hobb appeared. He started the deliberate process of sheathing his blades.

"That's hard to say?" Hobb answered; his eyes seemed to dart toward his pocket. Vidmar tried to ignore it. "I've bandaged the dislocated elbow and cleaned all the scrapes. He's lucky he didn't crack his skull, but he's still unconscious."

"I hope it doesn't affect his abilities. He's one hell of a bard, but I still don't understand what he was doing in the tower," Vidmar said.

Hobb either didn't hear the question or ignored it completely; either way, he looked over his shoulder to the watchtower before washing his hands. "Taldor is going to sit with him for a while. He will fetch us if he wakes," Hobb said. "Come with me. I have something to show you."

Vidmar nodded and followed Hobb. They walked slowly and silently. Vidmar kicked dirt into the air, desperately searching for a distraction. Suddenly, Hobb stopped. "Did you hear something?" he asked.

"Other than the wind in the trees and some wren, don't ask me how I know what kind of birds they are," Vidmar said, grateful that Hobb broke the awkward silence. Hobb furrowed his eyebrows and tilted his head. Then, a rough, harsh bark grew louder over the rustling leaves and chirping birds. "Is that Igni? What is he barking at?"

Hobb turned back toward the barn. "Wolves."

"Wolves," Vidmar said. Stay here." His instincts kicked in, and he trusted his hearing to lead him. Vidmar sprinted, paying little heed to the crops underfoot. He leaped over a fence, nearly falling when his back foot clipped the top of the waist-high barrier; a few hops and he regained his balance. The barking morphed into fierce growling. Low vibrating snarls seemed to multiply as Vidmar approached.

Vidmar slowed and crouched behind a fence post – not ideal cover, but enough for him to plan his attack. Fire was his weapon of choice against wolves, but it was too risky in the dry grassy fields of Hobb's farm. He didn't have much time. A pack of four wolves slowly pressed closer to Igni. The cattle galloped to the other side of the field. Igni growled, pacing back and forth to keep the wolves at bay, but they crept forward in unison. Vidmar needed to act while they were distracted. He reached into his boot, pulled out his favorite throwing knife, gripped the tip, aimed, and threw. It found its mark in the ribs of the closest wolf. The beast howled, turned, and charged Vidmar. Fortunately, it collapsed before Vidmar needed to make another throw. *Three left.*

The frantic mooing of the cows drowned the terrifyingly consistent growling of the wolves. Of course, the animals knew Vidmar was there, but that didn't change their goal – supper.

"What's going on?" Taldor yelled.

"Taldor. Get back in the barn now," Vidmar said over his shoulder. He didn't see Taldor's face. He didn't turn around to answer whatever question the boy asked next.

"Now," Hobb said, winded. "Damnit, boy. Move." He coughed between deep raspy breaths.

"Get in there too, Hobb," Vidmar said without turning around and inching toward the wolves.

"No," Hobb said in an inarguable tone. Vidmar didn't fight with the stubborn old man. Hobb leaned against the fence, pointing at the wolves with his cane. *What are you doing?* There was no time to think about the farmer, not if he wanted to save Igni, the cows, and possibly himself. These wolves looked different from typical wolves–darker and slightly bigger. Their eyes glowed with a greenish hue. He didn't have time to think about that either.

He crept into position and threw another knife, a small, poorly balanced blade usually used for cutting meat. It wobbled through the air and missed. It did, however, catch the attention of its target. The wolf attacked. There was a certain beauty to the way it moved: poised, confident, graceful, and powerful. Before he could line up another throw, the beast was nearly on top of him. Experience taught Vidmar that the wolf would bite one of two places – his legs or neck. He bent down on one knee, tilted his head, and exposed his neck. The bait worked like a worm on a hook. The wolf lunged for his neck. Vidmar rolled onto his back, unsheathed Acer's golden-hilted blade, and sliced the leaping creature from ribs to tail. Warm, thick blood spattered onto his chest and face. He somersaulted and positioned himself for another attack. Vidmar watched the terrifyingly beautiful animal whimper its last breaths. *Two more.*

The final two wolves continued to press Igni. Vidmar rolled quickly to his right. He had two knives remaining; Acer's knife, which wasn't great for throwing, and a perfectly balanced blade he had carried since he was a child. Just as Vidmar pulled back to throw, the wolves pounced on Igni. The old sheepdog growled, then yelped. The smaller of the two wolves bit into Igni's front leg. The black dog fell into the grass thrashing its hind legs to break free, while the largest wolf continued toward the cattle. Vidmar had to make a choice. With Acer's knife already in hand, he stood, spun, and released a perfect throw. The blade punctured the smaller wolf's neck, and Igni wriggled free as the third wolf died. *One.*

The final wolf was a giant among its companions. It stood a head taller and six hands longer. Green eyes glowed with an insatiable hunger. The dark beast rushed forward; it was done calculating the perfect attack. The cattle scattered. Vidmar narrowly avoided the cows as they ran from one end of the field to the other. Once the cows passed, he picked up his head to find himself face-to-face with the wolf, like they were in an honorable duel in a public square. The beast bared its teeth, snarling as another obstacle stood between it and supper. Vidmar reached for the sheath strapped to his thigh; it was empty. *Shit.* His final weapon lay in the dirt by the barn, where he absently fiddled while waiting for news of Vatis. *Shit, shit, shit.*

The wolf sprang forward. Its maw opened wide. Defense was Vidmar's only remaining option. He held his leather-bracer-covered forearm out like a shield. The wolf's jaws snapped shut around the sturdy, studded leather. He couldn't help but close his eyes. *Is this how it ends? A fucking wolf?* Vidmar could feel the giant teeth poke through the armor into his flesh. The pressure was incredible; a second longer, and his bone would snap.

He forced his eyes open, stuck his thumb out like a makeshift knife, and jabbed at the beast's exposed eye. His strike found the mark, digging knuckle-deep into the jelly-like organ. The wolf howled and released its grip. *Now.* Vidmar kicked. His boot connected with the wolf's throat. Tufts of hair fell into the grass like snow. Vidmar rolled backward. Igni, seeing his opportunity, leaped at the wolf's throat as best as his three working legs allowed. The wolf evaded the attack. The two canines became entwined in a hairy, bloody tornado. Vidmar ran, pulled Acer's knife from the third wolf, grimaced, and lined up a shot. *Shit. I don't have a throw. Fuck it.* Vidmar yelled and charged the wrestling animals to separate them. It worked. The wolf forgot its feud with Igni and attacked Vidmar, giving him the opening he needed. The wolf pounced. Vidmar rolled and sliced the creature's front leg off. The three-legged, half-blind, saliva-covered wolf still looked majestic as it lay in the grass desperately trying to stand, blood pooling in the dirt around it. Vidmar couldn't watch it struggle any longer. He crept behind its still-growling jaws and mercifully ended its life. Then, Vidmar collapsed on top of another victim of his blades.

Vidmar awoke in the barn next to, a still unconscious, Vatis. Igni was curled up at his feet with a bandage around his front leg. The smell of hay and manure didn't mix well with alcohol and blood. It reminded him of battle; it reminded him of her. *No. I can't.* He rubbed his eyes and rolled onto his side. Vidmar surveyed the area; luckily, a half-full bottle of alcohol sat on a hay bale behind him. He tried to push himself up. Pain exploded through his left arm. "Fuck," he yelled.

Taldor rushed in. "Are you alright, Vidmar?"

Vidmar shook as he pushed through the pain. Golden specs flickered in the dim barn light. "I'll be fine," he grimaced. "How are you doing, boy?" He asked as he scratched behind Igni's ears.

"He's got a few cuts, and his leg might never be the same, Pa said there was damage to his tendons, but luckily, he didn't break the bone. You're both lucky to be in one piece. Oh, shit, Pa wanted me to call for him as soon as you woke up. Don't move," Taldor said, sprinting out the open barn door.

"I'm not going anywhere," Vidmar said as he sat down cross-legged. He continued to pet Igni. "Good work out there, boy. Looks like we'll have matching scars." Igni whimpered and rolled onto his back, pleading with Vidmar to scratch his stomach. The dog's tongue fell out the side of his mouth as he relished the attention. Vidmar watched Vatis's chest slowly rise up and down. For the first time in days, the bard looked peaceful.

"Come on, Pa. Hurry," Vidmar heard Taldor yell outside the barn.

"This is as fast as I move, boy."

Taldor pulled the door open. Bright light erased the long shadows in the entryway. Taldor wedged the door open with a stone and raced to Vidmar's side. "Can I get you anything?" he asked.

"Water," Vidmar replied, licking his lips.

"Right away."

Hobb sauntered. His cane dragged behind him with each step. He looked at Vidmar, then turned away quickly. "How's he doing?" he said, nodding toward Vatis.

"He's still breathing," Vidmar said.

A prolonged silence filled the barn. Finally, Hobb cleared his throat and shifted his feet. "Thank you."

Vidmar nodded. He'd met plenty of men like Hobb – proud men, honorable men. There were few of them left in Emre. A simple nod said more than words ever could. Hobb smiled as wide as his stubborn lips allowed. Igni stood and limped over to Hobb. Taldor burst in with two mugs of water, somehow managing not to spill despite running from the well to the barn.

"Here," Taldor said, handing the mugs to Vidmar.

His mouth felt as dry as the dirt in the barn; his lips cracked as he brought the first mug to his mouth. He downed it entirely, water spilling over the sides onto his chest and neck. "Thank you, Taldor," he said, placing the mug on the ground and taking a small drink from the second. "Thank you."

Taldor nodded. He wiggled anxiously, watching Vidmar drink. "Yes?" Vidmar said, smiling. Soreness coursed through his body.

"How'd you learn to fight like that? I've never seen anyone move like that," Taldor asked eagerly.

"You were supposed to stay in the barn," Vidmar said.

"I did, but the barn has windows," Taldor said, pointing to an open window in the loft facing the pasture.

"I see," Vidmar smirked. "To be honest, the quickness comes naturally, and the fighting comes from too much practice. I used to be a scout in the army."

"You… you were in the army," Taldor said as he nearly jumped with excitement. His enthusiasm morphed into fear as he thought more. He grew quiet until he mustered the courage to ask, "But, you're young, too young to be excused from combat. Are you a deserter?"

Vidmar looked away. *Would I rather be labeled a deserter or a murderer?* He looked Taldor in the eyes. "Yes," he said.

Taldor's mouth hung open.

"Enough questions," Hobb said, turning toward Vidmar. "You don't have to say anymore. You saved us today. That's all I need."

"I'm sorry," Taldor said, twiddling his thumbs.

Vidmar drank slowly from the mug without looking at Taldor or Hobb. He set the empty cup down. It wobbled and fell sideways, drops of water spilling out and clumping in the dirt near the rim. Vidmar watched the dark rain cloud-like pattern expand in the dry earth. Hobb kneeled at Vatis's side.

"There comes a point in everyone's life where they have to decide what side they are on," Vidmar said after the prolonged silence. He liked Hobb and Taldor. *They deserve more.* "Do you believe in what you are fighting for?"

"You don't have to explain," Hobb said, looking up.

"No, I don't have to," Vidmar said. "But, you deserve to know. There's a crossroads in everyone's life, and you can choose one of two paths. The first path is fine; continue down the road with your caravan, never questioning why you are heading north as winter approaches, but knowing you are safer in a group. The other path is bumpier and foggy. You can't see far, and you will trip constantly, but you decide where you're going. You decide to go left or right, camp, or press on. You'll regret some of your choices, but they will be *your* choices. I won't go into detail, but I was asked to do something terrible. I was asked to follow along and trust that my superiors knew better. I told him that I couldn't do it. We fought. They nearly killed me. I ran and have been running ever since."

Hobb nodded. He continued examining Vatis.

"Were you asked to kill someone?" Taldor asked

"Taldor," Hobb yelled.

"It's fine, Hobb," Vidmar said, rubbing his chin. "Yes, not someone, but many people, women, and children too. That's all I will say about it. I've killed more than most, but I always believed there was a reason behind it: self-defense or they stood on the other side in battle or a duel, but never murder."

Taldor's eyes widened. He opened his mouth to speak, thought better, then began again. "You were in a duel?"

This kid needs to see more of the world. "A few." Taldor was about to ask another question when Vatis let out a raspy moan. They all turned and watched the bard's eyes flicker open.

"Oh, thank the gods," Vidmar said.

"What happened?" Vatis whispered.

HARAN

Vatis

V atis's head pounded. Imaginary painful knives stabbed his entire body as he packed dried meat into his bag and pulled out his purse.

"Here," he said, wincing as he offered the pouch to Hobb. "For the supplies. It's the least I can do."

Hobb pushed Vatis's hand away and shook his head. The farmer had been extra short with Vatis since he woke, his bushy eyebrows constantly furrowed like he was attempting to read Vatis's mind. *There's something in that tower. He wants to know if I found it. What are you hiding?*

Vatis placed the purse back in his bag. He watched Vidmar hide and sheath at least seven knives in his pants, shirt, jacket, and boots. The treasure hunter reached into his boot; his fingers scrambled up his leg and onto his hips. He searched the ground, ran inside, cursed, and ran back onto the porch.

"Has anyone seen a finger-length, green-handled blade? It has a sapphire in the hilt," he asked, turning his head rapidly as if the speed of this movement would somehow make the knife appear.

"Oh, yes. I'll get it," Taldor said, jumping to his feet. "You dropped outside the barn before the wolves attacked."

"Thank you, Taldor," Vidmar said. "Wait," he yelled as the boy ran toward the barn. He scratched the stubble on his chin. "You keep it. I've had that blade since I was your age; use it to whittle, filet fish, or practice throwing. It's a good blade and a trustworthy companion. It should be in," he paused. "Less practiced hands. If it's alright with you, Hobb?"

Hobb looked at Taldor. The boy grinned ear to ear, his child-like eyes pleading their case. The old man huffed once, then nodded.

"Thank you, thank you," Taldor said, running at Vidmar and wrapping him in a hug. "Do you have to leave so soon?"

Vidmar turned to face Vatis. "I need to get to Haran. We've been delayed enough already."

"Surely your wounds could use more time to heal," Taldor pleaded.

Vidmar looked down as if searching the dirt for an answer. Vatis interjected. "If we are going to reach Yimser in time for the tourney, we need to leave. Haran is just the first stop on the way. We can recover as we walk," Vatis slung his bag over his shoulder and tried his best to satisfy the boy's curiosity.

"You're going to try the tourney?" Taldor said, springing forward within inches of Vatis. The boy did not embrace him as he did Vidmar. Instead, he stopped short, keeping a little distance between them.

The distraction worked. "I believe so. If we can get there in time," Vatis said, winking at the boy and taking a step backward.

"Well, then, you better hurry," Taldor said, entirely wrapped up in the tourney idea. Hobb still studied Vatis with the scrutiny of a master fletcher stringing a bow.

"Hobb, Taldor," Vidmar said, tussling the boy's hair. "Thank you for everything. I hope our paths cross again someday."

"May your feet find the road," Taldor said, sniffling.

"And yours," Vatis said.

"Stay on the road," Hobb added.

"We will," Vidmar said, nodding at Hobb. Vidmar and the farmer seemed to have bonded when Vatis was unconscious. Vatis's stomach flipped over. *What did you say about me?*

"If you run into Evanor on the road, tell him to hurry home. He looks like me, except taller," Taldor laughed.

Vidmar smiled. "Ready when you are, Vatis."

"Onward," he said, waving his bandaged hand. The ominous tower to the west still whispered his name. *Vatis, Vatis.* It called as he took heavy northward steps.

A tedious, three-day journey through farmland and rolling hills led them to the expansive gates of Haran. Thick stone walls encapsulated the port city. Gulls cawed and circled above the walls, searching for scraps of food. Haran had been built on a hill. The walls and docks were at sea level, and the rest of the buildings gradually rose higher until they peaked at a four-towered castle with emerald flags flapping in the wind.

They continued up the cobblestone road; Vatis looked to his left beyond tall, wispy grass to see waves crashing onto the sandy coastline. The salty air felt strange, stinging his nostrils as he tried to acclimate himself to the new environment.

It felt odd to come to a city with no intention of performing. Nevertheless, Vidmar needed to come here, and Vatis needed the rest of Vidmar's story. He had gathered a few more details on the way as the treasure hunter opened up, but he never divulged anything substantial other than his escape from Jegon, which he described vividly.

A soldier approached adorned with steel plate armor, Haran's red and black eagle-like sigil painted on the chest. A well-polished helm with a triangular visor covered the guard's face. "The city is closed," a higher-pitched voice than Vatis expected announced. He examined the soldier, who had wide hips, narrow shoulders, and a slight sway as they walked forward. *A woman.* "The White Gull to the north has room for travelers."

Waves crashed against the shore, the calming sound growing louder as the tide came in. To their right, a man argued with another guard, desperately trying to get into the city. Dusk approached.

"Why is the city closed?" Vidmar asked.

The guard didn't answer but stepped back to her post. She planted her spear in the ground between her feet like a tree. Vidmar stepped forward with his hands raised. Before his foot hit the ground, the tip of the guard's spear nestled underneath his chin. A second guard stepped forward in unison.

"The city is closed," the woman repeated.

"I heard you the first time. Why is the city closed?" Vidmar said, gently pushing the spear's tip out of the way. He stepped backward and raised his arms again. "I don't want any trouble. I just want to know why the city is closed."

"Mayor's orders. Aye, come back on the 'morrow," the other guard answered in a brogue Haranian accent.

"Blindly following orders will get you far," Vidmar said. As he began to question the guards again, the woman twirled her spear with incredible speed and swung at Vidmar's head. He ducked under the blow with frightening casualness.

"The city is closed," she said, emphasizing the last word with a ferocious jab of the spear's blunt end toward Vidmar's ribs, but again the treasure hunter avoided the blow, deftly sidestepping the strike.

The guard held up her spear for another strike as Vidmar let out an exaggerated yawn. Vatis stepped forward before the situation escalated. "I'm dreadfully sorry for my companion," he said. "We will find other lodgings." The guards retreated to their posts, spears stamping the dirt with a rhythmic, coordinated thud.

Vidmar rubbed his eyes as they walked north along the road. "Fucking pricks," he said loud enough for the guards to hear.

"Are you trying to get us thrown in jail?" Vatis asked.

"The cells here aren't so bad," Vidmar said. "More comfortable than the dirt anyway. Follow me. There are other ways to get into this damn city."

After walking for some time, they veered off the road into a small yet densely packed forest.

"Where are we going?" Vatis asked, darkness thickening around them as they hiked into the woods.

"The city," Vidmar said. He ran his hand along a young oak tree. "Stay close. Stay quiet," he finished, whispering.

Vatis watched each step Vidmar took. His heel landed softly, then he rolled onto his toes and moved forward. He stopped; his left foot hung in the air like it was frozen in place.

"What's wrong?" Vatis asked.

"Traps. Don't step there," he said, pointing at what looked like a normal branch. Vatis mimicked Vidmar's movements, sliding sideways until his companion returned to his accustomed crouch. Vatis stood as a dull pain in his back grew from annoying to agonizing.

"Get down," Vidmar whispered as loud as he could without yelling.

"I'm not as young as you, Vidmar. My back can't handle this crouching too long," Vatis said, wincing into a more hunched crouch than before.

"Shh," Vidmar said, holding a finger to his lips. "We're almost there."

They slowly pressed further into the forest. Hot, shooting pain stabbed Vatis's lower back, but he continued to crouch. Vidmar's caution had saved them before; he decided to trust his instincts, even if that meant becoming a hunchback for the remainder of his life. *This story better be worth it.*

Vidmar stopped in front of a giant tree. It was as thick as three men standing shoulder to shoulder, easily the largest in the forest, at least that Vatis had seen as they crept through in the dark. They circled the tree twice before Vidmar knocked on some sort of door. A moment later, a small man appeared through a circular opening, holding a lantern in one hand and a crossbow in the other.

He eyed Vidmar suspiciously. "A king uncrowned seeks admiration," he said in a soft, accented voice. *Is that a child? Where are we?*

"The people unloved seek preservation," Vidmar said. *The people unloved seek preservation.* Vatis repeated the saying in his head, committing it to memory.

"Welcome," the boy said, pushing the door further open.

Vidmar walked into the tree, stopped, then tilted his head. "Jacob? Is that you?"

The boy shined the lantern at Vidmar, his long shadow in the corridor mirroring his movements. "Vidmar?" The boy wrapped his arms around him. The lantern nearly cracked as it crashed into the crossbow.

"Damn, you have grown. What are they feeding you?"

"Fish, mainly," Jacob said, letting go. "Too many damn fish."

"What would your father say about talk like that? You're supposed to be better than us, Jacob," Vidmar said, tussling the boy's hair.

"I'm not a kid anymore."

"Clearly."

Jacob led them through a narrow tunnel lined floor to ceiling with what appeared to be boat scraps. Vatis did not like enclosed spaces; he concentrated on breathing. He felt caged; the cool air struggled to enter his lungs. Fortunately, the boy's quick pace didn't allow Vatis time to panic. He thought he saw the word 'mermaid' painted in black along the wall. The Mermaid was one of Emre's most famous pirate ships until it sank in a storm off the coast of Numeria. Somehow the lumber made it into this escape route, or maybe Vatis's bard-eye urged him to look for a story that wasn't there. *It can't be The Mermaid.* He thought through frantic breaths.

"Did I miss anything?" Vidmar asked. "Oh, this is Vatis, by the way."

"Hello," Vatis said quickly in a nervous, unpracticed accent.

"What's with him?" Jacob asked.

"He's a bard. And we haven't exactly had a relaxing journey."

"Did you warn him?" Jacob said as he turned and stopped. *Warn me about what, where are we going?* Vatis wanted to interject, but he decided to focus on his breath. *In and out. In and out.*

"He's with me. He'll be fine," Vidmar said, nodding at Vatis.

"I hope so."

The smell of dirt and oil faded away as the spicy aroma of tobacco smoke flowed into the enclosed space. Jacob hung his lantern on a hook and pushed a circular door outward. Cloudy green light burnt Vatis's eyes. Dozens of tables were strewn about in what appeared to be a tavern. A long, glistening bar stood in front of three tapped barrels. Thick wood beams, seemingly placed at random, held up a low, planked ceiling. The murmur of conversation stopped abruptly as the door slammed closed.

"Who's that?" a dirty, dark-haired woman asked at a nearby table.

"You're not welcome here," a husky bald man yelled behind her.

Dozens of hard bloodshot eyes turned their attention from their games of dice or cards or empty mugs to inspect the newcomers. A man playing dice at the table closest to the door kicked his chair in as he stood, a maneuver that was somehow both extraordinarily violent and graceful. "What the hell are you doing here, Vidmar?" the man said, wiping beads of ale out of his graying beard.

At the mention of Vidmar's name, the tavern cohesively turned their attention back to their original vexes as if they rehearsed it. The uniform dismissive grunting and chairs sliding was almost sinister. "I could say the same to you, Kamet," Vidmar said, stepping forward. "What? Are you out of villages to burn down?"

Kamet grimaced. "Find a buried treasure yet?" The men at Kamet's table chuckled but did not look at Vidmar.

"I found a ring buried in a pond full of shit," Vidmar smirked. "Oh, also, I was digging somewhere quite familiar to you recently. I was searching, just for pleasure, deep within every hole in your mother's beautifully flabby body."

"You fucking piece of shit," Kamet said, charging forward. He towered over Vidmar. The expression on Vidmar's face didn't change. He looked up confidently, smiling like he knew something that everyone else in the tavern didn't.

"Stop," a commanding voice called to their left. A man sitting alone at a table scribbling in a leather notebook stood up and gently pushed his chair in. A hood concealed his face along with the dim, smokey light. "Sit down, Kamet." He pulled his hood back, revealing a clean-shaven, scarred face. Kamet sat down like a chastised toddler. "He's here to see me," the man said, walking forward. Despite a slight limp in his left foot, he still commanded respect as he marched. "Aren't you, Vidmar?" he emphasized the name like he knew a secret.

"I am," Vidmar said with unexpected sincerity.

"Who's this?" the cloaked man said, pointing at Vatis. His fingernail was painted black.

"Vatis, he's a bard."

"A bard, huh? Well, maybe he can entertain us later. I don't know how you ended up with such," he paused. "Questionable company, but it is a pleasure to meet you. I'm Alcin." The name carried weight and rang like a hammer striking an anvil. *The Alcin?*

Vatis bowed. He wasn't sure why. "An honor," he said, looking at Alcin's well-polished, jewel-studded leather boots. Vidmar elbowed Vatis in the ribs. He stood instinctually.

"Follow me," Alcin said. His cloak fluttered gracefully, emphasizing his movements.

A short, tense walk averting the eyes of other patrons led them to a small, smoke-free room where an ornate chandelier with dozens of candles outlined a polished wood desk. Two uncomfortable-looking stools sat in front, and an intricately stitched leather chair sat behind. The chair squeaked as Alcin sat down. Two muscular men took their posts: one at the door and the other behind Alcin. They each carried two black-painted axes, one on each hip. *What have you gotten us into, Vidmar?*

"Sit," Alcin said, gesturing to the stools.

Vatis felt like his stomach was going to explode like it was being inflated from the inside. "I can wait out in the bar. Perhaps I can entertain the guests with a story." *There's no need for me to be here.* The walls felt closer.

"No," Alcin said without explanation. His gaze struck Vatis like an arrow. Vidmar rubbed his face and looked at Vatis before wriggling onto the stool. Vatis brushed his pants, crossed his legs, and put on his best attentive listener façade.

"Tycar," Alcin said, gesturing toward Vidmar. The guard pushed him onto the stone floor and pressed his knee into his back. He searched roughly, placing each knife or weapon he found on the desk. Vidmar's silence surprised Vatis; he was reticent other than a few grunts. The guard dragged Vidmar up by the collar and threw him on the stool. It wobbled backward on two legs, but Vidmar calmly rocked back into place; blood dripped from his lip. Seven knives of varying sizes and one gray stone lay on the desk. Alcin examined each one.

"I've heard about this one," Alcin said, holding up the dagger Vidmar stole from Acer. "You stole this from a poor farmer. I thought you were a treasure hunter, not a thief."

"It depends who you ask," Vidmar said, wincing. It appeared like he was trying to resist his usual snarky retort. "Is there a difference? Is digging up graves different than pickpocketing a stranger?" Vidmar finished in an attempt to recover. Tycar stepped forward, anticipating a command, but Alcin signaled him to move back.

"Yes," Alcin said plainly. He finished his examination and neatly arranged the knives in a line from largest to smallest. "I've always wondered, what do you do with this one?" He said, picking up the smallest blade. It was thin and no bigger than his little finger.

"Pick food out of my teeth mostly, but it is also great at finding openings between helms and armor."

"Interesting. You're missing one. You always carry eight." *How often is Vidmar interrogated that this man knows precisely how many knives he carries?*

Vidmar scratched the back of his neck. "I lost it on the road, wolves attacked us, and I missed a throw."

"You never miss," Alcin said, smirking. The expression haunted Vatis.

Vidmar didn't flinch. "I miss often. A few lucky tavern wagers have exaggerated my skill," Vidmar said, shifting on his stool.

"Like your claim to be a treasure hunter?"

Vidmar nodded.

"Enough," Alcin said, raising his voice. "We aren't here to discuss your assassination abilities." Vidmar shuddered at the word assassination. His usual smirk flipped downward. "Have you made any progress?" He eyed the stone.

I shouldn't be here. Vatis's craving for drama lost to his selfish preservation. "Really, I can wait outside."

Alcin didn't look at Vatis. "I said no," Alcin said in a venomous tone. "Have you made progress, Vidmar?"

"Some," Vidmar said, looking down.

"What's some?"

"I've crossed off a few locations," Vidmar said, avoiding Alcin's darkening glare. "My lead in Numeria went nowhere. I need to find someone who can decipher the engraving. I've heard of a man in Yimser who knows all languages."

"He's a simple merchant, a raving lunatic," Alcin said.

"Some lunatics have answers buried within their disguise."

"Go to the library in Barna. There must be someone there who can read it. The hour grows late. I need results, and soon the burden of your secrets will be too much to bear."

"You know I can't go to Barna," Vidmar said, forcing his head up. "It's out of the question."

"I tell you what's out of the question. So, if I say you're going to Barna, you're going."

Vidmar nodded.

Why can't he go to Barna? "I'm sorry to interrupt, but perhaps this lead in Yimser is worth checking. I need Vidmar to accompany me on the road. You see, I'm entering the bard's tourney, and Vidmar's abilities have been priceless on our journey thus far," Vatis said, attempting to defuse the tension building in the room.

Vidmar looked at Vatis the way he did when Zidane had a knife to his throat—a deeply sympathetic look. Alcin's eyes widened but never left Vidmar.

"If you interrupt me again, Tycar will introduce you to one of Vidmar's blades."

Vatis wanted to run. He couldn't help Vidmar, but, more importantly, he couldn't die here. So Vatis bowed and obeyed Alcin's command.

"Danger follows Vidmar like a shadow," Alcin said, pointing at the treasure hunter. "I assure you that if there came a choice between your life and his, he wouldn't hesitate. Isn't that right?"

Vidmar didn't answer. His head hung lower like it was falling off his shoulders.

"See," Alcin said. "Didn't you notice how his demeanor changed in my presence? He's a different man, a different animal. That's the power of secrets, Vatis. I've domesticated Vidmar, the heroic, the feared, knife-wielding Vidmar, and all it took was a secret. He's a guard dog now, and like a guard dog, he obeys when commanded, but he keeps stealing scraps of food off my table, so he needs further training, or I'll be forced to set my other dogs on him. Understand?"

Vidmar's head plunged further downward. He rubbed his eyes with his left thumb and forefinger. Vatis forced a smile and nodded.

"Good. Now, I consider myself a connoisseur of the arts. So why haven't I heard of you, Vatis?" Alcin said, gesturing to a painting behind Tycar that Vatis hadn't noticed before. A gold frame held a canvas depicting a handsome man standing on a boulder, rallying a group of people with weapons raised in the air. *Is that Dinardo? Interesting choice.*

Vatis quickly looked at Vidmar. He *was* a different person in front of Alcin. His usual charismatic confidence had all but evaporated. "I'm a simple traveling bard. I have only performed around campfires and small taverns."

"Why enter the bard's tourney then?" Alcin asked.

"I was convinced that I could do well, possibly qualify for the King's Tourney."

Alcin stuck out his lower lip and bobbed his head. "Well, let's hear something. A song, a poem, a story. Give me a taste of the simple traveling bard Vatis."

"It would be an honor," Vatis said. He thought about what he might perform under such circumstances. He didn't sing, at least not in dimly lit rooms that seemed more like dungeons than studies. A tale seemed too long. A poem would have to suffice. He searched his mind for ideas, something fitting of this moment, nothing comedic, nothing fanciful. His eyes surveyed the room but always returned to the painting. *Dinardo. It must be. I do have a poem about Dinardo and the stolen crown. Yes, that's it.* He quickly ran the lines through in his head, cleared his throat, and began:

> *The coronation of a crownless king*
> *The subject's obedience it did bring*
> *A crown stolen from the unworthy*
> *Taken by a martyr without curtsey*
>
> *To a legend, the crownless king is bound*
> *Only a Pact knows where it is found*
> *'tis a search thousands tried*
> *In lonely homes, mothers cried*
> *'tis a search that all failed*
> *In broken homes, widows wailed*
>
> *A lone Pact knows where it has strayed*
> *Such treasure cannot be remade*
> *Rumors of ancient power reside*
> *In jewels of white the magic provide*
> *A simple ornament that brought fire*

A legend that toppled an empire

Is he a farmer with no crop
Is it affirmation or merely a prop
Is he king without a crown
His people have spoken.
They won't kneel down

Alcin clenched his fist and pounded the table. "What have you told this fool, Vidmar?"

Tycar pounced forward and threw Vidmar on the desk. A hollow thud echoed through the room. The knives and daggers scattered to the ground; a small black-handled one rested dangerously close to Vidmar's stomach. Vidmar tried to brace himself, but his hands slipped, causing his face to take the brunt of the fall. *What did I say?* Vatis thought, his heart pounded. Sweat beaded on his forehead.

Tycar grabbed Vidmar's hair, forcing him to look at Alcin. "What have you told him?" Alcin said, standing.

"Nothing. I swear. He knows nothing," Vidmar said, blood dripping into a pool under his chin.

Alcin turned to the other guard making an intricate hand signal. Calloused hands grabbed Vatis's throat and threw him against the wall; Vatis's feet dangled in the air. Alcin picked up a dagger off the floor near his feet; a menacing grin took the place of his stoic expression.

"You say Vidmar's abilities have been priceless on your journey. Well, I say everything has a price. I'm going to start," Alcin paused, searching for the words. "Trimming his fingers, knuckle by knuckle, starting with his right index finger. It will be awfully hard to throw a knife without that, won't it?"

"He doesn't know anything," Vidmar winced. The pool of blood was steadily growing into a lake. His eyes were bloodshot and horrified.

"We will certainly find out," Alcin said without looking at Vidmar. "I'll give you one chance to tell me the truth before I start pruning. So, Vatis, the traveling bard, what did Vidmar tell you about the treasure he is looking for?"

Vatis struggled to breathe, let alone talk; he croaked his first attempt at words. The guard's sweaty odor seared his eyes. *It was just a poem. What did I say? What did I say?* Vatis tried to speak again but could only muster a cough.

"Give him a chance to speak," Alcin said.

He could hear Vidmar struggling to free himself. Tycar laughed. He picked Vidmar's head up and slammed it back onto the desk. Vatis rubbed his throat as he coughed. His head was light and foggy like he had too much to drink. He tried to speak through the sore dryness in his mouth, but his words came out as a whimper. He inhaled deeply through his nose and tried again.

"He's telling the truth," Vatis choked. "The only treasures I know about are the ring he found in Basswood and Acer's knife. I know nothing of his current quest. It was a harmless poem; I saw your painting of Dinardo, and it came to mind. Please believe me." Tears burnt Vatis's eyes. The damp air stung his throat before it fluttered nervously in his lungs.

Alcin cocked his head to the side, stepping closer to Vatis. *No, no, that's the truth. I know nothing.* Alcin's tongue poked through his lips, and a hauntingly high-pitched laugh escaped. "You may have a chance in Yimser. I almost believe you." He stepped backward and turned toward Vidmar. "I hope you sharpened this recently," Tycar laid himself on top of Vidmar and braced his right arm into position.

I'm sorry, Vidmar. I'm so sorry. "Stop," Vatis wailed. It was all he could think to say, even though he knew it wouldn't help. The guard grabbed his throat again and lifted him into the air.

Vidmar struggled less than Vatis expected; defeated, he turned his face into the wood and closed his eyes. Alcin offered no comfort, no sarcastic remarks; he positioned the dagger's tip between Vidmar's index and middle finger and pressed down. He jumped and used his frail body to force the knife through the bone. Vidmar flailed and kicked the table, but he did not scream. His fingertip popped off like a cork and rolled onto the floor. Blood burst forth like water from a broken dam. Vidmar squirmed but somehow remained speechless. The once mahogany desk was stained crimson; the thick liquid rippled with Vidmar's breath.

"At least we can put one rumor to rest," Alcin said, dipping his finger into the pool of blood. "Vidmar-The-Coldblooded, your blood is warm and red like the rest of ours." The guards hollered like children. Vatis jostled up and down as his attacker vibrated with laughter. Alcin smiled, then sucked the blood off his fingers, his threatening demeanor returning terrifyingly quick.

"Let's try this again," Alcin said, turning towards Vatis. *No. I already told you the truth.* Vatis tried to think of a more believable story, but all he could focus on was the dismembered fingertip on the floor. "What has Vidmar told you?"

The process repeated five times. Vatis coughed inadequate answers with each interrogation. No matter how much he begged, no matter what he said, Alcin was not satisfied. Finally, after the fifth cut, Tycar cauterized Vidmar's wounds with a candle from the chandelier. Vidmar finally screamed, the deafening, agonizing scream of the useless prisoner. Fortunately, he passed out before the process could begin again. They dropped his limp body onto the floor and tied his blood-covered hands behind his back.

"Tie him up too," Alcin said, slipping into an elaborate emerald-colored jacket. "Allow them to get their story straight."

They threw Vatis on top of Vidmar and tightly tied his hands behind his back. He slipped onto his side with his head resting inches from Vidmar's mangled hands; the gruesome surgery left him with no right index finger or fingertips on his right middle and left index fingers. Alcin focused on the right hand until Tycar reminded him that Vidmar could throw with his left hand nearly as well as he could with his right.

"Come, we will check on them later. I've other business to attend to," Alcin said. "Tycar, guard the door; let me know when Vidmar-The-Eight Fingered wakes up."

"Yes, sir," Tycar laughed. Vatis rocked himself upward until he was seated with his back against the desk. He coughed. His throat was on fire. He searched for relief, a sip of water or wine, something to soothe the flames, but his injured arm pulsated with pain each time he moved. He shifted, trying to find a comfortable position. Tycar smirked as he watched him. The sweet metallic scent was overwhelming. A rhythmic drip, drip, drip of blood fell from the desk onto the floor near Vidmar's head, melodiously joining the guard's raspy breaths. The chaos of moments ago was lost in a temporary silence. Vatis closed his eyes as a tear ran down his cheek. *What have I done? Is it all worth it?*

Vatis listened—he listened as he did in the forest alone, as he did before he met Vidmar, as he did on the streets of Barna. He focused on Vidmar's labored yet calm breath, tuning out the horrifically consistent blood drops and Tycar's menacing snorts. A ferocious knock disrupted his momentary trance.

Tycar opened the door slowly. "What is it?" he growled.

"The boss wants to see you. He was raving about a missing shipment of Gar, asked me to take your place," a somewhat familiar voice said.

"Shit. I told him not to trust that cock-sure, hat-wearing fucker," Tycar said, stepping out of the door. "You're welcome, by the way. I'm sure if anyone can appreciate what's in there, it's you." His voice trailed off into the bustling common room.

"Good luck. Hey, Ty, stop and grab a drink on your way. I want a few extra minutes *alone* with our friend," the deep voice said. He heard Tycar's haunting laughter fade into the crowd. A huge, muscular man stepped through the door. It was the mercenary who nearly fought Vidmar when they entered the tavern, Kamet. *Shit, don't hurt him anymore.* He barred the door behind him as he stepped forward. *Don't hurt me.*

"Gods, what happened?" Kamet said, kneeling beside Vidmar and checking his pulse with his fingers. "Vidmar? Can you hear me? Vidmar? What happened?" he repeated, turning toward Vatis.

Vatis didn't answer immediately. His emotions were tugged around like a young whore. Seconds ago, he was confident Kamet was coming in to finish the job, but now he seemed genuinely concerned. His dark brown eyes flashed a kindness that contradicted everything about his appearance.

"What happened?" Kamet repeated.

"I'm not sure. It was going fine. It was going fine. I," Vatis said, trembling. "I recited a poem. A harmless poem, one I wrote about Dinardo and Greco's lost crown, and then," Vatis trailed off, unable to articulate what had happened. "I don't know what I did wrong," he cried after a long silence. "Don't hurt him anymore."

Kamet placed a hefty hand on Vatis's shoulder. "Vidmar is a friend, about the only loyal one I have," he said, cutting Vatis's bonds. "We like people to believe we are enemies. It's easier to get things done." *What does that mean?*

"We have to get him out of here. Alcin won't be long," Kamet continued. "Can you walk?"

Vatis nodded. He struggled to comprehend the turn of events. *Is he truly a friend? Or is this some cruel trick?* Pain shot through his arm as he pushed himself up. *I hope I can trust you.* Trust had never come easy for Vatis, he was skeptical by nature, but he didn't have any other choice.

"Good," he said effortlessly, placing Vidmar on his shoulder. "Stay close, stay composed, don't say a word. It might look better if you conjure up a few tears too." *That won't be hard.* All Vatis had to do was close his eyes, and the nightmares would do the rest. He nodded, gathered Vidmar's scattered belongings, and followed Kamet.

Kamet stayed in the shadows of the Tavern. They walked quickly around the edge, avoiding as many patrons as possible. A dark-haired man with a strange accent called out as they passed. "Taking out the trash, Kamet."

Kamet spun while walking backward and laughed so vigorously that Vatis's doubts about Kamet intensified. "I just want to see if rats can swim with their legs tied together," he said, turning again to face a guarded door. The brawny man's table erupted with laughter. They stepped toward the guards. Kamet's free hand rested on his mace.

A guard was about to speak when Kamet interrupted jovially. "Alcin asked me to take the trash out," he said, turning so the guards could see Vidmar's unconscious face.

"Is he dead?" one asked.

"Not yet," Kamet laughed.

The guards cackled like crows but opened the door to a moonlit cobblestone street. "Make sure you find out where his treasure is," the other guard called after them.

Kamet lifted Vidmar's hands into the air. "He's stubborn, but I still have eight fingers left. I'll buy a round next time I pass through." Their laughter reverberated as they returned to their posts. The door disappeared. Vatis stared at the city wall, mouth ajar, searching for seams or hinges or handles, something to indicate that a door was there, but he found nothing.

"Stay close," Kamet said, running down the dark street.

INTERLUDE

Zidane

Zidane gently tugged the reins of the carriage, slowing his horse. The familiar walls of Haran seemed different, taller, and more threatening. The salty air brought back memories of his childhood, his only joyous memories. The sun vanished from the sky; a faint orange glow reflected off the violent waves. His leg throbbed. The brutal wound Vidmar gave him was getting worse. Yellow puss oozed from underneath a bubbly black scab. He needed medicine. *I have to see Alcin first, though,* he thought as he approached the gate.

"Halt," the guard said. "The city is closed."

"Niare? Is that you?" Zidane said, straightening his hat. *It seems my luck has changed.*

The guard tilted her head. "Zidane. I should have recognized that dumb hat from a league away, but that's a different carriage. What happened?"

"Do you like it? I thought my carriage should better reflect my elegance, so I bartered, traded, and sold until I could afford this one."

"It does suit you. Where's your crew?"

"Oh, you know mercenaries," Zidane lied. "They follow the coin, and since I spent a hefty sum on this carriage, I could no longer afford them. So we parted ways near Vicus."

"The city is closed, Zidane. Mayor's orders," Niare said, her tone much less convincing than moments ago. "I can't let you in."

"What's this? I seemed to have saved a few coins for you, Niare," Zidane said, untying a pouch from his belt. He tossed it to her. "My favorite guard."

She caught it in her gauntleted hand, weighing it carefully. The coins jingled pleasantly like the wind chime hanging in his mother's window. "Seems a bit light for a person of such elegance," she said mockingly. "But fine. Be quick, and…"

"And if anyone asks your brother, let me in. I know," Zidane said. He carefully tucked his red-stained shirt into his new doublet as he ushered the horse through the gate.

After he stabled his new horse and stored his new carriage, he changed into a new shirt. Tarver had excellent taste in clothing. *It's a shame that only fish, snails, and crabs can admire it now.* He smiled as he adjusted the gray doublet's gold buttons, a perfect complement to his hat. His newfound wealth was a much-needed distraction. *I might be joining Tarver by the end of the night.*

He paced up and down a dimly lit street and cursed as he distractedly stepped into a puddle near a black iron lamp post. He kicked water off his new leather boots and caught a glimpse of his reflection in the muddy puddle. Dark stubble shadowed his sharp jawline. *I need to shave,* he thought. His breath fogged in the cool night air as he attempted to muster courage. *I should run, but I've worked so hard to get here. Alcin will understand. It can't all be for nothing.* Zidane's feet ignored his thoughts of escape and walked down a narrow alley that ended at the base of the city wall.

The door to lead thee Lies between diamonds three

He always felt like a child when he recited the rhyme, but he couldn't open the door without thinking of it. He approached the wall, the gigantic, ominous wall. To common folk, it looked ordinary, a barricade from the outside world, but to his guild, this was the front door. One only needed to know where to look. The first two marks were relatively easy to find. They looked like notches in the stone, but upon closer inspection, they were perfectly shaped diamonds. The two diamonds were engraved at eye height to the average man. Zidane had to look up slightly to find them. They were uneven and spaced about ten feet apart. The third diamond was harder to find. Some thought it was a star in the night sky. Others thought you needed to offer a diamond at the foot of the door, but the path to the third diamond required knowledge and courage. Between the two diamonds at waist height was a small hole in the mortar, just big enough for a man to stick a finger through. A thin piece of canvas camouflaged the opening. It was easy to find if one traced the line of mortar with a finger, but otherwise, it blended identically into the wall.

Alcin was fond of saying, "My men are like diamonds, hard to crack." This essentially meant anyone loyal to Alcin would offer up their diamond-like blood, and the door would appear–the third diamond. There was another part of Alcin's saying that Zidane overheard in the tavern. "My men are like diamonds, hard to crack but easy to sell." Zidane wasn't sure what the last part meant. Did it mean that they were all his slaves? Or that he sold their secrets? He tried not to think about it and gingerly stuck his finger into the hole, bracing himself for the impact of the needle.

Zidane winced as the mechanism pierced his skin. It hurt less each time he entered; his finger developed a protective callus. The apparatus was some intricately engineered machine that poked a needle into one's finger. Then the blood dripped into a vial and, when full enough, triggered a doorbell alerting two guards. He also didn't want to think about what Alcin did with all that blood. There were rumors of blood magic. It was most likely tavern talk; however, gossip in the guild turned out to be true too often for comfort.

The door slid open, the stone somehow retracting into the wall. The first time Zidane entered the tavern, the smell of alcohol and smoke was overwhelming, but now it was soothing and welcoming, like his mother's lavender garden.

"Complacency is rooted in stone," a voice said as Zidane's eyes adjusted to the hazy greenish light.

"Starvation is caused by the throne," Zidane said, reciting one of the dozen phrases he was forced to memorize.

"Welcome," the men guarding the door said simultaneously.

Zidane couldn't remember their names. "Thank you, gentlemen. It is great to be back." *Is it, though?*

The tavern was quieter than usual. He could hear individual conversations instead of the accustomed murmur. An attractive woman expertly dodged the vulgar advances of two drunks. "Sounds like you two could help one another," she said, leaving them.

Zidane straightened his hat as he meandered into the heart of the tavern. The conversational buzz grew louder until he heard a scream from Alcin's study. Alcin's torture chamber was more fitting; very few people left with their lives, even less left unscarred, at least that's what Tycar told him. He hadn't been with the guild long. Purchasing a new shipment of Gar was his first assignment of any significance, an assignment he failed. *Fucking Vidmar,* he thought. The patrons collectively turned their attention to the study; they fought the urge to stare. After a prolonged silence, the crowd returned to whoring, gambling, and drinking. Zidane veered his course closer to the study. A giant mercenary rushed past, nearly knocking Zidane over.

"Hey," Zidane said, picking his hat up.

The mercenary turned but didn't stop. His teeth snarled like a wolf through his beard while his hand moved to a mace on his belt.

Zidane had enough to worry about without angering this bull. "I apologize," he said, tipping his hat. After the incident with Vidmar, Zidane decided he needed to be more careful about who he picked his battles with. The man snorted and stopped a few paces away from the study. Upon closer inspection, the mercenary looked familiar, but he didn't have time to think about it. He had to tell Alcin that he missed the rendezvous with the dealer. *Fucking Vidmar*, he thought again. *I'm going to kill you*, but his thoughts of revenge dissipated into instinctual dread. *Not if I die first*. He approached the bar slowly with his coin purse in hand.

"I'll have a Numerian Brandy and a loaf of that brown bread. You know, the one with rosemary and the salted crust. I don't remember what it's called," Zidane said, placing ten Kan on the countertop. His hand shook when he let go of the tan drawstring, the last of his coin.

A few moments later, the bartender returned with a silver chalice and a wooden plate. Steam rose from the perfectly browned bread. The herbaceous fragrance momentarily distracted him from the butterflies that had been dancing in his stomach since he arrived in Haran. The bartender nodded, emptied the purse, and took the coin.

"Thank you," Zidane said, using the now-empty purse as a handkerchief to wipe the beading sweat on his forehead. He took a long, slow drink of the brandy. It was warm and smooth, sweet and bitter, a perfect combination of senses that made it the most sought-after brandy in Emre. He savored each sip like it was his last. The bread complimented the alcohol excellently; its warm, chewy center reminded him again of his childhood *and* his mother. At least he would see her again soon, according to most religions anyway. Zidane only seemed to find faith when his life was on the line. He raised his chalice to the air. *See you soon, mother.*

He was halfway through a bite of the bread when a chubby finger tapped on his shoulder. The butterflies in his stomach returned immediately, planning their coordinated escape through his belly button. Zidane's muscles tensed; he swallowed the bread and turned around.

"Alcin is ready," a ferocious, dog-like guard said.

Zidane chugged the rest of his brandy. The once-enjoyably warm liquid burned his throat like lava forced through a volcano. He coughed. His eyes watered. "Better not keep him waiting," he wheezed.

They walked into a storeroom behind the bar. Barrels of mead were stacked neatly along the back wall. A lantern swayed back and forth; its hinge mounted to the ceiling creaked softly. Crates of fruit and vegetables lined the other walls. A pleasant aroma of citrus filled the air. Alcin was drying his hands with an intricately stitched indigo towel; his flowing velvet cloak simmered in the lantern's dim light like a shadow on a crescent moon. The door slammed shut. Alcin turned, revealing a beautiful black tunic with a golden collar.

"Ah, Zidane, please excuse my tardiness. I had some urgent business to address," Alcin said, tossing the towel onto the ground near a crate of green apples. "I hope you will excuse the location. My study is occupied."

Zidane nodded. He didn't know what to say.

"Splendid. Well, don't delay. Is the shipment secure?" Alcin said, examining his nail beds.

Fuck, right to the point, Zidane thought. He opened his mouth. No sound came; a lump formed in the back of his throat. He swallowed, but it didn't help. "No," was all he could muster.

"What do you mean no?" Alcin said, focusing his intense glare on Zidane's stinging eyes.

Shit. How can I get out of this alive? "I was *delayed* and missed the rendezvous," Zidane croaked. He shook with each word. His fingertips were ice.

The guard grabbed Zidane's shoulders and forced him to his knees; his meaty paws threw his hat across the room, pulled Zidane's hair, and exposed his neck. *This is it.* Alcin bent down and met Zidane's tear-filled eyes. "You showed such promise, Zidane. I had high hopes for you." Alcin stood and pressed a knife onto Zidane's throat.

"Fucking, Vidmar," Zidane cried, forcing his eyes shut.

He could feel the blade release its pressure on his neck. He opened his eyes. Alcin stepped back but still pointed the tip of the knife at him.

"How do you know that name?" Alcin said quickly, biting his lower lip and baring his teeth.

"Vidmar," Zidane started. "He's the one who delayed the shipment."

"How?" Alcin demanded.

Zidane nervously told the story of his encounter with Vidmar, only embellishing a few minute events. Alcin listened without interruption; the veins on his forearms protruded as he gripped his knife tighter with each detail. The door opened. Zidane stopped. Alcin tapped his forehead with the butt of the blade. "No interruptions," he said, turning his attention to the newcomer. "Tycar, what are you doing here?"

Tycar looked around the room. His eyes bounced from the other guard to Zidane to the floor to the lantern, carefully avoiding Alcin. "Kamet," Tycar started kicking a stray potato against the wall. "Kamet said you asked for me. We switched places."

Alcin dropped the knife. It clanged against the stone floor. *Grab it,* Zidane thought, but he couldn't get his hands to cooperate. Alcin looked up at the ceiling, then dropped his head into his hands, rubbing his eyes like he was going blind, and somehow his fingers could massage his vision back to life. "Is Kamet part of my personal guard?" he asked, his hands still covering his eyes.

"No," Tycar said, scratching the back of his neck.

"Have I ever asked Kamet to guard my study?"

"No."

"Why the fuck are you still standing here?"

Tycar's mouth dropped open.

"Go, you fucking moron, go," Alcin said, ushering Tycar out the door. "Stay here, Lucius, and for your family's sake, do not leave." He followed Tycar. Zidane could hear him cursing as the door closed. He took a deep breath. His fingers tingled as he gingerly unclenched them. *Fucking Vidmar.* The thought brought a smile to his face. *You may have spared my life again, but I'm still going to kill you.*

WANTED COMPANY

Vidmar

Vidmar awoke with his face bouncing off someone's back. His world was a hazy blur as he tried to open his eyes. The last thing Vidmar remembered was Tycar grabbing a candle – the flame slowly cauterizing his wounds. Now, his entire body ached as he bounced up and down on his captor's shoulder. He tasted blood.

Waves crashed in the distance; the salty sea air grew thicker as they moved. Through the darkness, he could see sand. The big man left large, wet footprints. *Where are they taking me?* His fingers itched horribly. It felt like he still had all ten. He wiggled them around, assessing the damage. A dull ache evolved into excruciating pain as he moved the remnants of his right middle finger. He tried to remain silent, but the pain was immense; a cow-like groan escaped. Suddenly, the man carrying him stopped and set him down with his back against a rock. Vidmar blinked, trying to clear the fog from his dry eyes. Two shapes stood before him, one small, the other enormous. *Tycar and Alcin. Where's Vatis?*

The gigantic shape spoke first. "Vidmar, thank the gods," he said, kneeling in the sand. *That wasn't Tycar's voice.*

Vidmar tried to rub his eyes, but pain coursed through his hand as he put pressure on his missing fingers. "Fuck," he said, shaking his hand, hoping the pain would fall away like drops of water. "Kamet? Is that you," he grimaced.

"Yes, Vidmar, it's me. I'm sorry we don't have time to talk. We need to move. I'm sure they are looking for us by now. Can you walk, or do you want me to carry you?"

"I still have my legs. Don't I?" Vidmar looked down, genuinely curious about the status of his legs. He was relieved to find them mostly intact. He tried to stand but collapsed. He lost too much blood; he could hardly keep his eyes open.

"Come on," Kamet said, throwing him over his shoulder as gently as the maneuver allowed.

Kamet took off like a hound after a fox. Vidmar watched the receding tide erase their footprints and fell into a deep, uncomfortable sleep.

Vidmar rolled, face first, into something wet and coarse. The saltwater stung his parched mouth. He tried to move his fingers, but his hands were now neatly bandaged with blue fabric. He raised himself onto his knees, careful not to use his hands. Kamet slept a few paces to his left, snoring louder than the usually relaxing hush of encroaching waves. They were in a cave, or cavern, or hole, someplace damp and dark. Strange green, yellow, and orange plants clung to the walls. A crab scurried past his feet. He saw a familiar-looking pack on the ground next to Kamet. *Vatis.* He turned, searching for signs of the bard.

Vidmar found him watching the tide roll in at the mouth of the cave. He grimaced as he stood and approached Vatis, who swayed back and forth, clinging his knees to his chest. Vidmar tried to sit next to him, but he found it challenging to sit on the ground gracefully when his whole body ached, and he didn't want to use his hands. He plopped down and fell backward. Covered in sand, he finally rolled himself into a seated position with Vatis's help. He felt like a child learning to walk; any sudden change in direction meant he would topple over.

"Is this your work?" Vidmar said, extending his arms.

"The bandages?" Vatis said. He frowned and turned away. "Yes. I cleaned the wounds with the seawater and wrapped them with my blanket." He avoided eye contact.

"Thank you," Vidmar said. There was a long silence. Vidmar weighed his words carefully. The water now extended to his shins and toes crossed in front of him. "Tide's coming in."

The bard nodded.

"Vatis," Vidmar began. He took a deep breath. The cool sea vapors relieved growing pressure in his sinuses. "There's something I need to tell you."

"It's fine, Vidmar. It's my fault *again*," Vatis said.

"No. I need to say this. I work, well, *worked* for Alcin," Vidmar said. "I've helped him track down valuable items over the last few years. My task now, the treasure I'm hunting … he asked me to find Greco's crown." Vidmar felt a wave of relief wash over him; he hadn't told anyone of his quest.

Vatis's eyes widened. His mouth dropped open.

Vidmar looked at his hands, his livelihood; dark red blood crusted on the stumps of his missing fingers. "So, when you recited that poem, Alcin thought I told you about my task."

A tear rolled down Vatis's cheek. He wiped it away with his thumb. "I'm sorry, Vidmar."

Vidmar wanted to be angry with Vatis; he wanted to be angry with Alcin; he wanted to be angry at the world, but mostly he wanted to see her, and somehow those thoughts had calmed his rage. He had flirted with death most of his life. Last night, he was sure Alcin would kill him, so he gave up and pictured her one last time. Elisa: the only treasure he truly sought. Images of her distracted him from the pain. As he lost more blood, his distractions faded away into darkness. He screamed not because of the physical pain but because he had lost her again. His reverie washed away like footprints in the tide.

"I don't know that it would have ended differently, regardless of your unfortunate choice in poetry. I've been searching for too long, and I am no closer to finding this damn crown. Alcin is growing impatient with me and with his cause. He thinks if he has Greco's crown, he will have a claim to the throne. He's not wrong. To the people, the crown would be a symbol of his worthiness. Greco was the last king to wear the crown, the last king to come to power peacefully and not through brutal conquest. Many people, including myself, believe that Kandrian is unfit to rule. He is ruthless, unforgiving, and far too ambitious, but I can't say that Alcin is any better. The more power he gets, the more he wants. It's the curse of leadership. They fought so hard to achieve power that when the fighting is over, they forget the cause that garnered them love," Vidmar said. He hissed as the pain returned to his hands. "Sorry, talking distracted me from the pain." He examined the blacking bandages again. "Fuck."

"What if we found the crown? Would Alcin still want to kill you?" Vatis asked.

"He isn't known for forgiveness, but as I said, I am no closer to finding it than I was a year ago and now," Vidmar held up his injured hands. "I'm useless."

"Vidmar-The-Coldblooded, the only man to escape Jegon, useless, I think not," Kamet said.

"I'm not sure," Vidmar said. "If I can't hear an ox like you approach, I'm even more worthless than I thought."

"You never gave me enough credit. Just because I'm not a ghost doesn't mean I can't creep up on an idiot and cripple."

Vidmar looked at Vatis, then turned to Kamet.

"Too soon?" Kamet laughed.

Vidmar smirked. "Too fucking soon."

"We should thank the gods that Tycar is dumber than your friend here, or we would all be dead."

"There's only one way to thank a man like Tycar, and that's with cold steel nestled lovingly between his third and fourth ribs, but I doubt that I could hold a knife, much less use one effectively and even if I wanted to, Alcin has my knives." Suddenly, Vidmar's heart raced; his head felt like a cloud. *The stone. Alcin has the stone.* His legs started shaking uncontrollably.

"Alcin doesn't have your knives," Vatis said quietly. He stood and grabbed his pack, carefully setting five blades onto the damp sand. A wave splashed beneath them and rolled onto the weapons. "I didn't have time to grab them all. I'm sorry, but I did grab this." Vatis set the stone in the sand. "You're always playing with it, and Alcin kept looking at it, so I thought it might be important." Vidmar sprang to his feet.

A sincere smile forced its way through pain and gritted teeth. "Don't be sorry, Vatis. You saved the only clue I have left. I won't forget this."

"Do you know what it says?" Vatis asked. "The inscription?"

Vidmar's body trembled again, this time due to excitement, not nervousness. "No. Do you?" He said, trying to sound casual. *Please, please, please.*

Vatis examined the stone. "Unfortunately, no, but these are The Pact's symbols. Perhaps, if I had a copy of *Mysteries of The Pact* by Artgal Cairbre, I might be able to translate it." *Damnit,* Vidmar thought as Vatis rambled on about books. "…but Cairbre included a list of the symbols, so that's the book we need."

"Alcin suspected the stone had something to do with The Pact or Dinardo, but that's all he gave me. I've followed leads to Numeria, Wayland, and the edge of the Kaharn Desert. I have one lead left—an old friend in Yimser. Hopefully, he's still alive."

"The details of these leads would surely make an intriguing story," Vatis said.

"You saved my life. You will get your story. I'll tell you everything you want to know, but we need to move *now*. I've delayed us enough already."

Vatis strummed his fingers together while he licked his lips like a starving man in front of a feast. *Maybe I won't tell you everything*, Vidmar thought as the bard's frightening expression dissolved into his normally cheery smirk. Vidmar pocketed the stone and then bent down, trying to grab one of the knives with his right hand, but it slipped. It fell back into the sand. He tried again. He examined the blade, squeezing the hilt tightly with his three remaining fingers. He slashed the air. It felt odd and uncomfortable in his palm. The once reassuring feel of a blade was lost. He tried to jab, but the knife flew from his weak fingers. "See, useless. I couldn't cut cheese."

"That's why you have me, but we *need* to move," Kamet said.

Vidmar scowled at Kamet. "I just said that you pea-brained oaf." Vidmar turned back to the bard. "You didn't happen to grab my pack, too?"

"It's hanging on the rocks over there," Vatis said.

"I could kiss you, Vatis," Vidmar said, smiling. The bard took a step backward. *It was a joke.* "Maybe there's still hope. Alcin knows we were headed to Yimser. So where do we go? Do we try to catch a boat and loop back into Haran?"

"What about the bard's tourney?" Vatis asked, scratching his head.

"What about it?"

"Well, I'd still like to participate."

148

"Out of the question," Vidmar answered quickly. "Too many people know we were going there, and they know we are connected. You'll be killed."

"Vidmar, Alcin thinks highly of you. He values your caution. If he knew you were going to Yimser, he might think it's the last place you'll go," Kamet said, attaching his mace to his belt. "He knows how carefully you plan. You say your last lead is in Yimser, so maybe it's time to take a risk."

Vidmar thought for a moment. "That's the dumbest idea I've ever heard. Even if he doesn't believe I'll go, he'll still send a squad just in case. I don't like it. We should flee south, preferably on a boat."

"You know he has already offered every captain within twenty leagues of Haran a king's ransom to turn us in," Kamet said.

Vidmar sighed. "Yes, probably, but I can smooth-talk those mermaid-loving rum drinkers. It's less risky than walking into a trap in Yimser. How long were we pursued?"

Kamet shrugged. "We never had anyone chasing us, if that's what you mean. Once we were on the street, we sprinted toward the beach and started north. We're already on the way to Yimser. It makes the most sense."

Waves washed Vidmar's bare feet. The water now rose over his ankles. Orange rays of sunlight crept over the horizon. "I don't like it," Vidmar repeated. "Vatis can break the tie, but I know what he'll pick."

Vatis paused for a moment. Vidmar tried to communicate his apprehension telepathically and with a series of facial gestures that felt awkwardly lustful. "Yimser. I'm sorry, Vidmar," the bard said.

"Stop apologizing. I just want it to be known that I was against this plan, but let's get ourselves killed. I guess it's better to see the knife coming than to get stabbed in the back," Vidmar said as they started walking north along the shore.

Vidmar winced as Vatis changed his bandages. "Where's Hobb when you need him? That old man had the touch of a surgeon."

"My arm healed much faster than I anticipated. I only needed the bandage for a few days. My elbow is still a little sore, and my range of motion is limited, but it's mostly healed; nothing short of a miracle," Vatis said, moving his arm around haphazardly. He grimaced when he thrust it too far in the wrong direction.

"You're cheerful this morning," Vidmar said.

"It's amazing what a good night's sleep can do," Vatis said. He whistled an unfamiliar tune that harmonized with the hush of the waves and the caw of the gulls.

They traveled up the coast for two days until they stopped at an abandoned fisherman's hut with the decayed shells of two straw beds. Vidmar generously took the first watch. He passed the time by throwing knives at large pieces of driftwood, but try after try ended in the blade in coarse white sand. *Fucking useless*, he thought, struggling to adjust without two and a half of his fingers. He could barely piss without help.

Vatis transitioned from whistling to humming, stopping abruptly when a rock struck him in the back of the head. "Do you have to hum or whistle or sing all damn day," Kamet said, grabbing another rock. The bard looked as though he might retort but thought better of it. Vidmar laughed. The company and peaceful morning almost made him forget they were running from one of the most dangerous men in Emre. *I must find the crown*, Vidmar thought. *It's the only way to stop running, and I'm so tired of running.*

"Where are we?" Vatis asked, rubbing his head.

"I'd guess we are a day out, which should put us in Yimser two days before your tourney," Vidmar said.

"We don't need to be there for more than a day," Vatis said quickly. "We can take our time getting there. I'm sure they allow day-of entries."

"As nice as this shack was compared to sandy caves and forest floors, I desperately need a bath and a real bed," Vidmar said, stretching his aching back.

"The longer we are in Yimser, the more likely we are caught," Vatis said.

"If Alcin's men are in Yimser, it won't matter how many days we are there. I'm sure the hog over there would agree." Vidmar pointed to Kamet.

Kamet snorted before taking a large bite of bread. "Can I have one quiet, peaceful meal without being insulted before we die in the forest?"

Vatis tilted his head. "What forest?"

Vidmar had been avoiding thoughts of the Kokor Forest since he realized they would have to travel through it. *There's no other way.* "The Kokor. Today, we will have to cut through a small section of the forest to catch the road on the other side, and we need to do it as fast as possible and at midday. We do not want to be there longer than we have to."

"Stories are my business, and every story I've heard about this forest has been false. Other than the origins of 'May your feet find the road.' Do you know why we say that?" Vatis said.

Vidmar sighed, sensing a lesson coming from the bard. "No."

"Well, the phrase originated in Yimser. The northern wilderness is unforgiving. They say creatures and more lurk in the Kokor Forest. Some say the gods who created Emre dwell there; others say the spirits of tormented souls are trapped, never to escape. Of course, most of these rumors are categorically false. 'May your feet find the road' was said to people traveling to and from Yimser. There is only one road, and it bends around the forest. You do not want to veer off the road as it is nearly impossible to find again."

"I haven't seen any monsters or bird-sized wasps, but there are strange creatures, and the air feels *different* than any other place I've been," Vidmar said.

Vatis narrowed his eyes. "Thick air and strange noises do not mean the forest is haunted."

"Let's see how you feel when we are in it," Kamet said.

"You've been through this forest too?" Vatis asked.

"Once." Kamet did not elaborate. He slung his bag over his shoulder and adjusted his belt before letting out an obnoxious yawn.

Vidmar watched Kamet and joined in with his own slightly less exaggerated yawn. Vatis did not join the choir of howling wolves. "Let's go. Alcin probably knows where we are anyway. I'm sure they could hear Kamet's snoring in Haran," Vidmar said.

"Fuck off," Kamet said, launching another rock, this time at Vidmar. He instinctively tried to catch it with his right hand, but the small stone bounced off his palm onto the sand. He cursed under his breath. *Useless, I can't even catch a rock.*

A few hours later, they stood at the edge of the forest.

"Are you sure we can't go around?" Kamet asked.

"Not on foot," Vidmar replied.

"Fuck. I should have left you in Haran," Kamet said, pacing back and forth.

Vidmar pushed him with his right hand. Pain slashed through his joints like he was reliving Alcin's torture. He bit his lower lip hard, tasting blood. "Damn it," he said, spitting pink saliva. The pain lessened, leaving him again with the strange, itchy feeling. He sensed his missing fingers like they were wrapped in invisible cloth. He felt them open and close, open and close, but when he tried to remove the fabric, he felt nothing but air.

Kamet placed a hand on Vidmar's shoulder. "It's nearly midday; if we have to travel through this forest, we'd better do it now."

Vidmar nodded. "Ready?" he asked Vatis.

Vatis stared at the dark trees, their branches swaying haphazardly with the wind. A dark green leaf fluttered to the ground near his feet. He picked it up and held it in the sunlight. "What are all these brown spots?" he asked.

"I don't know," Vidmar replied. "A disease of some kind, but look closer. You see how the light struggles to pass through; that's how it is throughout the forest. Although it's midday, it will feel like we are walking in moonlight."

Kamet snorted his agreement and stepped forward, using his muscular frame to peel back a few low-hanging branches. Vatis exhaled and stepped into the forest first, impressing Vidmar with his uncharacteristic bravery. Vidmar looked back. The soothing safety of the beach begged him to turn around. He made eye contact with Kamet, exchanging the same shallow nod they used to in the army. The gesture offered good luck while acknowledging this may be their last adventure together. Kamet breathed deeply and released the branches; they snapped backward as the forest swallowed them in darkness

THE KOKOR FOREST

Vatis

I*should not be leading.* Vatis stepped carefully over the soft, muddy ground, holding his arms close to his chest to stop them from shaking. He tried to play a new character as he entered the forest, a brave hero like Dabin or Dinardo or even Vidmar, but bravery was something that he could not fake. So, he quit acting and focused on moving. Each breath caught in his throat. Vidmar was right about one thing: the air felt different. It was heavy in Vatis's lungs and clung to his skin like a misty rain.

His eyes toiled in the darkness, looking for anything familiar. Vatis stopped briefly to examine a coarse, abnormal plant. He touched one of the emerald leaves; it left a trail of slime on his fingertips. He pushed the leaf away and pressed forward, mud clinging to the heels of his boots.

Everywhere Vatis looked dark trees grew in twisted patterns as if the branches had to fight the air to taste the sun's rays. Crimson and violet tulips drank in the sour nutrients between gnarled roots. He heard Vidmar breathing heavily behind him, but nothing else. No crickets chirping, no birds singing, nothing, except the disturbance they caused. The silence sent shivers down his spine.

Your story better be worth it, he thought as he felt Vidmar's hand against his waist. Vatis kept walking, one careful step at a time, but stopped when he heard a humming noise like a mother rocking her baby to sleep. *What's that?* The tune was vaguely recognizable. "Do you hear humming?" Vatis asked.

"No. I don't hear anything. Vidmar?" Kamet answered.

"Everyone hears different things in this forest; don't think about it," Vidmar whispered. "Just focus."

How can I focus? I know that tune–the Giant and the Lamb? Vatis felt an almost irresistible urge to investigate the noise, but every time he stopped, Vidmar nudged him forward. He tried to remember all the stories he knew about The Kokor Forest. The subject had never interested him: stories of fairies, magic, and legends. They were all tales for childish bards who never outgrew their youthful whimsy. *They can't be true,* Vatis thought while trying to ignore the increasingly terrifying humming. Sweat dripped from his forehead. The air smelt like recently fallen rain, reminding him of his childhood on the streets of Barna.

We are the Kokor Forest, Vatis. A voice whispered in his head, not his voice, not one of his characters, but a familiar voice.

"Did you hear that?" Vatis said. His knees quivered, but Vidmar still pushed him forward.

Vidmar whispered. "Keep moving. Don't get distracted."

Vatis, the voice called again. *We know who you are–what you are. You are one of us; join your brothers and sisters and rest.* Vatis swallowed. His throat dried like he had eaten a spoonful of salt. He bit the insides of his cheeks to stop his teeth from chattering. Suddenly, a dark shape sprinted across their path.

"Please tell me you saw that," Vatis begged. The forest seemed to be playing tricks on him. Vatis no longer trusted his usually keen senses. Even his taste was obscured; a queer, sour flavor lingered on his tongue.

"Yes, keep moving," Vidmar said, increasing the pressure of his push against Vatis's back.

"Can't you move any faster?" Kamet whispered. "I feel like something is watching me."

"Something is watching us," Vidmar said. "I saw it in the trees. It's been following us. Here." He handed Vatis a blade.

Vatis examined the gold hilt; the object felt foreign in his sweaty, shaking hands. The voice hissed in his head. *Put that away, Vatis.* His fingers opened involuntarily, and the knife fell into the mud. He bent down and reached for the dagger. Something slithered between his feet. He jumped back, nearly falling over, but Vidmar caught him, wincing as Vatis crashed into his injured hands.

"What is it?" Vidmar said, grimacing.

"I think it was a snake," Vatis answered, shaking as he bent down again to find the knife. *I hope it was a snake.*

Kamet snarled. "Let's get the fuck out of this forest."

Vatis scrambled to find the dagger. The closer his nose came to the ground, the harsher the smell of mud became. He was blindly searching for the blade. His hands dragged through mud and leaves and twigs until, luckily, they collided with the knife. The hissing voice screeched desperately.

"Did you find it?" Vidmar asked.

"Yes," Vatis said, standing up. He wiped his hands on his pants, alternating which hand carried the knife. The blade felt better in his left, and he slowly convinced his feet to move. He hadn't taken more than ten steps when he stopped again.

"What is it now?" Kamet called.

A figure loomed in front of them, cloaked in shadow. It was no larger than a child with a vaguely human shape. *Fairies and monsters and legends, what is that thing?* Vatis watched its outline shimmer like a reflection on a pond. He felt a need to call out to it, but he couldn't force his voice to cooperate. Vidmar slid in front of him, fiddling with a blade in his left hand as he nudged Vatis backward. The shadow remained in their path, observing them. Its head twitched as Vidmar took another step forward. The voice returned, its tone teetering somewhere between anger and hatred. *Sheathe your blades. We decide who passes through the Kokor.*

Vatis tapped Vidmar on the shoulder. "Did you hear that?" he whispered. His voice cracked on the last words.

"No," Vidmar answered sharply, never taking his eyes off the shadow.

The dagger felt hot in his hand as he watched the creature shift back and forth along their path. "The voice said to sheathe our blades," Vatis said, handing Vidmar the dagger. Vidmar pushed the knife toward Vatis but kept his eyes on the shadow. "What voice?"

I don't know what voice. The heat from the blade intensified as the hissing monster's call tickled the hairs on the back of Vatis's neck. "The voice, its voice, the forest's voice, it's talking to me," Vatis said, trying to articulate his scrambled thoughts.

"The forest's voice?" Kamet asked.

"Yes, put your weapons away," Vatis said, forcing the dagger into Vidmar's hand. "Now."

"No chance," Vidmar replied quickly.

"Vidmar, please, trust me."

Vidmar looked at Vatis. "Fine. I trust you." He exhaled and faced the creature again.

Vatis watched Vidmar slowly store his knives, placing one in a sheath on his hip and the other in a slit in his jacket. The maneuver took much longer than it used to. The treasure hunter grunted each time the blades missed their mark. Before the injury, it seemed like Vidmar could conceal several knives in seconds, but now he could hardly replace two without cutting himself. Vatis heard Kamet's mace clink into place a few seconds later.

Good, the voice called. The shadow didn't move. *Now join us, Vatis. You're tired; you need rest.*

"What now?" Vidmar asked, turning back toward Vatis.

Vatis rubbed his temples as the voice hissed louder in his head. *Leave these thieves to their fate. Come, rest.* The voice was right; Vatis *was* exhausted. *When was the last time I slept more than a few hours*, he thought as he stepped off the path.

Who are you? Vatis asked in his head as he stepped further into the forest. *Can you hear me? How do you know who I am?*

Of course, we hear you; we are brothers. The voice screamed as Vatis felt his collar jerk backward.

"What are you doing?" Kamet and Vidmar asked in unison.

The creature screeched again; its head twitched. Then, a shrill cry escaped, and it darted forward. Vidmar threw Vatis sideways, yelling as he stepped in front of him. The shadow passed through all of them like a cloud, encapsulating Vatis in a blizzard as an icy wind crystallized every joint in his body. The pain forced Vatis to his knees. Kamet groaned. Vidmar hissed through gritted teeth, and Vatis cried. The screeching surrounded them. Even after Vatis covered his ears, the high-pitched wailing wouldn't stop.

We are the Kokor. We decide who passes, Vatis. Join us.

Vidmar was screaming now. Vatis saw his knees shake as he tried to stand. The screams were relentless. Kamet's roars softened into whimpers. Somehow, Vatis stood. "Stop," he yelled.

The unbearable noise ended abruptly, leaving Vatis feeling like he had stuck his head in a ringing bell. He swallowed to break the painful bubbles clogging his ears. After an excruciating pop, Vatis felt like he was underwater; every sound was muffled, though the lack of sound was a welcomed replacement to the screaming and bell-ringing. He shifted his jaw left and right. Vidmar and Kamet slowly rose to their feet. Vidmar inserted his little finger into his ear. Kamet took a more vigorous approach, smacking his ears with the heel of his hand and shaking his head.

"What was that?" Kamet yelled.

"What?" Vidmar yelled in return. They both seemed to struggle to adjust to a normal conversational tone. They each tried their preferred method of sensory recovery once more.

"What the fuck was that?" Kamet said, slightly softer than the first time but still louder than his usual tone.

Vidmar stretched his mouth open. "What?" he said, leaning forward.

Vatis swallowed again. "I think it was the forest," he said as normally as he could. *Or whatever lives in the forest. What does it want from me?*

"Follow me," Vidmar yelled, either not hearing or ignoring Vatis. He took off, tilting his head and scratching his ears as he moved.

Vatis tried to keep up as Vidmar jogged through the forest. The treasure hunter's pace was unsustainable; Kamet pushed Vatis every time he fell back like a carriage driver whipping a stubborn horse. Vatis gasped for air. The thick forest fog burnt his lungs and throat. He felt like they had been running for hours. He could barely hear; he only saw vague outlines of shapes, and his mind raced faster than his feet. Vatis didn't know if it was his imagination or if the creatures were running beside them. Every time he looked, a dark shape ruffled the foliage alongside the narrow path and hissed in his ear. *Join us, Vatis. Before it's too late.* If it weren't for the mercenary pushing him from behind, Vatis would have collapsed and given in to the forest. *I'm so tired.*

We know. Come, rest, Vatis. The forest answered his desperate thoughts.

The outer edge of the Kokor Forest glowed a translucent jade as more light filtered into Vatis's line of sight. Vidmar ran faster, extending his lead. He leaped through a narrow opening. Sunlight poured into the forest, creating the most beautiful, golden door Vatis had ever seen. Dust danced in the yellow light, illuminating their path to safety. The voice screamed in his head. *No!* Vatis felt as though vines were pulling him backward.

"Go, go," Vidmar said, ushering them through the branches.

Vatis forced his body forward, ignoring the forest's pleas, and jumped through the opening.

Bright sun temporarily blinded him. Golden specks twinkled in the knee-high grass as he blinked furiously to regain his vision. He squinted gently, easing his eyes all the way open. He looked up and sneezed; pain shot through his body, and the stars returned, dancing more voraciously amongst the white flowers in the tall grass. Vidmar and Kamet fought through similar reactions.

Finally, Vidmar spoke, "Never, again," he said, breathing hard.

"Fuck," Kamet said, rubbing his eyes.

Vatis searched for words. He didn't know what to say. He didn't know how to feel. The forest talked to him, and he spoke back telepathically. *Was that magic, or am I going crazy?* Rarely had his travels taken him north of Barna. In fact, he had only been to Yimser once as a boy with his mother, and they had stayed far away from the forest. Yet, he *still* felt pulled toward the Kokor like the watchtower at Hobb's farm – he needed answers. Something tugged on his natural curiosity; something or someone knew too much. *Why? What does it know?*

Vatis tried to remember their trip through the forest, but everything was a blur besides the voice in his head and the shadow creature. The journey seemed to last days, but judging by the sun, Vatis guessed they only spent a few hours in the Kokor. A tap on the shoulder brought him back to the present as Vidmar handed him a waterskin. "Drink," he said.

"Thank you," Vatis said. The water cooled his aching throat.

"Easy, that's all I have until we get to Yimser," Vidmar said, extending his hand.

Water dripped down Vatis's chin as he swallowed one last gulp. "Sorry." He handed Vidmar the nearly empty waterskin. Vidmar jostled it, listening to the hollow splashes, and shook his head.

"What was that?" Kamet asked. "We've been through twice before and have never encountered anything like that."

Vidmar looked back at the forest. "I don't know what that was. Was it talking to you, Vatis? You said you heard voices."

Vatis nodded. "I don't know if *it* was talking to me, but something spoke to me."

"Why?" Vidmar asked.

"I don't know. I don't know if it was some spirit, fairy, or monster trying to lure me to my death or if it was trying to help me, but it could hear my thoughts," Vatis said as tremors reverberated down his legs. "It could hear my thoughts."

"How do you know?" Vidmar asked. He and Kamet stepped closer, but Vatis backed away.

I don't know, but I can't reveal too much. Simple is better. "I asked it something, and it replied."

"What did you ask?"

Vatis struggled to stand. His teeth chattered. He hugged himself to stop the shaking. Vidmar lightly rubbed his back. "It's alright. We're out. We're safe."

"For now," Kamet said.

"Shut up," Vidmar snapped. "We can be in Yimser tonight if we hurry."

Vatis nodded. He didn't want to be in Yimser any longer than he had to, but he wanted to put as much distance between himself and the Kokor as possible.

"Give me a moment," he said. Vatis knelt in the tall grass. The rough fescue itched his exposed ankles. Nearby, a dove cooed. The soothing, familiar music reinvigorated him. He adjusted his boots, straightened his pants, and stretched his neck. He looked back at the forest. In his mind, a faint, distant voice called, *Vatis*. He forced his feet to move north.

YIMSER

Vatis

lurry clay tiles came into focus as Vatis winced on blistered feet. Tall, steeply pitched roofs poked over the top of a wooden wall that could barely be considered a fence. Beyond the wall at the center of the city, a black spire towered above the other buildings, shimmering beneath a crescent moon. Chimney smoke created dark clouds that hung ominously below the tower's peak. *The Church of Eternal Darkness,* Vatis thought, absently humming as a distraction. He had forgotten how popular the religion was in Yimser.

A putrid, sulfuric scent drifted on the cool evening breeze. "What is that smell?" Vatis scrunched his nose.

Vidmar laughed. "That's Yimser. There's a tar pit northwest of the city. They say you get used to it."

"It's not that bad," Kamet said.

"That's because you've been smelling yourself for 30 years. Nothing smells bad compared to that," Vidmar said.

I should have known about the tar pit, Vatis thought, ignoring the banter between his companions. He couldn't concentrate. His mind drifted like the foul-smelling wind, elevating everything unpleasant: the Kokor Forest, the shadow creature, his aching feet, and his always-present self-doubt. *We're too early.*

They walked along a road that transitioned from dirt to gravel to unmaintained cobblestones. Weeds grew through the cracks, breaking the once-perfect symmetry. Tall, wooden lamp posts lined the remainder of the road. The flame in the lanterns somehow burnt with a faint green light. Vatis paused to examine the lantern to his left; however, movement beyond the post distracted him. He looked closer. Two hooded corpses swung rigidly from a lone oak tree as crows pecked at their decaying skin. A sign hung around one of their necks. Vatis squinted but couldn't read it in the dim light.

"Vatis," Vidmar called.

Vatis spun backward. "I'm coming," he said, rubbing his eyes. They were close now. The smell from the tar pit intensified. Yimser was a new town. Vatis needed to get in character, but he quit acting a while ago. Vidmar would notice a change in his demeanor. *Still, I need to be Vatis-of-the-Road,* he thought, trilling his lips and gently slapping his cheek, seeking the familiar comfort of his favorite character.

"What are you doing?" Kamet asked.

Shit. "I'm exhausted. I'm trying to make it to an inn without collapsing," Vatis lied, bouncing on his toes and shaking his head. Kamet furrowed his eyebrows and whispered something to Vidmar.

What are you saying? Vatis watched Vidmar and Kamet laugh as they walked. *It was a joke at my expense, I'm sure. Fine, keep it to yourselves.* They walked a few more paces before approaching a red-painted shack with a tiled roof. One of the tiles near the edge looked like it was about to fall off, but it hung on with a desperation that Vatis admired.

"What in the everlasting darkness do you want?" a guard said, stepping out of the roadside shack.

"Hello, we'd like to enter the city," Vidmar answered in an unusually cheery tone. Kamet nodded, and Vatis decided an enthusiastic wave was the best greeting he could muster.

"What's with him?" the guard said, pointing at Vatis. Vatis pulled his arm down with his opposite hand and stopped waving.

Vidmar smiled. "It's been a long journey. We could all use some rest."

Kamet nodded again. This time, Vatis followed the mercenary's lead.

"What brings you to Yimser?" the guard asked, returning his gaze to Vidmar. "And darkness, what happened to you?"

"My friend wants to participate in the tourney," Vidmar explained.

The guard laughed. "He looks like a bard, but Feya *always* wins the tourney."

"Well, they haven't heard Vatis-of-the-Road yet. And this," Vidmar said, holding up his hands. The bandages were filthy. "Wolves attacked us on the road. I wouldn't be here if not for the bravery of my friends."

Vatis knew Vidmar was lying to the guard, but sincere appreciation glimmered in his eyes when he looked back at them.

"I see," the guard said, squinting. "We don't hear of many wolf attacks north of the forest."

"It happened near Vicus," Vidmar answered quickly.

"Then, you have traveled a long way to get to Yimser. You seem like honorable men, a word of caution; most of us aren't fond of foreigners, especially foreign bards. A local almost always wins the tourney," the guard said, nodding to the executed corpses.

"Do the losers hang?" Vatis asked, following the guard's eyes to the hanged men. His stomach twisted into a tight knot.

"No," the guard said without emotion. "Not unless they are criminals."

"Well, we are no criminals, and as I said, they haven't heard Vatis yet. The man could make the King weep. Are there rooms available at Geoff's?"

"I believe so but don't take my word on it. Lots of *people* in town for the tourney," the guard said, strangely lingering on the word people as if it were a threat.

"Thank you. May your feet find the road," Vidmar said.

"And yours," the guard said, returning to his shack. He poked his head out of a narrow window as they passed. "Stay out of trouble."

Vidmar spun, bowed, and held a hand to his heart. "On my honor."

"Like you have any," Kamet whispered.

Vidmar laughed. "More than you."

They walked through the gate and down a well-lit street. The lanterns inside the walls glowed with normal yellow-orange light, casting shadows on multiple-level homes painted in various colors. The buildings were constructed so close they left no space for allies or side streets. It was difficult to see all the shades in the dark, but the homes seemed to range from yellow to red to blue to white. Vatis wondered if the paint had any significance. *Members of different guilds, perhaps.* He looked at a large, rectangular stained-glass window next to a golden door. Unfortunately, he couldn't tell what image the window depicted.

Vatis continued to admire the architecture as they walked when a shop on his right caught his eye. At least a dozen baskets with vibrant, cascading flowers hung from hooks beneath a balcony. A man with a hunched back perched precariously on a stool watered the plants with a bowl. He grumbled and went inside as fast as his elderly body allowed. *That's odd,* Vatis thought as the old man slammed a blue door shut. Petals fell from the two hanging plants closest to the door. He had been too enamored with the buildings and didn't realize that hardly anyone was on the street. *It isn't that late. There should be more people out.*

A woman carrying a basket with bread and cheese scowled as she passed them a few moments later. Of the ten or so people Vatis saw, only two didn't act like he carried a plague, but even those two didn't offer any greeting. *They* really *don't like outsiders,* Vatis thought as the street turned north. The buildings curved with the road; one's face bowed to match the street. Its black window frames stood out against a red-painted wall. A bright blue building distracted Vatis, and he stumbled over a protruding cobblestone, hopping to regain his balance. A bearded man sitting in a chair outside the home huffed at the display. Vatis tried to ignore the people, but they only made him more nervous.

The sound of running water and a fragrant, inviting aroma prevailed over the inhabitants' annoyance and the smell of tar. The sweet, spicy scent of cinnamon and nutmeg warmed Vatis's nostrils and rumbled his stomach. "Are those sweet rolls?" he said, sniffing the air like a dog.

"I think they call them mammoth ears," Vidmar replied. "They are huge discs of fried bread with a sweet, sugary topping. I haven't had one in years." Vidmar cleared his throat. "I'm drooling already."

Kamet licked his lips. "I haven't eaten anything except dried meat and fish for a week. I would kill for one of those right now."

Vidmar slapped Kamet on the shoulder. "We'll get some tomorrow. But, first, let's get to Geoff's."

Soon, the road widened and split into two separate paths. One path led to a bridge where the buildings seemed to become even more elaborate than they had been. The other went east down an eerie path with fewer lampposts and unnerving shadows.

"This way," Vidmar said, turning right down the dark path toward a decaying building. He walked slower, staring at each shadow. "Why is no one on the street?"

"I don't know, but I don't like it," Kamet said, pulling out his mace.

Why are we going this way? "Maybe everyone is at the inn?" Vatis said, looking at a building that appeared to be a mild storm away from collapsing.

"Maybe," Vidmar said, but he didn't sound convinced.

They continued their deliberate path toward Geoff's; Vidmar checked each shadow thoroughly while Kamet stayed close to Vatis with his mace in hand. The smell of tar and sulfur reemerged and overtook the pleasant cinnamon fragrance. *I hope the inn is near,* Vatis thought, watching a rat scurry out of the street with an apple core in its mouth. He dried his sweaty palms on his shirt and thought he saw eyes watching him from a window, but when he looked closer, the window was filthy, if not entirely ordinary.

Vidmar scouted a few paces ahead, moving from lamppost to lamppost and waving them forward when all was clear. *Is this necessary?* Vatis thought, then reconsidered when a cat darted into their path from the shadows. He jumped and crashed into Kamet. "Sorry," he said, patting Kamet on the back. The giant mercenary scowled and mumbled something under his breath. A few scares later, they approached the first building with any sign of life; it had a rickety, unkempt porch, and the murmur of conversation and drinking escaped from glowing windows.

"Is that the inn?" Vatis asked. *It looks more like a barn.*

"That's Geoff's," Vidmar answered. "There are more inns and taverns on the other side of the city, but they are crowded. Besides, these are *my* people. Maybe we can find a game of dice, Kamet."

"As long as we get off this street, and it has ale, it's fine by me," Kamet said, stepping onto a creaky stair. "A woman wouldn't hurt either."

Vatis stretched, hummed a merry tune, and followed Vidmar and Kamet into the inn. *Whatever it takes to get off this street,* he thought, before his mind drifted to an improvised song. *Once, there was a teeny, tiny, crooked goose.* He sang internally as Vatis-of-the-Road came to life. He felt better every time he entered an inn, even one so run down as Geoff's. Each contained a new audience, another chance to tell a story.

Geoff's was two stories tall. A balcony outlined the sides of the square inn. The railing looked like it was one wobbly drunk away from toppling over onto the tables below, but somehow, three men leaned over it, smoking pipes and calling to waitresses. In the center of the room was a firepit. The stones were caked in black soot, and the remnants of old fires poured over the edge. Four small birds roasted on an iron spit. A middle-aged woman brushed something over each bird's crisp, brown skin. She wore a ratty apron, and sweat dripped from her wild, curly gray hair. She grimaced as they approached.

"What do you strangers want?" she said, basting the birds. *Those aren't chickens,* Vatis thought. *Maybe pheasants, maybe pigeons.* Vatis stepped forward to speak, but Vidmar nudged him backward.

"Any rooms available?" Vidmar asked.

"Aye," she said, never diverting her attention from the birds.

Vidmar looked at Vatis, played with his bandages, and slightly changed his tone as he spoke. "Two rooms, three chickens, and six ales." Vidmar's ability to match the cook's demeanor surprised Vatis; it looked like it shocked the cook too. The wrinkles on her forehead multiplied as she furrowed her brow. She examined each man slowly before letting an exasperated sigh escape. She rubbed her twisted nose with one hand and counted on her fingers with the other. "Twenty and two," she said, wiping her hands on her apron.

169

Vidmar patted his hip. When he couldn't find what he was looking for, he turned to Vatis, pointed to the coin purse on his belt, and held out his hand.

Vatis smiled and untied the pouch from his belt, remaining silent as he followed Vidmar's lead. He counted twenty-five Kan and slid the coins into Vidmar's hands. Some coins fell onto the floor as Vidmar tried to pass them to the cook. The men leaning over the railing looked as they heard the metallic click of coins colliding with the wood floor. A long, tense silence filled the room as Vatis helped Vidmar retrieve the coins.

"Fuck," Vidmar whispered so only Vatis could hear. "I just put a target on our backs."

Vidmar struggled to pick up the coins. He cursed each time the Kan clung to the floor instead of his fingers. Vatis gathered most of the money and waited for Vidmar to pick up the last coin. "Damnit," he hissed as it fell back onto the floor.

Vatis looked up. A group of tattered-looking men shifted in their seats. The waitresses stopped clearing tables and watched Vidmar closely. The cook's uninterested gaze turned terrifyingly sour. Finally, Vidmar picked up the coin, gathered the others from Vatis, and gave the money to the cook, who gobbled it up ravenously. Vidmar scowled as he stood up. It was a look that would have petrified the tavern in Haran, but the occupants of Geoff's saw it as the frustration of a crippled man. The men to their left stood up; however, they sank back into their seats when Kamet stepped forward with his hand on top of his mace. *Thank you, Kamet,* Vatis thought.

The cook stiffened as she placed the coins in her pocket. "Rooms are upstairs," she said, gazing between Vidmar and Kamet but avoiding eye contact. "Margaret, make sure they don't get lost," she called to one of the waitresses, who walked over slowly. Margaret looked only a few years younger than the cook. She wore a frayed green dress with a dirty rag slung over one shoulder. Her bloodshot, green eyes hid beneath wavy red bangs. "Three and four," the cook said, handing the waitress two keys.

Margaret grabbed the keys. Her fingernails were painted green to match her dress, but most of the paint had chipped away. "Come, I don't have all night," she said, her curvy hips swaying as she walked toward the stairs.

"Thank you, you are most kind," Vatis said, mustering as much courtesy as his weariness allowed. The waitress gave him a sidelong look, rolled her eyes, and continued up the stairs. *I hope the audience at the tourney is more friendly,* Vatis thought as they walked up the unstable steps. Nails protruded like spikes along the edges of dark wood boards. Vatis tried to put as little weight on his feet as possible. He tiptoed to the top and exhaled.

"The last two on the right," Margaret said, pointing to the other side of the balcony. "Here." She handed Vatis two iron keys.

"Thank you, Margaret. If the rest of the women in Yimser are as lovely as you, I might have to make this my home," Vatis said, kissing one of her hands as he bowed. The waitress bit her lip flirtatiously but pulled her hand away quickly when the cook called from below.

"What was that?" Vidmar chuckled as they walked around the balcony.

"What? A little chivalry can go a long way," Vatis said, winking as he slipped a key into the first room's lock. It clicked as he struggled to turn the mechanism open. He tried the second key, the lock slid, and the door swung into a dark room. The room was ordinary. In the left corner, two narrow beds lay adjacent to a rickety nightstand with one drawer. Three candles of varying heights oozed white wax onto the splintered surface. An iron chamber pot sat next to a three-legged stool in the right corner. The only other object in the room was an oil lantern hanging on the left wall inside the door. The flame burned low and blue and did little to light the room.

"I'll take this one," Kamet said, pushing into the first room.

"Very generous of you," Vidmar said. "Come on, Vatis. I guess you're with me."

Vatis followed him into the next room. It was nearly identical to Kamet's except for a few more candles and a broken window. It was clear that the beds had been made quickly, and whatever had been spilled in the center of the room left a dark stain and an even darker smell. Vidmar's pack thudded to the floor before Vatis closed the door. "Shit," Vidmar said, collapsing onto one of the beds. "The floor might be more comfortable." He wriggled around the bed, arching his back like an exhausted cat.

Vatis sat down on the other bed and set his pack on the floor at his feet. "It's better than the beach," he said, opening the drawer to the nightstand. A cockroach scurried out, vanishing between a narrow gap in the floorboards. Vatis jumped and slammed the drawer shut before pulling a fresh shirt and journal out of his pack.

Vidmar sat up and examined his bandages. "Would you help me change these before we go downstairs?"

Vatis nodded, unwrapping Vidmar's hands slowly. The bandages stuck to the partially scabbed skin. Vidmar grimaced as Vatis tugged the wrapping and scabs free. Vidmar's left hand was in decent shape. He lost the tip of his left index finger and nothing more. The finger had a healthy-looking red scab. Vatis guessed he would have normal function back in a few weeks. His right hand was a different story. His missing index and middle finger were now puss-filled stumps; the smell was worse than the room.

"Shit," Vidmar said. His hand trembled as Vatis examined it.

"Do you have any alcohol?" Vatis asked.

Vidmar laughed. "I wish."

The treasure hunter winced as Vatis touched his warm skin. "It's infected," Vatis said, looking up at Vidmar's right arm to see if the infection had spread. Fortunately, the rest of the arm looked healthy—*for now.*

"Just cut the whole thing off. It's useless anyway."

"Then your arm would be infected in a week."

"Then take my arm. Repeat the process until I'm just a head and a torso. Kamet can carry me around everywhere, and you'll have quite the story to tell," Vidmar said as his tone wavered dangerously close to serious. "Just wrap it. I'm starving. Kamet has probably eaten our food by now."

Vatis fumbled around his bag, looking for a small vial. "Here we are," he said, pulling out a glass tube containing a clear liquid. Vatis popped the cork off with his thumb and smelled the contents. "This is pure alcohol. I use it for cleaning my writing supplies," he said, eyes watering. "It will help, but it's going to be painful." *I can't have you dying halfway through your story.*

"Thank you, Vatis," Vidmar said, looking away. His knees shook.

You're getting too close, a voice inside his head whispered. Vatis tried to ignore it. "Don't thank me yet," he said, holding the vial over Vidmar's hand. "Ready?"

Vidmar nodded. Vatis returned the gesture and poured the alcohol on Vidmar's wounds. The treasure hunter scrunched his face, but the only sound that escaped was a dog-like growl. The alcohol bubbled on Vidmar's swollen, red skin. Vatis rewrapped the wounds in silence—he didn't know what to say. It was clear that Vidmar was struggling to deal with his injury. *Stubborn oaf,* he thought as he finished wrapping Vidmar's hands. "Buy the strongest spirit they have when you're down there and put some in this vial. We will have to do this a few times a day until the infection clears," Vatis said, retrieving the cork from the floor. Vatis gave the empty vial to Vidmar.

"You're not coming down?" Vidmar asked, looking at the vial.

"No, I'm tired and must prepare for the tourney."

"You'll have time to prepare. You could test a story out on those degenerates," Vidmar said, pointing down. "Besides, you need to eat something."

"Bring me the leftovers. I don't mind if it's cold. I'm sorry, Vidmar. I need some time alone."

"Alright, if you hear trouble, stay put. We can handle ourselves."

"Are you planning to start trouble?"

"I never plan to start anything," Vidmar smiled. "But when Kamet and I drink, well, you never know what could happen."

"Then don't drink."

Vidmar snorted. "I'll see you tomorrow."

Vatis watched Vidmar leave. He noticed that Vidmar had moved Acer's knife to his right hip instead of his left. *Don't get into trouble.* Vatis took off his dirt-covered green shirt; a strand of thread escaped the careful weave on the frayed bottom. His shoulders ached as he stretched his arms over his head. His bottom ribs were now visible through his slender frame. Even the top of his hip bones stuck out like they were trying to poke through his skin. The joints in his neck popped. He slipped into his only other shirt, a simple, short-sleeved off-white garment. He grabbed a quill and a nearly empty ink vial from a pocket in his bag. He flipped to the next blank page of his journal, dipped his quill into the ink, inhaled, and wrote two lines.

The voice is back. I'm so tired.

QUESTIONS & ANSWERS

Vatis

Thud, thud, thud. The door to Vidmar's room shook.

"Wake up, you lazy shits," a deep voice bellowed. Vidmar rolled onto his stomach. The room spun. His dry lips cracked as he opened his mouth. The sour, stale taste of mead clung to his tongue like shit on a shoe.

"Wake up," the voice hollered.

The door and a soft buzzing in his ears altered the gruff shouts. Vidmar sat up. Golden specs of light danced in the room. He blinked and hit his forehead with the palm of his hand. Not only did the stars remain, but pain coursed through his stumps, reminding him of his uselessness.

"Vidmar," the voice called again, followed by an even more aggressive knock.

Vidmar pushed the imaginary stars away as he shuffled to the door. He slid the lock open, turned the knob, and Kamet burst into the room. "Rise and shine," he said, almost knocking Vidmar over.

"I'm up," Vidmar said, rubbing his face with his less crippled left hand. "What do you want?"

"Where's the bard?"

"I don't know. I just woke up."

"Fine," Kamet said. "But midday approaches, and I can only sharpen my knives and clean my mace so many times. I'm starving. Let's get one of those mammoth ear things."

"Why do you need me? Go," Vidmar said, sitting down on the bed.

"Never scout alone," Kamet recited, standing straight.

"We aren't scouting. We are one of Emre's largest cities. I'm sure you can manage breakfast on your own."

"You don't remember last night, do you?" Kamet said.

"Is it that obvious?" Vidmar said, laying down and pulling a blanket over his head.

"We *may* have made a few enemies."

"We have plenty of enemies. What's a few more?"

"Nothing normally, but we took these poor bastards for everything they had," Kamet said, jingling his coin purse.

"I still don't see the problem," Vidmar said, peeking over the blanket.

"Normally, there wouldn't be a problem, but those fucking unlucky pigs are downstairs, and I don't want to leave you alone."

Vidmar sat up. "You don't think I can handle a few drunks."

Kamet didn't answer.

"You don't." Vidmar stood. The stars returned, spinning around the room. "Fine, but I'm not going anywhere until I get some water."

"I thought you might say that," Kamet said. He tossed his waterskin to Vidmar; it sloshed as he bobbled the catch. He pulled the cork out with his teeth and took a long, slow drink.

"Ah," Vidmar said, wiping his mouth with his forearm. He took another deliberate drink. "Boots," he said, pointing to his worn leather pair near the door. Kamet set them at the foot of the bed. "Thanks."

"What *do* you remember?" Kamet asked as Vidmar tied his boots.

"Ah. We had a drink while we waited for our food. I brought a chicken up to Vatis. He was writing something in that journal of his, I asked him if he was coming down, and he said, 'No, I'm working on my story.' He asked me a few more questions about my escape from Jegon. Then I went downstairs, and you were playing dice. I sat next to you; you handed me a pint of mead and the rest is hazy," Vidmar paused, rubbing the bridge of his nose with his bandaged palm. "Did I, ah, throw a knife at you?"

"Yes," Kamet laughed.

"You *let* me throw a knife at you," Vidmar said, looking at his hands.

"I never miss," Kamet mimicked.

"Did I miss?" Vatis asked, wrinkling his nose.

"Depends on what you were aiming at. If you were aiming at the apple in my hand, then yes, you missed. If you were aiming at my forearm, then no, you didn't miss. Either way, it made us about thirty Kan each," Kamet said, rolling up his sleeve and revealing a small, scabbed gash on the top of his forearm.

"You're lucky I didn't kill you."

"What can I say? I trust you. You were much closer than Simon, or was it Samon or Semin? Anyway, you won the bet," Kamet said, rolling up his pants. He peeled back a dark red bandage. A deep, wet slice still dripped blood down his leg.

"Why were you holding the apple? Why didn't we put it on a shelf or something?"

"They paid double if I held it."

"You're an idiot," Vidmar smiled. He rubbed his left hand, packed his knives into their hiding places, stretched his hands over his head, and vomited in the chamberpot. "Let's go," he wheezed through teary eyes.

Vidmar followed Kamet down the rickety staircase. Three men rolled dice at a table near the door. "Boys," Kamet said, nodding. All three stood. The stools screeched against the wood floor. The hollow thud echoed in the nearly vacant tavern. "No hard feelings," Kamet said, walking to the bar. "Miss, a round of mead for my friends."

A choir of grumbled insults followed them out the door. "That wasn't so bad," Vidmar said.

"No, but it helped that they were a few pints in already," Kamet said, straightening his belt. "Now, where can we get one of those sweets I've heard so much about?"

An hour later, Vidmar savored the last bite of the soft, warm pastry. "Damn," he said, licking his lips.

Kamet mumbled incomprehensibly with a full mouth.

Vidmar's stomachache dissipated, but his headache lingered like a long winter. He rolled his head in a circular motion—a merchant selling fresh vegetables and herbs called to them from across the street. "Go back to where you came from," the haggard man with warts on his nose yelled.

Vidmar bowed. "And a fine day to you as well." The street brightened as he bent down, almost knocking him off balance. "Folk around here are so pleasant."

"Aye, they treat us like royalty. My mother isn't as welcoming," Kamet said loud enough for the merchant to hear.

"Don't be silly, Kamet. Your mother is *very* welcoming," Vidmar winked.

Kamet punched Vidmar in the shoulder. "Fucker."

They walked through the market, basking in the insults slung their way from merchants and townsfolk. "Do you know where you are going?" Kamet asked after a long silence.

"A shop called Gaffer's," Vidmar said.

"The yellow building with the crooked sign," Kamet said, squinting. "Yeah, Gaffer's Goods. We have passed that place already."

"Three times."

"Why?"

"I'm waiting for it to be empty. Someone is in there, some snob who has tried on at least three different shirts," Vidmar said.

"How do you know that, and how will a tailor help you find the crown?"

Vidmar hushed Kamet, putting the bandaged remains of his left index finger to his lips. "Every time we pass, a skinny little shit is wearing a different shirt. And Gaffer, he's more than a tailor. He sells a little bit of everything." They walked by a fourth time. As they passed, a chime rang, and the door opened. The meticulous model ambled onto the street, carrying a pile of neatly folded clothes. The familiar melodic bounce of his steps could not be mistaken. *Of course, it was Vatis.*

"What are you doing here?" Vidmar asked.

"Gods," Vatis said as he jumped, fumbling with the clothes. "Vidmar, ah, where did you come from? What are you doing here?"

"I asked you first."

"I'm buying new clothes for the tourney," Vatis said, straightening the pile.

"Right. So, you were able to sign up?"

"Indeed. With little time to spare."

"Well, I'm looking forward to your performance, but I don't know why you aren't telling the story of Montalvo," Vidmar said, stepping closer to Gaffer's.

"The people of Yimser are not fond of Montalvo, but that is a story for another day. Now, your escape from Jegon is a tale worth telling."

Vidmar shrugged. "I should never have told you about that. Can you at least change my name?"

"Why? I could surprise the audience and bring you on stage if all goes well," Vatis said, his voice changing in demeanor and inflection like he was performing.

"I think that's a bad idea," Kamet interjected.

"Since when do you think? Also, why are you talking like that, Vatis," Vidmar added.

"One must prepare themselves for a performance, get into character as it were," Vatis said, shifting on his feet and avoiding eye contact. *He's hiding something,* Vidmar thought. "Are you sure you want me to change your name? Such a heroic tale could yield the companionship of a fair maid or maiden," Vatis said, tilting his head.

Vidmar looked at Kamet and smiled. "Yes, I'm sure. It's never worked before, well, except on Kamet's..."

"Talk about my mother one more time, and I'll finish what Alcin started," Kamet said, bumping his chest against Vidmar's.

"Gentlemen," Vatis said, stepping between them. "I don't mean to be rude, but I must change into these garments and prepare for the tourney." Vatis bowed gracefully and spun on his heels.

Vidmar rolled his eyes. "Good luck."

"Thank you, sir. I shall see you, gentleman, after the tourney," Vatis said, prancing away. He hummed a strange tune, garnering equally strange looks from the men and women he passed.

"He's odd," Kamet said as they watched Vatis disappear around the corner of a building. "I can't get a read on him."

"Vatis is strange, and I think there is more to him than his traveling bard gimmick," Vidmar said, shaking his head. "But he's not so bad, we've been through a lot together in a short time, and he's a fine companion to have around a campfire, maybe the best storyteller I've heard. I don't know how long he plans on following me. He has most of my stories. I've told him almost everything, probably too much."

Kamet spat onto the street and nodded. "Definitely too much. Are you sure we can trust him?"

Vidmar looked down. "No," he said after a moment's hesitation. "Not yet. Come on, let's go inside before another customer enters."

The chime rang as they entered Gaffer's Goods. Vidmar gently closed the door, sliding the lock into place as it clicked into its frame. A cat jumped down from a shelf on Vidmar's left. Two glass jars wobbled but didn't fall. The feline landed silently and approached Kamet. It took a careful step forward, smelt his boot, and bolted toward the other end of the shop.

An old man appeared, dragging a burlap sack behind him; his legs shook as he took slow, deliberate steps. The cat darted between his feet. "Who spooked you, Meeza," he said, dropping the sack. Small black beans spilled out of the top of the bag. "Meeza," he said, clicking his tongue. "What's gotten into you?"

"Hello," Vidmar called.

"Hello. I'm coming," The old man said, approaching slowly. His shoulders arched rigidly, swallowing his neck like a turtle. He moaned as he sat on a nearby stool. Specks of dust floated in a beam of light pouring in through a high cat-nose-smudged window. A musty aroma hung in the air. "How can I help you?" he said, wheezing. Vidmar stepped forward. "Vidmar. Is that you?" the old man coughed.

"The one and only," Vidmar said, waving. *I've spent too much time with Vatis.* He thought as he finished the awkward gesture.

"Let me have a look at you, boy. Darkness, what happened to your hand?"

"We ran into some wolves—they got both hands," Vidmar corrected, holding up his bandages. The left hand was healing as nicely as he could have hoped. His diligently sharpened knife had cut clean, but an infection coursed through his right hand. Black veins spread from his knuckles to his wrists. Oozing scabs itched on the stumps of his missing fingers. He hated to admit it, but the pain worsened by the hour. *I can't die, not yet, not here,* Vidmar thought, pulling his hands away.

"Come closer. Let me see your hands," the old man asked, scooting forward on the stool.

Reluctantly, Vidmar stepped closer, placing his hands in Gaffer's upturned palms. "I'm fine."

"We will see about that," Gaffer said, unwrapping Vidmar's left hand. "This looks ok, though I've never seen a wolf bite so clean," he said, looking up. Vidmar felt the intense scrutiny of Gaffer's gaze but remained silent. The shopkeeper unwrapped Vidmar's right hand. "Everlasting Darkness. This infection will take your arm in a week if you aren't careful."

Kamet stepped around Vidmar to look at his hand. "Gods, Vidmar, we need to get you to a medic."

"I'm fine," Vidmar insisted. "I've been cleaning it with alcohol."

Gaffer stood, using Vidmar's shoulder for support. "You need something more than alcohol, boy; the rot has sunk in. I might have something back here." Gaffer moved behind a wooden desk with stacks of books on each corner like towers on a castle. He groaned as he bent down out of sight. Vidmar heard a lock click and a door slide open. Meeza returned, jumping onto the desk to watch Gaffer. "Ah, here we are," he said, closing the door. He emerged a few seconds later with clean bandages and a black canister.

"What's that?" Vidmar asked.

The old man mumbled something to himself as he scratched the cat's ears. "More than you deserve. We haven't seen you in years, and you show up at our shop dying."

"I'm not dying," Vidmar said.

"We all are welcomed by the Darkness sooner or later. You're just on an accelerated path," Gaffer laughed. "But don't worry, I'll save you…again." Gaffer winked at the cat. He opened the canister and rubbed a white, speckled paste over Vidmar's wounds. It burnt at first, but after a moment, a cool, numbing sensation invigorated Vidmar.

"What is that?" Vidmar said, feeling like his fingers had grown back. "The pain is gone."

Gaffer closed the container. "It's made from the Axiro plant that grows near the tar pit. It will save your life," Gaffer said, sticking his tongue between his teeth and bandaging Vidmar's hands. "There. Leave them wrapped for a few days, then clean them with the alcohol you're fond of; then, you should live another few weeks before you run into *wolves* again."

"Thank you, Gaffer," Vidmar said, wiggling his unwrapped fingers.

"You're welcome, Vidmar. It is our duty to help those in need before we can rest, though I don't think you came here for medicine," Gaffer said.

"Nothing gets by you. I need your help," Vidmar said seriously.

"He needs our help, Meeza. What do you think of that? We just saved his life, yet he needs more help," the old man said, petting the cat.

"Please, Gaffer. I'm out of leads," Vidmar said, stepping closer. The cat jumped off Gaffer's lap.

"You wouldn't be here otherwise. No one comes to visit us, Meeza. Where did you go, girl?" Gaffer said, slowly turning his head from side to side. "What is it this time? Provisions, poison, another book, another name?"

Vidmar felt anger boil to the surface of his cheeks. *I never use poison, a coward's weapon,* he thought. He inhaled slowly. "I need you to translate something. You claim to know every language in Emre," Vidmar said, pulling the flat circular stone from his pack. Narrow silver markings shimmered on its face. He handed it to Gaffer.

"What's this?" Gaffer said curiously.

"My only lead, and I paid dearly for it. Do you know what it says?" Vidmar asked.

Gaffer examined the stone, running his fingertips over the markings. "Where did you get this?" he said, holding the stone into a light beam.

"Does it matter?" Vidmar asked.

Kamet shifted from side to side. He tapped his foot on the floor.

"I suppose not," Gaffer said. "Quit that tapping."

Kamet stiffened and stopped.

"Interesting," Gaffer said, examining the stone like a banker inspecting a counterfeit coin. "I've seen these markings before. They…"

"What does it say?" Vidmar interrupted.

Gaffer huffed. "Follow me," he said, then turned to Kamet, waving a crooked finger. "You. Yes, you. Guard the door. If anyone comes by, tell them I'm out for a walk. We love a good walk, don't we, Meeza? Where'd that cat go off to? Anyway, don't let anyone in. Vidmar, come."

Vidmar nodded at Kamet. "This way," Gaffer said. He followed Gaffer through the shop. They passed shelf after shelf of various goods. One wooden shelf sagged in the middle as it struggled to hold what looked like a perfect iron sphere, another had carved figurines of soldiers, and another held a single boot leaning against a stack of leather-bound books. One shelf, in particular, captivated Vidmar's attention. It held knives and daggers and other weapons arranged haphazardly. The sharp metal gleamed in the dim light. He extended onto his toes to get a better look at the blades. A door creaked open.

"In here," Gaffer said. They walked into a dark room; Gaffer lit the lantern on the wall. The air was heavy and smelled of mold. He stepped into the cold room. Gaffer rummaged through a chest against the wall. "Vidmar, do an old man a favor and grab those stools," Gaffer said, pointing to the opposite end of the room.

Vidmar dragged the heavy stools into the center of the cellar. Goosebumps rose on his forearms.

"Ah, here we are," Gaffer said, carefully shutting the lid. Vidmar heard two clicks. *Two locks. Whatever is in there must be valuable,* Vidmar thought, examining the chest further as Gaffer wandered over carrying something wrapped in white cloth. Metal straps bolted the chest to the stone floor. The trunk wasn't made of wood but solid metal inlaid with silver veins. *That chest is worth more than his entire shop.*

"Vidmar," Gaffer said, adjusting his seat. "I don't know where you found that stone, and I don't want to." He uncovered the object under the cloth, a nearly identical stone with slightly different markings. "Members of The Pact traded and communicated with these stones. Some stones held secrets, some stones held locations, and some stones held names." Vidmar didn't speak. *Vatis was right – it is The Pact. God's I always believed they were a fairy tale, something orphans made up to escape their reality,* he thought, leaning closer as Gaffer continued.

"My stone holds a name, Dinardo. The founder and leader of The Pact. It is the most common of the stones. They exchanged these while recruiting to confirm validity. Your stone isn't the same," Gaffer said, pulling Vidmar's stone out of his pocket. "This appears to be a secret as it is neither a name nor a location."

Vidmar clenched his fists; searing needles stabbed his tender wounds through the numbing ointment. *Of course, it's not a location.*

Why is it always difficult? "What does it say?" Vidmar asked through gritted teeth.

"Patience," Gaffer said. "It takes time to read The Pact's code. It's like mathematics; it takes many steps for a simple answer." Gaffer traced the markings on the stone and drew intricate shapes in the air with his other hand. He squinted and scratched his chin before letting a solitary sigh escape.

"What?" Vidmar asked.

"Hush," Gaffer said, never taking his eyes off the stone. "Very clever." Gaffer paused before he retraced his steps. "Better to confirm than to report inaccurately, eh Vidmar?"

Vidmar bit the insides of his cheeks and nodded. *Tell me what it says, old man.*

"It lies near the dead," Gaffer said.

"What?"

"That's what the stone says, 'It lies near the dead,' I'm sure, oh there you are, Meeza." The cat's eyes glimmered atop a high shelf in the dark room. It jumped down gracefully.

Vidmar watched the cat stretch its back. "What the fuck does that mean? 'It lies near the dead.' What is *it*? The crown? Fuck, damnit, shit, this is no help," Vidmar's voice grew louder with each curse. *Why can't anything be simple?* He looked at his mangled hands. *After two years of searching, I now have another riddle to solve, another clue that leads to another mystery.* "What do I do now?" He asked more to himself than Gaffer, but the old man answered anyway.

"I think this is good news. 'It lies near the dead' must mean the crown is in Barna, in the palace. Many believe masons constructed the palace over the tomb of The Nameless King."

"It could mean the crown lies with Greco, and no one has found his tomb," Vidmar mumbled, covering his face with his hands. "Or it could mean it lies in a random graveyard. Or it might not refer to the crown at all. It's another riddle, and I am sure another will appear when I solve this one."

"Isn't that the task of a treasure hunter?" Gaffer said. "To solve riddle after riddle until the treasure is found."

Vidmar stood. He kicked the stool. It shot backward, bouncing loudly off the stone floor. Meeza hissed and scattered out of the room. He bent over, collapsing onto his knees. "I'm tired, Gaffer–so tired. Every time I wake, I feel like my fingers are still there. It is a haunting feeling. I can feel my missing knuckles bend. I can feel the tip of a blade between my fingertips, and then I look down at emptiness, and icicles stab my wounds. I don't know if I did the right thing. I don't know if I'm working for the enemy. Even if I succeed and find this damned crown, I don't know if I'll be remembered as a traitor or a savior. Either way, I will be on the run for the rest of my life." He blinked away tears from his itching eyes. "I believed him, I believed in him, but now, I fear I'm supporting another monster, a less obvious but equally ruthless monster."

Gaffer didn't respond. He watched Vidmar closely. *One, two, three, four, five,* Vidmar thought, counting his breath. He sighed, relaxing his shoulders and cracking his neck. "I'm sorry, Gaffer."

Gaffer stood. "There's no need to apologize, my boy."

"Thank you for your help," Vidmar said, looking at the ground.

"Hope is not lost, Vidmar," Gaffer said, picking up Vidmar's chin with shaking, crooked fingers. "There's a reason the crown has stayed hidden for centuries. The path was never meant to be easy. But I feel that you're closer than anyone has come since The Pact disappeared. So, compose yourself, collect the information, and continue your search. I'm sorry I couldn't offer more aid, but I may have something that could provide some support."

Vidmar furrowed his eyebrows. "What is it?"

"A book."

"Of course," Vidmar laughed.

Gaffer shuffled out of the room. "Come, follow me."

Kamet stood statuesque at the door. He peered around a table holding miscellaneous traveling supplies mouthing the word "well." Vidmar shook his head. Kamet bit his lip, punched his thigh, and returned to his post.

Gaffer searched through stack after stack of books. "Where is it? Darkness. A book doesn't simply walk off on its own."

"What's the matter?" Vidmar asked as he piled fallen books into a neat stack.

"I can't find it," Gaffer said, half answering the question and half talking to himself. "By night's long rest," he said after throwing another book onto the floor. It fluttered like a bird with a broken wing before knocking over Vidmar's stack. "Mia," he finished as he sat in a chair. "Mia."

Gaffer breathed heavily. Meeza shyly jumped onto his lap. He took a deep, wet breath like he was inhaling water. He coughed. Green mucus splashed against his wrist and his upper lip. The cat scurried away under a small table.

"Can I get you anything?" Vidmar asked as the coughing slowed.

"No. I'm fine. Thank you," Gaffer said. He exhaled smoothly through pursed lips. "Ah, there we are. I'm afraid the long dark is beginning to cast its shadow on me, but nonetheless, I know where the book is. Mia has it."

"Who's Mia," Vidmar asked.

"Oh Mia, there aren't many like her. She's a brilliant girl, quick as a cat and sharp as a knife. She likes to come in every once in a while."

"I'm sure she's a fine woman. Where can I find her?" Vidmar interrupted.

Gaffer narrowed his eyes and cleared his throat. "Not a woman, a girl, but as I was saying, she likes to come in and borrow books. She lives on the other side of the bridge, but she hangs around the market during the day. She's no more than ten and has brown hair, usually tied in a bun. She loves books, histories, and stories. I'm sure she will be at the tourney."

"Why are you telling me all this?" Vidmar said.

"Because I'm rather fond of the girl, and she can help you *if* she likes you. She's rather particular in that regard. Probably had something to do with abandonment and raising herself in a tough city. You know you two have a lot in common. Anyhow, she has a book on the disappearance of The Pact. It might be able to help you with your search," Gaffer said, scratching his chin.

"Mia?" Vidmar asked.

"Yes, Mia."

"Well, I guess I'll go searching for my next riddle. Thank you, Gaffer," Vidmar said. "Someday, I'll repay you for your kindness; maybe I'll see you at the tourney."

"I never miss it," Gaffer smiled. "Good luck, Vidmar. May your feet find the road."

"And yours."

Vidmar and Kamet walked onto the busy street. Herds of people passed by in both directions. "What now?" Kamet asked.

"There's still some time before the tourney," Vidmar said, looking at the descending sun above a steeply pitched roof. "Let's go back to Geoff's."

THE TOURNEY

Vatis

People passed Vatis in all directions, giving him sour looks as he stood in the middle of an unfamiliar street. He bounced on his toes and played with the loose sleeves of his new emerald-colored shirt as he searched for the arena. The shirt wasn't a perfect fit, but it would have to work—he didn't have any more time. His tan trousers were shabby yet presentable. He wore no boots as his only pair would have been more shameful than his bare feet. His matching green hat held a duck's feather in the brim to complete the ensemble. He spent every coin he had on this outfit. He needed to make a good impression.

"Good luck, Vatis-of-the-Road. I can't wait to hear your story," the organizer's words echoed in his head from earlier this morning. *This is my chance,* Vatis thought, pulling out the parchment the organizer gave him from his breast pocket. He examined it thoroughly like a navigator with a map; it didn't matter; Vatis couldn't decipher the informal shorthand. *Where's the arena?* He tried to retrace his steps from this morning. All the streets looked the same. The once beautifully random-colored buildings that charmed Vatis when they entered Yimser now infuriated him as he couldn't remember any landmarks.

"Get out of the road," a deep voice called from behind Vatis.

"Terribly sorry," Vatis said, looking for the voice. After a short search, he gave up and tapped a man in a gray tunic on the shoulder. "Excuse me. Where is the arena?"

"Go back to where you came from," the man said, shouldering Vatis out of the way.

Next, Vatis approached a woman with two children by her side. *Perhaps a mother will be a little more kind.* "Pardon me, miss. Where is the arena?" The woman pulled her children into a protective embrace. The boy of about five began to say something, but his mother tugged him closer. "Go below the bridge where you belong," she said, herding her kids in the opposite direction.

Vatis shuffled further up the street. The smell of freshly baked bread was a welcomed distraction to his infuriating search. A woman sat on a bench eating a sweet roll with creamy white frosting. Vatis gamboled toward her in what he assumed was a friendly, if not funny, greeting. "Hello, would you be so kind as to tell me where I can find the arena?" The woman did not answer; she didn't even look at him. Vatis stomped. *What is wrong with these people?* He clenched his fists. *I cannot miss my chance. Will none of these forsaken people help me?* Vatis thought, looking through the crowd for a kind face when a quiet, gentle voice called to him.

"Hey," it said softly.

Vatis looked around.

"Hey," the voice repeated. "Over here." A girl no older than ten waved at him. Her brown hair was tied in a messy bun atop her head. She sat on a barrel tossing bread to a flock of pigeons.

"Hello," Vatis said cheerily.

"The arena is up the road on the left. You can't miss it," she said.

"Thank you very much. What's your name?"

"Mia, you know, like Mia-The-Maiden," she said proudly.

"That's a powerful name. Are you coming to the tourney?"

"No," Mia sighed. "Feya wins every year. And she plays boring music on her flute."

"I don't play music. I tell stories. Wonderful, heroic, tragically true tales. Would you come see me?"

The girl shrugged. "You look like a bard. Last year, this stranger came to town and butchered my favorite story of Mia-The-Maiden. So, I threw a tomato at him," Mia said. Vatis furrowed his eyebrows as he scratched his chin. "Don't look at me like that. I missed. Everyone else threw things too; some people threw rocks."

"I promise not to butcher your favorite story," Vatis said, smiling. "I'll tell you a new story. Who knows, it might even become your new favorite?"

"I doubt it," she said. She hopped off the barrel and chased most of the pigeons away. "Just a warning, they don't like foreigners, so you better be really good."

"Thanks for the advice, Mia," Vatis said.

"But, you seem nice, so maybe I'll come. Good luck," she said, running after a straggling bird.

A few moments later, Vatis turned left down a wide road. Dozens of people funneled between two carved pillars; familiar faces of ancient heroes, bards, and kings looked down on the audience as they wandered toward their seats. The arena was two stories tall, primarily wooden, except for its stone foundation. Orange clay tiles lined a roof, covering only the seats reserved for the rich. The exterior was painted in a rainbow of colors; each entrance, arch, and window displayed a different vibrant color. The benches and marvelous architecture formed a half-circle around an elevated, square stage.

Vatis drifted with the flow of patrons into the arena, taking a seat in the row furthest from the stage. The sun sank beyond the roof, illuminating the sky with a brilliant red light. Vatis arrived minutes before the first act: a local jester who juggled balls, scarves, and knives. The crowd laughed at his juvenile performance. *Jugglers should be sent to freeze on Jegon, but at least he's putting the people in a good mood,* Vatis thought as the jester blindfolded himself and began juggling four knives. The crowd roared with applause when he finished his act by catching the hilt of a dagger in his teeth.

The subsequent acts were local singers. First, an elderly woman sang a painfully pitchy version of *The Widow in the Window,* but the crowd awarded her with flower petals. Next, a young, elegantly dressed man with a well-groomed beard captivated Vatis with his rendition of *The Road Around the Forest.* Vatis sniffed back tears and swallowed a lump in his throat. The crowd seemed to have a similar reaction, as it took several seconds before they stood on their feet and cheered.

The fourth act was a foreigner like Vatis. The audience appeared to straighten in their seats. A man sitting to Vatis's right scowled and pulled a rock from his pocket. The foreign bard told the story of *The Fairy and the Giant.* He performed well; his pacing was a bit too slow, and the accent he gave the fairy was too childish, but overall, Vatis enjoyed the tale he hadn't heard in years. The audience didn't agree. They yelled and threw rocks and fruits at him until he left the stage in tears.

Vatis rose from his seat, nearly falling onto a woman in front of him. His head spun; he needed space. His vision blurred as he pushed passed the crowd back into the street; fiery breath came through as his chest convulsed. He grabbed a nearby bench like an overboard sailor grasping for his ship. The sounds of wagon wheels, conversations, and street vendors blended into a dull hum. *I can't do this. I can't do this,* Vatis thought, closing his eyes and rubbing his temples. He sat like that for a long time; he didn't know how many acts he had missed. Then, someone tapped his shoulder.

"Did I miss it?" a vaguely familiar voice asked.

Vatis opened his eyes. Mia looked down at him, standing just a few inches taller than he was sitting. He met her gaze. "No. I just needed some air," Vatis said, wiping sweat from his forehead. He took a deep, raspy breath.

"Are you alright?" Mia asked, sitting beside him.

"Yes. I'm fine," Vatis said, trying to conceal his panic.

Vatis could feel Mia looking at him. "When I get nervous, I pretend I'm Mia-The-Maiden, leading soldiers into battle. It helps a little," she said.

Vatis tilted his head, looking at Mia's large hazel eyes that appeared to glimmer with genuine concern. *You have no idea how close to the mark you are, girl,* Vatis thought, standing up. *We all need an escape from reality.* He shook his arms and legs, cracked his neck, and smirked. "Brown bunnies bite brains because bored bunnies brought beavers," Vatis said in a deep, performance-worthy voice.

"Bunnies bite what?" Mia said, laughing so hard that she held her stomach.

Vatis smiled. "It helps loosen my tongue so I can enunciate better. Thank you, Mia. You reminded me why I love stories. I am in your debt, but I'm on soon. I hope you'll come in and watch my performance."

Mia shrugged. "Brown bunnies bite," she stumbled over the words as Vatis waved goodbye.

Vatis skipped to the other side of the arena. His confidence slowly returned as he sang himself into character. A pot-bellied man with a white beard and a tall, sapphire hat ran up to Vatis as he rounded the corner. "You're on next. My audience does not respond well to late arrivals. Hurry, Cal is about to introduce you," he said, pushing Vatis through a narrow door leading to the stage. He almost crashed into the announcer waiting at the bottom of the stairs.

"Easy, son," Cal said, sliding gracefully out of Vatis's way.

"I apologize," Vatis said, adjusting his clothes.

"You nearly gave my brother a heart attack, but I knew you would show. Gregory's song is almost over," the announcer said, wrapping Vatis in a sideways hug. He smelled strongly of spiced wine. The last few notes of a song faded away into cheers from the audience. A thin man wearing a blue tunic carried a lute as he walked down the stairs.

"Wonderful, Gregory, simply wonderful," the announcer said. "That performance could earn you a nightly spot at the White Raven."

"Thank you, Cal. You're too kind," Gregory said, smiling. His expression turned into a frown as he glared at Vatis. The look sent butterflies dancing in his stomach. Gregory huffed. "Goodnight."

"Goodnight, dear Gregory," The announcer blew Gregory a kiss goodbye and turned to Vatis. "He's a decent luthier, but Alec will never let him play at the Raven," he said, laughing at a joke that Vatis didn't understand. "Are you ready?"

Vatis nodded.

"Splendid," Cal said, walking up the stairs. "Follow me. Good luck, son."

Paralyzing nervousness returned as Vatis followed the announcer. He walked on stage silently, looking down as he confronted the crowd. Tremors reverberated through his body. Thin hairs stiffened on his neck and forearms, and sweat pooled on his lower back, trickling down his legs. A burnt smell filled the thick air like smoke, suddenly changing directions, making his eyes dry and foggy.

Vatis rehearsed Vidmar's escape from Jegon diligently. He knew where to pause; he knew what to emphasize. He hoped the crowd would love a true story, not a new spin on a classic tale like *The Fall of the West,* but something unique they could tell their children and grandchildren. He always thought true stories were the best, the most believable, and the most memorable.

He dipped forward into a clumsy bow as the announcer introduced him. The audience was an unidentifiable blur in front of a rosy sky. As the introduction finished and his performance began, the crowd came into focus. Cruel, judging faces, eagerly awaiting a chance to throw rotten fruit and stones at a foreigner. His tremors became more violent, moving from his arms to his legs as the light applause ended.

"Thuh…" Vatis began. "Thank you. I… I am Vatis of the Road." He stuttered his well-rehearsed introduction, the easiest part of the whole performance. The audience cohesively sat straighter, anticipating the chance to rise and pelt Vatis with an array of vegetables.

"Guh, go on," a heckler mocked.

The audience cackled wickedly. Vatis's tremors worsened, and sweat dripped from his forehead into his left eye. He winced. He repeatedly blinked, trying to regain his vision as he surveyed the crowd for a familiar face. He took a deep breath, shaking his arms to release the tension. *Where are you, Vidmar?* Vatis needed something to focus on, someone to single out. Luckily, he found Mia standing in the back. She leaned against the right-side wall and smiled at him. His muscles loosened, and Vatis-of-the-Road reemerged. *This story is for you, Mia,* he thought, focusing on the girl, not the crowd.

"I would like to tell you a story, a true story of an unknown hero," he said, confidence returning to his voice. "Our story begins with our hero, Davas, in the small town of Aswar," Vatis started, happy with how his chosen name of Davas sounded in replacement of Vidmar. *I wish I could have used his real name, but I need to earn his trust. He will be Vidmar in his next story.* "Davas was the leader of King Kandrian Ambita's Outriders – an elite group of scouts who helped him win and keep his throne. Davas earned the King's trust by finding and *eliminating* his enemies. He saved the village of Wolvesbarrow from an angry mob with no more than a knife and a torch. He killed the rebellious leader, Coil, with the criminal's own sword and wounded the legendary giant Anaar, forcing the monster into hiding, but this isn't a tale of assassination and trickery. No, this is a tale of bravery, morality, and love."

Mia looked engrossed as Vatis finished Davas's introduction, well, Vidmar's introduction. He didn't bother to look at anyone else in the audience. Yes, he shifted his gaze, but it only bounced from blur to blur to keep up the appearance of speaking to the whole crowd. He always returned to Mia. *Thank you, Mia. You have given me a chance.*

After a short pause, Vatis continued. "Davas scouted Aswar for a week, watching its people go about their everyday chores from the shadows. No one noticed him. The simple townsfolk's lives centered around their mill. Men cut down trees, moved logs, and stacked wood. Most young women operated the saws or cleaned up sawdust and other debris; the others either taught the children in a small school or tended their homes. At night, each family would return home from an honest day's work and have supper together – Aswar was an admirable town full of hardworking men and women. Davas didn't understand his assignment. He returned to Barna and delivered his report to the King.

'Aswar seems completely mundane, sir,' Davas said, ending his report.

'Tell me about this school,' Kandrian demanded.

Davas detailed the school's structure and lessons from the day he spent in the rafters like a hawk watching field mice. 'It seems like a standard education, not up to Numerian standards, but enough for future millers.'

Kandrian stood up from his throne, bit his thumbnail, and spat it on the ground. 'Davas, do you remember how we usurped that idiot Pavao Begic and ended his dynasty that lasted decades too long?'

Again, Davas was confused. 'We garnered the support of the people, then snuck into the palace and killed him.'

'Yes, that's what the stories will say,' the King said. 'But it's because we were smarter. We had all the information. We struck at the opportune time because we planned and look at what we have created – a better world, a brighter Emre. The people are happy, though happiness only lasts so long. I cannot take the chance that another will match my intelligence and steal my throne. So I want you to burn down the school and kill the teachers as well as any students over ten years old. This will be our message to the world, our warning before we destroy all the schools in my kingdom.'

Davas nearly fainted. The King's words pierced him like a spear through the gut. 'Sir, there must be another way.'

The King strode in front of a tapestry of himself, smiling. 'I want this message sent in two weeks. Do not fail me, Vid..."'

Vatis caught himself before he revealed Vidmar. '"Do not fail me, Davas,' Vatis repeated. He paced back and forth across the stage like an angry king. Mia twirled her finger around her hair, eating bread and listening with wide eyes. Vatis dropped to his knees for the next line. '"Please, sir. I can't do this. I'll burn down the school,' Davas relented. 'But why do the women and children have to die?'

Kandrian took Davas's chin in his hand. 'Because I commanded it. You have two weeks,' the King said, holding out his enormous emerald ring for Davas to kiss. Davas's fingers lingered on a dagger sheathed in his boot for a moment. He thought about killing the King and ending this madness, but his cautious mind told him the guards would kill him before the King hit the floor. Reluctantly, he bent forward and kissed the King's ring. He knew there had to be another way, but he had to be alive to see it through. For now, he needed to confront Elisa."

Vatis let the King's threat simmer in the audience's minds. Mia had moved closer, sitting on a bench behind a muscular, dark-skinned man. She was harder to see, but he managed–he still needed the distraction. "Now, you all have heard of our warrior princess Elisa Ambita; some say she's the greatest fighter alive. Some say she's the one truly ruling Emre. Others say she's a witch or a sorceress. One thing is certain: Davas loved her, and she loved him. She often accompanied him on scouting missions. They challenged each other in all the ways that a good couple should. Davas was one of the few men alive who could spar with Elisa without bruising his ego. When Davas was in Barna, they spent their days and *nights* together, enjoying their loving company. But, unfortunately, it was all about to end."

Mia leaned forward, resting her chin on her hands; her attention seemed to hang on every word. Vatis did a lap around the stage; when he reached upstage right, he sprinted downstage. The audience jumped back. "Davas ran to Elisa's room. She wasn't watching people from her balcony or reading in her study. Instead, Davas found her practicing her spear in the garden. It should have been the first place he looked.

'Tell me you didn't know about Aswar, Elli,' Davas demanded, catching her spear. Fury burnt in his eyes. 'Tell me you're not ok with this madness.'

Elisa pulled back her spear, holding it in front of her defensively. 'I tried to talk him out of it, Davas, but you know how he is when he gets his mind set on something.'

'I won't do it,' Davas replied. 'How can you be ok with this?'

Elisa shouldered her spear and stepped closer to Davas. 'What other choice do we have? If you don't do it, he will find someone else. You can save most of the children. They don't need to die.'

'No one needs to die. The people of Aswar have done nothing wrong,' Davas said, stepping back.

Elisa gently tapped her spear to her forehead, her long black hair flowing in the breeze. 'One of the teachers spoke *unkindly* of Kandrian.'

'Then, this is all about revenge. Did all the men I killed speak *unkindly* of the King? I've sacrificed everything because I thought we were building a better world. If Kandrian goes through with this plan, he will be worse than Begic. Power has corrupted his mind. He's not your brother anymore; he's a monster,' Davas said, clenching his fists.

'Careful, Davas. Kandrian has ears all over this palace. He will kill you for talk like that,' Elisa said, gesturing around the garden. She stepped closer. Davas wanted to embrace her, but he forced himself to back away. 'Davas, please,' Elisa pleaded.

'I don't care if he fucking hears me. Whose side are you on, Elli? We did all of this to rid the world of tyrants, to save people like the millers in Aswar,' Davas yelled.

Elisa took a small step closer to Davas, dropping her spear on the ground as she walked. 'Please keep your voice down. We're on the same side, Davas.'

'I almost killed him, Elli. My hand was on my dagger; I should have killed him, but I'm too much of a coward,' Davas said, holding back tears.

Elisa wrapped Davas in a tender hug. He resisted at first, keeping his arms at his sides, but eventually, he gave in. He cried as he nestled his face in her neck and held tight. 'I'm on your side,

Davas. We can figure this out.' Deep, coughing laughter interrupted their embrace.

'How adorable,' Kandrian said from the doorway to the garden. 'It's about time that I ended this fanciful romance. Guards seize him. Davas, you have committed treason against your King. There is but one punishment for betrayal.'

Six guards swarmed Davas and Elisa. Two ripped him from her arms; Davas didn't fight back. 'Kandrian,' Elisa started.

'Shut your mouth. I'll deal with you later, sister,' the King said, walking toward Davas. 'Betrayed by a man I saved, a man I called brother.'

'How have I betrayed you?' Davas said as one of the guards tied his hands behind his back.

'Don't play dumb, Davas. I heard every word,' Kandrian said, drawing his sword. 'Your head will make a fine warning atop the wall.'

'Brother, if you love me, you'll spare Davas's life,' Elisa pleaded, grabbing her brother's arm. The King slapped her with the back of his hand, knocking her to the ground.

'Do you want your head to join his?' Kandrian said, facing her.

Elisa sprang to her feet like nothing had happened, grabbed her spear, and stepped in front of Davas. 'If you want to kill him, you'll have to kill me too.'

The King cocked his head to the side, laughed wickedly, then screamed. 'Move, Elisa.'

Elisa stood firm.

Kandrian screamed again before sheathing his sword. 'Fine, sister. You win,' he said, his hauntingly jovial laugh returned. 'Jegon. I'll send Davas to Jegon.'

'No,' Elisa yelled.

'This is my compromise, sister; I am not without compassion. Davas served me well for many years, but he must be punished.'

'Jegon is the same as death,' Elisa pleaded, looking back at Davas with love and fear in her eyes.

'Argue again, and I will cut off his head right here,' the King said, turning to one of his guards. 'Put him on a boat for Jegon immediately. Davas is slippery; I don't want him to escape. So long, old friend. Try to stay warm.' Two guards followed the cackling King out of the garden. The other four stayed close to Davas.

'Don't let him do this, Elli. Promise me,' Davas said as the guards hauled him away.

She mouthed, 'I promise' as she wiped tears off her cheeks."

Vatis shuffled to the center of the stage, paused, and rubbed his eyes. He dragged his hands down his face, pulling his skin tight before hooking his thumbs in his belt. "For the conservation of time, I will spare you the details of Davas's trip to the island Jegon and his first few months in prison high in the mountains. Aside from this, from the first day he entered his frozen cell, Davas planned his escape," Vatis said, sitting down. He looked up. Mia had moved another row closer. He smiled as the girl seemed desperate to hear every word. He rolled backward and jumped to his feet as he continued the story.

"Davas had been in Jegon for nearly four months. It was a miracle that he was alive; three cellmates had either died from the conditions or killed themselves, two of his toes had turned black from frostbite, and he even survived a game of Shadow. But Davas was resilient. He observed everything; his skills as a scout proved invaluable. He knew the guards' schedules, and he knew which guards were lenient and which were strict. Davas memorized the prison's layout, tracing a map in frost each morning as he recalled his trip to the mines. Luck found Davas one morning as he chipped away at the ice, mining for gold. A finger-length shard of rock flew into the air, landing between his feet. He deftly hid the shard in his ice-crusted hair. He finally had what he needed to escape. That night, he formalized his plan. In the morning, he would either be free or dead."

Vatis watched Mia move yet again. He mirrored her movements, walking upstage as the girl drifted to the second row of the arena. Once she sat, he twirled on his heels and faced the audience for the climax of his tale. "A piece of stale bread bounced off the cell floor after a guard threw it at Davas. He listened to the groans and complaints of the prisoners about their breakfasts. He needed to move as soon as the deliveries ended. Davas knew he didn't have much time before the next two guards would escort them to the mines. Once the guard moved to the next level of the prison, Davas pulled the shard of rock from his hair and began picking the lock. His frozen fingers didn't have the same dexterity they once did, and the sliver of rock was more brittle than a pick, but it had to work. After several attempts, he finally heard the life-saving sound of the lock turning. Davas gently opened the door, but it squeaked on its rusty hinges, alerting the other prisoners.

They whispered, 'Let us out.'

'I'll come back for you,' Davas lied.

One ragged prisoner, nearing The Welcoming Darkness, screamed. 'Guards, he's escaping.' Davas had hoped this particular prisoner would react obnoxiously. The old man shrieked from nightmares quite often, and the guards didn't have their accustomed urgency when they checked on him. Davas slunk into the shadows and waited for the guard.

'What is it now, old man?' a guard asked, walking down the stairs.

'He's escaping. He's escaping. He's escaping,' the man howled, pointing in Davas's direction.

'What? Who?' As the guard turned around, Davas plunged the shard into his neck. The rock bit into the exposed flesh. Davas covered the guard's mouth as he fell to the floor, twisting his head for a merciful death. Certainly, The Darkness is better than guard duty on Jegon.

Davas dragged the body to his cell and changed into the uniform, leaving the dead guard in his undergarments. He fastened the sheathe on his hip and slid the sword out - the feel of cold steel in his hand gave him confidence. The first part of his plan was a success. Now, he had to actually escape. He closed the door and threw the ring of keys into the cell across from him. 'I don't have time to figure out which key works, but I wish you luck in your escape. May your feet find the road again,' Davas said to the other prisoners. He didn't wait for their reply.

Davas marched through the prison with the authoritarian entitlement that most guards have as he made his way to the yard. He walked by one guard unnoticed. In the next hallway, he slipped by a group of three, avoiding eye contact as they passed. The yard was one hallway away. With no guards in sight, Davas sprinted through the dim stone passage; his head light from hunger and exhaustion, he nearly tripped while looking back over his shoulder. His feet ached in the too-tight, stolen boots. He glanced back again. It can't be this easy, he thought. Turning around, he knocked over a barrel. It splintered against the wall, spilling grain out in front of him. The barrel knocked him off balance, and the slippery grain helped his feet slide out from underneath him. He twisted slightly and crashed onto his right shoulder. A sudden, sharp pain reverberated across his upper body. He let out a muffled cry into the stone and closed his eyes. A brief moment of rest was all he allowed himself, a moment to clear his mind and find his strength.

'I just need to make it to the yard,' Davas said, dusting himself off. 'Through the yard, over the wall, and down the mountain.' He finally reached the door to the yard, but it was locked. He cursed himself for giving away the keys and leaving his makeshift lockpick behind. Fortunately, a guard walked up the hall a few moments later.

'Dermont, what are you doing up here? They are looking for you downstairs.' The guard called. Davas didn't turn around. 'Dermont,' the guard repeated. 'What are you doing?'

Davas didn't want to kill another guard, that wasn't part of his plan, but he needed to escape. He waited for the guard to get closer, clenched his fist, drew his sword, and charged, driving the blade into his opponent's ribs before the guard could defend himself. The sentry collapsed, his helmet clanging against the stone floor. Davas pulled the keyring from the guard's belt and tried to unlock the door. The first key didn't work, and neither did the second, or the third, or the fourth. His hand shook more with each key he tried. Finally, the eighth key fit and turned. Davas opened the door and stepped into the yard, locking the door behind him. He hadn't made it more than ten steps when he heard shouts from inside.

'He went this way. He's escaping,' shouts came from all directions. Davas sprinted to the stack of crates near the southern wall. He still was in disbelief that the guards let him stack the containers in a stair-like fashion, but no one had ever escaped Jegon, so they paid little attention to the escape-aiding stack.

'There he is,' guards called from behind him. 'Archers, take him down.' Now, one man might seem like an easy target for archers, but with no enemies and no reason to stand ready, the archers were not quick enough to even fire at the lightning-fast Davas. Before so much as a bow was drawn, Davas was atop the wall. He looked down at the snowy slope below, gazed back at the prison, and jumped off the wall."

A shocked murmur floated around the arena as Vatis jumped off the front of the stage. He looked to his left. Mia clapped. A few others near her tentatively joined in. Vatis smiled at the girl as he walked up the stairs back on stage, whistling an ominous tune to fill the momentary silence. When he returned to center stage, he began again, "Davas had escaped, but his life wasn't saved yet. It took him three days to descend the snowy slopes. Another toe succumbed to frostbite. He nearly starved before he managed to catch a fish in a stream at the base of the mountain. Somehow, Davas reached the coast of Jegon without dying. He knew he didn't have the strength left to swim across the channel, but he had to make it back inland. Again, it would be the crates that saved his life—the containers he filled for months with nuggets of gold, iron, and other minerals.

In the cover of night, he crept to the docks. Once all but two guards were asleep, he slipped onto the boat, hiding behind a pile of crates in the ship's storage. Luck was on his side that night. In the morning, the boat crossed the narrow channel. Davas slunk off the ship unnoticed through a porthole near the stern. He dove into the cool water, floating with the current as far as his exhausted body would allow. Before he let the water take him out to the open sea, Davas swam ashore. He had done it; Davas escaped Jegon. He looked back at the mountainous island across the water; its snowy peaks shivered his bones, but the euphoria of escape warmed him quickly. Yes, Davas had escaped Jegon, but at what cost? He would have to run for the rest of his life. He lost friends. He lost his place in the world, and he lost his love, but he had his life, and maybe he could still try to make Emre a world worth living in," Vatis said, finishing his tale with a bow. He stood tall, inhaled, and awaited applause.

IN THE CROWD

Vidmar

Vidmar and Kamet sat in the back of the arena as they waited for Vatis to perform.

Kamet gobbled down his third pastry of the tourney, washing it down with a pint of something strong. Vidmar savored a bag of candied nuts like a squirrel preparing for winter. The performers were disappointing. One man from Greenbriar, the only city north of Yimser, told an interesting story, but the crowd heckled him relentlessly. He left the stage in tears, using his forearms as a shield. A jester from Yimser told some of the worst jokes Vidmar had ever heard, but the crowd roared with laughter. Kegs of ale flowed like water. The audience grew rowdier as the evening wore on.

"How much longer?" Kamet asked. His breath reeked of alcohol.

"Soon, I hope," Vidmar replied, looking around the audience, examining the groups of people that joked and talked in between the performances. One group in the back of the arena gambled on arm-wrestling contests. A man nearly as big as Kamet hadn't left the table in four or five rounds; other, smaller men shook their arms out painfully as they watched each match.

A thin woman with curly red hair slid into the row in front of Vidmar. "Look what I found," she said, tapping a big-eared man on the shoulder.

"What?" he yelled.

"Quiet, James," she put a finger to his lips and looked around. Vidmar averted his gaze momentarily. "Look." She held out a coin purse. "We're rich. Found it this mornin' on the street. Just layin' there."

The man put his arm around her shoulders and hugged her tightly. Vidmar couldn't hear the rest of the conversation. *I wish I had her luck,* he thought, continuing his unbreakable habit of scouting the crowd. He saw Gaffer a few rows ahead. The old shopkeeper waved to him; Vidmar returned the gesture as Gaffer pointed to a thin girl hiding in the shadows. Vidmar mouthed *Mia* to Gaffer, and he nodded. As he stood to approach the girl, the announcer burst into his introduction. "Our next performer is a bard. A man from nowhere and everywhere, ladies and gentlemen, it is my sincere honor to introduce Vatis-of-the-Road."

Light applause rolled through the audience as murmured conversations faded into eager silence. *I'll find the girl after Vatis performs,* Vidmar thought, sitting back on the bench. Kamet drained his mug, smacked his lips, and whistled piercingly. Vidmar elbowed him in the ribs. "Sorry," the drunk mercenary whispered.

"Thuh…" Vatis said. "Thank you. I… I am, Vatis of the Road." *Oh, no, he's terrified.* A group of men in front of Vidmar reached into a sack for moldy fruit. A woman next to Kamet smiled devilishly. Gaffer rubbed his eyes. Vatis took a deep breath.

"Guh, guh, go on," a man sitting close to Gaffer yelled. Vidmar wanted to throw something at the heckler. If he had all his fingers, a small knife would have been wiggling between the bastard's shoulder blades already, but he no longer had the fingers or confidence to make such a challenging throw through a crowd. The audience laughed. Light shined off Vatis's sweaty forehead as he shook himself again and cleared his throat.

"And I would like to tell you a story, a true story of an unknown hero," he said smoother. *Better.* "Our story begins with our hero Davas, in the small town of Aswar," Vatis said. *He actually changed my name.* The audience relaxed as Vatis told his story. He looked like a seasoned professional as the story reached its climax.

The audience was silent, waiting for each word like a dog begging for scraps at the supper table. As the tale ended, Vidmar noticed a sudden shift in a few audience members. Figures in dark cloaks approached random members of the crowd. Those few audience members sat straighter as if instructed, then searched for rocks, dirt, fruit, and anything they could throw.

"This isn't good," Vidmar whispered to Kamet.

"It's fantastic. He makes you look like a real hero," Kamet said, watching Vatis. Kamet looked like a child discovering dragons for the first time.

"Kamet," Vidmar demanded in a rash whisper. He elbowed him again, not playfully but forcefully.

"Enough," Kamet said. Flames of anger sparked in his eyes.

"Listen, you oaf," Vidmar said, leaning closer. "Something is going on. Do you see those men in cloaks? Don't point, you fool. Look, they are up to something. Be on your guard."

Kamet nodded.

"Yes, Davas had escaped Jegon, but at what cost? He would have to run for the rest of his life. He lost friends. He lost his place in the world, and he lost his love, but he had his life, and maybe he could still try to make Emre a world worth living in," Vatis finished. He looked regal and proud.

A tall man sitting next to one of the cloaked figures threw a tomato at Vatis. It exploded on the bard's cheek. The rest of the crowd joined in happily; dozens of projectiles shot onto the stage.

"What a load of shit," another man sitting near a cloaked figure screamed. He threw a fist-sized stone; luckily, he missed.

"No one escapes Jegon," a man behind Vidmar yelled. *No, this isn't right*, Vidmar thought. He watched the cloaked figures slink into the shadows. *What did they say?* He stood to chase after them, but the tip of a blade poked into his back.

"Where are you going, Vidmar?" a familiar shrill voice uttered.

Vidmar turned and saw the brim of a ridiculous purple hat before a rock struck his temple, and he collapsed into darkness.

LOST

Vatis

Rocks, tomatoes, apples, and onions flew onto the stage; Vatis put his arms over his face for protection and tried to escape.

He looked through a small slit between his forearms, searching for the narrow wooden staircase upstage. A rock hit him in the thigh, knocking him off balance. He tried to steady himself, but his left foot found a smashed tomato instead of the sturdy wooden planks. He slipped and fell, landing on his side. His makeshift shield split as he grabbed his leg in pain. He crawled to his knees, fruit continuing to bruise his body. He found the staircase. Reaching up, he pulled himself to his feet with the support of the railing. Another rock whizzed behind his head, bouncing off the wall with a loud thud. He fell down the last two steps as he rushed to get out of the audience's range, landing on the muddy, worn grass at the bottom of the staircase. He rolled onto his back, covering his face with his hands.

"Are you alright, son," the announcer said, running up and kneeling beside Vatis.

Vatis did not answer. He rolled onto his stomach and pushed himself to his knees with all his remaining strength.

"It's a ruckus crowd today, son. And you are a foreigner. But, for what it's worth, I loved your story. I had only heard rumors of this, Davas," the announcer asked, helping Vatis to his feet.

Vatis brushed the announcer's hand off his shoulder.

"Take it easy," the announcer said, resting his hand on Vatis' lower back.

"I'm fine," Vatis said sharply, moving out of the announcer's reach. "I'm fine," Vatis repeated with more fervor.

"I'm sorry. It always hurts me when a young man like you gets treated like that. You're talented. Who knows, in another town, you may have won," the announcer said as he walked onto the stage to introduce the next performer.

"I am fine," Vatis repeated, more to himself than the announcer.

"Thanks for getting them all worked up," a shrill voice muttered to Vatis' right.

A woman in a gray lace dress with straight blonde hair dangling just above her waist walked toward the stage carrying a flute. Her pungent, flowery perfume almost forced Vatis to sneeze. She looked like a trained musician. Her eyes scolded Vatis as she passed him and climbed the stairs. Her look of pure, unfiltered hatred turned to jubilation as she saw the crowd from the top of the staircase. She casually kicked a rock backward with her heel down the stairs toward Vatis while waving to the audience. It narrowly missed, ricocheting inches in front of his head.

"It is my pleasure to introduce the best musician in all Emre, four-time consecutive champion and last year's runner-up in Barna, your home-grown maiden, Feya," the announcer called with much more vibrato than he expressed for Vatis's introduction.

The crowd hushed momentarily before deafening applause shook the stage. The praise seemed to last hours. *How could this simple flutist garner such admiration?*

He stood up; pain seared across his body. A rock had sliced his right eyebrow; he felt a trail of blood trickle down his cheek. His left side was a cornucopia of bruises and cuts. Despite his many injuries, no pain was worse than the few seconds of utter silence after his tale ended. The occupants of taverns had always enjoyed his stories. Vidmar and Taldor praised him endlessly. *What's different here?* He desperately waited for approval, recognition, and the cheering of his name; instead, the silence saturated his body, numbing him for the beating that followed. *Why didn't they like the story? What did I do wrong?*

He limped toward the main road before the announcer returned. He heard faint music through the buzzing in his head, an enchanting melody skillfully played, never missing a note. Feya's skill infuriated Vatis. She was a great artist, and her performance assured his defeat. He quickened his pace, covering his ears with his hands until he could only hear the bustling street conversation and merchants peddling their wares.

"Sweet treats and mammoth ears for sale. Get 'em while they last," an older gray-haired woman called from a cart that smelled of spices and roasted nuts. This morning, he cheerily told her he would buy the whole cart after winning the prize. He was confident he would win. This was a small-town competition, not the grand competition in Barna, and recognized performers didn't bother coming this far north.

"Hey, did you win?" the woman called in Vatis' direction. "I made sure to stock the cart."

Vatis turned the other way, ignoring the vendor's call.

"I guess not, you know, nothing soothes pain better than a sweet treat."

He thought about turning around, but he couldn't; he couldn't face another person, another judge. All he wanted to do was gather his things and leave town before anyone else could berate him.

Vatis found an alley between two buildings, hobbling as fast as possible. He made it to the next road; it was less busy and ran parallel to the main road. His bag was at Geoff's, almost a mile away on the city's southern edge. The Braymore Inn was closer. Sure, he fit in with the ragged patrons of Geoff's, but he wanted to taste the elegance of the Braymore before he left. He was unsure if he could walk there, not in his battered state. He inhaled deeply through his nose like he was starting his performance again. Vatis put his head down, avoiding eye contact with passersby, exhaled, and doddered to the inn. He didn't rehearse this act. He didn't fret over word choice or body language; Vatis performed.

The Braymore Inn was like many of the inns throughout northern Emre. A large sitting room was decorated with eight wooden tables; simple blue embroidered runners spanned their lengths. A gray stone fireplace on the back wall with a dark wooden mantle held various items: a framed painting of a beautiful, green-eyed woman, an expertly crafted brass box, a black figurine of a soldier raising a sword above his head, and a crystal vase with pink and white flowers. The room had an inviting aroma of mead and freshly baked bread. A well-polished bar with wooden stools lined the left side of the hall. Three barrels of ale sat between shelves full of wine, bread, herbs, and dried meats. Two elderly men sat side-by-side at the bar, joking with the bartender. Empty silver mugs adorned the table nearest the entrance, hinting that guests had left recently. A young blonde barmaid unsuccessfully scrubbed what appeared to be red wine out of the table runner. She looked up as Vatis entered.

"Darkness, what happened to you?" she said.

Vatis did not respond. He limped towards the nearest table, scaring the barmaid as she piled empty mugs onto a round tray. He almost fell through the wooden bench as he sat down. It tottered back and forth before settling into its proper place. He crossed his arms on the table, resting his chin on his wrists.

"You look like you've had better days. What can ole Jonathan get you? Ale? Mead? Something stronger?" the chiseled, broad-shouldered bartender asked. He filled a mug of ale from one of the barrels behind the bar. "A hot bath and a meal might help," Jonathan smirked as he slid the frothy ale toward the older of the two men sitting at the bar.

"Thanks, Jon," the white-haired man said with a thick northern accent.

Jonathan nodded and collected the coins, pocketing them in his elegant black apron.

Vatis remained silent. His head throbbed. He didn't notice it on his way to the inn; the pain in his knee seemed to be the worst at the time. A dull ache pulsed from his forehead to the back of his neck. He lifted his head, rubbing his temples with two fingers on each hand.

"Here, on the house," Jonathan said as he sat on the bench opposite Vatis. He pushed a mug halfway across the table.

Vatis blinked his swollen eyes briefly before he covered them with his hands. Blood dripped from his chin, missing the table and soaking into his muddy trousers. He dragged his hands down his face, irritating his cuts and bruises.

"Everlasting Darkness, who did this to you?" Jonathan asked.

Vatis didn't answer. Instead, he grabbed the ale, downing its contents in three long swallows. He coughed as he set the mug down. "Another," he said, wiping froth from his lip.

"Right away," Jonathan stood and filled the mug again.

Vatis remained silent. *Why?* He thought. He watched a fly buzz around his table. It landed in a small pool of ale, rubbing its forelegs together like it was washing its hands. Vatis slammed his palm down. The puddle exploded outward, sending tiny drops of ale onto the table runner and his shirt. Vatis lifted his hand—nothing. The fly mocked him as it flew around his head. Vatis flailed both hands, growing more frustrated with each miss.

"Here you are," Jonathan said.

Vatis slammed his palm down again. The dull thud echoed in the small tavern. Ale spilled from the mug. "Fucking fly," Vatis yelled. He swatted the air around his ears. He picked up the cup, finishing the ale faster than the first. "Another."

AN INVITATION

Vatis

Darkness's icy breath filled the unfamiliar room. Sunlight tried to slither snake-like between narrow cracks in meandering walls, leaving faint golden streaks. Vatis winced. He touched the tender skin around his eyes. The putrid stench of dirt, sweat, and alcohol created a revolting combination. His stomach convulsed. He lurched forward, covering his mouth with his hand. The sour rising bile resisted his recovery attempts; acidic liquid burnt his aching throat. Saliva dripped from his lips. Fuzzy, spinning shadows mocked him on the edges of his vision. He blinked.

"Are you alright?" a gentle voice asked behind him. He spun around too quickly. He imagined he felt like a new sailor in his first storm. *Where am I?* Vatis thought as his head continued to spin.

"Vatis? Are you alright? Here," the voice said as a small hand appeared holding a waterskin.

A girl sat on the floor with her back against the wall. The golden sunlight outlined her petite figure through the wall's cracks. His new shirt, stained by food and mud, lay on a tattered blanket near his feet. *What happened?* Shivers ran down his spine.

Vatis rubbed his eyes. "Mia?"

"Vatis," she said, mocking his tone. "Vatis-of-the-Road. You know, that's a strange name."

"What happened? Where am I?" Vatis asked.

"You're in my castle–the coziest place in the world. I found you sleeping in the alley behind Braymore. I was looking for dinner. Jonathan has the best day-old bread, but instead, I found you," Mia said.

Vatis uncorked the waterskin and sniffed its contents.

"It's water," Mia said.

Vatis sipped tentatively. The cool liquid temporarily soothed his smoldering throat. "Thank you," Vatis said before taking another drink. "Oh gods, Braymore. The last thing I remember is falling over the table, trying to kill a damn fly. How did I get here?"

Mia laughed. "You wouldn't stop talking about that fly. You don't remember?"

"No."

"Well, I didn't want you sleeping on the street uptown; it would only be a matter of time before the guards found you, so I woke you up. By the way, you're tough to wake up. I kicked you; I shook you. Finally, I found a fish–it smelled awful. I put it under your nose, and boom, like magic, you were on your feet. Then you used me as a crutch on our way here. It's ok. I didn't mind. Then you cursed about a torn seam, ripped off your shirt, and passed out."

"You dragged me all the way here? Did I talk about anything other than the fly?" Vatis asked. The hairs on his forearm stood.

The waves in his stomach ceased momentarily as they retreated into the depths before tsunami-like devastation wrecked his gut.

"You mumbled some stuff about some guy named Vidmar and complained about being tired—that's it, but it's alright. I felt bad for how they treated you after your story. I wasn't going to let them hang you on top of it," Mia said, standing. She tightened a braided belt on her waist and adjusted an empty sheath.

Vatis sighed. His shoulders relaxed. "Hang me?" he said, returning the waterskin. The storm in his belly dissipated slowly.

"A foreigner sleeping on the street uptown, people have been hanged for less."

"Why do people in Yimser hate foreigners?" Vatis asked, sitting up.

"I don't. But most of the elders do, especially the donkeys uptown. Gaffer says it's because of some old rebellion, but he didn't have any books about it."

"You can read?"

"Of course, my Papa taught me."

"What's your favorite book?"

"Maiden's Tales," Mia said proudly.

"I should have guessed," Vatis smiled. "I saw you in the crowd. What did you think of my story?"

Mia's eyes widened. "It was incredible. I loved Davas. He was so resourceful and smart. Did he have any other adventures?" She paused and bit her lower lip. "I'm sorry. I can't believe what they did to you because you aren't from this dumb city. That fake Feya won again, and she played the same songs last year. I threw a tomato at her, not while she was on stage, but later when she was prancing around with her dumb medal."

Vatis laughed. His head pounded, and his gut didn't like the sudden movement. "Thank you, Mia," he said. "I can't tell you how much you've helped me. I owe you my life."

"Alright, don't get sappy. I did you a favor. Now you can do *me* a favor," Mia smiled. She straightened a stack of books in the corner of the room. She ran a finger down the spines, then stopped on a dilapidated book; its torn cover barely held on.

Vatis watched her thumb through the book. "How can I repay you?"

"What do you know about *The Lost Forest?*"

Vatis felt his eyebrows nearly leap off their perch. "Nothing more than that book. Why?"

"I want to find it. They say Mia-The-Maiden had a secret hideout in the forest and that fairies used to help her. I don't know if I believe in fairies, but this book talks about magic, real set-things-on-fire-with-your-mind magic. I want to have adventures like Mia and Davas. I don't want to scavenge for food in Yimser my whole life. I'm not saying I need to go on a quest to find The Lost Forest, just take me with you when you leave. Please."

Vatis sighed as he itched his chin. His long, dirt-covered fingernails scratched against his stubble; it had been far too long since he shaved. The sound of running water trickled peacefully nearby.

Mia inched closer. "Please, Vatis?"

"I," he said. *Mia can't come with us. Vidmar will kill me.* "I have to consult with Vidmar."

"Who is this Vidmar guy?" Mia asked, looking up from her book.

Vatis paused again, unsure of how much information to divulge. *I owe her.* "I'm traveling with him and collecting his stories. Vidmar is the one who escaped Jegon – Davas was a pseudonym."

"A pseudonym?" Mia said, struggling to sound out the word.

"A fake name."

"Wait, you know Davas, I mean Vidmar—the hero from your story?"

"Yes. He's in Yimser now."

"Really?" Mia said, springing to her feet. Her head came dangerously close to banging into the ceiling each time she jumped. Mia covered her mouth with her hands to muffle her screams. She grabbed Vatis's wrist. "Can I meet him?" Her big hazel eyes beamed with excitement.

"Yes, you can meet him, but I have to get my things from Geoff's, and we must leave Yimser today. We've already lingered here too long."

"Let's go," Mia said, unlatching a small crude lock. "Wait, I need to pack."

She shoved most of her possessions into a burlap sack with a frayed drawstring: a tan shirt with a hole in the side, a loaf of bread, and a carved figurine of a woman holding a sword above her head. *Mia-The-Maiden*, Vatis thought. She added a spool of thread, a small knife, a lockpick, and a silver coin. A brief deliberation between three books ended with her packing *The Lost Forest* and *Maiden's Tales*.

"Don't bring *The Lost Forest*. I have that one in my pack," Vatis said.

"Alright," Mia said. She stuffed a book called *The Mystery of The Pact* into her bag and tightened the drawstring.

"*The Mystery of The Pact*–interesting choice. A few of the stories are good, but most of the book is like reading an accountant's ledger. I would have gone with *The Eternal Darkness*. The message is a little frightening, but it has some wonderful stories. Although I can't blame you for connecting with Dinardo and his cause," Vatis said.

"*The Eternal Darkness* is a bunch of lies. At least most of *The Mystery of The Pact* is true," Mia said, slinging her bag over her shoulder.

"I can't argue there."

An hour later, Vatis gathered his possessions in his room at Geoff's, placing each item carefully into his pack. Vidmar wasn't there, and neither was Kamet. *Maybe they're looking for me. Why is Vidmar's gear still here, though? Where is he?* Vatis wrapped two apples in a cloth and corked his bottle of ink.

"What's this?" Mia said, opening Vatis's journal.

"Don't," Vatis said quickly. Mia froze and put the book down on the nightstand.

"I'm sorry," Vatis said, grabbing the book and carefully setting it into his pack. "That's mine. It contains my notes and the beginning of a story I am working on."

"You're writing a book? What's it about?"

Vatis smiled. "It's a collection of stories. The same stories I tell in taverns and campfires."

"And tournaments," Mia added.

"No more tournaments—not anymore. But, yes, this is a collection of those stories. *The Stories of Emre*, I call it. It's more of a history than a standard book of stories, as each of the tales I plan to include is true. Although, instead of focusing on royal lineages, wars, and cataclysmic events, I am focusing on individual tales of heroic, everyday people like Vidmar."

"Is Mia-The-Maiden's story going to be in it? You can't have a book of heroes and not include her," Mia said, pacing back and forth.

"Mia's story is well documented. I may include a few of her lesser-known deeds, but not the same events from *Maiden's Tales.*"

"She has more stories?" Mia said, temporarily ceasing her patrol.

"Yes, many. Why are you pacing like that? You're making me nervous."

Mia looked out the window, examining the street below. "I don't like this place. Nothing good ever happens in Geoff's. Do you have everything?"

"Yes, but I must gather Vidmar's gear too. As soon as we find him, we need to leave Yimser."

"I'm coming with you, right?" Mia asked, still looking out the window.

"Yes, but this would go faster if you helped," Vatis said, pointing to the other nightstand. "Grab those knives and anything else that looks important."

Mia reluctantly left her post. "Why does he need so many knives?"

"Every time I ask him that, he says, 'Would you rather have too many knives or too few?' Vatis laughed.

"Too many, I guess," Mia said, examining each blade. She passed the last knife to Vatis and slung her leg over the windowsill.

"What are you doing?"

"Leaving, better safe than sorry. I'll meet you in the alley. But hurry, please," Mia said, swinging the rest of her body out the window. She hung by the sill for a moment, raised her eyebrows, and disappeared onto the street below.

Vidmar is going to like her, Vatis thought. He walked downstairs with each bag slung over his shoulders. *Maybe the bartender has seen him.* A group of men playing dice at a table stared at Vatis as he passed. Their carnivorous eyes caused shivers to run down his spine. One gigantic, bearded man slammed his fist on the table. Two thin wisps of men whispered while examining Vatis, and three men reached for the blades on their belts. Vatis walked faster. He approached the barkeep.

"Have you seen my companions?" Vatis asked.

The barkeep turned, snorted, and returned to washing mugs. "Excuse me, please," Vatis said. He reached into Vidmar's bag and found a full coin purse. *Where did you get all this coin, Vidmar?* He tapped a coin against the bar and called again. "Excuse me, have you seen my companions?"

The barkeeper turned, noticed the coin, and stepped forward. She slid the small metal piece into the pocket of her apron. "Haven't seen 'em."

Suddenly, a thick, sausage-like finger poked his shoulder. He didn't hear anyone approach. It was the man who slammed his fist on the table. *How did he move so quietly?* He looked even bigger standing. Tight leather armor accentuated his muscular figure. He was smaller than Kamet, but not by much. His left hand rested on the hilt of a longsword strapped to his belt. "I know what happened," he grimaced. Water sloshed in a bucket as the bartender scrubbed mugs clean.

"Splendid, where did they go?" Vatis said, retreating against the bar.

"That'll cost ya," the man said, trapping Vatis between himself and the bar; his tongue slid between missing teeth like a snake—his breath smelt of alcohol. The men at the table watched like vultures. The sound of water splashing and scrubbing ceased.

"I can pay," Vatis said, holding his hands up defensively.

"I'm sure you can," the brute said, poking Vatis in the chest. "We all watched you yesterday, Vatis-of-the-Road, and we think it's past time you left Geoff's and found your home."

Vatis pressed against the bar, sliding down as the man moved closer. "I intend to."

"Good," the man said, taking a step back. "Now go."

Vatis started walking to the door, averting the gaze of the other occupants of the tavern. "Sorry, I truly am, but you said you knew where my companions went."

"No," the man laughed. "I said I knew what happened, and it will cost you."

"How much will it cost?" Vatis said.

"Everything you have," the man laughed. The table of ruffians joined in like a pack of wolves howling.

Vatis reached into Vidmar's purse, nimbly tucking a few coins into his sleeve. *Thank you, Vidmar,* he thought as he finished the coin trick the treasure hunter had taught him on the road. "Is twenty and two enough?"

The big man laughed. "No."

The other men seemed to drool as Vatis pulled out more coins.

"Thirty is surely enough," Vatis said, making his hands shake. He played a nervous merchant better than most of his other characters. It was almost natural.

"I said everything. Give me the purse," the man said, closing the distance between them.

"Fine," Vatis tossed the leather pouch and slid sideways.

"Well, boys. It seems bards are better paid than I thought," the collector said, tightening the drawstring. He threw the pouch to the table. The wolves pounced on it like it was a bone. "Now get out."

"What happened to my companions?" Vatis asked.

One of the men cackled and mimed hanging himself. The others howled with laughter.

The big man smiled. "Crow's food."

"Excuse me."

"Town guards arrested them during the tourney. They are probably swaying from a tree right now, fucking cheating foreigners. Leave now if you don't want to join them."

"You're lying," Vatis yelled. "You're lying."

A man from the table called out. "I saw it with me own eyes— damn cheatin' foreigners. I laughed when that fella in the purple hat knocked the small one out. Hit him right in the ole temple. The big man put up a fight before…."

"Shut yer mouth," the apparent leader said, turning around. "Did you say a man in a purple hat?"

"No. Now leave before I take the clothes off your back."

Zidane? It must be. What is he doing in Yimser? Vatis slung the bags over his shoulders and turned around. He heard footsteps following him when the front door crashed open. A hefty man dressed in vibrant clothing stepped into the tavern. Streaks of black makeup ran down his cheeks. His bloodshot eyes examined the scene. "There you are," he said, out of breath, looking at Vatis. His voice sounded like a frog croaking. As he approached, Vatis noticed he was still wearing his announcing attire.

"Hello," Vatis said, grateful for a momentary distraction. "Good morning."

"Ah," the announcer cried. "Ah, I wish it were." He continued to wail. He snorted, and his lips trembled. "Alas, our sweet, my love, Feya. She was welcomed to the darkness last night. She has passed on," he cried more. Vatis stepped close and rubbed his back. The announcer cleared his throat and stood taller. "I can do this," he whispered to himself.

"My brother and I have decided that you shall take Feya's place at the tourney in Barna," he said, mustering his strongest announcing voice. "We agreed that your story of Davas was not fairly received, and you deserve a chance to perform in front of a less biased crowd. As a traveling bard, I knew I needed to catch you soon, so forgive the hour and my appearance." He breathed heavily when he finished. Tears flowed down his cheeks.

"I," Vatis started.

"Please, Vatis," the announcer interrupted. "I don't have a medal for you, but take this letter. It has our official seal. It will grant you entry to the tournament. My love for the arts gave me the strength to deliver this message. You deserve another chance to perform, but I must go. Forgive me. I cannot hold it together much longer; congratulations, Vatis-of-the-Road." He bowed, turned, and jogged out of the tavern. The tail of his coat flapped like a flag in the wind. "May your feet find the road," he cried from the street.

What happened to Feya? Vatis couldn't breathe or think. He leaned against a nearby table, petrified like a statue. His mind ran in circles; excitement battled with terror, relief fought dread, and confusion encapsulated elation. For a moment, he forgot about finding Vidmar. He closed his eyes and took a deep breath. Images of himself on Barna's stage appeared like a new dawn. He heard applause; he felt rose petals on his feet—*finally, a stroke of luck for me.*

"What the fuck happened to Feya?" a man cried from the table of gamblers.

Vatis's daydream shattered like broken glass. The man at the bar charged forward. "It's your lucky day. A young, beautiful woman dies suddenly, and look who has an invite to Barna. What happened to Feya? What did you do?"

"Nothing. I was at the Braymore Inn. Ask the bartender," Vatis said, wiping his sweaty palms off on his pants.

"You hear that, boys? The rich bard went to fucking Braymore last night," the big man said, surging forward. The table spewed sinister laughter forth like an erupting volcano. The men at the table stood, hovering like ash in the wind.

"I was at the Braymore," Vatis cried.

"Leave him alone, Alec," a voice called from the door. *Mia.* "He's with me."

"Stay out of this, girl. He's a foreigner," Alec said.

"He killed Feya," a pair of voices called from the looming storm.

"Alec, let him come with me, and we're even," Mia said.

Vatis continued to back toward the door. Rage flared in Alec's eyes. "Letting him live is too high a price."

"A higher price than your life," Mia snapped. "Who slipped you a pick when you were being carted off to jail? Who stole medicine and brought it to you when you were sick last winter? You owe me, Alec."

The big man looked at his feet and shuffled like a scolded child. "I told you never to come to Geoff's again, but fine, Mia. We're even."

"But, what about Feya," a shrill voice interjected from Alec's pack.

"I said we're even. Get out of here before I change my mind," Alec growled.

They walked along the narrow river that ran through Yimser. It smelt of dead fish and urine. Vatis tried to comprehend the events of the last day. He finally played in front of a tournament crowd, and that same crowd shattered his expectations. He drank enough ale to knock out a bear, woke up in a strange shack, and a ten-year-old girl saved his life not once but twice. Vidmar and Kamet might be dead, but he could only focus on a chance to perform in front of the King. He was going to Barna. He was going to perform on the most revered stage in Emre. A smile slithered onto his face.

"Why are you smiling like that? It's creepy," Mia said, knocking him back into reality.

"What? I don't know. That's how I smile," Vatis said.

"Well, quit."

"Fine. I can walk somberly, not relishing my stroke of luck," Vatis said, dropping his head low like it had trouble attaching to his shoulders.

"Oh, you're something else, your friends are in trouble, but all you can think about is that damn invitation. I should never have pulled you out of the alley. I thought you were different from the rest of the artists and bards, or whatever you call yourself. You're all liars who crave fame and fortune," Mia said, throwing a rock into the river.

"Why is it so bad to want fame and fortune?" Vatis asked. He stopped walking. A duck flew away as Mia missed it with another stone. He kicked a small pile of rocks into the river. The current erased the small cascading ripples.

"It's selfish. You don't care who you have to climb over to get to the top as long as you're the one standing at the end. Your friends are in trouble. They might be dead, and you don't even want to know what happened," Mia said, sitting down and dipping her toes into the water.

"What do you know? You're what, eight years old?"

"I'm eleven."

Vatis snorted. "Anyway, Vidmar and Kamet are two of the most capable men in Emre. So, if they aren't dead, what chance do I have of rescuing them? And why should I?" Vatis said. He paced the riverbank.

"They're your friends."

"They are my companions. Nothing more," Vatis said. *They can't be anything more.* "There are other stories in this world to gather, other heroes to uncover. You have to know when to cut your losses."

"Aren't you lonely?" Mia said, pushing a loose strand of hair behind her ear. "I am," she whispered. "If you won't save them because they are your friends, save them for the story. You'll have a front-row seat to a heroic rescue mission. Please, Vatis. I want to meet Vidmar, and there has to be a part of you that wants to save him too."

Vatis bit his lip. *Damn, she's perceptive, but she's right.* Vatis exhaled and sat beside Mia. Frothy waves splashed against his bare feet. "If you ever want to see more of this world, we should make for Barna right now, but if you want to play hero, I will follow you. The second there is too much trouble, I'm fleeing. There are too many stories I haven't told to die in this poor excuse of a city." *This is a mistake.*

"Really," Mia said.

"Don't make me have second thoughts. Do you know where they might be?"

"Yes," Mia said, jumping to her feet.

BENEATH YIMSER

Vidmar

Water dripped onto his head. The darkness of his cell concealed everything. He raised his hand in front of his face and saw nothing; he remembered he was missing two fingers on that hand, so he waved. His useless thumb, ring, and pinky finger flashed by like two bats chasing a fly. He almost smiled. Vidmar knew the key to escaping captivity was to stay sane. The slow torture from the dripping water was not a good start. Water found a way to drip onto him no matter where he moved. He decided that water splashing onto his shin was the least annoying spot to endure the torture for now.

"Kandrian's ball sack, I hate these fucking holes," A deep voice bellowed.

"Kamet," Vidmar called.

"He lives. You had me worried," Kamet said.

"Where are we?"

"Yimser's asshole. But honestly, I liked the company of those pricks at Geoff's better."

"So, we are still in Yimser? What happened? Is Alcin here? Did they capture Vatis?"

"One at a time, Vidmar," Kamet laughed. "Shit, fuck these damn holes. The bottom of my cell is like Numerian cheese."

"I'll trade with you. I'd rather have holes than these tiny leaks dripping water onto me wherever I go; I hope it's water. It smells awful."

"Deal. Let's put in the transfer request next time we see a guard."

Vidmar rubbed his head. He felt a tender lump just above his left temple. "So, first question, are we still in Yimser?"

"Yes," Kamet said. Iron bars creaked as the big man shifted against them in his cell. Vidmar heard his leather pants scrape against the stone floor. "Wait until I get my hands on that stupid, purple-hat-wearing sack of shit."

"Did you say purple-hat-wearing?"

"Yes, the dumbest hat I've ever seen."

"I knew I should have killed him," Vidmar said. He bent forward. Water dripped onto his neck, tickling his spine as he returned to a comfortable position.

"You know him? I thought he was just one of Alcin's lackeys," Kamet grunted.

"Yes, at least I think so, Zidane. A Gar smuggler, he tried to rob Vatis and me on the road." Vidmar scratched his chin. "That's the last skirmish of my life when all my skills and limbs were intact against armed men anyway. You would have been impressed. Me and Vatis against Zidane and four or five guards, well, just me. Vatis was useless except for distracting Zidane." Vidmar recalled his encounter in the forest with Zidane, sparing no details.

"You sure know how to make an enemy. Remember Gibbon, the one who called himself a knight? He hated you," Kamet said as Vidmar finished his story.

A dim light swayed into the dark cellar. Two long shadows followed it. "Vidmar, Vidmar, Vidmar," a shrill, familiar voice called before two lanterns appeared. The sound of boots against stone grew louder as they approached. The voice cackled with laughter as Zidane's skeleton-thin frame emerged from the darkness.

"I'm going to kill you, Vidmar," Zidane said, crouching in front of Vidmar's cell. "God's, I've wanted to say that to you for a long time. Look at you. I can't believe people feared you. You look like a stick that lost a fight with the wind. Didn't your mother tell you to eat your vegetables?"

"Hello, Zidane, you look well, like a fourth son grasping for your unloving father's attention," Vidmar said. Kamet coughed a dry laugh.

"Shut up, you overgrown shrub," Zidane barked, turning toward Kamet.

Vidmar chuckled. "Clever."

"You two are having far too much fun; perhaps we should let the hounds down here to play for a while," Zidane sneered.

"Aye, sir, they haven't been fed in days. I'm sure they would enjoy it," one of the guards escorting Zidane said.

"I'm rather busy. I don't have time to train your dogs, Zidane, but we would like to request to trade cells. I'll take the one with the holes, and Kamet will take the leaky one."

Zidane hit the iron bars of the cell with his palm. The lock rattled. *Interesting,* Vidmar thought. "If Alcin didn't want to kill you himself, I'd do it right now," Zidane shouted. He smacked the bars again. A rock fell from the ceiling, bruising Vidmar's shoulder as it rolled onto the ground. Vidmar grabbed the stone before Zidane noticed. The stone wasn't large, but it had a jagged edge that could be useful in a pinch. *Better than nothing.*

"So loyal," Kamet said. "You'd make a great dog yourself. I'll get you a collar to match that hat of yours."

Vidmar snickered. Kamet laughed so hard he nearly choked. "Alcin didn't say anything about you." The twang of unsheathed metal sliced through their laughter. "One more word, and I'll fill those holes with your blood." The iron bars cried as Zidane scraped his blade against them.

"What do you want, Zidane?" Vidmar said.

"I want to kill you. I thought I clarified that, but Alcin wants to finish what he started. You know how he is," Zidane paused. Vidmar couldn't see his expression in the dim light, but he could almost feel Zidane sneer. Ding, Ding, Ding, Dong went the bars of his cell as Zidane dragged his blade across them. Vidmar noticed a different sound each time Zidane hit the furthest bar. *Also interesting.* Vidmar focused on the steel while Zidane rambled off numerous threats from Alcin. "He had your fingers made into dice, but the annoying part is, the smith only had enough bone to make a single die, and what games can you play with a single die?"

"Shadow," Vidmar said coldly.

"Nobody plays Shadow." Zidane's arrogance wavered.

Vidmar remembered the only time he played the ancient game. His stomach sank as the guards pointed at him. He could hear them snicker as he rolled a two. His opponent's wicked, toothless grin was scarred in his memory as he threw a five. Shadow was less of a game and more of a death sentence.

Two players rolled one die and fought to the death using whichever weapon the die chose. Roll a one, and the player fought with nothing more than their fists; a two, and they could use a small knife. A three was a sword, four a mace, five a crossbow, and a six was a spear. He remembered playing with the small, dull knife. The comforting feel of steel between his fingertips. Guards and prisoners chanted in a circle around them. His bare feet were so cold that they burnt against the icy stones in the courtyard. A guard shouted the rules with bard-like gusto, but Vidmar didn't listen. He watched his opponent crank the heavy crossbow. The barbed tip pointed at Vidmar's stomach, but it wavered. He didn't hear the click of a fully wound crossbow. His opponent's finger trembled above the trigger, waiting for the signal.

"I have," Vidmar said.

Zidane huffed. "Liar."

"Call me a liar, but there isn't much in the way of entertainment on Jegon. Every few days, the guards would pick two prisoners to play. I won a two against a five. The crossbow jammed, and my knife found its mark."

"Is there nothing the great Vidmar can't do?" Zidane mocked.

He remembered the snapping bolt and the collective gasp that followed. Vidmar seized his opportunity and charged after his opponent, screaming. Even though his opponent was twice his size, fear glossed over his green, bloodshot eyes. He threw the knife. It stuck in his opponent's thigh, but his assault was only beginning. He spun and pulled the blade from the big man's quivering leg. He ducked. The crossbow swooshed over his head. Vidmar turned again and slashed the back of his opponent's knee. The tendons snapped like a cut bowstring. The other prisoner collapsed, and Vidmar mercifully ended his life by slicing his throat. Dark red blood pooled on the frost-covered ground. Haunting lifeless steam rose into the air around his victim, leaving a ghostly trail into the dark sky.

"I was never very good at cooking."

"Enough," Zidane yelled.

He remembered the sound of guards groaning as they lost their bets. The other prisoners cheered. None of them had bet against Vidmar. They knew better.

"Come," Zidane ordered his guards, their heavy boots clanging against the floor. Desperately, Vidmar pressed against the bars. Zidane limped. He watched their lanterns swing down the corridor; their long, jagged shadows melded into the darkness.

"Why are we down here? Alcin doesn't leave Haran," Vidmar called as the lanterns disappeared. Water dripped onto the top of his head.

One lantern bobbed quickly back into view. Zidane's sinister grin appeared in the light. "Our ship is being prepared. I'll be sure to find a leaky cell for you."

"I request one with fewer holes," Kamet said.

"My dear barbarian. I have made special arrangements with a sailor particularly fond of keelhauling, and you are lucky enough to have a cage on the ship's bow. That is, until we get out to deeper waters. Then you can begin scrubbing barnacles off the bottom of the ship with your back," Zidane said. His high-pitched laugh sounded like a goat choking. "Come. We have more preparations to make."

The lanterns disappeared, leaving Vidmar and Kamet in darkness once again. Vidmar moved back against the wall and positioned his shin under the drip. The steady tap, tap, tap, and Kamet's slow breathing were the only sounds Vidmar heard for a long time until Kamet broke the silence.

"Vidmar, what's keelhauling?" he said in a low voice.

"Not something you have to worry about. We are not getting on that ship."

"Give up. It's not going to work." Kamet sighed. Vidmar had been sawing the hollow bar with a small rock for hours. First, he tried to pick the lock using a pick woven into his hair, but after several attempts, the lockpick slipped from his grip and fell into the darkness. Lockpicking seemed to be an unrecoverable skill. So, he turned his attention to the hollow-sounding bar. He tried wriggling it free first, a strategy that seemed promising but yielded little results after a half hour. Then, he tried the sawing method.

Cramps coursed through his bleeding left hand, and the rock kept slipping from his mostly useless right hand.

"Just tell me what keelhauling is so I can pray to the right god," Kamet pleaded.

"You don't pray," Vidmar said, trying a new grip by pinning the stone against his palm with his two remaining fingers. He tried a backhanded sawing motion that worked slightly better. He didn't know if he had made any progress. The work rendered the annoyingly consistent drip obsolete, but his damp shirt clung to his back. The bar seemed weaker. One strong kick should knock it out. Then, there would be enough room for him to squeeze through. He didn't know how he would break Kamet out. One thing at a time. "I'm close." He sawed until the rock slipped from his fingers again. He slid back and lined his left foot up with the bar. He rocked and kicked with as much force as he could muster in the tight, dark space. The bar sprang free and clonked against Kamet's cell. The metallic twang echoed like a bell.

"Shit. It worked," Kamet said.

"You had doubts," Vidmar whispered through gritted teeth as he squeezed between the wall and the bars. He stretched and dusted himself off. "I hope that wasn't too loud." Vidmar picked the bar up and listened for commotion in the direction where Zidane and his guard had disappeared. Again, the only noise he heard was the dripping of water and Kamet's raspy breathing. He waited.

"How are…." Kamet began.

Vidmar hushed Kamet like a mother soothing a crying baby. He waited. He stepped further down the hallway. Heel, toe, heel, toe, moving silently closer. He listened. He heard nothing except the slow drip of the water in his cell. *How far down are we?*

"What's the plan?" Kamet whispered. Vidmar hushed him again, poking him in the chest with his ersatz weapon. "Stop that.

If someone heard, they would be down here by now. How are you getting me out?"

"Every man for themselves," Vidmar whispered.

"Funny," Kamet said seriously.

"Well, I can try to pick the lock. It will be easier from this side," Vidmar said. "But I have to find the damn pick."

"Stop whispering. We were talking before; Zidane can't hear us," Kamet said.

"Fine," Vidmar said in a normal tone.

"Can you pry the lock open with that bar?" Kamet asked.

"I sawed this with a stone. I don't think it can handle much force."

Kamet exhaled. "Damnit. Crassus would have lost his mind if he saw how you broke out of there."

"'These new homes are like children, getting weaker with each generation,'" Vidmar said, mimicking the old mason's raspy voice. "I think he would have been impressed. A cripple breaking out of a prison cell without picking the lock or outside help. He would have scrutinized the stability of the cell, though."

Kamet tested each bar on his cell by jostling them back and forth. "Of course, no luck for Kamet—as usual. You remember when you and Elisa were sparring, and you tried to trick her with one of her spinning lunges, and you knocked over Crassus's limestone. His face was as red as an apple, but he blamed me. I spent the rest of the day shoveling stones while you two went off doing whatever," he trailed off.

Vidmar lost the will to speak. Her name had that power over him—the sweet, loving sound of her perfect name made his eyes water. His stomach dropped through the floor, leaving a tight knot that slowly made its way up toward his throat. He closed his eyes and saw her wavy, black hair whirling through the air; its vexing, shimmering beauty constantly distracted him while they sparred. He never doubted his choice to betray Kandrian; he only regretted that he fell in love with his sister while in his service. *Perhaps her decision to stay with him was better,* Vidmar thought. *Better for Emre, maybe, but not better for me. She is the only thing keeping that monster tethered between this world and madness.* His remaining fingertips were ice; the frost expanded into the joints in his wrists and elbows. Vidmar scowled in the darkness, clenching his jaw to push the rising knot back into his stomach. The sound of the rotten smelling water dripping onto the floor was the only noise breaking the silence. The uncomfortable quiet lingered until a metallic creak interrupted the steady drip, and a dim light emerged down the corridor. Instinctively, Vidmar scrambled back into his cell. His damp shirt ripped against the stones as he slid through.

Two elongated shadows appeared in the orange light. Vidmar could see Kamet pressed against the bars of his cell. He avoided eye contact. Two guards in light infantry armor approached cautiously; their chainmail jingled. Zidane was not with them. Short swords hung loosely from their belts. Each guard threw a loaf of bread and an apple into the cells like they were feeding rabid dogs, careful not to get too close. The bread must have been a week old; it sounded like a stone as it hit the floor. The apple hit Vidmar in the chest. It wasn't much better; bruised and misshapen, it felt more like a ball of clay than an apple. The guards turned on their heels and began marching away. Vidmar had to act.

"Impressive swords. I bet they don't see much action," Vidmar said.

One of the guards stopped. He was twice the size of the other guard, but the smaller guard spoke. "Deliver the food. Do not engage. Those are our orders."

The big guard brushed the smaller one aside. "I don't take orders from Zidane. Major Aislin didn't seem interested in their petty squabbles. Besides, what's the harm? They aren't going anywhere."

"No, we aren't," Vidmar said. "This is quite the prison you have here."

"This isn't the...." the big guard began.

"Fergus," the undersized guard whispered harshly. *Not at the prison. Good to know.*

"It doesn't matter, Liam. I'm just going to have a bit of fun with the only man to escape Jegon," Fergus said wickedly. "I've heard everything about you, Vidmar or Davas or whatever you call yourself, and, boy, Zidane doesn't like you."

Vidmar adjusted the grip on the weapon behind his back. The guard stood in front of Vidmar's cell but didn't notice the missing bar. "Well, we aren't exactly friends, but exemplary guards like yourselves surely have better things to do than tend to that maniac's needs."

"Fergus, let's go," Liam said. "We have to report to Zidane."

"I. Do. Not. Take orders from fucking Zidane," Fergus said, unsheathing his blade.

"You know that blade looked more fearsome in its sheath," Vidmar said, feigning disappointment.

"How does it look now?" Fergus said, pushing the tip underneath Vidmar's chin.

"Fergus. Enough!" Liam yelled.

Vidmar rubbed his chin against the blade. "Oh, thank you. I've needed to shave for days but don't have the time." The lantern's light reflected in Fergus's eyes like tiny flames. His nostrils flared. *Good.*

"I'll give you a fucking shave." The sword pressed against Vidmar's throat. He winced at a slight prick and felt blood begin to trail down his neck. *Now.* Vidmar sprang back. As he hoped, Fergus tried to push the blade into Vidmar's neck, exposing his hand as it moved to the prisoner's side of the bars. Vidmar struck his hand with his makeshift weapon. The bar snapped in half, but Fergus dropped his sword. It clanged against the stone floor. The lantern clipped to Fergus's belt oscillated as he tried to recover the sword, but Vidmar was too fast. He dropped the bar and grabbed the blade with his left hand. It felt strangely comfortable, like meeting an old friend, but he didn't have time to reminisce.

Liam pounced to Fergus's side. "I told you to leave him alone."

"Shut your mouth and give me your sword. He's dead," Fergus said.

Liam reluctantly handed his sword to Fergus. Vidmar was right about one thing. These guards didn't see much fighting action. Their slow exchange was enough of an opening for Vidmar. He thrust forward, stabbing Fergus in the gut. The blade nearly slipped in his hand as he pushed it through the poorly made armor. Fergus collapsed to his knees. Liam stood, shocked. Fergus reached for Liam desperately, their doe-eyes trying to comprehend this turn of events. The other sword ricocheted off the stone floor. Vidmar tried to kick into Kamet, but it only made it halfway. Fergus choked on his blood as he fell onto his stomach. Liam's lips quivered; he looked for his sword, giving Vidmar enough time to slip out of the opening behind Liam.

"Go on. Pick it up," Vidmar said.

Liam didn't pick up the sword. Instead, he raised his hands and scooted away from the desperate man, grasping at his leg. Fergus croaked. A dreadful sound Vidmar had heard too much in his life, his last blood-soaked breath. His forehead squished dully against the stone as he died. Vidmar watched Liam's hands. They were stiff and frozen with fear, not relaxed, playing coy. He wouldn't try anything, but Vidmar didn't take chances.

"Let him out and get in," Vidmar said, pointing at Kamet's cell.

"I don't have the key," Liam said. His voice cracked like a child's.

"Does he?" Vidmar said, nodding toward Fergus but never taking his eyes off Liam's hands.

Liam nodded.

"Well, get them."

Liam's arms trembled as he bent down and reached for Fergus's belt. The big man's body convulsed, and Liam shot backward.

"They do that sometimes," Vidmar said. "He's dead."

"Are you sure?" Liam stuttered.

"Yes, I'm sure. Now grab the key, unlock my friend, and get in the cell."

Liam's head bobbled as he crawled toward Fergus's body. He winced and unclipped the key.

"Good. Now unlock the cell and get in," Vidmar said.

Liam's fingers shook as he tried to insert the key. He kept missing the narrow hole.

"Give it here," Kamet said, ripping the key from his hand. He reached through the bars and slid the key into position, turning it carefully. It clicked, and the door swung open.

"Thank you," Kamet said to Liam as he pushed the guard into the cell. "Watch out for the holes."

Kamet locked the door and picked up the sword from the ground. "Hello, friend," he said, looking at the blade and twirling it through the air.

ROOFTOPS & RAINDROPS

Vatis

Will you put that stupid letter in your pack," Mia said from a nearby roof.

Vatis had read the letter a hundred times since he received it the day before.

> *Fellow Bard, Jester, or Musician,*
> *Congratulations, you are hereby invited to perform on my grand stage. The Tourney is one of our finest traditions, dating back centuries. Past winners include Gawen Tomkin, Candace Paine, and countless others. I hope to add your name to that storied history. The Tourney begins on the first day of winter. Arrive early. Performance times will be assigned upon arrival.*
> *I look forward to your act.*
> *Your righteous King,*
> *Kandrian Ambita*

Barna. I am going to perform in Barna. Finally, Vatis thought. It was a dream he had given up long ago, but now it returned with the fervor of childish imagination.

"Vatis," Mia yelled. "Hello."

"Huh," Vatis said, stuffing the letter into a secret compartment in his pack. "What?"

"Does that change every time you read it?"

"No," Vatis searched for a valid reason as to why he kept reading the letter, but he didn't have one. He was still in shock. Nothing good ever happened to him. Yet, a stroke of luck fell his way, and for some reason, he was risking his life to save someone else. *I should be on the road to Barna.*

"Then climb up here. We have to hurry," Mia said.

"How am I going to climb up there?"

Mia sighed and jumped down. She landed lightly, hardly making a sound as she hit the hard dirt. "Watch," she said, climbing on top of a barrel. "Climb up here. Then up here. Put your foot here." She climbed onto a stack of two barrels, then stuck her foot in a narrow crack in the wall. "Then grab the roof and pull yourself up. Easy."

Yeah, easy. Climbing onto the first barrel was difficult for Vatis. It wobbled back and forth, almost tipping over as he stood.

"Now, climb on those," Mia said, pointing to the stack of barrels. "Be careful. They aren't as heavy as that one." The barrels teetered. Vatis pushed himself up, stomach first. His arms shook as he pressed himself onto his knees. The barrels wobbled again. A terrifying crack popped in the wood below him, but the barrels didn't fall. He slowly stood, balancing on his precarious perch. "Good, now put your foot there," Mia said, pointing at a crack in the wall.

Vatis stepped forward, wiggling his foot into the crack. The fissure allowed room for his big toe and not much else. "Now, push and grab the ledge," Mia said. Vatis bit his lip and released himself from his perch. The barrels crashed onto the ground; the contents sounded wet. Vatis reached for the ledge but couldn't manage a consistent grip. His loose foot scraped at the wall, searching for more support. Mia grabbed his forearm; her long fingernails dug into his skin as she tried to pull him up. Vatis finally found footing and pushed himself over the edge. Mia tumbled backward. "Graceful," she said, brushing her hair out of her eyes.

"I'm not a cat like you," Vatis said, trying to catch his breath.

"It would have been easier to drag a pig up here."

"Please, don't call me a pig."

Mia stretched onto her tiptoes, searching the city below. "If you want to walk through town, go ahead. I'll have to rescue three of you instead of two," she said. Vatis looked back at the alley. A pile of small, silver fish scattered between the broken barrels. The smell of salt and vinegar eclipsed Yimser's foul tar-like smell for a brief, extra putrid moment. He hated vinegar. "Are you coming?" Mia said, poking her head over the ridge of the roof.

Vatis checked his pack to ensure his letter didn't slip out in the pother. It was still there. The King's golden seal smiled at him from the safety of its compartment. He pulled the drawstring tight and flipped his pack over his shoulder. It bounced off Vidmar's bag, which was so heavy that Vatis questioned whether it was worth the trouble. *Is this story worth the risk? Would Vidmar rescue me?* The answer was yes, of course. Vidmar had saved him twice so far in their brief relationship.

"Vatis, come on. We have to hurry," Mia said, throwing a loose shingle at his feet.

"I'm coming."

Mia led them over roofs, down alleys, and through one particularly damp tunnel until she stopped abruptly. Vatis bent over, trying to catch his breath. He interlaced his fingers and placed them on top of his head; his lungs felt deflated like two overused bellows. The river stretched out in front of them, its slow current rocking a docked ship. Pink-highlighted clouds drifted above the jade water. Only the top of an orange sun was visible above the western mountains like a crown upon a king.

"Why are we stopping?" Vatis said. He watched a gull land on the ship's railing, tilting its curious head as men carried wooden crates aboard.

"We're here," Mia said, pushing a strand of hair behind her ear.

"The docks? Why would they be here?"

Mia pointed at a decaying stone structure near the dock. "There's a not-so-secret jail beneath that building. If I were going to kidnap someone, that's where I would take them."

A dark-skinned man kicked the wooden door of the stone building open. He struggled to carry a crate that sat atop his shoulder. "There are guards all over. How are we going to get in there?" The gull fluttered away as another guard dropped a sack onto the deck.

"I don't know. Don't you have any ideas? I got us this far," Mia said, crouching in the shadow of a taller building to their left.

"How do you know about this place?"

"I had a friend," Mia paused. She brushed a strand of hair behind her ear and twirled it around her finger. "Recruiters captured him and locked him in there. I guess he had dodged them for months, and it finally caught up with him. I don't know what they did, but they broke him. He left Yimser shortly after and left me with no one – again." A thick curl of her brown hair dangled behind her ear as she pulled her finger out. The coil slowly disappeared into the knotted amber forest covering her head. She sniffled. "So, any ideas?" she finished, looking backward, not directly at Vatis but in his direction.

Vatis hummed while he thought. *I could go down there, asking for passage on their ship. If it's Alcin's men, they are probably looking for me too. So, that doesn't work. She could go down there, but what would she say, and do I want to put her in danger?* "You could pretend to be a little girl looking for her father?"

Mia glared at Vatis and stepped toward him. "What would I say? 'I'm sorry, sir, please. I can't find my father anywhere.' Wait, that might work. If I could force a few tears, they might buy it. Punch me in the nose." Mia stepped closer. "Come on."

For the first time, Vatis noticed how thin Mia was. Her sunken cheeks, her angular jaw, and her clavicles were almost entirely visible; she was starving. "Absolutely not," Vatis said.

Mia grabbed his wrist and pushed his fingers into a fist, aiming it at her nose. "Come on. Hit me." She pressed against his loose fist.

"Even if you weren't an eleven-year-old girl, I wouldn't hit you."

She sulked into a squatting position on top of the swallow ridge. "Fine, then tell me something sad. You're a bard, after all."

"I cannot move people to tears at the drop of a hat. If I had that power, I would never have started this ridiculous journey to this foul-smelling town. Think about your friend—the one they captured."

Mia huffed. "Fine. I guess I'll figure it out. Stay here."

Vatis watched Mia slide down the roof nimbly; she leaped, vanishing beneath the building. *Vidmar is going to like her,* Vatis thought. He tapped his foot to the rhythm of a song, but he couldn't remember its name. *Tap, tap-tap, tap, tap-tap, what is it called? Miner's march, Mine, Marching Miner's. Something about a mine or miners. Ah, it's no use. Where is Mia?* Vatis stood on his tiptoes, trying to find her.

Despite its location, Yimser was well populated. On the roof, he could see almost everything below: a gray-haired man pulling a small wagon, a thin, blonde woman carrying a swaddled baby, a black-and-white cat sulking in the shadows, and a dole of doves cooing atop a neighboring roof, but no Mia. *Where is she?* He felt

247

the sensation of eyes watching and realized that he had been standing, exposed for far too long; he slunk behind the cover of a brick chimney.

The guards near the dock continued working, carrying supplies aboard the ship. A man wearing a purple hat emerged from the ship's cabin. He directed two guards holding a wooden chest. Vatis's hands shook. His lips quivered; he felt the memory of a blade pressed against his throat. *Zidane.* He rubbed his neck, trying to wipe away the feeling of the imaginary knife. Of course, no one was there, but it felt like Zidane had him at knifepoint all over again. He tried to clear his head. The longer he watched Zidane, the more intense the flashbacks became. He saw the guards Vidmar killed, their gruesome injuries, and the golden fire of rage in Vidmar's eyes as he stared down Zidane. He winced again and felt the wind of Vidmar's dagger pass his leg; he heard the nauseating squish of a blade in flesh and Zidane's cry of pain. Vatis squinted and saw Vidmar's smile as he approached; that terrifyingly confident smile. He blinked repeatedly and pinched his forearm. *Snap out of it.* It worked, temporarily.

Zidane stood on the bow of the ship, inspecting an iron cage. He fiddled with the lock. Vatis wanted to run. He wanted to save himself. *Don't get attached—never get attached to a story.* He stood, knees shaking, and turned away. *I can't.* He looked toward the dock one last time, intending a ceremonial goodbye when he saw her. Mia. She had rustled her hair and disheveled her clothes, playing the perfect lost child; there were few things Vatis respected more than a good performance, and Mia acted admirably. She even added a limp to her character, or her dismount from the roof wasn't as graceful as it looked. She kicked dust into the air as she approached a guard. Vatis couldn't hear anything other than the nearby doves and the low whistle of wind between the roofs. The guard tried to shoo her away like a pesky fly, but Mia kept pressing. Vatis couldn't tell if she had tears, but she wiped her eyes anyway.

The guard retreated, fidgeting with his hands like he was trying to find some way to console the little girl. *She's good.* Vatis heard a loud bang, and a guard ran out of the stone building with his sword drawn. He thought he heard the guard yell 'escape' when all the men on the dock drew their weapons and lined up in front of the door like an infantry unit. Zidane stayed on the ship. Mia retreated to the shadows.

Five men waited outside the door; two others slid around the side out of sight, their hands resting on their swords. The guard's formation loosened as they waited. Men swayed back and forth impatiently. These men didn't look like soldiers but mercenaries, fierce fighters, and less disciplined. Vatis didn't know if that was good or bad for Vidmar. Seconds felt like hours. He lost track of Mia. *Where did she go?* He desperately wanted to run now; then he heard Mia's soft yet frantic voice. "Vatis, Vatis," she yelled, her tone getting louder and angrier with each call. "Vatis."

Vatis exhaled and called back. "Mia, what's happening?" He gingerly slid down the roof until Mia came into view in the alley below.

"Where's our stuff? We need to go." Mia said, jumping up and down.

"What's happening?" Vatis repeated.

"Get the stuff. Hurry. I'll explain on the way."

"Fine," Vatis said, crawling back to their supplies. *Go to Barna.* He thought as he grabbed their packs. *Run.* A shingle popped off as he slid down the roof. *Run, you idiot.* He tossed each bag into the alley. *Why aren't you running?* Mia carefully caught hers but let Vidmar's crash into the dirt. "You better catch mine," he said, holding its strap tightly and lowering it as close to the ground as he could without falling off the roof. Mia rolled her eyes and opened her arms. *Just run, damnit. What are you doing?* He dropped his bag. There wasn't anything particularly fragile in there, but it contained everything he owned and, most importantly, his invitation to Barna. Mia caught it and carefully placed it on the ground.

"Come on," Mia said.

Vatis swung his legs over the ledge and lowered himself down as far as possible without letting go of the roof. He struggled to find a comfortable grip. "I'm working on it," he said through gritted teeth.

"It's not far; just jump."

Vatis clenched his jaw and dropped into the alley. It turned out that it wasn't a far drop, and now he felt silly for imagining how painful the fall would be. He threw the packs over his shoulders and dusted himself off. "What's happening?"

"I said I would explain on the way. Come on." She jogged down the alley. "Come on," Mia yelled, waving.

Vatis stretched his neck, noticing dark clouds floating ominously overhead. The quickening wind whistled between the gabled roofs.

"I'm not waiting any longer," Mia yelled as she ran out of sight.

There's still time. Run. Forget them. Find a new story. Vatis bit his lip, exhaled, and chased after Mia.

Mia smiled as she saw Vatis chasing after her. "This way."

They jogged down the alley. "What is going on?" Vatis said.

"I guess Vidmar didn't need our help," Mia said, stopping briefly. She looked left, then right, but ultimately decided straight was the best course.

"What do you mean? He doesn't need our help," Vatis said, nearly colliding with an elderly man walking the other way. The hunched-backed man grumbled an insult, but Vatis couldn't tell what he said.

Mia laughed as she watched Vatis hop to regain his momentum. "They escaped. Or they are escaping. We have to help them. There's a lot of guards down there." She turned left down a narrow street. As he turned the corner, Vatis heard the spine-shivering sound of swords clashing. The metallic twang grew louder as he followed Mia down a tighter alley. Sickening screams overshadowed the clanging weapons when they popped into the open. Kamet bulled over a soldier and buried his sword into his exposed neck. Three other mercenaries lay dead around the stone building. Kamet charged two men, cornering Vidmar. Lightning flashed in the distance, and thunder joined the battlefield symphony. Vatis crashed into Mia.

"Sorry," Vatis said, trying to help her up. Her eyes were wide; her head jerked side to side. Vatis knew that look. She was in shock, a state that seemed to welcome all of Vidmar's new companions. He pulled her to her feet just as the rain started. A drop landed in the middle of her forehead. "Mia."

"I've never seen a battle before," she said, staring at a dead mercenary. Again, she played with her hair unconsciously. "What do we do?"

"Nothing, wait," Vatis said.

"I can't wait," she said, pulling a dagger from her belt. She looked at the blade like it was foreign, an object she had never seen before. Her fingers tightened around the leather hilt while she ran a finger down the knife's edge. "What if they die?"

"There is nothing we can do to help in these situations. We'll get ourselves killed, too," Vatis said, resting a hand on her shoulder. *God's, she's all bone. She'll shatter like glass if she runs out there.* A sinister thought crept into his mind. *But the story. A new Mia-The-Maiden. Even if she dies, she'll be a hero. It may even be a story worthy of the King.* Vatis watched Mia bounce up and down as she observed the battle. Kamet and Vidmar were fighting back-to-back, surrounded by four mercenaries. Vidmar twirled his sword around in his left hand; he even smiled. *That fucking smile.* His practice on trees, flowers, and tall grass appeared to work. A fifth guard appeared atop the stone building, slinking into position, aiming a crossbow. "Mia-The-Maiden fought young, twelve-years-old," Vatis lied under his breath.

Mia tore into the battle like a hound after a fox. "Look out," she screamed. "On the roof." She picked up a stone and threw it at the archer. *A heroine, indeed.* Her shot missed, but it was close enough to buy Vidmar and Kamet an extra second. One of the mercenaries surrounding Vidmar and Kamet turned. Kamet seized the opportunity and struck him down; his deathly wail faded into the blood-stained sand. Vidmar spun and rolled between the two guards in front of him; one of the guards tried to strike Vidmar, but his blow sliced his partner's reaching arm off above the elbow. Mia threw another stone at the archer who had been aiming at Vidmar; this time, she hit her mark squarely on the archer's nose. The crossbow misfired, and the bolt whizzed over Vidmar's head, embedding into the side of a building. Kamet finished his last opponent with a vicious thrust that went through the mercenary's stomach and out his back. He kicked the corpse off his sword. Vidmar had one opponent left.

"Kamet," Vidmar yelled, pointing at the roof; he spun, narrowly avoiding the guard's strike. The archer cranked the crossbow, loading another bolt. Kamet knelt, hands turned into a platform, nodding to the charging Vidmar. Vidmar leaped onto Kamet's hands. Kamet hurled him upward, and Vidmar landed on the roof next to the archer.

Mia's mouth hung open. "Woah," she said, a small stone falling out of her hand.

The hooded man turned. Vidmar dropped his sword as he went for the killing blow. Both men stared at the fallen sword briefly, enough time for Vidmar to devise a new strategy. He yelled and charged forward, tackling the archer off the roof. They landed in a crumpled heap near Kamet's feet. Vidmar rolled away, and Kamet finished the archer with a downward thrust through his chest.

Vidmar picked up a sword from one of the fallen mercenaries. "Put your sword down, and we'll let you live," he said to the only remaining guard.

"We will?" Kamet barked.

"Yes, we will," Vidmar said. "All you have to do is tell me where Zidane went." Heavy raindrops showered the docks, puddles scattered like ponds expanding by the second. An empty iron helm had rolled near Vatis's feet during the skirmish. The rain created a tinny percussion that was almost musical until he thought about the helm's owner who was facedown dead in the mud—*another tragic ending.*

"They'll kill me," the guard said, pointing his sword at Vidmar, then at Kamet.

"You could run," Vidmar said. "Do something better with your life. We all have choices. There has been enough blood spilled today."

The guard took off his helm, holding it upside down on his hip. He stuck his sword into the ground. "No one has a choice," the guard said after a long silence. He threw the water that had pooled in his helm at Vidmar, grabbed his sword, and thrust forward. Vidmar spat and leaped backward. The rain poured. Vatis could hardly see; he tried to keep the water out of his eyes by holding his hand above his brow. A figure fell into the mud.

"You, girl, come in," Vidmar called to Mia. He signaled her to the stone building.

Mia looked back at Vatis.

A NEW PLAN

Vidmar

Vidmar sat cross-legged on the damp ground, drying his face with another victim's shirt. He listened to the relentless rain drumming atop the frigid stone building and ripped the garment, passing the dry half to the girl beside him. "Sorry it smells, but at least it's dry."

The girl hadn't stopped staring at Vidmar since they entered the guard's shack. She sniffed the shirt, then wiped her face. "Thank you," she said quietly.

"No, thank you. If you hadn't shown up, we'd both have arrows sticking out of our necks. And you brought Vatis with you. What are the chances? I thought we were going to have to leave him behind," Vidmar said, looking at Vatis standing in the corner by a torch. "What's your name?"

"Mia," the girl said shyly, looking at her feet and twirling her hair around a finger.

Brown hair, about ten years old; it must be her. "Mia, do you know Gaffer? He has a shop uptown."

She smiled. "Yes."

Vatis cursed, interrupting their conversation. He held a piece of parchment over the flame, trying to dry it without setting it on fire. "What is that, Vatis?" Mia sighed. Her thin eyebrows furrowed as she glared at the bard.

"My invitation," Vatis said. He frowned. The nearly translucent parchment cast a vicious dog-like shadow on the wall behind Vatis, with the bard's knuckles as the beast's teeth.

"Did you win the tourney?" Vidmar said with a surprising amount of excitement. "I, ah, didn't see the announcement."

"No," Mia whispered.

Vatis returned her poignant scowl. "Yes, after a series of events, I have been declared the winner."

"Well, congratulations," Vidmar said. He watched a confusing nonverbal exchange between Mia and Vatis. *What's going on there?* He thought. Vatis carefully folded the letter and set it on a wooden table next to his wet pack; its content scattered throughout the room, drying out. Mia took a few items out of her bag to dry, but she neatly organized her possessions near her feet. *The Mystery of the Pact* lay open and drying on the floor. *That's it.* Vidmar opened his mouth to speak but was once again interrupted by Vatis.

"Thank you. What did you think of the story? I tried not to exaggerate too much, but you didn't exactly provide me with a thrilling narrative."

Kamet coughed. "As *thrilling* as this news is, we need a plan." He emerged, shirtless, from a pantry holding a pile of tunics and trousers. On top of the clothing sat apples, bread, dried meat, and a flask. "If it weren't raining, we would be surrounded by now. God's we might be. I can't hear anything other than the damn rain."

Vidmar sighed. He wanted to ask Mia about the book but decided it could wait until they were safe. "We could tough it out and run now; it would be hard to track us in the rain or wait for nightfall and slink out of the city, or we could commandeer that ship on the dock. Does anyone know how to sail?"

Mia shook her head; Vatis didn't respond. An apple fell from his arms onto the floor, rolling toward Vidmar's feet. "I'm not getting on a ship unless it's our only option," Kamet said, slamming his fist against the wall "I vote we tough it out and leave now."

"I say we try the ship. How hard could sailing be? And it probably has a cabin to keep us dry," Vidmar said. He scratched his chin, thinking of other options. "Where's Zidane? Did you see him, Kamet?"

"No, only cheap mercs," Kamet said, setting his pile of supplies on the table near Vatis. A long, pale scar ran diagonally down his rigid, muscular torso from his left shoulder to his navel.

"He was on the ship," Vatis said, wringing out his blanket.

Water splashed onto the floor. A dark stream flowed down the shack's uneven surface toward the pantry, forming a small puddle next to a decaying board. Vidmar shot up. Arrogantly curious pain wandered through his limbs, reminding him of his age. His day in a tight cell, combined with his first action in weeks, bore him down like an anchor. Ten years and a hundred battles ago, he would have already been at Zidane's throat, throwing him into the river, but now he couldn't stand without pain somewhere. His father had warned him about the price of a soldier's life. Slow cane-steadied walks, cries in the night, and somber silence in the day were practically the only memories he had of his father, but Vidmar wanted to play the hero, and he paid dearly for it. At least his father had escaped that life. *I should have listened to you, Pa.*

Vidmar lifted the barricade and pushed the door open. The wind moaned in concert with the heavy drumming droplets. A thick fog rose above the shimmering ground. Persistent gray sheets decreased visibility substantially, but he could see the ship floating down the river, no longer tied to the dock. *Fuck*. He pulled the door closed.

"Well, Zidane escaped, and the ship is no longer an option," Vidmar said, brushing his wet hair backward.

Kamet smirked. "Damn, I guess we will have to go on foot."

"You know, keelhauling is when you are tied to a rope and dragged beneath the ship and pulled up on the other side," Vidmar said. "I didn't tell you because I know you hate water, and somehow Zidane knew the absolute worst form of torture for you, but that ship was our best option."

Kamet shuddered. "That's what I fucking thought it was."

Vidmar kicked the door. "Well, you don't have to worry about it now. Fuck. I don't want to run in the rain." The rain brought back images from his first battle: soldiers collapsing around him as arrows plummeted their lines, charging forward with little hope of survival, waking up covered in blood amongst his fallen brothers. Vidmar shook his head, sighed, and walked in circles around the room. "There is some good news; there are no guards out there. Does anyone have an idea? There has to be another way."

"I say we wait until the rain stops," Vatis said, examining a book from his bag. He pulled two pages apart and dried them over the torch.

"That's not an option," Kamet said.

"Why not? You two probably killed half the city guard."

More blood on my hands. Vidmar looked at Kamet, nodded, then turned away. A crack in the stone floor looked like a canyon cutting through a vast gray mountain.

"Those weren't trained guards," Kamet scowled. "They were mercenaries. If the town guard finds us, we'll be hanging in a tree by morning."

Mia coughed gently. "We could take the tunnel."

"Tunnel?" Vidmar asked.

"Beneath the chapel. I don't know where it leads, though."

"How do you know about this tunnel?" Vatis asked.

Mia looked down. Vidmar noticed her callused heels and painfully thin wrists as she played with a droplet of water on the floor, tracing the letter 'm'.

"Does it matter?" Vidmar said. "Mia, how far is the chapel?"

"Not far," Mia said, still looking at the ground. A faint letter 'i' appeared beneath her fingertip. "I used to live there."

"You don't have to explain, Mia," Vidmar said.

"It's alright. I want to be honest," Mia said, glancing at Vatis. "I lived there after my mother died. That's where all the orphans go. It was fine until they tried to convert me. Stupid, death-worshiping priests. I used to sneak out of our room and read books in the library." She finished writing her name with her fingertip and scribbled it away with another water droplet. "One night, I followed a priest into the cellar because I always wanted to know what was down there. He kept going lower and lower until he came to a tunnel. Then, a cloaked man appeared carrying a baby, and I ran. I don't know what they did with the baby, but I never saw it again." Mia's face reddened, and she covered her mouth like she had to force herself from saying any more.

Vidmar put a hand on her shoulder; the sharpness of her bones surprised him. "How do we get to the chapel?"

"Why can't we wait until the rain stops?" Vatis pleaded.

"Go ahead," Kamet said, squeezing into a clean shirt that was clearly too small. His arms looked like sausages poking out of the casing. "But I'm not sticking around to say hello to the guards." His short black hair pressed flat against his forehead, laying over his eyes like dark curtains.

Vatis huffed. "Fine, are there more shirts?"

Kamet threw one at him. Vatis didn't put it on. Instead, he stuffed his invitation inside his book, wrapping the shirt tightly around it. "Are there more in the pantry?"

Kamet snorted as he strapped two swords around his waist. "Yes, but we will leave without you if you don't hurry."

Vatis jogged to the pantry, leaving a trail of wet footprints on the stone as he moved. Vidmar examined his pack. It contained four knives, the golden-hilted dagger, a spool of thread, an empty waterskin, his cloak, a small cast-iron pot, and, most importantly, the stone–his first and last clue. Gaffer told him Mia's book might provide some insight. He examined Mia as she placed the book into her bag. *It lies near the dead. What does that mean?* He left Yimser with more questions than answers, as he did in every city for the past two years.

"Damn," Kamet said, throwing the suit of mail on the ground. "Underfed children, the lot of them. No offense. Might fit you, though, Vidmar."

"I hate mail, too loud," Vidmar said.

"Fine, but it seems a shame to waste it."

Vidmar filled his waterskin with a pitcher that was left on the table where Vatis dried his gear. He smelled its contents; unfortunately, the pitcher contained water and nothing stronger. A few moments later, Vatis ambled out of the pantry, holding a stack of blankets and a wooden shield.

"What are you doing with that," Kamet laughed, pointing at the shield.

"I'm trying to stay dry," Vatis said, stuffing a blanket into his pack. It barely fit. The frayed tan edges poked out of the top.

"Everyone ready?" Vidmar said.

Vatis slung his bag over his shoulder then draped another blanket over the top of the pack. Kamet adjusted his swords and spat an apple seed onto the floor. It bounced in front of Vidmar's feet. Mia stood at the door waiting for them; the strap of her bag hung between two bony shoulder blades. She scratched the back of her neck. Vidmar stretched, cracked his remaining knuckles, and grabbed his bag with his left hand. He preferred to hold it while running instead of it draped over his shoulder - it helped him move faster. "Alright, go," Vidmar said, following Mia out the door.

The chapel was further than Vidmar expected, but fortunately, they did not run into anyone dangerous on their way, only a mother chasing her two children back indoors. Heavy, relentless rain poured their entire run. Vidmar was the first to arrive at the chapel. Once the tall black spire was visible, he sprinted, but Mia was on his heels; he held the massive door open for the others, his back pressed against a stained-glass portrait of a black knight galloping across a battlefield. Kamet burst in, shaking wildly. They waited for Vatis; he jogged, more like stumbled – it was hard to tell in the rain. He held the shield over his head like he was deflecting arrows and moved in a zigzag pattern. Vidmar didn't know if this was intentional or if the heavy shield pushed the small bard in different directions. Kamet laughed ferociously. Mia wrung out her hair. The shield came sliding through the doorway, and Vatis clumsily followed.

"Graceful," Kamet chuckled.

Vatis slid against a bench, clutching his knees. His breathing was short and inconsistent as he gasped for air. Mia held out a hand. "It's easier to breathe standing up," she said. Vatis's chest vibrated as he tried to stand. Kamet stopped laughing.

"Here," Vidmar said, offering his shoulder as a perch. Vatis accepted; his breathing slowed.

"What brings four travelers to our humble chapel?" a black-robed figure said in a deep, penetrating voice.

Vatis nodded, signaling his recovery. Vidmar set him down on the bench. "We seek shelter from the storm."

"The Darkness welcomes all wanders," the priest said, eyeing Mia. "You look familiar, girl."

Vidmar slid in front of her. "She's my daughter, Verle. I'm Joris. These are our traveling companions, Arvid and Jesper," Vidmar said, gesturing to Kamet and Vatis, respectively. Mia's eyes widened when Vidmar called her daughter. A smile crept onto her cracked pink lips.

"Very well. Please, sit. Take shelter," the priest said, pointing to a row of wooden benches. The armrests had been carved into the shape of bats. Vidmar brushed one of the bat's wings, the wood carved so thin he could nearly see through it. He sat. "Tell me," The priest continued, looming over them like a dark cloud. "Do you welcome The Darkness?"

Vidmar looked at Kamet, who clenched his jaw. Mia picked up a black leather book that sat next to her and opened it. Vatis stood, made an intricate gesture with his thumb on his chest, cleared his throat, and said, "We find peace in The Darkness."

The priest nodded. They passed his first test. "Please rest, travelers. May The Darkness embrace you when your light fades," he said, turning away. His gaze lingered on Mia; he turned back briefly, exhaled, then marched toward a black stone altar with a single candle lit atop it. Vidmar watched the priest kneel, gesture like Vatis, then pivot and face the nearly empty chapel.

Vidmar leaned forward and whispered to Vatis, "I didn't know you followed," Vidmar paused, searching for the right words, 'this' was the best he could come up with.

"I don't," Vatis said, pretending to pray with a fist balled on his forehead. "But I have always found *this* interesting and remembered some of their customs."

Vidmar shook his head. "I have avoided these places like the plague."

"Me too," Kamet said. Vatis shushed him.

"What now?" Vidmar whispered, facing Mia.

"We could run for it. Egon isn't very fast," Mia said as she flipped a page in the book.

"You know him?" Vidmar asked.

"I lived here for a year. Of course, I know him. There are only five priests; the children do all the work."

"Where are the other four? Where are the children?"

"One is probably in the library, one is probably in the kitchen, and the other two are in their rooms resting. They rotate throughout the day. The kids are probably in their room over there," Mia said, staring at the priest, who looked away when he noticed she was watching. "The stairs to the cellar are behind that door." She nodded to an ironclad wood door to the right of the priest.

The priest squinted and walked toward them. Heavy boots echoed through the vaulted chamber as the priest marched with his hands crossed inside his robe's sleeves. His piercing, green eyes never left Mia. "Verla, was it?" the priest asked Mia.

"Verle," Mia corrected. Vidmar was impressed that she remembered the random alias he had given her.

"Right, Verle. I can't help but notice that you're reading *The Book of Patience and Prophecy*, I don't mean to be presumptuous, but a girl your age reading is quite rare. What is your favorite passage?" The priest asked with a hint of sarcasm in his tone.

Mia flipped through the book.

"Her education was quite important to her mother before she passed," Vidmar said.

"Before The Darkness embraced her," Vatis corrected, adding a sniffle to round off his performance.

The priest began to speak, but Mia interrupted, reciting a passage from the book. "The Darkness is both cold and warm. Inevitably, The Darkness will embrace the world. Only the devoted will feel its warmth, while heretics and heathens are frozen in sin." *Well, that's fucking terrifying,* Vidmar thought.

"Ah, Prophecy, passage thirteen," the priest said, nodding.

"Fourteen," Mia said, pointing to the dark number fourteen in the book.

"Very astute," he said, narrowing his eyes. "You remind me of an orphan who lived here not too long ago. Smart girl, but I expect she is frozen in The Darkness now, too curious for her own good. The Darkness is not fond of curiosity." His tone shifted from astonishingly happy to darkly sinister. Mia remained calm. Vidmar jumped as the chapel's bell rang. Intricately designed candle holders wobbled on each of the bell's ten rings. "Alas, my respite with The Darkness has arrived. Goodnight, travelers, do not fear The Darkness. Embrace her and rest."

"We long for our final rest," Vatis said, bowing. The priest returned the bow and marched in the direction of the library.

"Is he going to kill himself?" Kamet asked as they watched him walk away.

Mia snickered. "He's going to sleep, but this is our only chance." Mia tiptoed down the aisle, ensuring the priest was out of sight.

They grabbed their gear and followed Mia, Vidmar behind Kamet, and Kamet behind Vatis. A trail of water droplets and wet footprints marked their path; the priests would know precisely where they went. Vidmar tried to scrub the watermarks away, but it was useless. *We have to hurry.* They slithered one by one to the ironclad door. It creaked as Mia opened it. "Come on! Go," she said, pushing them through the doorway. It thudded shut behind them, and Mia crept to the front of the line again, grabbing a lantern off the wall. "This way."

There was only one way to go, down a steep stone staircase, through an arched doorway, and into a narrow, unlit tunnel. Vidmar held Kamet's belt and nearly bumped into him when they stopped abruptly.

"Why are we stopping?" Vidmar said. He heard the door's creaky hinges open from behind them. The door crashed shut, echoing down the chamber; heavy footsteps chased the echo.

"They're coming," Kamet said, moving aside.

Vidmar noticed why they had stopped. A tiny skull had been mounted to the mouth of the tunnel. Vidmar's entire body convulsed as he held back an identical reaction. *Fuck.* "Mia, we have to move," Vidmar said, rubbing her back and swallowing bile. His palm bounced off each protruding vertebrate. "The fact that you got us here is amazing, but I'll lead now. You follow behind me, Kamet take the rear in case they catch us, and Vatis keep up." Vidmar scooted up to the front, grabbing the lantern. Kamet drew a sword. The heavy footsteps behind them seemed to be closer.

Vidmar had been jogging down the tunnel for what felt like hours before he stopped. "Everyone here," he asked, catching his breath. They weren't moving fast, but the air was heavy and thick. Fuzzy black mold grew on the jagged walls.

"Yes," Mia said flatly. Vidmar could sense her behind him.

"We're here," Kamet called through raspy breaths. "The bard needs a break, though." Vidmar heard Vatis's labored breathing. "I don't think they followed us," Kamet continued as his voice returned to normal. "Haven't heard their boots in a while."

"Why would they stop?" Vidmar asked.

"They probably know what's on the other end of this tunnel, or maybe there's no way out," Kamet said.

"Maybe word spread about what you did to those men at the docks, and the priests aren't so eager to welcome The Darkness as they seem," Vatis said through heavy breaths.

Whatever caused the priests to stop following, Vidmar still wanted to hurry. He didn't want to take any chances. "Maybe.

Let's take a moment to rest. Here," Vidmar said, passing his waterskin to Mia. She accepted with shaking hands. "Go slow, then pass it back," Vidmar added. She did. He couldn't help but be impressed by the girl. Mia didn't freeze in battle; she was nimble enough to keep up with him, adapted quickly, and hopefully, she could help him find the crown. When the waterskin returned to Vidmar, it was nearly empty.

"Damnit, Kamet, you better have filled yours too," Vidmar said, taking a sip.

"It wasn't me," Kamet said. "I have some vodka."

"Of course," Vidmar said.

"I'm sorry," Vatis said. "It was me. I can't seem to quench this burning in my throat. It's like I've transformed into a dragon."

"It's called endurance, and you have none," Kamet said. He seemed to be growing more annoyed with Vatis as his usually kind-hearted jests teetered too close to genuine criticism.

"Again, apologies," Vatis said. "I'm ready."

Vidmar decided it was best to ignore the escalating tension between Vatis and Kamet. He listened for followers, heard none, and tightened his grip on the lantern. It was nearly out of oil. "Let's go," he said and jogged down the tunnel.

Vidmar slowed his pace as he heard rain pummeling the ground above them. The lantern only had minutes left of light, if not seconds.

"It's still raining," Vatis sighed as he and Kamet caught up.

"Yes, but we have to be close. We've been jogging uphill for a while," Vidmar said as the lantern went out. "Shit. We will have to take it slow the rest of the way. Mia grab my pack, Vatis take Mia's, and Kamet hold Vatis's." He felt Mia pull on his bag.

"Anyone want to trade? I don't want to ruin the champion's pack with my greasy fingers," Kamet said.

"Just grab it," Vatis said.

"Vatis, there are children present," Kamet said.

"Will you two shut up and hold on?" Vidmar said, taking careful steps in the dark.

They inched forward, step after step. Vidmar wanted to move faster but withheld in case the tunnel diverted at some point. As they climbed, the rocky floor transitioned into carved steps. Vidmar tripped over the first one and the second before he realized they were stairs. Dim, gray light gleamed into the tunnel ahead of them.

"We made it," Vatis said, sounding exacerbated. Vidmar picked up his pace as the tunnel brightened, taking a long, deep breath of the fresh, albeit damp air. They emerged in a clearing of tall pine trees, standing at the mouth of the tunnel as the rain stopped.

INTERLUDE

Zidane

Zidane paced across the ship's bow as it rocked gently near the dock, shuffling his feet across the wet surface. Rain dripped off the front of his hat. *How did he escape?* He bit the insides of his cheeks to stop himself from screaming. Vidmar and the big mercenary took down guard after guard as they emerged from the shack; he couldn't remember the mercenary's name, Kameer, Kal, Kamen, something with a 'k,' and it didn't matter. They would come for him if he didn't act fast.

"Get those crates," he called to the guards on the dock. "Get the fucking crates."

If I lose Vidmar and the shipment, I'm worse than dead. "Hurry." There were only two crates left—each full of freshly harvested Garvasta flowers, worth almost as much as the entire city of Yimser. "I said hurry," Zidane yelled through the heavy rain. The guards looked distracted. They didn't know whether to join the battle or load the ship.

"Sorry, sir," two guards said simultaneously, carrying the second-to-last crate aboard while watching the mercenary strike down another of their comrades.

Zidane raised his eyebrows as he saw an archer climb onto the shack's roof. *Yes,* he thought. *Shoot the big one. Shoot the big one.* The archer loaded his crossbow and peered over the edge. He hesitated. "Shoot, you idiot," Zidane said. The guards carrying the final crate of Garvasta looked at him despairingly.

Rain pelted the deck; its hollow thudding drowned out all other noise. The archer aimed, fell backward, and missed. A small, dark-haired girl threw something at the crossbowman. "Who the fuck is that?" Zidane yelled. She attacked again, hitting the archer in the head, and another shot misfired. He fell, grabbing his face.

While Zidane focused on the exchange between the girl and the archer, Vidmar and his brute murdered three more men. Only the archer and one guard remained until the mercenary launched Vidmar into the air and onto the roof. Zidane couldn't believe his eyes. Vidmar tackled the archer off. A second of hope led to gut-wrenching despair as the Vidmar's oaf-of-a-friend drove a sword into the archer's chest. Zidane's enemies confronted the last guard, who met a similar fate as most of the men he had hired. *Useless.*

Vidmar and the brute ushered the girl forward, who in turn motioned to another man carrying two packs. *The bard.* He watched them take shelter in the shed, breathing a sigh of relief while thanking every god he knew that they didn't board the ship.

"Come on, untie the damn boat. Hurry," he screamed at his two guards on the dock. The rain worsened; Zidane could only make out the dark outlines of the guard's shack. "Man the oars," Zidane said, adjusting his hat. Water poured down his face.

They obeyed but appeared reluctant; with only three of them left, there was no one to push the boat away from the dock. "Why aren't we moving?" Zidane yelled.

"The anchor," one of the guards explained.

"Gods. Pull it up. Pull it up," Zidane said, pushing the closest guard to the anchor. The guard snarled at him for a second but still wound the anchor upward.

"We need someone to push us out," the other guard said, pointing to a long oar-like stick on the ship's starboard side. The boat began to sway now that the anchor was up. Wind whipped against the mainsail.

"We need to row. You need to push us off," the guard yelled, struggling to keep his oar steady. Finally, the other guard locked the anchor and returned to his seat.

"Fine, fine," Zidane yelled. *Fucking Vidmar*, he thought as he tried to lift the long wooden oar; *he killed my whole crew.* The oar slipped from his grip, smashing his toes. "Damnit," Zidane yelled before he tried again.

The obtuse stick wobbled as he held it over the edge, growing heavier and heavier as he extended it. His forearms burned. He was losing his grip on the slippery surface, but he finally struck the dock. He pushed with all his strength, but the ship wouldn't budge. It was too windy. The oar slipped off the pier, and Zidane crashed into the railing, nearly falling overboard.

"Help," he yelled.

The guards pulled him and the oar aboard. The ship collided with the dock. He heard wood splinter through the downpour and hoped it was the dock, not his escape vessel.

"Go. You row on the port side. We'll push off," a guard said. Zidane wasn't sure which one. *Insolate, subordinate fool, you can't tell me what to do,* Zidane thought, but he pushed his way through the rain and grabbed the oar. His clothes were heavy, and his hat drooped over his eyes. He felt the boat jerk; both guards wielded oars and pushed the ship away. They were close now. So close. The wind blew them off course, sending them back into the dock;

luckily, the guards used the momentum expertly and gave one final push. The current grabbed hold of his ship.

"Check her down," one of the guards yelled. "Check her down." One guard returned to his oar, and the other dropped his stick and sprinted toward Zidane. He slipped on the deck. "Check her down," he repeated as he tried to stand.

"I don't know what that means," Zidane yelled.

"Push the oar down. Hold it in the water."

Zidane hesitated.

"Put it down," the guards yelled.

Zidane dropped the oar into the water. The force jerked him out of his seat as he tried to hold it in place. "I can't hold it," Zidane said, grinding his teeth.

"Move." The guard grabbed the oar, pushing Zidane out of the way. Zidane felt rage boil in the pit of his stomach. He hated feeling useless and hated it even more when someone below his station pointed it out. *Just wait until we are on dry land.*

"Steady," the other guard called out.

The ship teetered back and forth but eventually evened out and began floating down the river.

"Keep her steady, boys," Zidane said, trying to regain his composure and standing amongst his men. Satisfied, he bowed, entered the ship's cabin, and hung his hat on a peg by the door.

WATCHTOWERS

Vidmar

Vidmar leaped over a fallen tree. Mia was on his heels while Kamet and Vatis brought up the rear.

"Can we not have a moment's rest?" Vatis said, gasping for air. They had been running for no more than a few miles.

Vidmar held up his hand, signaling a stop. He turned around to face the group. "Fine, but be quick," Vidmar said. Mia and Kamet nodded in agreement.

Vatis exhaled and fell to his knees, placing his hands above his head and breathing deeply. Kamet huffed, then broke a dead, low-hanging branch off a nearby tree, fashioning it into a makeshift spear. Mia threw pinecones at the trees. She hit the center of a sparse pine three times in a row. "Impressive," Vidmar said as they waited for Vatis to catch his breath. "I'll show you how to throw a knife once we get somewhere safer."

The girl jumped up as she grabbed another pinecone. "Really?" she said, bursting with excitement that quickly faded. Her face reddened, and she looked at the ground as if she were embarrassed. I mean, I would like that. Thank you." She shuffled through the pine needles.

Vidmar smiled. "How long have you been on your own?"

Mia threw the next pinecone at a different, thinner tree–a direct hit. "A year, I think," she said, searching for more ammunition but still avoiding eye contact.

Vidmar kicked a pinecone over to her. She smiled as she picked it up. "It's hard. I was only a few years older than you when my Pa died."

"You're an orphan, too?" she asked, throwing her pinecone and spinning around in one flawless motion, meeting his gaze. There was a special bond between orphans–not unlike siblings. Orphans understood pain; they knew real hunger, real kill-for-your-next-meal hunger. Dark memories of the streets of Haran bubbled to the surface of Vidmar's memory, but he pushed them back–popped the bubbles. Those recollections did more harm than good.

"I never knew my mother; my Pa died when I was thirteen. Pox. I was on my own for a while before…." Vidmar paused for a moment, watching Vatis listen to the conversation while his breathing returned to normal. "…. before I joined the army. Are you ready yet, Vatis?" He said, changing the subject.

The bard slid his bag around his back and stretched his arms. "Yes, but can you slow the pace a bit?"

"I'll try."

Vidmar jogged slower for the first mile or so but picked up the pace again as the sky darkened. He wanted to be far away from Yimser when they rested, but for the first time in years, Vidmar was lost. He didn't know which direction the tunnel had taken them. The cloudy sky and tall trees blocked his chance of finding a landmark. He ran his hand across a mossy stone and examined a footprint in the mud.

"What is it?" Vatis asked.

"A deer or a boar, maybe."

"God's, I hope it's not a boar," Vatis said. His disposition significantly improved each time they stopped. "Years ago, I was traveling near Numeria, and one poor member of our party was speared through the gut by a charging boar. Sweet man, too, though his name escapes me."

Vidmar looked for more tracks. "If you leave boars alone. They will leave you alone," he said sternly. He was in no mood for one of Vatis's rambling road stories; they were far worse than his campfire tales. *Pointless*, Vidmar thought. However, he found it quite odd that the bard's demeanor changed so quickly. He found a better set of prints perfectly preserved in the mud a few paces away. "Luckily, these are deer tracks, and they are more skittish than Vatis in a tavern brawl."

Mia laughed, a quiet hissing laugh like she was trying to hold it in. She snorted, gasping as her fluttering laughter escaped. Kamet joined her with his contagious, deep, booming laugh.

"It wasn't that funny," Vatis sneered.

Vidmar chuckled. "For once, Vatis. I agree." He followed the deer tracks for some time, stopping repeatedly to reexamine the trail until he heard a loud trickle of cascading water. He stopped. "Do you hear that?"

"Yes," Kamet said from behind him. "Sounds like a stream."

"A waterfall," Vidmar corrected.

"A waterfall," Mia echoed excitedly. "I've never seen one."

Vidmar exhaled happily. He knew where they were—the foothill of the Islingrey Mountains east of Yimser. He worried that the tunnel ran west toward the coast or, worse yet, south toward the Kokor Forest and Haran. "My first lesson of scouting, Mia, trust your ears and nose. Don't rely solely on your eyes. You have five senses for a reason–use them."

After a treacherous uphill hike over slippery rocks and across a fallen tree, they arrived at the waterfall. Two winding falls splashed into a calm, dark pool. White, frothy water fell against the gray stones, turning them almost black. Moss-covered boulders lined the pool like chairs while tree branches extended over the pond, trying to get a drink of cool water. Vidmar was speechless. He had traveled all over Emre but cherished sights like the falls before him. Mia climbed on top of one of the boulders, dangling her legs over the pond. Her jaw hung open as she surveyed every inch. Vidmar climbed up next to her. "Beats Yimser."

"Yeah," she said, watching the water plummet into the pond.

"This seems like a decent spot to rest," Kamet called to Vidmar. "There's enough coverage that we could light a small fire, but the falls are loud; we wouldn't be able to hear anyone approach."

"Can we please stop? I can't go any further," Vatis pleaded. He knelt at the pond's edge, drinking the clear water with a cupped hand. He splashed his face. "Please."

"We can rest here," Vidmar said reluctantly. "We will gather some firewood and set a few traps. Come, Mia. I'll show you how to set a snare."

Mia did a backward somersault off the boulder, landing perfectly before she tucked her hair behind her ears. "Show off," Vidmar smiled.

They hiked uphill around the waterfall, Mia's arms full of firewood, following the creek cut into the foot of the mountains. She struggled. A few twigs escaped the pile each time she added more. Vidmar held back his laughter. He knew her feelings of wanting to impress; they often led to overexertion or embarrassment. "We should have set the traps before we grabbed firewood," Vidmar laughed, dropping his sticks in front of Mia. She followed his lead, but a protruding branch scraped against her on its way down, creating a pink scratch that outlined her jaw. She hissed, trying to conceal her pain.

"Are you alright?" Vidmar asked.

Mia rubbed the scratch. "I'm fine."

Vidmar had to ask her about the book. He had wasted enough time already. "Mia, do you remember when I asked if you knew Gaffer? Are you sure you're alright?" Vidmar said, watching her rub the darkening scrape. He needed to approach the subject carefully. It was too dangerous to let Mia know too much. He couldn't risk another person's life over his perilous quest.

"It's just a scratch. I'm fine. But, yeah, seemed random," Mia said, twirling her hair.

"I've known Gaffer for a long time, and I came to him for answers. He told me to find you, but somehow, you found me like we were meant to meet, although I don't believe in that shit," Vidmar said, choosing his words carefully.

"Answers to what?"

Vidmar ignored the question. "There are few as cunning as that old man; don't let his demeanor fool you. Gaffer said you borrowed a book that could help me."

Mia tilted her head, scratching behind her ear. "I'm sorry, most of my books are in Yimser."

"Well, I saw the book I am looking for when you were drying your things—*The Mystery of the Pact*. It could help me," he paused. *How much can I say?* "It might help me decipher something. Does the book refer to anything as 'The Dead'?" He removed the spool of thread from his bag as he talked, cut three long pieces, and braided them, trying to appear as casual as possible.

Mia watched him closely. "Um, there's a story about a battle–lots of people died in it. I don't know what you mean."

Vidmar finished braiding, trying a loop in one end of the string. *Shit, what do I ask her?* "Does the phrase 'It lies near The Dead' mean anything to you? Is it said in the book?" He decided the phrase itself was ominous enough to avoid incriminating her.

Mia hummed. "I'm not sure," she said before clicking her tongue. "Oh, wait. Maybe the burial grounds. At the end of the book, there's this list of members. I only skimmed it, but I think it says something about them all being buried together before they disappeared."

The knot slipped as Vidmar perked up. *Of course,* he thought. *Why didn't I think about that?* The Pact's burial grounds weren't exactly a secret. They were rumored to be at the Kaharn Desert's western edge, but the desert was the most dangerous place in Emre. Violent sandstorms, volatile temperature changes, and much worse lurked in the Kaharn. Vidmar had only been near once, and it was the closest he came to finding out if The Darkness was what he feared. "Will you show me this passage when we get back?"

"Sure, but it's the most boring part of the book, just a long list and some symbols. The story of Dinardo is much better," Mia said.

Vidmar shook his head as he retied the snare. "You like Dinardo?"

"Sometimes. I don't know how much I believe. Some of his stories are a little crazy."

"I agree. My Pa used to tell me a story of Dinardo–how he freed his men the night before they were supposed to be hanged. Dinardo controlled people's minds and ignited fires with his bare hands. You know, *real* magic." He finished tying the snare and tested it with a twig. The branch shot into the air and hung from a nearby tree at waist height. He reset the trap.

Mia stood, resting her hand on Vidmar's shoulder. "You're going to need *real* magic for that to work. How is that going to catch a bandit?"

Vidmar chuckled, ushering her backward. "This one isn't for bandits. It's for rabbits. You know, so we don't starve when Kamet eats all the food. We're going to set three more of these, and then we will set a few traps for *bigger* game."

Vidmar showed Mia how to set traps for rabbits, boars, and men. By the end of his lesson, Mia could set a snare about as well as a seasoned scout. "You're quick," he said, watching her test the last trap. A thick log launched into the air, dangling above their heads. "Well done."

Mia smiled, admiring her work.

"Let's see you reset this one," Vidmar laughed. "There's no way you can reach it." He would have to jump to grab the log but might have trouble catching it now that he was crippled; regardless, he could still reach it. Vidmar had no idea how Mia would grab it. He watched her survey the surroundings, then bolt toward a tree, run up the trunk, and leap backward, pulling the log on her way down. She smirked as she reset the trap. "You really are a show-off."

Mia smiled, picked up her sticks, and waited for Vidmar.

"We should head back," Vidmar said, their shadows disappearing into the surrounding darkness. Mia nodded. He grabbed his firewood and followed the stream back to the waterfall.

When they returned, Kamet was humming on a boulder he had pushed in front of the campfire. Vatis sat cross-legged on the ground, writing in one of his books. "What took you so long?" Kamet said. "I almost had to send Vatis after you."

"I showed Mia how to set some snares," Vidmar said, dropping the sticks behind Kamet. Mia added to the pile. "She's a better scout than you ever were."

"Yeah? Did she save the lives of an entire battalion by finding a path around a blockade?"

"I'm the one who spotted the blockade."

"Yeah, but I was there," Kamet said.

"Fair enough. What did we miss?"

Kamet poked the fire with a long stick. "A peddler stopped by and sold us a magic cow. Can't you see her? Wait, where did she go? Vidma, where are you, girl? Damn. She's invisible now—magic and all that," Kamet said, holding a hand to his mouth and mooing like a cow. "Vidma, where'd you go? I'm starting to think we were tricked, Vatis. Well, besides our missing cow, you only missed a bard bathing and an old soldier farting."

"You know, I thought your mother finally caught up to us," Vidmar said, nonchalantly adding a log to the fire.

Kamet pulled his stick out of the fire. Its smoking, charred tip glowed orange. "What did I tell you about my mother?"

"Nothing the sailors haven't told me at The Portly Carp."

"Watch it," Kamet growled, pushing the stick closer to Vidmar's face. Vidmar blew on it, watching the embers glow brighter.

"What's The Portly Carp?" Mia asked, grabbing her pack.

Vidmar smiled and nodded to Kamet, who returned a menacing glare but remained silent.

"It's a tavern of sorts that encourages young women to become independent entrepreneurs, so long as they pay the house a small tax," Vatis chimed in without diverting his attention from his book.

"What?" Mia said, scrunching her face like she'd just smelled manure.

Kamet still held the stick in Vidmar's face. "Put that thing down, Kamet. It's a whore house in Haran, and that's all she *needs* to know."

"I'm watching you," Kamet said, pointing the stick at Vidmar's chin one last time before adjusting a log in the fire.

It was quiet for a while. A crescent-shaped moon appeared amongst the stars through a hole in the forest's canopy. Stars always seemed brighter in the north, more peaceful. Vidmar listened to the calming hush of the waterfall behind them and forgot, for a moment, that they were running from one of the most dangerous men in Emre. *Am I running? I'm still searching for the damn crown.* Then there was the issue with Zidane. Did he work for Alcin? How much does he know? They also might have made enemies with The Church of Eternal Darkness. It seemed like every day, Vidmar created a new enemy. What was one more? Hundreds of questions pleaded for answers in his mind; for now, he enjoyed the waterfall's serenity and the company of his companions.

Vidmar felt a gentle tap on his shoulder. Mia. She handed him *The Mysteries of The Pact.* "Here," she said. "But be careful. I told Gaffer I would give it back."

Vidmar hoped she would have a chance to give the book back someday. He opened it slowly. "Thank you, Mia." The fragile pages crinkled as he flipped through. A chapter called *The Destruction of Tyranny* caught his eye, but he didn't stop to read further. Instead, he skipped the remaining pages and opened the back cover. *Why didn't I do this in the first place?* He only had to turn three pages before he found the list. Each name had a date and a symbol next to it–Azariah Emmitt 3 Harvest 627 with a triangular shape next to the date, Zacchaeus Templeton 12 Winter Solstice 627 with a similar triangular shape as well as two circles, one with a dot in the middle and one with a line through the top. He pulled the stone out of his pack.

"What's that?" Mia asked, leaning in.

Vidmar jumped. He didn't realize how close Mia had gotten. "It's just a stone with some markings that I hope to translate."

"Oh," Mia said. Vidmar heard skepticism in her voice.

The stone and the list had the same triangular markings, but the stone had three others that were nowhere on the page. "Damn," Vidmar said louder than he intended. *These markings mean nothing to me.*

"What's wrong?" Mia asked. "The book doesn't help?" She looked hurt.

Vidmar bit the insides of his cheeks, exhaling while rubbing the bridge of his nose. He didn't answer as he dropped the book and threw a log on the fire; embers danced into the night sky, burning out like his ever-decreasing optimism. Vidmar's gaze followed the path of one of the orange dots. It rose higher and higher until the orange glow disappeared, and a trail of smoke fell to the ground by his toes. *Wait. Vatis can help,* Vidmar thought, remembering the bard's initial examination of the stone. For a second, hope returned like an old friend. "Vatis, can you make anything of this?"

Vatis looked up from his book. The reflection of flames frolicked in his dark eyes. "*The Mystery of The Pact,* a tedious but mostly accurate recollection. In the excitement of winning the tourney, nearly dying, and running until exhaustion, I had forgotten that Mia's book might be able to help your quest. What are the chances?" He closed the book he was writing in and stuffed it into his pack. Vatis held out his hand. "Let me see."

Excitement boiled in his stomach, rising higher into Vidmar's chest. He quickly handed the book and stone to Vatis.

"Interesting," Vatis began. "Luck is on your side tonight, Vidmar."

He choked the elation back into his throat. "Do you know what it says? Gaffer thought the symbols said: 'It lies near the dead.'"

"Hmm," Vatis said, scanning the page. He licked the tip of his finger and flipped through the book. "It lies near the dead. Yes, well, maybe. Perhaps, it's buried with the dead. No, no, I don't think so." He mumbled under his breath as he continued to think out loud.

"What?" Vidmar asked, growing impatient.

Vatis bit his nails. "It could be nothing. Maybe it's just my skeptical outlook." He continued his examination.

"What?" Vidmar and Mia said simultaneously.

Vatis traced the symbols on the rock with his finger. "I think Gaffer was right. It most assuredly says: 'It lies near the dead.' But I think 'lies' does not mean to lie down but rather to be untruthful. However, I haven't the slightest clue what 'it' means. Hmm. There might be a sister stone. It's rare, but sometimes, The Pact used two or more stones to deliver a message. One stone was brought by different couriers, an extra bit of caution when Dinardo gained more power. That way, the enemy wouldn't have the full message if a courier were killed or captured."

"And you think my stone is part of a longer message?" Vidmar asked.

"Perhaps."

Vidmar shot up and kicked the dirt. The tiny particles sizzled as they passed through the fire. "How the fuck am I going to find the other half? Why is there always another clue?" He ground his teeth to keep himself from screaming.

"Isn't that the job of a treasure hunter?" Vatis asked softly.

"I'm not a damn treasure hunter. I'm a soldier, a scout, a killer. I'm done pretending."

A terrible silence fell over them. Vidmar rubbed his eyebrows and watched a beetle dive into the fire like it had nothing left to live for, and the warmth of the fire appeared to be the best remaining option. He didn't disagree. It would have been easier if he had died. If Alcin had killed him or if he had frozen to death on Jegon. It would have been easier still if he had died when he turned on Kandrian. Vidmar was one of the few loose ends the King let escape. Yet, it would have been easiest if Elisa had never pulled him out of the sand and left him to die in the desert. Fuzzy shapes mumbled as he focused on the fire. It felt so warm, so inviting. If he were a beetle, he would have flown into the flames.

"Vidmar," Kamet said, grabbing his shoulder.

"What?" He snapped. He felt a weight bearing down on him; his head sunk as the stress pushed against him. He could barely keep his eyes open. *When was the last time I slept?*

"I don't think he heard you, Vatis," Mia said.

"What," Vidmar repeated. He crouched forward, grabbing his opposite elbows and curling into a ball.

"Hobb might be able to help," Vatis said.

"Hobb, the farmer. How could he possibly help?"

Vatis stood and walked in front of Vidmar and Mia. He kicked leaves away to clear a patch of dirt. "Can I borrow your stick?" the bard asked Kamet.

Vatis began drawing a rough sketch of what looked like a map. Vidmar couldn't help but watch. As it took shape, Vatis elaborated. "This is Emre, well, what we know of Emre. We don't know what lies beyond the Kaharn Desert to the east." He scribbled out the eastern half of the map, then continued. "We don't know what lies across the sea and beyond these mountains." He crossed out most of the northern half of the map. "We don't know how or why The Pact disappeared, so let's focus on what we know. From Yimser to Jegon and everything in between, Western Emre is well documented, and it just happens that two confirmed monuments of The Pact remain." He drew two small rectangles—one near the desert and one near Numeria. "These towers once belonged to The Pact. Watchtowers, beacons of their strength. Do you remember the tower near Hobb's farm, the one I fell from?" Vatis asked, rubbing his arm.

Vidmar tilted his head. "Yes," he said, drawing out the word while thinking through the implications.

"I believe it might be the third tower of The Pact. It's much more decayed than the others, but there's something strange about it. Why would a random watchtower be in the middle of a farm?" Vatis said, drawing a third rectangle on his map. Next, he drew lines connecting the three towers. "Look at this," he said. The lines formed a perfect triangle. "It's The Pact's symbol, a triangle pointing east. Hobb's tower is directly north of the tower in Numeria. You cannot tell me this isn't an interesting coincidence," Vatis said.

"Is that why you were in it? To look for symbols or signs of The Pact?" Vidmar asked. Mia shifted on the ground next to Vidmar, trying to get a better look at Vatis's map. Kamet fiddled with the fire.

Vatis stopped drawing. "Yes." He didn't explain.

"And you think Hobb is part of The Pact? He *did* seem like there was something he didn't want us to find out," Vidmar said, trying to think through this revelation.

"Can you put another log on, Kamet? It's getting hard to see." Vatis asked, ignoring the question and drawing a circle around what appeared to be Barna.

Kamet looked at Vidmar for approval; they didn't want the flames rising too high. Vidmar nodded, and Kamet added another log. "Thank you," Vatis said, itching his upper arm. "There hasn't been a confirmed member of The Pact in Western Emre in centuries, not since Benino Cuaya helped Cairbre write this book, then vanished as if into thin air. That's one of the greatest mysteries in my profession. Ah, well, I'm getting distracted. Sorry, I don't often get a chance to talk about history when I'm not telling a story. Where was I?"

"You don't think this Hobb person is a part of The Pact," Mia quickly answered before she slouched backward.

"Ah, right. Thank you, Mia. I *don't* think Hobb is a part of The Pact, but I agree that there is more to him than he lets on. He knew of Dabin and was a spectacular medic for a simple farmer. So he might know something."

I am constantly moving backward on this quest. Vidmar thought as he sat down. He rubbed his brow with the scabbed stump of a missing finger. "Well, how are we getting back to Vicus?"

DARTMORE

Vatis

Vatis panted, stretching his hands into the air. A cramp ate through the back of his leg, burying its teeth into his femur. "Can we please stop?" he asked, forcing the air out of his burning lungs.

Silver specs shimmered on the river's current. He wondered how much running he would have to do to have endurance like Vidmar. The treasure hunter skidded to a stop as he made a gesture with his right hand; it looked odd with two of his fingers missing, but it was still effective. "Catch your breath," he said, circling behind the group.

"I," Vatis began. His hot breath stung his throat like bees defending their hive. "Why are we running?"

Vidmar glanced toward Kamet. The mercenary shrugged. Mia jumped on top of a large piece of driftwood; she had more energy than Vidmar. "I thought I saw someone or something behind us," Vidmar said, looking upstream toward a sparse grove of pine trees.

Vatis sipped the remaining water from his waterskin, smacking his lips unsatisfyingly. "What," he said, shaking the waterskin upside-down into his mouth. A single drop landed on his tongue, which was worse than nothing coming out. The droplet was absorbed instantly in his desert-dry mouth. "Did you see?" he finished. Each word withered his mouth further.

"A dark shape, I'm not sure," Vidmar said. "But I'm not taking chances."

Vatis's breath slowly returned to normal. He bent over the river's edge, filling his waterskin. "Let me get this straight," he said, attaching the full waterskin to his belt, then bending back down. "We are running from a dark *shape*, not a man or a beast." He splashed water onto his face and cupped a large handful into his mouth. The gritty, slightly sour water quenched his thirst after two more handfuls. Kamet bent down next to him, pretending to push him into the river while reeling him in by the collar of his shirt. The rough canvas irritated his skin.

Kamet laughed. "Careful."

Vatis rubbed his neck and scowled.

"Is it following us?" Mia said, stepping behind Vidmar.

Vidmar jumped, then stretched onto his tiptoes. "I don't think so."

"We are running from shadows now?" Vatis said, still rubbing the skin around his neck.

Vidmar turned slowly, his expression deadly serious. "Do I need to remind you of the Kokor Forest?" He said, looking over his shoulder.

"You went into the forest?" Mia asked. She held a hand over her mouth until a finger meandered to a curl in her hair.

Vidmar shifted his gaze from Vatis to the ground. "We didn't have a choice, but that's a story for another time. Dartmore is not far. If we run the rest of the way, we can make it before sunset.

Then the three of you can laugh at how silly I was for making us run all the way there."

Recently, Vidmar's abundance of caution verged on paranoia. *Maybe it always has,* Vatis thought. *I'd be paranoid, too, if the King and the King's most prominent rival considered me an enemy.* He slung his pack onto the ground and checked on the status of his invitation. *Still there.* He tightened the straps as he stood. The last thing he needed was his pack falling off and rolling into the river while they ran from Vidmar's ghosts. However, he had seen the shadow in the Kokor Forest, though he wasn't afraid. It spoke to *him*, not Vidmar or Kamet, offering the rest he so desperately craved. He closed his eyes and imagined a soft feather bed underneath a dark tree. Shadows hugged him like blankets. *Rest.*

"Are you ready?" Vidmar asked.

The feather bed beckoned him. He squinted the dream away, forcing himself to speak. "I'm ready."

Kamet slapped his back as he jogged past. "Try to keep up."

Apparently, Vidmar and Vatis had drastically different definitions of not far. They had been running for hours, stopping only briefly for Vatis to catch his breath. Each stop came seconds before he passed out. Golden stars evolved into orange-green planets collapsing in on his vision and sucking the mass from his head. His movement became more difficult with each stop, like getting an old horse to pull a wagon. Then he saw it as they crested the final hill, smoking chimneys and slated rooftops beyond a wide, fast-moving river, Dartmore.

Rest.

Vidmar made his three-finger stopping gesture. There was something familiar about Dartmore; repressed memories forced their way to the front of Vatis's mind. He had performed here, but he couldn't remember how long ago. *Years, decades, maybe.* It had been one of the first taverns he dared to enter. Dartmore sat at the intersection of the Camil and Fox rivers. The Camil River flowed east toward Barna, and the Fox river ran north and south from the Islingrey Mountains to Vicus. The structures of Dartmore were laid out in a circular fashion revolving around a tall spiraling chapel with a cracked bronze bell. It had been painted blue at one point in its history, but now only a faint hint of the color remained. Vatis watched an eagle pluck a fish from the river. The majesty of the creature awed him.

"Eagle," he exclaimed to the group.

Mia jumped beside him. "Where?" Vatis watched her green eyes widen with similar awe. "Wow," she whispered. "Gaffer said that The Pact used to use eagles as weapons."

"That's terrifying," Kamet said without turning around. His head followed the bird as it soared over Dartmore.

"Actually, The Pact used them for intimidation. Eagles are quite difficult to train; very few were ever trained well enough to strike on command, which is why the King employs his regimen of falconers, not eaglers. I don't know if that is the correct term," Vatis said as the regal bird disappeared beyond the horizon.

"Are you all done gawking at the bird?" Vidmar said.

Vatis tried to remember his performance in Dartmore but couldn't; however, he did recall the force of the swift-moving Camil River. A mill across the river spun, powering a wood saw in the adjacent building. Constructing a bridge was impossible, and the current was too strong to swim; they had to take a ferry across. Fortunately, one was docked nearby; its captain sat on a stool fishing with a rod.

"Hello," Vidmar said in a friendly tone as they approached.

The pot-bellied man held a finger to his lips, then yanked the rod upward. He stood faster than Vatis thought possible for a man of his stature. He frantically reeled in his line.

Vatis froze. The man grunted, pulling his line closer and closer to shore. He dove onto his stomach, reaching his hands into the water. Vatis heard frantic splashing as the man wrestled his catch. He emerged shortly after holding a murky-green scaled fish by its gills. It was nearly as long as Vatis's arm, with a pointed mouth and sharp teeth that jutted outside like a boar's tusks.

"Haha," the man exclaimed, holding the fish above his head. Blood dripped down his forearm. Vatis couldn't tell if it was his or the fish's.

Vidmar held up his hands triumphantly. "Is that a pike?"

"It sure is, friend," the fisherman said in a deep yet comforting voice. He grabbed its tail with his free hand and examined it closer. "Might be the biggest I've ever caught, enough to feed my family for a week."

Vidmar stopped in front of the wooden dock. "Impressive." Vatis, Mia, and Kamet lingered behind.

The fisherman abruptly ended the pike's life by sticking a thin knife through the side of its skull. Vatis found the efficiency of the kill terrifying.

"Is this your boat?" Vidmar asked after the fisherman stored the fish in a barrel brimming with salt.

"Aye," he said, using a wooden mallet to seal the barrel.

"We seek passage across the river," Vidmar said, pointing to the town in the distance.

The ferryman laughed. "No need to be so formal, friend. 2 Kan each."

Vidmar reached back toward Kamet, holding his hand out like a beggar. "Toss me the purse."

"Don't you have any coin on you?" Kamet asked, untying the pouch on his hip.

"No. I gave it to you."

"Fine, but are we sure there is no other way across?" Kamet said, his voice shaking slightly.

"You could walk to Barna and around the other side, or you could swim," Vidmar said, narrowing his eyes. "We are crossing a river, not sailing uncharted waters. I'm sure this fine ferryman has made the journey hundreds of times."

The ferryman coughed. "It's my first time."

Kamet's face turned ghostly pale. Then the ferryman burst out laughing. "A little water-feared, I see, aye, you've nothing to fear. Ole Oto's the most experienced ferryman this side of the Camil," he said, stepping near Mia. He bent down and whispered loudly. "Oto's the only ferryman this side of the Camil."

Kamet threw the purse at Vidmar's feet. "Let's get this over with."

A smooth ferry ride and a few hours later, Vatis watched the sunset through a small rectangular window; a dull orange light fell below his sightline. The bathwater cooled rapidly. His body ached, muscles he didn't know he had pulsed beneath the lilac-scented water. This was his first proper bath in months, not since the Raue Tavern in Basswood. He was going to relish every second of it. Vidmar had knocked twice, Mia once, but Vatis wasn't ready. He needed this bath. He'd earned some rest. A fourth knock came at his door, "Sir, another guest requested a bath. Are you nearly finished?" An unfamiliar woman's voice called through the door.

Can't I have a moment's rest? Vatis respected the tavern business too much to dawdle when another customer was waiting. He had been that customer, and he hated waiting. "I'll be out shortly," he said, rinsing his hair. He shivered as the cold water ran down his neck. *How long have I been in here?* His fingers looked as though he had aged fifty years. His moments of rest were always too short. He thought briefly about the shadow figure in the Kokor Forest and his vision of a luxurious bed beneath a large oak tree. He didn't know if he could resist the creature's offer again.

"You look … refreshed," Vidmar said a few moments later as Vatis joined their table in the tavern's common room.

"Are you a woman?" Kamet asked. "What took you so long?" Vatis could smell the mead on his breath.

Vatis sat next to Mia; dirt still clung to her face and clothing. "I just lost track of time."

"I saved you some stew," she said, sliding a wooden bowl in front of him. "It's cold now, but it's good."

Vatis lifted the bowl to his lips. It was good. He couldn't tell what kind of meat it was—most likely some type of fish—but it was well-seasoned with pepper and rosemary. He wiped his mouth clean with the back of his hand. "Thank you."

Mia played with a loose nail on the bench. "Kamet tried to steal it."

"Why doesn't that surprise me?"

Something about a tavern made Vatis feel at home, perhaps because he hadn't had a home in decades. The ambiance, the people, the food, the history, and the potential all varied drastically from place to place. The Troubled Pike in Dartmore was nothing special. It didn't even have a proper bar or at least one where people could sit. Rectangular tables were scattered about the common room, not in a lined sequence, but randomly, like they had been moved by patrons, and the owner didn't care enough to push them back. He ignored Vidmar and Kamet's mindless banter as they argued about something involving boats. Vatis finished his stew, enjoying one of his favorite hobbies – people-watching. At least, that's what he called it. He sat back and observed, watching for the details that made humans, well, humans.

A dark-skinned man scratched the back of his neck while playing cards; his fingers were blistered and callused, a millworker most likely. Dozens of patrons gathered around their tables, projecting a pleasant murmur that's only heard in a well-occupied tavern. A gray-haired man with cloudy eyes held the leash of a slender black dog as they sauntered out the door. "Goodnight, Ister," a man in a black apron called while sweeping. *Blind, perhaps, that must be one well-trained dog.* Vatis thought before turning his attention to a thin woman with white streaks speckled throughout her black hair. She wore a long lavender cloak and looked familiar. She pushed a stool into an opening between the tables. Crow's feet wrinkled next to her hazy, azure eyes. "What are you playing tonight, Kytia?" someone called from a nearby table. Vatis now realized that the tables were all lined up to face her. A bard. Vatis couldn't remember the last time he listened to a bard in a tavern. *Kytia,* he thought, trying to place the name.

Mia elbowed him in the ribs.

"Hey," he said, scooting onto the edge of the bench they shared.

"Sorry. Do you know her?" Mia asked.

Vatis scratched his chin. "She looks familiar, but I can't place her."

Mia began to ask another question as Kytia cleared her throat. The simple noise silenced the tavern.

"Thank you," she said in a gentle yet commanding voice. She brushed a wrinkle out of her gray skirt. "As I was saying, what would you like to hear, Thad? You haven't requested anything in a few weeks. A song?" She pointed to the lute case leaning against the stool. "A story? A poem?"

The man called Thad said something, but Vatis didn't hear, and apparently, neither did Kytia. "Stand and annunciate, Thad," Kytia demanded like a schoolteacher. The broad-shouldered man stood; mead spilled from the mug in his hand.

"Um," Thad began quietly. The young man shuffled his feet.

"Louder, Thad,"

"Sorry, miss. Um, can you tell us the story of Durgia," Thad said. His voice faded into the attentive crowd.

Kytia sat on the stool, adjusting her spine to appear taller. "Durgia," she started. "Interesting choice. Are you sure you don't want to hear of Dabin again?" Thad nodded. "Alright then. How does our crowd feel about the story of an ancient creature that roamed the Camil long before Dartmore's establishment? A tale of a being larger than a barge, more powerful than a tornado, and faster than an eagle. A creature that was hunted for its indestructible scales, only to repay our hatred by saving a child that would one day become the most powerful man in the world." The crowd collectively raised their glasses in agreement.

Vatis listened attentively until he was stabbed in the ribs again by a dreadfully sharp elbow. "Quit that," he said.

"Sorry," Mia smirked. "Is it true? This Durgia creature."

"There's always some truth in myths. But, alas, no one has seen this creature in centuries, at least no one credible. Just enjoy the story," Vatis said, sipping the last of his stew.

Kytia finished her introduction, scanning the crowd. Azure eyes met Vatis's, and he thought Kytia stiffened like she had seen a ghost; her eyes widened before they continued their examination. She cleared her throat. The growing murmur stopped immediately. "Thank you," she said, placing her hands on her lap. "This tale could start in many different places, but most bards agree that it is fine to skip the creation of Emre and the age of evolution that followed." Her eyes lingered on Vatis as she said, 'most bards.' She blinked repeatedly. "Let's start our story with the settlement of the finest city in the world, Dartmore." The crowd roared. *Pandering,* Vatis thought. He ordered an ale, adjusted his seat, and listened.

"A dark sapphire shape thrashed in the river as the gathering townsfolk watched in horror. A seamstress fainted, nearly joining the boy in the violent water below," Kytia said, approaching the climax of her story. *She's good,* Vatis thought. *Too good for a tavern in Dartmore.* Mia watched with bated breath, soaking in each detail of the story like a sponge.

Meanwhile, Kamet had passed out with his forehead on the table, snoring loud enough to draw menacing looks from a table of men to their right. Kytia stood and began walking through the crowd. "The water went deathly still. The crowd's heavy, raspy breathing was the only sound for what seemed like miles," she whispered, crouching behind a table of women in the back of the room. Then she stomped her foot. Vatis jumped; he wasn't expecting such theatrics. The hollow thud echoed through the room like she knew exactly what floorboard would produce the best sound to emphasize her story.

"Suddenly, the boy flew through the air and landed on the dock," Kytia glided through the common room, eyeing her audience. "The stunned crowd gasped as the boy rolled onto his stomach and coughed out a lungful of water," Kytia paused as she poked her head over Kamet's shoulder. She stared at Vatis. He felt cold as the room blackened until it was just the two of them, her stare delving deep into his soul. She bit her lip and tried to focus but stumbled over her words. Her gaze slipped from Vatis to Mia, displacing her from the reverie. The room had gone eerily quiet; not even the fire responded with its usual cracking.

Kytia gently slapped Kamet's back. "I must be losing my touch," she said. "I haven't put a man to sleep in years." She smiled, deliberately avoiding the vacuum of Vatis's lingering stare. The crowd responded by booing Kamet. One man threw an apple core that struck the back of the mercenary's head. A black seed landed in front of Vatis. Kamet didn't move; however, his snoring grew louder as his subconscious fought when his body betrayed him. "If he wasn't snoring like a hog, I would have guessed he was dead," Kytia said, returning to her stool. The crowd laughed. "Now, where was I?"

Vatis couldn't focus on the story as she finished; he barely heard the room erupt with applause. He and Kamet were the only two patrons sitting as she performed her final curtsy. Mia kicked him in the shin, and he jolted to his feet, joining the crowd for the final seconds of their ovation. He remained standing as the rest of the patrons returned their attention to drinking and gambling.

"Why didn't you stand? I thought the story was incredible," Mia said, watching Kytia visit with a table of dark-skinned men toward the front of the room.

The trance clung to Vatis like sap to a maple tree. "What?" he squealed as Mia kicked him again. A tender lump formed on the top of his shin.

"Why didn't you stand?"

Vatis barely heard the question. Instead, he focused on Kytia, who greeted another table with infectious laughter. *Is she in the guild?* The thought terrified him. He hadn't associated with a guild member in over a decade; most members thought he was dead. Vatis's palms began to sweat.

"What's with you tonight?" Vidmar asked. "You seem distracted, more distracted than usual." Kytia neared their table as she continued her rounds. Vidmar raised his voice. "Vatis?"

"Vatis," Kytia's butter-smooth voice repeated from the head of their table. "I," she stopped, swallowing hard. "We thought you were dead." Vatis *did* know Kytia. He tried to deny it. He searched for a response, but fortunately, Kytia continued. "Vatis, what happened?" She asked, looking like it took all of her training to keep her composure. Vatis saw the tension behind her smile.

He needed to say something, anything; her questioning stare ripped his stomach apart. The edges of his vision darkened, blackening out the shadows that Mia and Vidmar and the entire tavern became until it was just the two of them. Kytia and Vatis. Classmates. Old friends. "Hello," was all he could muster.

Her accusatory tone softened into comforting velvetiness. "Vatis, it's me, Kytia Versil, from the guild."

He watched her lips roll like waves from happiness to confusion to concern. "I know," he said softly.

"Where have you been all these years?" She asked, gently touching Vatis's forearm as she leaned over the table.

Thoughts raced through his head. *What can I say?*

"You know Vatis?" Vidmar asked. His voice was like lightning, illuminating the darkness for a second before the storm passed and the tavern returned to normal.

"... we studied together," Kytia said. Vatis only caught the final few words of her answer.

"You mean people go to school to tell stories," Mia's friendly voice said, casting a ray of sunshine into the exchange.

Kytia laughed. "The good bards do." She smiled, then returned her attention to Vatis, beaming like a child with a new toy. "I can't believe you're alive. The guild will be shocked."

Vatis straightened as if he had been stabbed in the back. "Don't tell the guild."

Kytia's brows furrowed against her long eyelashes. "Why? They *deserve* to know."

"I can explain."

"Don't forget about us, Kytia," A group of men called from a nearby table.

Kytia backed away, nodding at Vatis. "Fine, meet me in my room in an hour." She pointed to a room in the back corner of the tavern. "It was a pleasure to meet you all," she said, slapping Kamet again. He snorted what seemed like an answer. "Vatis," she finished, spinning on her heels and embracing the table behind them with open arms.

Vatis tried to listen to Kytia's exchange with the other table. It seemed so friendly, so warm. Pain vibrated up his shin. "I said stop it," he said, baring his teeth at Mia.

"What was that about?" Vidmar asked.

"It's nothing," Vatis whispered, rubbing his shin with his opposite heel.

Vidmar looked back at Kytia, who, in turn, kept glancing at Vatis. "Didn't seem like nothing."

"It's nothing," Vatis yelled. Kytia stole another glance at Vatis with wide, scared eyes.

BARDS

Vatis

Vatis waited by Kytia's door, tapping his foot and trying to come up with a believable story; he couldn't tell the truth. Most of the patrons had either gone home or retired to their rooms. Vidmar and Mia dragged Kamet upstairs shortly after Vatis's outburst. *I should never have chased Vidmar's story*, he thought. *Don't get attached.*

He watched the innkeeper silently curse his guests as he picked fish bones and clam shells off the floor. A door hinge creaked as Kytia emerged. "Come in," she said, emotionless.

She pushed a stool out for Vatis and sat cross-legged on the edge of her bed. Her black robe appeared metallic as the firelight reflected off its surface. Hay inside the mattress crinkled when she adjusted her seat, waiting. Again, Vatis searched for words. For a man who knew hundreds of stories and delighted in conversation, words seemed to evade him now. He could see them in his mind: *Hello. I should have written. I'm sorry.* His tongue and lips wouldn't cooperate until he finally managed something, an observation as his curiosity exceeded his apprehension. "Is that a copy of *Timun's Bestiary?*" Kytia didn't acknowledge the question. "It's incredibly rare," Vatis continued. Kytia remained silent. Her penetrating stare wanted no part of the diverting question. "May I see it?"

"No." Her flat answer ended his inquiry without debate. She was a different person in her room. Her façade in front of the audience melted like snow in spring, revealing shriveled foliage beneath.

"Kytia, I don't know where to begin," he relented after another torturous minute of enduring her gaze.

Kytia laughed, not playfully but forcefully. "We searched for you for months." She closed her eyes and bit her lip, smudging her black eyeliner as she rubbed her face.

Vatis inhaled deeply as if he were about to perform. In some ways, he was. He had to tell her something, anything, but it didn't have to be the truth. *She deserves honesty,* his subconscious interjected. *But I can't; there's too much at stake.* His aching shoulders relaxed as he exhaled, beginning his story. "After the attack, I hid," he began. "I hid from the bandits, from the Guild, from you, from myself. It was my fault, after all." Vatis paused for a potential response, but Kytia was unmoved. He thought that an admission of guilt would move the lie along quicker. It didn't work. "I was in shock. They slew Kleon in front of me." He paused, adding a stutter for dramatic effect. "I can still see the arrows in his chest." At least this was true; the best lies are forged from small truths. He *did* see images of Kleon lying dead, blood dripping from the corner of his mouth when he couldn't sleep or worse when he was asleep.

"It was chaos."

Kytia's scowl intensified as he built upon his lie. "Do *not* perform for me. Tell me the truth or leave," she said.

The urge to continue the lie was undeniable; however, Kytia remembered him too well. She knew all the tricks and subtleties of a good performance. "I was taken captive," he began again.

"I said, tell me the truth."

How did she know that was a lie? Vatis bit the insides of his cheeks to stop himself from shouting. The floor creaked beneath his bouncing toes. He couldn't hold the truth back any longer. "I ran," he said, looking down at a knot in one of the floorboards. "They killed Kleon, and I ran. He was the brave one; I was only there to keep him company."

The sound of hoofbeats rumbled like thunder in his head. He closed his eyes. Two dark arrows splintered as Kleon fell face-first next to him. Vatis squeezed his temples like the pressure could somehow erase his memory. Finally, he forced his eyelids open only to face Kytia's unchanged executioner's expression.

"If I hadn't been lying down, they would have killed me too. There were too many. I rolled under a bush just before they passed, and then I heard screaming and swords clashing, and I ran. I ran until I collapsed in the tulip field outside of Wayland. When I woke, I ran until I reached Curma. Truthfully, I haven't stopped running. My pace has slowed, but I never stopped. I can't stop."

Kytia sniffed, wiping her nose with a silk handkerchief embroidered with the Guild's emblem – an open book with a quill in the center encased in a diamond. "I can't believe Likhas was right. How could you abandon us? We lost three bards that day; I lost four friends. Where have you been for the last twenty years?"

Vatis saw the pain and confusion in Kytia's eyes. His stomach twisted into a tight knot. "I ran for the first year, maybe longer; honestly, I've lost track of time. I made it as far as the Emerald Isles before I stopped. I met a shipwright there who dreamt of constructing a vessel strong enough to sail west into the uncharted waters."

"Focus on *your* story," Kytia interrupted.

Vatis scratched his chin and nodded his apology. *How much does she need to know?* "I lived on the isles for a while, mostly out of guilt. I couldn't return to the mainland, not yet. So, I wallowed in my cowardice and became a wretch to anyone who crossed my path. I *allowed* things to happen that harmed many people; I may have caused more than a few deaths, though not directly. I am a coward, not a murderer. My home for that time was a seaside shack that looked almost as decrepit as I felt. But, again, I don't know how long I tarried there; I only left because a hurricane destroyed my home. That storm did far worse to the villages a few miles south," Vatis said as his body convulsed, and his long-hidden secrets revealed themselves like starfish on low tide.

He hunched into a ball to stop the shaking, but the wobbly stool only accentuated his movement. Vatis looked up, meeting Kytia's gaze; she didn't respond. Instead, her look of perplexed horror reminded him of his walk through the destroyed villages after the hurricane – buildings toppled, corpses floating in the water, and children crying for their parents.

He choked back tears and continued. "After the storm, I ventured from village to village, helping the locals rebuild their homes. It was then that I rediscovered my passion for storytelling; talking with the villagers about their lives, struggles, and dreams led me to my current endeavor. *The Stories of Emre*, I call it. It is a collection of tales and poems about the everyday heroes and villains who truly affect our world, not just kings and knights and wars, but a recollection of history from the people who experience it," Vatis paused, waiting for Kytia to comment on his idea, his life's work. She did not.

Vatis rubbed the bridge of his nose and exhaled. "I knew if I wanted *The Stories* to be accurate, I would have to return to the mainland. It took months to work up the courage and even longer to accumulate enough coin for passage, but I returned. I landed in Numeria a few years ago and began searching for stories."

Kytia shook her head. "How has no one in the Guild seen you? It doesn't make sense."

Vatis shrugged. "I searched for stories far to the south, between Numeria and Jegon, where I knew the guild was seldom active. It took a while to develop a character who could persuade others to divulge their secrets, but after some trial and error, I uncovered some marvelous stories. Unfortunately, though, there are only so many tales worth telling in that region, so a few years ago, I began venturing further north. It wasn't until I met Gunnar that I began performing again. Now, there was a hero whose story ended too soon. His unmatched charisma, incredible swordsmanship, and proclivity for helping those in need could have made him the next Dabin."

"Focus," Kytia said, adjusting her position on the bed.

Vatis nibbled on his thumbnail and forced a curt nod. "Sorry, Kytia. As I was saying, it wasn't until a few months ago that I began performing again. I didn't realize how difficult it would be to regain my confidence. With Gunnar as my guide and muse, I played a few small taverns south of Basswood. I perfected my voice around campfires, though my presentation still needs work. Yet, somehow, I've been invited to perform in Barna at The King's Tourney," Vatis said. He felt a smile creep onto his face. "More importantly, I may have finally found the story that will mend my relationship with the Guild and make Vatis-of-the-Road known throughout Emre."

"I do not care about your petty accomplishments or your ideas. You're still as arrogant as you were when we were students – arrogant and overconfident. Do you truly think a story can repair the damage you've done?" Kytia said. Vatis tried to respond, but she held out a finger, silencing him. "What aren't you telling me?" She furrowed her eyebrows and forced each word out slowly. "Why haven't you aged?"

As Vatis searched for an answer, someone pounded relentlessly at Kytia's door like a battering ram. "Kytia," the muffled voice called. "Kytia."

Kytia huffed as she stood, tightening her robe as she walked. "Coming."

An old man burst into the room a second later, followed by a black dog. It was Ister. The blind man from the common room. "I've got a story for you," he said, pointing to his eyes. "I can see again."

Kytia didn't respond to Ister. Instead, she turned toward Vatis, her eyes wide with comprehension.

ESCAPING DARTMORE

Vidmar

What's going on?" Vidmar asked, rubbing the sleep from his eyes as someone shook him awake. No one answered, so he rolled over, looking for the culprit. He blinked and saw Vatis slide to Kamet's bed to perform a similar awakening. *Bad idea.* Growling, Kamet turned over. Somehow, he lifted Vatis into the air by his neck while still lying down.

"Wake me like that again, and I'll kill you," Kamet said, throwing Vatis to the floor and rolling back onto his stomach.

Vatis shot up faster than Vidmar had ever seen the bard move. "We must hurry, please." He pulled back the curtains, but only a faint glow entered the room.

His sore joints cracked as Vidmar stretched, still groggy. "I'm not leaving until you tell me why?" Vidmar said, sitting up. Vatis now knelt over Mia, whom he woke much more gently.

Mia yawned. "What's happening?"

Vidmar pulled on his boots. "Ask Vatis."

Mia turned toward Vatis, who was now back at the door, strumming his fingers against the wood. "Vatis?" she asked.

Vatis tapped his foot. "We need to leave. When Vidmar says we need to leave, nobody questions it. But the one time I request a bit of urgency, you all look at me like I murdered somebody."

"Did you?" Kamet groaned into the mattress.

The tapping quickened. "What? Of course not."

"It seems like you murdered someone," Kamet said, rolling onto his back. "Gods, my head. If you all could stop spinning, we might be able to get somewhere."

Vidmar looked out the window; only a sliver of the morning sun appeared beyond the horizon. "You can't drink like you used to," he said, trying to button his shirt. Vidmar had adjusted to his handicap, but the task he hated most was buttoning his shirt. He wasn't particularly good at it before the injury; it never seemed like a task that required more than minimal effort or attention, but now it was nearly impossible. The smooth, black button slipped from his grip. "Shit."

"At least I can button my shirt," Kamet said.

The last button slid into place. "Normally, your mother helps me with my buttons, although it's with my trousers, and the buttons are being undone."

Kamet stood quickly, then fell back onto the bed. He tried to stand again, using the bedpost as a cane. "You're lucky I'm seeing three of you right now. I don't know which one to hit."

Vidmar laughed as he packed his bag. He watched the bard pace back and forth, occasionally putting an ear to the door. *What's gotten into Vatis?* Vidmar was used to quick, early morning escapes, but he liked to know what he was running from. *What did that other bard say?*

"Let's go," Vatis insisted.

Mia shuffled between Vidmar and Kamet, meeting Vatis at the door. "I'm ready."

"Thank you, Mia. At least someone here takes me seriously," Vatis said.

Mia looked away as she twirled her hair.

"She's young. She's excited to explore," Vidmar said. The leather strap around his left thigh was wearing thin. *I'll have to replace this,* he thought as he tightened it and slid a dagger in place. "Kamet and I have seen enough of this world to know that we must cherish these calm moments before…"

"Before it all goes to shit," Kamet interrupted.

"Not exactly what I would have said, but yes, before it all goes to shit."

Vatis clenched his fists, grinding his knuckles together in front of his mouth. "That's what I've been trying to say. It's all gone to shit. We need to leave."

"I told you he killed somebody," Kamet said, slinging his pack over his shoulder.

After a frantic trip through the backdoor of the Troubled Pike, they found themselves in an alley that smelled of stale mead and rotting fish. Vatis led the way onto the main thoroughfare in Dartmore. Merchants and shop owners began opening their establishments as the first rays of sunlight shined on the eastern half of the town. Long shadows hid the faces of the people they passed. Beads of dew streaked the store windows. Dartmore's entire merchant district could fit into a single city block in Haran. The quaint shops had a peaceful aura, making Vidmar wonder why he hadn't spent more time here. *Too close to Barna,* his subconscious answered.

"What happened with Kytia last night?" Mia asked as they walked down the brick-paved street.

"Nothing of note," Vatis said, breathing hard. He walked briskly, only pausing to look down side streets and alleys. "We reminisced. She was my teacher at the Bard's College."

"Then why are we leaving in such a hurry?" Mia asked. Vidmar was thankful that the girl had taken over the questioning. Vatis was more receptive toward her.

Vatis sighed but did not look back at the group trailing a few paces behind him. "I will explain everything once we get out of this forsaken town. Darkness. What's the fastest way to Vicus?"

Vidmar jogged to catch up to the bard. "Probably a ship, but I doubt any ferries sailing at this hour."

"Fuck," Vatis said. Vidmar eyed the bard after his unaccustomed curse. He looked like a deserter with recruiters on his tail – a look Vidmar was all too familiar with. *Fucking recruiters.* Dark circles emerged below the bard's brow; his heavy lids hung low, disguising his swollen red eyes. *He hasn't slept in days.*

"We might be able to *persuade* a sailor or fisherman to take us south," Vidmar said as the street turned southwest toward the Fox River.

"There has to be a wagon or caravan going south," Kamet urged from behind Vidmar.

"We'll see. I think the docks are at the end of this street."

Vidmar smelled the docks before he could see them. The fishy, musky scent from the quick-moving river brought back memories of his youth in Haran. He could hear the chatter of dock workers beginning their day over the gentle lapping of waves against the ships. Two cogs sat docked next to well-kept wooden piers while a small crew prepared a fishing vessel. "Hurry," Vidmar said. "We might be able to catch them before they push off." Vidmar ran to catch the captain; he heard Vatis's frantic breathing as the bard tried to keep up.

"Good morning," Vidmar called.

Two workers looked at each other confused, nodded, and carried on with their work without a word. A tall, slender man appeared and handed the two perplexed men a net. "Mornin'," he said, pulling up his trousers that were clearly too large.

"A fine day for fishing," Vidmar said with his hands on his hips.

"Aye," the man said. "It is."

"Can you take us to Vicus?" Vatis interjected. "We can pay."

Vidmar shook his head. *Damnit, Vatis, let me handle this.* He scowled at the bard and clenched his fists.

"Vicus, that's a ways south. I can't afford two days without fishin'," the sailor said.

Vatis began to speak again, but Vidmar quickly interjected. "I apologize for my companion's impulsiveness. Where are you fishing today?" Vidmar knew if they didn't want to spend every coin they had, he would have to negotiate a fair rate, which started with getting on the captain's good side.

"A few miles downriver, good fishin' next to the sandbar," the sailor said.

"Well, if you're heading downriver, perhaps we can ride along. We aren't afraid of a hard day's work, and my friend here is a terrific bard; he could entertain the whole crew," Vidmar said, draping his arm over Vatis's shoulders.

"My crew doesn't need help, and stories can't feed my family," the captain said. "If you want passage to Vicus. It'll cost ya 100 Kan, not a coin less."

100 Kan, how dumb does he think we are? "What about 50? Half now and the other half in Vicus," Vidmar said. *I doubt we've got 50 between us.*

The sailor spat into the river. "The price is 100."

Vidmar watched Vatis reach into his bag as he thought of another counteroffer. "What about…"

"Is this enough?" Vatis said, holding up an emerald the size of his thumbnail. *Where did you get that?* Vidmar thought. The gem had to be worth more than ten times the fare the captain was charging.

The captain's eyes widened, but he appeared to restrain himself as he scratched his chin, pretending to ponder the offer. "Aye, that'll do."

Damnit Vatis. I could have gotten him down to 50. "I hope this *generous* offer buys us a little urgency," Vidmar said, hoping Vatis picked up on his disappointment.

"Aye," the captain said.

A few miles downriver and a couple of hours later, Vatis finished his explanation for their hasty departure. *He's withholding information. It doesn't make sense.* Vidmar wanted to ask Kamet what he thought about Vatis's story, but the mercenary was too busy getting seasick to debate the merits of the bard's explanation.

"I'm going to kill you, Vidmar," Kamet said as he wiped his mouth with the back of his hand. "I'm," he started before vomiting over the ship's railing.

Vidmar rubbed his back like a mother soothing a sick child. "No one forced you to come," he said before turning his attention back to Vatis. "So, you deserted your guild, your friends, because you were *scared.*"

Vatis bit his thumbnail, avoiding eye contact with Vidmar. "I suppose you could say that," he said as his gaze drifted distantly to the sky.

"I told you he was a coward," Kamet said. The mercenary curled himself into a ball with his back against the ship's mast.

"I don't think you're in a position to call anyone a coward," Vidmar said, handing him a piece of stale bread.

Mia leaned over a rail near the bow of the ship. Vidmar was glad he sent her away while Vatis explained what had happened. For some reason, she seemed to admire Vatis. *It's better that she doesn't know the whole truth,* Vidmar thought. *Although I doubt Vatis told me everything.*

"I still don't understand why," Vidmar said, stepping next to Vatis. The bard slid further away. "If you ran then, why didn't you run from Zidane or in Yimser? Why did you save me in Haran? Those men are much more dangerous than common bandits."

Vatis licked his lips. Waves crashed against the slow-moving ship. "I want your story," he whispered.

"I gave you my story. It's not that interesting."

Vatis met Vidmar's gaze but quickly looked away. "You gave me a few chapters of your story, exciting chapters, no doubt, but far from whole. Your current quest is groundbreaking. The world will want it. I want it and intend to be there for the climax."

A piece of Vidmar was flattered that Vatis still wanted his story—a small piece. He didn't have children, so this would be a way to leave his mark on the world, a way to be remembered. Another part of him was outraged. He dragged Vatis halfway around the known world just for him to have another tale to tell in taverns. He'd lost his fingers because of Vatis. Worst of all, he thought they had become friends. Vidmar had never had many friends aside from Kamet. He succeeded alone; he survived alone. Vidmar had accepted being alone. *It's not worth it*, he thought, pushing his anger into his gut for it to simmer a little longer.

A gull scooped a scrap of bread off the deck, swooping over their heads, close enough to grab. The water thrummed in the wake of the silence between Vidmar and Vatis. The bard hung his head and walked away.

Vidmar followed Vatis to the stern, looking over the railing at the wake in the murky river behind the ship. He exhaled and turned toward Vatis. "The climax of my story happened long ago, Vatis. Everything after has been filler, padding before the inevitable conclusion. I have made enemies with two of the most powerful men in Emre. There is only one way my story ends, and it's not a happy one. Don't let yours end the same way."

Vatis stared vacantly into the water. "Unfortunately, that's how most stories end," Vatis said without blinking. Vidmar nodded, trying to think of something to say, but Vatis hummed a few ominous notes and began again. "It's what we do before the ending that matters. I want to help you finish your task. I want to be there when you find it and when you decide what to do with it." Vatis turned his head away, shielding his eyes.

Vidmar patted Vatis on the back. The bard still looked away. "So, you believe it's real, that there's actually a chance we can find it?" Vidmar asked.

Vatis finally met Vidmar's gaze. "It is real. I think you're closer than anyone has come before."

A bell rang as Vicus's docks appeared on the river's western shore. Vidmar couldn't help but smile. For the first time in years, he had hope. He still believed that Vatis was hiding something, but Vidmar was no stranger to secrets of his own. He decided to trust the bard and trust that whatever secrets Vatis had were better left hidden.

"Thank you, Vatis. I hope you're right."

MORE THAN A FARMER

Vidmar

Vidmar led the group down a dirt path that followed a meandering creek. The sound of the water trickling over stones distracted him from the constant thoughts of Vatis, Hobb, the crown, and his task. He watched a frog jump into the stream; it joined several croaking cousins who seemed to mock their slow pace. Mia ran off the road after a frog, at least half a dozen scattered in different directions. Her innocent smile as she rejoined the group reminded him of how young she was.

My path is too dangerous for her, Vidmar thought as he stepped over a remarkably well-maintained bridge that looked like it had been repainted recently. It had a deeper red hue than he remembered. Soon, the wispy tops of corn stalks came into view as they crested a small hill.

"Vidmar," Taldor said, leaping from the cornfield into the road. The dog, Igni, tottered out of the field behind the boy with its tail wagging.

Vidmar ruffled the boy's hair. "Not so loud, Taldor. You don't want Acer to hear."

The boy grabbed Vidmar's hand on top of his head and furrowed his brow. "What happened to your hands?" he shouted.

"Wolves."

Taldor tilted his head. "I'm starting to think you attract them or something," he said, peering around Vidmar's back. "There's more of you." His voice grew an octave deeper when he saw Mia. Vidmar smiled. "Where's Vatis?"

Vidmar turned, pointing down the road. "He's taking notes on a bird. He said something about a blackbird. I don't know. One minute, he's rushing us out of bed; the next, he's charting birds."

Taldor grinned. "He's a little strange."

"That we can agree on."

Another young man appeared out of the corn stalks to their left. He was a head taller than Vidmar with a patchy beard and broad shoulders. Two baskets of corn swayed in his hands as he strode forward. *Taldor's brother?* There was no denying it; they were practically twins aside from the older brother's height and sorry beard.

"Who is it, kid?" the young man called as he set his baskets down.

"Don't call me kid," Taldor said, his face reddening. "This is Vidmar–the one who stopped the wolves and saved our cows."

The young man raised his eyebrows. "You're something of a legend around here. I'm Ev."

"Nice to meet you, Ev," Vidmar said, shaking his hand. "These are my friends Kamet and Mia. The slow-moving bard down the road is Vatis."

Ev waved. "Hello. I've heard of Vatis. He was with you before, right?"

"The best bard I've ever heard," Taldor added.

"He's the only bard you've heard other than Pa and his after-dinner tales."

Taldor stomped his foot. His face grew beet-red. "That's not true. I've heard Steffen a few times at Cat's."

Ev laughed. "Fine, but compared to Steffen and Pa, a frog could be the best bard you've heard if it croaked loud enough."

Taldor rolled his eyes. "You're so funny, Evanor," the boy said, sticking his tongue out. "Come on, Vidmar. Pa will be excited to see you."

"Pa, excited?" Ev spat. "No chance."

Vidmar answered unrelenting questions from Taldor as they walked across the farm. It seemed like the boy's curiosity could never be satisfied. "I wouldn't put Yimser on your list of cities to visit when you get off this farm," Vidmar said after Taldor's last question. "Nothing good happens in Yimser, and it smells."

They passed through a wooden gate that led to the barn, where Hobb knelt in the dirt near a groaning cow. Acrid sickness wafted through the air, sour and deathly, overpowering the sweet scent of straw. Large, calloused hands stroked the cow's head as Hobb pushed water into its mouth with a syringe. His cane lay beside him. Etched into the side was a familiar triangular shape. *He is hiding something,* Vidmar thought. *How did I not see it before?*

"Pa," Taldor shouted.

"What is it, boy? Keep your voice down. You'll spook her," Hobb said, patting the cow.

"Sorry," Taldor said in an exaggerated whisper. Hobb sighed. "It's Vidmar and Vatis."

"What about them?" Hobb said, snatching his cane quickly.

"They're here."

"Hello, Hobb," Vidmar said warmly.

312

Hobb grunted as he pushed himself to his feet. Vidmar lunged to help him, but Ev tugged him backward. "Don't help. It only makes him angry," he whispered.

After a moment of struggle, Hobb straightened his back; he seemed to double in size. "I never thought we would see you again."

"Certainly not so soon," Vidmar said, eyeing Hobb's cane. "How are you faring?"

"My bones ache, and my grandsons are lazy," Hobb said. It seemed like a well-rehearsed answer. He rotated the etching on the cane backward like he noticed Vidmar's examination. "And my cow is dying," he added before Vidmar could reply. "Has the eternal darkness reached our farm? Have all the crops died?" Hobb asked, pointing his cane at Ev.

Ev shrugged and elbowed Taldor. "No."

"Good. You had me worried. Why else would you be putzing around when there is work to be done? You can catch up with these men at supper. You there, girl. Yes, you. Help Taldor pick cherries. He has a tough time on his own," Hobb said, his rough voice issuing an undeniable command. Mia looked at Vidmar for approval. He nodded. There was something about the ease of Hobb's authority that both comforted and scared him. Taldor shuffled his feet. "Go on."

"This way," Taldor said quietly to Mia. She looked back to Vidmar. He reassured her by mouthing 'go on.' "Mia, right?" Taldor asked as they walked out the door.

"Now for you," Hobb said to Ev.

Ev tilted his head sideways. "What about me?"

"Did you harvest the corn?"

"Yes."

"Did you take care of those wasps on the side of the house?"

Evanor held out his left arm. Two bright red bumps protruded from the skin. "Yes."

Hobb looked around the barn. "Well, then cut the grass," he said, pointing to a scythe leaning against the wall.

"I did yesterday."

Hobb snorted like a horse coming to a stop after a long ride. "Here," he said, handing the syringe to Ev. "She needs water every half hour."

Ev took the syringe and knelt beside the cow. "Is she going to make it?" Flies swarmed around the sick creature. One landed on Hobb's forehead; he brushed it away with his sausage-like fingers.

"If you do what you're told, boy," he said, walking out of the barn. Vidmar, Vatis, and Kamet followed closely behind without being told. Vidmar turned to see Ev shaking his head but following Hobb's orders. "And pick some radishes for dinner," Hobb called without breaking stride.

"Yes, Pa."

They followed Hobb to the house. Igni bathed in the sun on the porch. His black and white speckled head remained perfectly still, but his long tail thumped against the wood as they approached. Vidmar scratched behind the dog's ears. Igni, begging for more, rolled onto his back, directing Vidmar to move from his ears to his stomach, to which Vidmar smirked and obeyed.

Hobb grunted and gestured to the table. "Tea," he said as more of a statement than a question, like it was time for tea, and Vidmar and his friends happened to be in the right spot at the right time.

"Yes, please," Vatis said, sitting down.

Kamet leaned against the doorframe, scanning the house, probably for points of entry. That was a hard habit to break. The house had an inviting aroma of oak with a subtle herbaceous hint. Everything had a proper place; mugs were aligned neatly on a shelf to the right of the window, the floor was immaculate for a farmhouse, and even the coats hanging on hooks near the stairs were aligned in order of length. Vidmar pulled out the chair facing the window, his back to the fireplace.

Hobb returned with a black kettle and hung it above the fire to warm. "Do I want to know what happened?" He said, sitting at the head of the table, gesturing to Vidmar's hands.

"Probably not," Vidmar said. He closed his fist, itching the stumps of his missing fingers.

Hobb nodded and moved on. "How's the arm?"

Vatis flailed it about haphazardly. "Good as new. Thank you."

The old man sniffed and narrowed his eyes. "You're a fast healer," he said, studying Vatis. "Very fast."

The whistling kettle broke an awkwardly long silence. Worn floorboards creaked as Hobb meandered to the kettle, towel in hand. He grabbed four mugs with one hand and placed them on the table. "I hope you take your tea black. I don't have sugar, and I'm not sharing what little honey I have left," he said, filling the mugs.

"Thank you," Vidmar said. Steam rose from the warm mug between his hands. "Are we intruding, Hobb? If so, I apologize."

Hobb glared at Vidmar, then exhaled. "No, you're not intruding, but I don't take kindly to mercenaries on my farm. No offense." He said, nodding to Kamet. "How much did you have to pay for one that big?"

Vidmar laughed. "Kamet is one of my oldest friends. We didn't hire him."

"But he is a sellsword?" Hobb asked, sipping his tea.

"He is many things."

Hobb snorted, then nodded. "What about the girl? Why is she with you?" Vidmar clenched his jaw. *I'm supposed to be questioning you, old man.*

Luckily, Vatis answered before Vidmar. "She helped me in Yimser, and in return, I told her she could travel with me for a while."

"How did she help you?"

"She guided me through the city."

"Yimser is not large. You shouldn't need a guide," Hobb said, looking out the window toward the grove.

What are you getting at? Again, Vatis replied before Vidmar could. "In my experience, it is best to have a guide in a new city— a local. Mia was excellent. She showed me what to avoid and what shops had the best food."

Hobb huffed. He didn't appear satisfied with the answer. "The road is no place for a girl that young. How old is she? Nine?"

"She's eleven," Vidmar answered. "And truthfully, she's more useful on the road than Vatis."

"That I cannot deny," Vatis said, laughing.

"Very well," Hobb said. He leaned forward. His inquisitive expression turned grim. "Why are you here? To give Taldor more weapons? Or to snoop around the tower again?"

Vidmar looked at Vatis, then at Kamet. It seemed he was going to be the one to answer the question. It was his quest, after all. "I meant no offense when I gave Taldor the knife, but as for the tower. Yes, it's why we returned." He paused. *How do I ask this? Hobb doesn't play games. I might as well get straight to the point.* "What association do you have with The Pact?" Hobb's expression didn't change. His eyes never wavered from Vidmar's. "Are you a member? A descendant? I saw the symbol on your cane, and no farm has ever needed a defensive tower," Vidmar continued his line of questioning. "What are you hiding?"

Silence filled the room until scratching paws strummed against the floor. Hobb's tongue poked out through his lips before it retreated snake-like into his mouth. Gray hairs on his chin stood out like spikes. "Get out," he growled.

I've gone too far, Vidmar thought. "Hobb, please."

"Get out," He repeated, standing and pointing to the door.

"Hobb. I need answers," Vidmar pleaded.

"Get out. All of you." He opened his mouth to yell louder, but Ev appeared through the back door.

"What's going on?" Ev said. A dirty rag in his hand dripped onto the floor.

"None of your concern, boy,"

"Hobb, listen. Please," Vidmar said, holding up his hands defensively.

Hobb's lip quivered, but he looked at Ev before sitting down. Red flames reflected in his cloudy eyes.

"What's going on?" Ev repeated, sounding much older than he appeared.

Vidmar and Hobb ignored the question. Instead, they stared at each other as if searching the other's soul. The farmer grunted when his examination was complete. Vidmar didn't flinch. "Please, Hobb," he said without breaking eye contact.

"You need to leave, boy," Hobb said to Ev while sipping his tea.

"Why?" Ev said. "I'm a man. Taldor won't be back for another hour."

"You're a boy. Help your brother. Don't come back until sundown."

Ev clenched his fist, biting the knuckle of his index finger. "Pa."

"It's not up for debate. Take the dog with you."

Ev ground his fist into his thigh. "Fine, keep your secrets – like you always do. Come Igni." The dog followed, head hanging low like he was disappointed he didn't get to stay either. The crackling of the fire, Vatis's slurping, and shuffling footsteps outside were the only noises that dared to emerge while they waited for Ev to disappear behind the cornfield; then Hobb nodded toward Vidmar.

Vidmar decided to use a friendlier, less direct approach. "What can you tell me about this?" he said, pulling the stone out of his pack.

Hobb's expression remained stoic. "Looks like a rock."

Vidmar closed his eyes. *So that's how you're going to play it.* "It has been confirmed to be a messaging stone of The Pact by a reliable source in Yimser. And Vatis. They believe it says: 'It lies near the dead.' Vatis thinks 'lies' means to be untruthful, but Gaffer was unclear."

At the mention of Gaffer, Hobb perked up. "Did you say Gaffer? The shopkeeper? Wiry old man likes coffee for some reason."

How do you know Gaffer? I thought you never left your farm. This revelation only raised more questions. "Yes," he said. "Gaffer's Goods. He's a friend."

"And he helped you willingly? Or did this oaf *persuade* him?"

Vidmar could hear Kamet's teeth grind; his chainmail jingled as he shifted. He was showing remarkable restraint. *He knows how much these answers mean.*

"Vidmar is more," Vatis started. Vidmar scowled at him. "Persuasive than Kamet. There aren't many who are more *persuasive* in all of Emre." *Are you threatening him?* Vidmar didn't think the bard was capable of threats.

Hobb looked as if he was having the same thoughts as Vidmar. "So it seems," he said plainly, taking a long drink from his tea. An orange sun began to fall behind the cornstalks. Crickets chirped their synchronized, unchanging song. Hobb set his mug down, rubbed the bridge of his nose, and exhaled. "Why do you think I can help you? Did Gaffer mention me? What else did he say about this stone?"

Vidmar felt a weight lift off his chest. His tensed muscles relaxed into the chair. "He told me it says, 'It lies near the dead.' Vatis thought the same thing, but he thinks lies could have a double meaning; he also thought that you could help, something about your watchtower."

"It's not my watchtower, and I don't care what a bard thinks," Hobb said quickly. Vatis grabbed his chest and mimicked, pulling a knife out. "It lies near the dead," he said slowly, savoring the words. "I haven't the slightest clue what that means. What's 'it'? Or what do you hope 'it' is?"

Do I tell him? It could put him and his family in danger. I must. "Greco's crown."

Hobb rocked like he was soothing a baby. Again, his tongue poked through his lips; his cheeks reddened. Red-hot anger boiled beneath the surface like lava. "Tell me you're joking," he said at last.

"Let me explain," Vidmar said. Desperate for answers, Vidmar told his story. The whole story, with one exception. Elisa. They didn't need to know about her, at least not everything. He started at the beginning, his childhood in Haran, the death of his father, Kandrian's recruitment, his role in his uprising, and his eventual betrayal. He quickly retold his escape from Jegon before he divulged his relationship with Alcin before power corrupted him. Vidmar described work as a treasure hunter but didn't disclose specifics until his quest to find Greco's Crown. He finished with what he remembered from his confrontation with Alcin, how he lost his fingers, and how they arrived back in Vicus. "We boarded a ship in Dartmore yesterday, and here we are today."

INTERLUDE

Mia

Why does Vidmar keep sending me away? Mia thought, shuffling her feet alongside Taldor as they approached the grove. The boy hadn't stopped talking since they left the barn. Question after question, Mia's short, sharp answers did nothing to deter him. Neither did her silence.

"What's life like in Yimser?" Taldor asked, rephrasing his question for at least the third time.

Mia didn't answer last time, so she felt obligated to humor him. "It's great. There's a murder every day, and most foreigners are killed for no reason," she said, exaggerating Yimser's worst rumors. But, in truth, it was fine. Life on the streets of Yimser was all she had known, and she was alive. *That's more than most people can say.*

"Really?" Taldor said, either terrified or excited. Mia couldn't tell. "Pa says it has a bad reputation, but it's not nearly as bad as Haran or Barna–in terms of safety, I guess. He has an old friend who lives there. He runs a shop or something. I can't remember his name."

Mia sighed. "You talk a lot."

Taldor laughed. "Pa always says curiosity will be the death of me. I'm sorry. I get excited about new things, especially about places other than Vicus. It's just so dull here, day after day, it's the same: breakfast, tend the crops, do more chores, then dinner and lessons. Sometimes, Pa changes the lessons to stories, but other than that, it's the same every day. Ev gets to go away once a season, but I'm stuck."

"I know how you feel," Mia said, twirling her hair. She liked the way her hair felt wrapped around her finger. It comforted her.

"At least you get to travel with Vidmar. I would give anything to travel with him; he only stayed here two days, but he seemed smart and funny and saved our cows. And he gave me this knife. I've been practicing throwing but still can't get it to stick. I must be doing something wrong," Taldor said, fumbling with a green-handled blade with some gem embedded in the hilt. He threw the knife at a tree. It struck hilt-first and fell into a mess of rotten cherries on the ground. "Damnit," he said, wiping the blade off on his pants. "How long have you been traveling with him?"

Mia was never good at identifying time; some weeks felt like days, and some days felt like weeks. She never found it an important thing to track. It just seemed to be a way to calculate the hours between meals, and meals for her came very infrequently.

"I'm not sure. A couple of weeks, I guess," Mia said. She stopped and pulled her finger from her knotty hair. "Vidmar is great. He taught me how to set traps, start a fire, and throw a knife properly."

She held out her hand. Taldor slowly handed the blade over. His fingers clung to the hilt like it was a solid bar of gold. Mia cracked her neck, set her feet, and threw; the blade whizzed through the air and stuck in the tree. Taldor's jaw dropped; for the first time that afternoon, he was speechless. Mia retrieved the knife and handed it back to the unusually silent boy. She smirked. "Nothing to say?"

Taldor's face reddened. He quickly placed the knife back in its sheath. "What about Vatis? Pa doesn't like him. He complained about him for a week after they left. Too nosey, I guess."

Vatis. Darkness, I don't know. Mia prided herself on her ability to judge people. It was a skill she developed to survive on the streets of Yimser. Who would spare food? Who to trust? Who to avoid? "He's a little strange, but he's smart," Mia started, carefully choosing each word before she decided to focus only on his positive traits, glossing over his questionable ones. "And he's a terrific storyteller."

"Oh, I know. He told us a couple of stories about Dabin. They were incredible."

"He told the story of Vidmar's escape from Jegon at the tourney. I wonder what he will tell in Barna."

"Vatis won the tourney?" Taldor said, leaping in front of her. "I had to convince him to enter. I knew he would win," he said, his eyes beaming with excitement.

Mia stepped around Taldor. "Yes, he won." *Kind of.* "But don't ask him about it. He finally stopped playing around with his invitation."

A furry, brown creature with a bushy tail nibbled on a cherry, then darted up a tree to their left as they got too close. Mia watched the small rat-like animal leap from branch to branch. She ran to get a better look. Small twigs vibrated in the air, marking its path. It chirped like a bird before she lost sight of it in a small nook. "Was that a squirrel?" Mia asked. "I read about them once."

Taldor chuckled. "Yes. Are there no squirrels in Yimser?"

"We have rats and crows and cats, oh and Sal," she said, hoping the cute animal would pop its head out of the hole.

"Vidmar showed me how to set a snare for a squirrel, but I've never seen a real one before. I'm never setting one of those traps again. They're too cute."

"Pa hates them. They like to eat our corn."

Mia tried to mimic its chirping sound, but the stubborn creature remained hidden.

"It won't come out until we've gone, but you'll probably see another. They're all over the place. Them and rabbits."

"Really? I saw some rabbits in the forest, but I want to see more squirrels."

Taldor laughed and began climbing a tree. He looked like the squirrel, hurrying up the tree confidently without fear of falling. "Who's the big, scary-looking guy?"

"Huh, oh. Kamet?"

"Yeah. Toss the basket up here."

Mia threw the woven basket up to Taldor. He caught it with one hand. "I like him. He's a little intimidating, and as long as he doesn't drink too much, he's fun. He's Vidmar's friend, so that's good enough for me. Are there any squirrels up there?"

"No, but you'll be the first to know if I see one."

Taldor filled the basket with cherries that were more purple than red, different from any she had seen in Yimser. She picked one off the ground, wiped it on her shirt, and bit into it. It was delightfully sweet, less tart than the red cherries her mother had been fond of, simply delicious. She spat the seed out and searched the ground for more. "These are so good," she said, pulling the stem out with a cherry between her teeth. A brownish crack ran down the next cherry she picked up. It seemed like a waste, but she threw it away.

"When the merchants come through, Pa always buys a small bag of sugar and makes a pie. If it weren't for that pie, I would have run away by now," Taldor said, jumping off the tree, basket in hand.

"Really?" Mia asked. She was warming up to the curious boy. There weren't many kids around her age in Yimser, not under the river anyway. Most kids died before their fifth birthday. "Your farm is amazing. I would never leave."

As Taldor began to speak, a tall man stomped into the grove, cursing worse than any drunk she'd heard on the streets near Geoff's. "Fucking unbelievable. Goddamn secrets. I need to get the fuck out of here," the man said. Mia stiffened and hid behind a tree reflexively.

"It's alright," Taldor said, tapping her shoulder. "It's only Ev."

Mia poked her head out, watching Ev approach. He continued to curse as he kicked off the tops of mushrooms; the gray porous material exploded into the air. An innocent tree was his next target. He slapped the trunk so hard that pieces of bark fell off. "Damnit," he screamed, shaking his hand.

"What's wrong," Taldor asked timidly.

Ev rubbed his palm. "He fucking sent me away like a little kid."

Taldor looked at Mia. "They sent us away too." He stepped closer to his brother.

Ev put a hand on his shoulder, relaxing. "I know. I'm sorry," he said, taking a deep breath. "I shouldn't have yelled. I'm just, ah, I'm pissed. He lets me go to Haran and Barna but won't let me listen to a conversation."

Taldor shuffled away from Ev and leaned against a tree. "At least you get to leave."

Ev's anger seemed to dissipate. "You'll get to leave soon. I didn't get to go anywhere until I was fifteen."

"I know. I just want to see the world."

Mia couldn't believe the petty argument between these two brothers, who lived on an enormous farm with enough food for a small village. "I don't understand," she said softly at first, then grew more confident as she continued. "You both have a wonderful life." Mia paused, biting her lip to restrain herself. "Last winter, I had to eat a cat. A cute, scared cat that trusted me, but there was no food. The bakeries didn't even throw out their moldy bread." She sniffed back tears. "I lived in a shack under a bridge for the past year. Then, I spent a month in a prison cell. If I hadn't been a girl, they would have killed me. And now, I've traveled; I've run from guards, mercenaries, and worse. I haven't seen much of the world, but what I have seen isn't that great. You have a wonderful home; I don't understand why you are so eager to leave."

Taldor rubbed the back of his neck. "I get bored of the same chores every day. I'm sorry, Mia."

"Me too," Ev said, still rubbing his palm.

Mia ate another cherry. She didn't mean to talk so much, let alone lecture two strangers about their lives. Her face felt hot, and her palms were sweating; she needed a distraction. They spent the next hour talking about the world, eating cherries, and taking turns throwing the knife at various targets. Mia couldn't remember a time when she had more fun. When the last rays of sunlight disappeared, they walked back to the farmhouse, laughing and exchanging stories.

A STORY WORTH TELLING

Vatis

Vatis watched Hobb and Vidmar measure each other like masons debating the best way to build a castle. They had gone back and forth for hours but hadn't progressed far. Much to Vatis's chagrin, no secrets had been revealed. Sure, he learned a little more about Vidmar, and yes, that would help with his current story, but no secrets.

He craved secrets. They were his trade, after all. Every story was a secret until it was written or performed, and nothing was more thrilling than revealing a shocking tale.

Hobb stood and sighed. His chair screeched against the hardwood floor. "That's enough for tonight," he said, rolling his head shoulder to shoulder. His joints popped, and his cane tapped against the floorboards. "The boys will be back soon. We can pick this back up in the morning."

Vidmar rubbed his eyes. "I've been searching for this damn crown for years. What's another day?" Vatis was unsure if he was sarcastic. His voice sounded weary.

Hobb groaned and disappeared into the kitchen. The farmhouse had a different feel than it had just a few weeks ago. It felt heavy, like a mist on a brisk morning. Nothing blatant had changed; everything still had its proper place. All the knickknacks, tools, mugs, and books were lined up perfectly on their corresponding shelves, precisely the same as they had been. *What's changed?* Vatis thought, feeling his throat tighten. He needed to move; he needed to do something, go somewhere. *Is it the tower?*

"Do you need help in there, Hobb," Vatis called, mustering as much enthusiasm as he could and hoping that preparing a meal could distract him from his meandering thoughts.

"No," Hobb snorted over the clanging of pots and pans. The old farmer had been cold to him since they arrived.

Just tell Vidmar what you know, old man, Vatis thought. He didn't want to stay another day; they needed to keep moving. *Vidmar has to find the crown soon. I need his story for Barna.* Also, the tower loomed large in his mind, casting a shadow over their meeting; if it called to him again, he didn't know if he could resist.

Vatis started pacing, occasionally stopping to examine the spines of the books on the shelf next to the fireplace. One book caught his eye, *Beyond the Kaharn Desert* by Artgal Cairbre. *How did I miss this before? Why would a farmer have a book about crossing an impassable desert? It's a Cairbre – just facts and theories; this isn't a bedtime story.* His head felt light, searching for answers. Vatis slunk back to the table and sat down as Kamet approached Vidmar.

"Are you sure he can help?" Kamet whispered. It was the first time the mercenary had spoken since they entered the farmhouse. "Something about him rubs me the wrong way."

Vidmar didn't look up. He just nodded and whispered. "He knows something."

A few moments later, Mia, Taldor, and Ev strode onto the porch with a basket brimming with dark red cherries. The old dog followed lazily behind, distracted by a sudden itch near his tail. They seemed tense too. *What happened to them?*

Vidmar seemed to notice as well. "Are you alright, Mia?" He asked as they entered.

She spat a cherry pit through the window onto the porch. Her lips were dyed a deep red like many of the noblewomen in Barna. "I'm fine," she said, sitting in the chair next to Vidmar.

"Um, that's Ev's chair, Mia," Taldor said

Ev laughed. "It's fine, little brother. I'll get a stool from the barn."

"Check on the cow while you're in there," Hobb called from the kitchen. *If Hobb heard that, did he hear Kamet and Vidmar?* Vatis thought. Every new revelation about Hobb raised more questions.

Ev huffed, clicked his tongue, and stomped out the front door.

The ripe cherries on the table looked delicious. "Can I have some of these, Taldor?" Vatis's mouth watered in anticipation.

The young boy looked distracted as he watched his brother through the window. "What?" he asked.

"Can I have a cherry or two?" Vatis repeated.

"Oh, yes. Have as many as you want. Mia has eaten a whole tree's worth already," Taldor said, sliding the basket closer to Vatis.

He grabbed a maroon cherry with an emerald stem, popped it into his mouth, and bit. The flesh was crisp; the juice was sweet and not too tart. "Wow," he said, grabbing a handful. "These are delicious."

Kamet grabbed one, pulled the stem out, and spit the seed through the open window behind him. "Hmm, good. I like the bright red ones better. You know, the cherries that are more sour than sweet."

"People tell me you're a bit too sour," Vidmar said.

"Who?" Kamet said, biting through another cherry.

Vidmar started to speak. "If you say, my mother. I will shove cherries down your throat until you choke." Vidmar winked at Taldor as the boy and Mia laughed.

Vatis ate his pile of cherries as he watched Mia and Taldor throw seeds at each other. Vidmar and Kamet talked in the corner, and the old black dog slobbered as it slept near the front door. Mia threw another pit at Taldor, but the boy ducked, and it struck an unsuspecting Ev as he returned with two short stools.

"Hey," he said. Vatis couldn't tell if he was smiling or grimacing.

"Sorry," Mia said, twirling a finger through her hair. Her cheeks grew almost as red as the cherries.

Ev picked the seed up and threw it at Taldor. It hit the boy in the middle of his forehead.

"Ouch," Taldor said, rubbing the red spec that the cherry pit left behind.

"If you're going to throw something at Taldor, make sure you hit him," Ev said, tussling his brother's brown hair. Taldor pushed Ev away.

"Nobody is throwing anything else in my house," Hobb said, emerging from the kitchen with a large ceramic plate full of dried meat, cheeses, and an assortment of vegetables, all neatly sliced into bite-sized pieces. "It's time to eat."

They ate in silence, aside from the chomping of teeth and the slurping of ale. To his credit, Taldor tried to break the increasingly uncomfortable quietness by asking Vidmar about his escape from Jegon, but Hobb stopped Vidmar before he could respond. "We can have a story after supper, but not that one."

"Why?" Taldor asked with a mouthful of meat.

"Not that one." And that was the end of the discussion. They finished in even deeper silence; drinks were quieter, teeth chewed softer, and even Igni stopped whining for scraps.

What felt like hours later, Taldor and Ev cleared the table while Mia disappeared to the outhouse. Again, Vatis, Vidmar, Kamet, and Hobb examined each other. Vatis felt outmatched in this game. He didn't know what he was looking for; all Vatis saw was a mole he hadn't noticed on Hobb's cheek, Vidmar's insistent itching of his missing fingers, and Kamet's boar-like breathing. *What do they see in me?*

"Done," Taldor said excitedly. "Will you tell us a story tonight, Vatis?"

Darkness, anything to take a break from this game. "Why, of course. That is, if it's alright with you, Hobb?"

Hobb grumbled something under his breath. "I said we could have a story."

"You're grouchy tonight, Pa," Taldor said, sitting in his seat.

Hobb scowled. "Never tell a man they're grouchy, boy. It only makes matters worse."

"Especially when they are always grouchy," Ev added from the stool that he had moved closer to the fireplace.

Vatis thought he saw a hint of a smile underneath the old man's beard, but it quickly evaporated with a dismissive grunt. "Well then," Vatis started. "What story would you like to hear? A classic tale like Mia-The-Maiden, another story of Dabin, maybe a romance?"

"No, not a romance," Taldor answered quickly, sticking his tongue out like he tasted something foul.

Vatis laughed. "How about a story about Vidmar?"

Taldor and Mia nodded excitedly, but Vidmar frowned. "I'd like to hear something else," he said. Hobb grunted in agreement.

"Fine, no Mia-The-Maiden, no Dabin, no romance, no Vidmar. Any suggestions?" Vatis asked.

Mia shrugged. Ev held out his palms unknowingly. Taldor hummed and looked at the ceiling as if it might have an idea written up there. Hobb grumbled more softly than usual. "Tell us of the fall of Slavanes Greco," he said, looking directly at Vidmar.

Vatis scratched his chin. "That is a story I know, a formidable tale. Not many stories of Emre are more powerful, and powerful stories have consequences. Some who tell this are killed, some become heroes, and others are forgotten – a bard's worst fate. I'll start with a poem, and I hope it is received better than the last time I told it." He nodded at Vidmar before he began.

The coronation of a crownless king
The subject's obedience it did bring
A crown stolen from the unworthy
Taken by a martyr without curtsey

To a legend, the crownless king is bound
Only a Pact knows where it is found
'tis a search thousands tried
In lonely homes, mothers cried
'tis a search that all failed
In broken homes, widows wailed

A lone Pact knows where it has strayed
Such treasure cannot be remade
Rumors of ancient power reside
In jewels of white the magic provide
A simple ornament that brought fire
A legend that toppled an empire

Is he a farmer with no crop
Is it affirmation or merely a prop
Is he king without a crown
His people have spoken. They won't kneel down

Vidmar fiddled with his missing fingers, contrasting the thick fingers that scratched beneath Hobb's chin. "That's a dangerous poem," the old man said, drinking from his mug. Mia and Taldor looked at each other, confused.

"You have no idea," Vatis said, avoiding eye contact with Vidmar. He exhaled. "I began that story with a poem because it's challenging to convey the legend of Slavanes Greco in a single story. He's the king who burned witches, the king who killed monsters, the king who destroyed magic, and the king who reigned both too long and too short. Greco has puzzled bards for centuries, but we have reached a consensus regarding his origin and downfall. Tonight, you will hear a tragic tale of the collapse and death of the most powerful man Emre has ever known."

"Pfft," Kamet said into the bottom of his ale. It echoed like a trumpet in the small room. "Dinardo was the most powerful man in the history of Emre."

Hobb cracked his neck when Kamet mentioned Dinardo. "Who's that?" Taldor asked.

"You don't know about Dinardo and The Pact?" Mia said, uncurling her finger from her robin's nest hair.

"The Pact sounds familiar," Taldor said.

"It's not real, is it?" Ev said, leaning closer.

Hobb has hidden The Pact from them. It looked as though Vidmar had the same thought as the treasure hunter eyed Hobb more thoroughly than before.

"The Pact is real," Vatis said, continuing his story. Hobb bit his upper lip, his crooked lower teeth sticking out like a boar, but he didn't stop Vatis. "The Pact is real," he repeated. "And they do play a part in this tale." *I'm sure Hobb knew that. So why would he suggest this story?* Vatis took a drink and continued. "But let's not get ahead of ourselves. No more interruptions, Kamet. This is a long story, and I cannot afford to get sidetracked."

THE FALL OF SLAVANES GRECO

Vatis

Vatis looked around the room; everyone waited patiently, except for Hobb; the farmer seemed to study every move he made. Vatis tried to ignore the old man and focus on the rest of his audience. No one was too drunk or had a generational hatred of foreigners. He was in his element – a fire gently warming the cozy house, a crisp breeze in the late-summer air, a bittersweet ale in his mug, and a story frolicking on his tongue.

"Right," he began. "Our story opens in Barna, as one might expect. King Slavanes Greco has been on the throne for nearly three decades. He has grown old and fat and complacent. His only son, Davor, leads his armies against the Numerian uprising in the south. Rumors have started to spread of another threat growing in the north. A group of rebels called The Pact with a simple mission – protect the forgotten and dethrone Greco."

Vatis stopped. *How can I coax more information out of Hobb?* "Greco didn't consider them a threat. The technologically advanced Numerians had innovative siege weapons, the world's best navy, and a tribe of loyal giants – they were the *real* threat. The Pact was a group of uneducated rebels led by a charismatic trickster named Dinardo. Some say he could use magic. Others say he was a fantastic performer who deceived his opponents with sleight-of-hand, but all agree, he was deadly with a blade."

Vatis sipped the last of his ale, pushing the empty mug toward Taldor. The boy took the hint and quickly retrieved a pitcher from the kitchen. *Where do I go from here?* Dethroning stories were usually straightforward – rebels rise quicker than expected and overthrow a complacent king. This story happened many times throughout the history of Emre; in fact, it happened just eight years ago when Kandrian Ambita unseated Pavao Begic. Begic was a thoroughly idiotic and delusional king who focused on trifles like crossing the Kaharn Desert and preparing for The Final Darkness. The Church of Eternal Darkness owed Begic thanks; without his devotion, the religion would have stayed tucked in caverns where it belonged.

Vatis realized he'd exaggerated his pause too long as Mia's curt nods urged him to continue. "As I was saying," he said, clearing his throat. "Greco did not view The Pact as a threat and paid them little heed, but in the Islingrey Mountains, that acorn grew into a sapling, and its bark began to harden. Now, we know the players: Greco, Numeria, and The Pact; let's advance to the Harvest feast. Greco held an enormous festival with bards, performers, exotic merchants, and duels yearly. This year, Greco opened the duels to everyone in the Emre except for Numerians. Anyone who could pay the modest entry fee and hold a sword was eligible for the grand prize – the lordship of Numeria. As you can imagine, hundreds of vagabonds, rogues, sellswords, farmers, and soldiers entered. With a field this large and a prize so valuable, Greco felt a need to raise the stakes. Yields were outlawed; every duel was to the death."

Igni interrupted the story as he scratched the door, wanting to go outside. "Sorry," Taldor said, opening the creaky-hinged door. He sat back down with his head propped up by his upturned palms.

"Can you pass that pitcher?" Vidmar asked. "Thank you." He filled his cup, and Kamet's after the mercenary leaned forward eagerly.

Once everyone returned to their comfortable, attentive postures, Vatis continued. "Once the new rules were announced, a few dropped out, but fewer than you would imagine. The chance to become lord of Numeria was too great, even if it meant losing one's life. The leader of The Pact, Dinardo, entered the tourney. His skill with a blade was legendary, but his captains felt the risk was too significant. If he were to die, their cause would be lost.

Dinardo laughed at his pessimistic captains. 'Greco has invited me to his doorstep and given me lordship of his biggest rival. We cannot fail; our cause is just, and our hearts are strong. If I falter, another shall take my place.'

His enthusiasm and confidence persuaded his captains. A week later, Dinardo and two companions left their stronghold in the mountains and began the journey to Barna. During this time, Greco grew proud of his scheme for the entry fees alone paid for the feast, and he felt that a simple duelist would be easy to control in Numeria, even if his hand-selected champion, Pylades, didn't win. Pylades was Greco's personal guard, a half-giant, natural-born killer whose gold-handled morning star's spikes were dyed crimson from its victim's blood. Other than Greco, there was no man more feared in all Emre. The giant was only Greco's guard because the King was the only man ever to defeat him in combat, but that is a story for a different day," Vatis took a long drink of the sour ale, notes of cherry sang sweet songs on his lips.

Taking advantage of the pause, the ever-inquisitive Taldor asked a question. "I thought Pylades was a full giant, and his flail could anchor a boat on the Camil River."

"Common mistake," Vatis said. "Many of my predecessors had a penchant for exaggeration. While there was still one tribe of pure-bred giants in those days, most cherished nature and detested violence. Half-giants like Pylades were cruel, hard folk who lived on the desert's outskirts. Though I'm still not entirely sure why they are called half-giants, men were about half as tall as real giants by all accounts, and I've seen a half-giant who was twice the size of me. Most texts and scholars agree that giants are thinner and taller, while half-giants are thicker and more broad-shouldered. Anyway, we have gone off course. Pylades was a menacing half-giant who used a morningstar, not a flail."

"Sorry," Taldor said shyly.

"No need to apologize, Taldor. It was a good question."

"Show me a decent warrior who uses a flail, and I'll show you the path through the Kaharn," Kamet said, slurring his words slightly.

Vidmar laughed. "I saw a young officer ride into battle waving a flail about like a child with a stick, only to have an arrow plunge into his chest as soon as he was in range. They look frightening mounted on a wall, but I agree with Kamet. A flail is useless in a real fight."

"We aren't here to debate the merit of weapons. Continue, please," Hobb said.

"Thank you, Hobb," Vatis said. *Why is he so keen to hear this story?*

"Where were we? Dinardo and his companions are traveling to Barna. Greco is preparing for the feast. I've introduced Pylades; ah, yes, to Numeria we go. Alanas Fadus, the self-proclaimed King of Numeria, led an assault on Davor's forces outside a small lumber mill that would later become the town of Aswar. Well, I suppose I should back up slightly; Fadus valued knowledge and technology above all things. He craved it. While Fadus was quite the scholar and inventor, most of Numeria's advancements can be attributed to Euclio, his Master of Knowledge. Euclio recently invented the ballista, not as deadly as the modern version we have today but effective enough to wreak havoc on a battlefield. Let's summarize without getting into battle strategy by saying Davor led the world's finest infantry unit, so fine that he brought little to no cavalry. The legion of one hundred ballistae mowed down the infantry like grass under a scythe. Davor himself was brought down by one of the massive bolts. His body was later displayed like a flag on the walls until his corpse fell into the moat. It was a devastating defeat for Greco, personally and militarily."

Vatis scratched his chin. *Where do I go from here? We can skim the Numeria conflict and focus on Dinardo, Greco, and the duels.* He ripped off a chunk of fresh, brown bread; the light, airy inside was sweet, melting in his mouth. He tore off another piece and continued.

"Greco was outraged. In one defeat, he lost his only male heir and his foothold in the south. There was only one small regiment of Cavalry keeping Numeria from marching. He wrote in his journal the day he heard the news:

'My heart has been ripped from my chest. I am empty. After the festival, I shall muster my final assault on Fadus, the usurper, and put this nonsense to rest.'

Greco's descent into madness had begun. His advisors urged him to show restraint; Greco wanted to join the duels to prove his worth, but Pylades vowed to win in his honor. While unhappy, the King was satisfied. Now, let's return to Dinardo. Word had reached him of the Numerian's victory and the death of Davor. He knew the King would be desperate.

He said to his companions, 'Fortune favors us, my friends. For the gods have distracted our enemy and left him vulnerable.'

His companions were weary; they thought that Greco would become reckless. And they were right. Reckless is the best way to describe Greco's actions over the next week. He drank himself into belligerence by noon every day, executed every prisoner in his cells, and dispatched his navy toward Numeria. Meanwhile, Dinardo and his friends arrived in Barna with a day to spare before the first duels."

Vatis looked at Hobb, but the old man scowled and nibbled on a piece of dried beef. The rest of his audience eagerly awaited the climax of the story. Ev pulled his stool closer, Taldor's wide brown eyes rarely blinked, and Mia stopped eating cherries.

"Right, here we are, the first day of the duels. Now, I must include this, in his impulsive rashness, Greco added traps to the arena. He wrote this in a nearly ineligible script the night before the duels:

'If the cowards won't let me duel, I'll take lives with spikes, pits, and flames.'

We don't know what he meant by flames, but we know that he added a ring of spikes to impale any duelist who ventured too far away from their opponent and two large pits, one with snakes and the other with stakes. Dinardo toured the arena before his first duel. His companions once again urged him to reconsider and withdraw.

He said, 'It's too late, my friends, but this is good news; perhaps my more qualified opponents will find an unfortunate death.'

Dinardo's optimism was a trait many admired, a quality that won him many followers. His first match was against a rabid-looking beggar, who somehow collected enough coin to enter the duels. Most duelists will tell you that desperation is not ideal for competition; it works well on a battlefield but leads to mistakes in the arena. The match was over seconds after it began. Dinardo positioned himself in front of the pit. The crazed branch-wielding beggar charged, trying to push Dinardo into the hole, but he sidestepped and watched his opponent tumble to his death."

Hobb coughed. The spasms escalated from a short throat-clearing to violent tremors. Ev and Taldor seemed unconcerned. *This must happen often,* Vatis thought. *Maybe that's why he's humoring us. His days are numbered.* Hobb wiped a speck of blood off his lip with a handkerchief.

"Are you alright?" Vidmar asked.

Ev and Taldor shook their heads simultaneously as if urging Vidmar to stop his questioning. "I'm fine," Hobb said sharply.

Vatis took this signal to continue the story. "Dinardo breezed through his next two opponents, sending another eager challenger into the pit of stakes and pushing the other into the ring of spikes before mercifully ending his life with one deft stroke."

Hobb coughed again, muffling the sound with his fist before he waved at Vatis to proceed.

"Pylades, conversely, dominated his first three opponents, decapitating two and throwing another into the snake pit. He laughed as the venomous cobras sank their fangs into his opponent, barely old enough to be considered a man. The first day was nearly finished, but both Pylades and Dinardo had one more match. Blood, urine, ale, and mud covered the sandy arena floor. Pylades drew his match, a boy, no more than ten. The boy had fought valiantly, catching two bandits by surprise with his quickness and a throwing knife; his other opponent was so drunk that he wielded a mug of ale as his weapon. He was the snake's first victim of the day. The boy's mother wailed when he drew Pylades, but the boy stepped forward bravely, spinning his daggers around like a juggler enticing the crowd before his act. The match lasted longer than expected. The boy used quickness to keep his distance from Pylades; he even dazzled the crowd by weaving in and out of the exterior spikes. But Pylades was too patient and cunning. He waited for the boy to make a mistake, and soon, the boy slipped on the muddy surface. The half-giant lunged forward, driving his sword through the boy's chest as he tried to rise. The crowd wailed with disappointment, but Greco smiled. His champion had made it to day two."

Mia tried to cover a yawn with her hand, but Vatis noticed—a bard always sees a yawning audience. It either means the story is boring or too long. Although, in Mia's case, he was sure it was exhaustion.

"We can finish the story another time," Vatis said, looking at Mia.

"No. I'm fine," she said, rubbing her eyes.

I don't plan to be here tomorrow night, so we must finish, Vatis thought.

"Put another log on the fire, Evanor," Hobb commanded. Ev didn't respond, but he obeyed.

Vatis waited for Ev to sit on his stool; the boy's muscles tensed, and his eyes glared wide with anger. *He's teetering on a knife's edge. One more push and he's gone.* Vatis found it strange how much Ev seemed to resent Hobb. *Maybe he's just a young man with ambition, or perhaps, he has reasonable cause.* Vatis took a sip of ale and continued his story, putting aside his thoughts of Hobb and Evanor's relationship.

"Dinardo's final match of the day was a man he knew well, a soldier called Storm. He was smaller than Dinardo, but there wasn't a faster man in all of Emre; he wielded two short swords and liked to spin at his opponent like a tornado, hence the nickname. We don't know his real name, but that is of little importance to this story. He is one of the more sympathetic figures that served Greco – another tale for another day. Storm and Dinardo had history. They met on the battlefield two times before the duel; the first time they met, Dinardo forced him to yield, and Storm was held captive for two weeks before he escaped. The second time, Storm beat Dinardo and left him to die on the bank of the Camil River. Fortunately for Emre, Dinardo survived. Now, on to the duel. The only contestant Greco openly rooted for other than Pylades was Storm, his backup plan. Until this point, Greco had not realized who Dinardo was. He looked like a common soldier, tall but not giant, muscular but not enormous, with long brown hair and a scarred face. He looked like half the contestants in the tourney. It was another reason people flocked to him; he was the common man. The two men walked into the arena smiling.

'Storm, it's been too long,' Dinardo said.

Strom stepped back; his smile vanished. 'I thought you were dead, Dinardo.'

The King leaped from his throne, spitting over the guardrail that separated him from the audience. 'Dinardo,' he screamed. A murmur flowed through the crowd. The King sensed the audience's admiration. 'This is the Dinardo my advisors are so worried about,' Greco said, laughing. 'At least they can sleep better tonight knowing you're dead. Show no mercy, Storm.'

Dinardo didn't acknowledge the King. Storm bowed. 'As you command.'

Dinardo walked the arena's edge, never taking his eyes off his opponent. 'So obedient, Storm. You disappoint me.'

Lightning coursed through Storm; he bolted forward, pressing Dinardo in range of the spikes. Greco waited on the edge of his seat, watching as if his life depended on it, and perhaps it did. Dinardo countered the fierce blows, parrying both swords and reversing their position in the arena. Storm's back was to the ring of spikes; he tried to push forward to create distance, but Dinardo held his ground.

'You need to learn some new tricks, Storm,' Dinardo said, blocking another flurry of strikes. His quips enraged Storm. Dinardo ducked under a horizontal slash, then rolled sideways to avoid the other blade's downward stroke. 'See, there you go. That's a good trick. You nearly had me,' Dinardo said, panting.

This back and forth went on for some time. The orange setting sun cast long shadows on the arena floor, making the slippery footing even more precarious. Finally, Storm's strikes began to slow. Say what you will about speed, but endurance wins challenging duels, and Dinardo's was renowned. His opponent tried to continue his hurricane onslaught, but the tempest had lost most of its power. Storm launched his final attack, mustering as much force as he had left. He spun. Dinardo parried. Dinardo leaped backward over the pit onto the other side with one carefully calculated flip. Storm's momentum was unstoppable. He screamed as he slipped into the pit of snakes."

Mia gasped. There was nothing quite like a gasp from an audience. It meant they were listening and engaged, and the bard had done his job conveying the drama. Vatis smirked. Mia was quickly becoming his favorite traveling companion. Not only had she saved his life, but she was one of the most interested audience members he had ever performed for. *She deserves better,* Vatis thought. But, as much as he liked her, Vatis needed to find a way to separate from her. *Nothing good happens to anyone that's with me for too long.* Another one of his dramatic pauses had lingered.

"Greco wailed, stomping his feet like a toddler. 'Save him,' he yelled. 'Pull him up.'

Dinardo furrowed his brow and looked through the crowd before he addressed the King. 'Are you not a man of your word?' he said.

Greco's eyes reddened with rage. 'Shut your mouth, you vagabond. I am King, not you; you will never sit upon my throne. Save Storm or face my judgment.'

A voice echoed from below. 'It's too late,' Storm called wearily. 'Dinardo, hasten my death. I'd rather die by the blade than poison.' Dinardo looked to the King, who was biting his lower lip so hard that blood dripped down his chin. 'Please,' Storm called again.

Finally, Greco relented with a single curt nod.

'I'm sorry, Storm. You deserved a better death, but I can grant you your request,' Dinardo said, throwing a hidden blade into the snake pit and ending the life of one of Emre's greatest warriors. The crowd cheered for Dinardo louder than they had for any fighter that day.

Greco's rage worsened. 'You're only delaying the inevitable, Dinardo. Tomorrow, Pylades will massacre you like the dog you are.'

Dinardo continued waving to the crowd. 'Let him try. There are plenty of dogs in my Pact,' he said. The crowd's cheers echoed throughout the city.

A brief stop in the story allowed crickets to voice their chirping song. Igni added percussion as he scratched another itch behind his ear. A barn owl hooted to complete the melody. Vatis rubbed his thumb against his opposite palm, opening his hand like a merchant showcasing his wares.

"So we can go to sleep at some point tonight. I will skip to the main event. Pylades and Dinardo drew each other in the semifinal match. They both breezed through their first two opponents. The first semifinal match was between two knights who fought classically with swords, shields, and heavy armor. Sir Boethus, an older knight who served Greco loyally for over a decade, advanced to the final with a well-placed stab between his opponent's breastplates. Greco was pleased; he was sure a loyal subject would win the prize. Nobody could defeat Pylades in single combat, or so he thought. The crowd cheered as Dinardo entered the arena; they erupted as he slithered between the spikes and handed a white rose to a girl in the front row.

'Enough pageantry, Dinardo. Your death is nigh. May the beggars that follow you meet the same fate.' Greco said, obviously drunk.

Dinardo bowed one final time to the crowd before he responded. 'If I die, another shall take my place. We have given voice to the voiceless, and they will not be silenced.'

The crowd's roar shook the arena until Greco extended a fist. 'See, they will always obey me. No matter how much you flatter them. They know who keeps them safe.' A murmur weaved through the crowd like a rat. 'Enough. It's time to end this nonsense. Fight.'

Pylades wasted no time and charged Dinardo, swinging his morningstar above his head. The half-giant won most of his fights with intimidation and a quick stroke, but if one could survive the initial onslaught, they stood a chance. Dinardo took notes from the unfortunate boy, who almost beat Pylades. He had to move quickly and strike swiftly."

Vatis refreshed himself with a sip of ale, then continued.

"Dinardo spun out of the way of the first attack and rolled between the legs of Pylades, slicing the half-giant's calf as he passed through. Pylades hammered his weapon into the ground, but Dinardo sidestepped. The colossal weapon left a hole in the mud.

'Get him,' Greco commanded from his perch.

Dinardo tried the same trick as the boy and began weaving in and out of the ring of spikes. Pylades' frustration boiled over, and he swung his weapon, destroying the carefully constructed trap and making more room for Dinardo to run.

'Kill him, kill him, kill him,' Greco screamed desperately.

Dinardo kept moving; he kept running, using his legendary endurance to wear down his opponent. He slid under another blow and stabbed the half-giant behind the knee. Pylades shrieked and wobbled but didn't fall.

'No,' Greco wailed.

The half-giant faked an attack with his morningstar, then backhanded the swerving Dinardo across the arena onto the edge of the spike pit. The crowd gasped collectively. Pylades pounced like a lioness on her prey and swung his mighty weapon down. Dinardo rolled with inhuman speed, but the blow nicked his left shoulder. He winced. The weapon's crude spikes tore a deep gash; blood trickled down his arm. Pylades sprung again, and once more, Dinardo rolled away with indescribable speed despite his injury. The half-giant roared in frustration.

'How?' Greco cried from his seat.

Dinardo's arm hung low, but he dove under a barehanded strike, somehow managing to stab Pylades behind his other knee. A thunderous bellow escaped as the half-giant fell. He swung his weapon around, but his momentum carried him too far forward, and he landed face-first in the mud. Dinardo leaped on this back, buried his long sword between his helm and armor, and somersaulted backward to avoid any last effort. The crowd was silent until Greco released a drawn-out, 'No.'

"What happened next?" Taldor asked excitedly. He covered his mouth with his hand after the question like it had escaped of its own accord. "Sorry."

Vatis laughed." No need to be sorry, Taldor," he said.

"The crowd showered Dinardo with flower petals and praise, cheering until Greco held his fist in the air.

'Settle down. Sir Boethus is too disciplined to fall for your tricks. He will not fail me.'

Dinardo smiled. 'Boethus is admirable. I hope you are not disappointed tomorrow.'

Greco glowered, signaling Sir Boethus forward. 'There's been a change of plan,' he said, grinning wickedly. 'The championship duel is now.'

Dinardo was exhausted, and his shoulder needed urgent care, but he grinned and said. 'Good, I have plans to dethrone a king tomorrow.'

Greco scowled. 'Sounds like treason to me, and my dragon grows hungry.'

Dinardo held his injured arm, saluting the king with a crimson palm. 'My great King. I was referring to that scoundrel Fadus and his Numerians. Or is lordship no longer the prize?'

Dinardo stepped backward as Sir Boethus entered the arena. The old knight's squire tightened the straps of his armor, handing him a circular wooden shield with an azure-painted dragon on its face, as well as a neatly polished longsword with an ornate jeweled pommel and long curved guard atop its handle. 'It seems you've upgraded your sword,' Dinardo said. It was, in fact, the King's sword, Wyvern's Fang, made from the finest steel in all Emre. There wasn't a finer blade ever crafted before or since."

"Well, that's debatable," Kamet said.

"Shut up, Kamet. Let him finish," Vidmar said, holding out a hand in apology.

"As I was saying, Greco lent his sword to Sir Boethus.

'That sword has never lost a battle, Dinardo.' The King said, satisfied with the trap he had sprung. Although he had been disappointed with the results of his first two plans, an exhausted, injured Dinardo against a rested, well-equipped knight was a duel Greco believed he would win.

'Mine has lost plenty,' Dinardo said, holding out his ordinary-looking blade. 'But it's honest and true.'

Greco held up his arm to begin the duel. 'Anything you want to say to the rabble that follows you,' he said, but as Dinardo started to speak, he lowered his fist and called, 'Fight.'

Dinardo laughed and settled into a defensive stance. He expected Sir Boethus to be aggressive, and he was right. When the king gives you his sword and watches your every move, what choice do you have but to assert dominance? He parried each attack decisively, displaying more discipline than in previous duels. The knight slid into a series of progressively aggressive attacks, but Dinardo parried each one. His last block left Sir Boethus's left side open; he riposted, landing a piercing blow under the Knight's arm into his heart, ending the fight minutes after it started. Some say it was the most accurate strike in the history of duels as if Dinardo somehow slowed down time around him. To avoid a calculated attack, parry, spin, then stab at a narrow, closing gap with enough strength to follow through to the heart–why it's a move instructors awe young squires with today. Sir Boethus perished almost immediately. Greco's face turned purple before he erupted over the roaring crowd.

'No,' he shouted as ale and spit poured out his mouth. 'This isn't possible.'

Dinardo grabbed the King's sword from the dead knight's hand and thrust it over his head. The crowd exploded with praise.

'You will never be lord of Numeria,' Greco shouted. Dinardo gestured for the crowd to quiet.

'I never expected to be,' he said. 'You know this sword is remarkably light. I thought it would be heavier.'

'Put it down,' Greco shouted before whistling twice. A second later, ten archers appeared on the roof of the arena. Of course, the King had another plan. Greco always had another plan. That's why he had been king for nearly three decades, but he continued to underestimate Dinardo.

'So, this is how you treat the winner of your tourney. I'm glad the people will see the kind of man you truly are.' Cries of 'monster' and 'craven' emerged from the mumbling crowd.

Vatis paused and tried to dislodge a piece of dried meat from his teeth. *Where should I end the story?* He thought while sipping the last of his ale. *Where does Hobb believe it will end?*

"Greco addressed the crowd. 'This man would not protect you. Bandits and rogues would ravage our city, yet I'm the villain. Your King, who freed you from slavery. Your King who has kept you safe for thirty years. My punishments are harsh, but that's what keeps you safe. Don't come crawling back when vagabonds leave you homeless, you ungrateful whelps.'

The crowd quieted, weighing the king's words.

'To me, freedom is worth more than safety,' Dinardo said. 'And I think the people will agree.'

A murmur of agreement waved through the crowd.

'Ha, an ideal of the young, you don't know the cost of freedom. No matter. Your rebellion ends here. Archers.' Greco commanded, holding up his hand.

The crowd gasped. Dinardo planted his sword in the ground, knelt, and rested his head on the pommel.

'Loose.' Ten blue feathered arrows flew from the roof, darting at the defenseless champion. The arena was silent. The birds ceased chirping; the wind stopped whistling, dogs quit barking, and the packed, blood-soaked arena was still. Then, a blinding flash of light rose from the ground around Dinardo, and he vanished. His sword remained planted in the ground as ten arrows lodged into the mud where he had knelt. A crash shook the arena like thunder after lightning, and Dinardo reappeared behind the King.

'You are no longer worthy of this crown,' Dinardo said, ripping the golden crown from Greco's head. Before the King could react, Dinardo disappeared again, only to reappear next to his sword between the crude circle of arrows meant to end his life.

'Citizens of Barna, of Haran, of Emre, your time is now. Claim what is yours. Take your freedom from the tyrant who stole it from you. Do not squander this opportunity. We will return. For now, I have another battle to fight. Do not fail me here,' Dinardo said.

Light flashed around him again, and he disappeared, taking Greco's sword and crown with him. The crash that followed him ignited a riot that lasted two months. Without his sword or Pylades to guard him, Greco was beaten and stuffed into his torturous dragon. The blood-thirsty crowd cheered as they roasted their former king alive, suffering the same fate that he condemned so many. Thus ended the second-longest reign in Emre's history. Some say Dinardo returned as they burnt Greco alive, which caused him and his Pact to move east. Others say he intended to cause chaos. Either way, Barna's rebellion and the disappearance of Dinardo and The Pact are tales for another night. Let us end here: Dinardo prevailed, magic existed, and for three centuries, heroes and villains alike searched for the power he wielded; some still search to this day."

A LOST STORY

Vatis

Vatis exhaled slowly, watching his audience digest the ending of the story. Vidmar and Kamet seemed content. *Perhaps they had heard a version of this tale before.* Mia twirled her finger in her hair, smiling as she contemplated. Ev furrowed his brow like he was putting a puzzle together. Taldor clapped, looked around, then counted on his fingers as if trying to decide which question to ask. Hobb's white mustache twitched, but otherwise, his expression remained unchanged.

"Vatis, you said you only tell true stories. There's no such thing as magic," Taldor said timidly.

Vatis ran his tongue over his gums as he thought. He looked at the boy with keen, penetrating eyes. "No, not anymore, but there used to be."

Hobb huffed but didn't voice his opinion. Ev added to Taldor's concerns before the boy could respond. "You mean to tell me that this Dinardo could fly or something."

Taldor scratched the back of his head. "I don't believe it."

Vatis smiled. *Farm boys are too stubborn to challenge their beliefs, and these two need to see more of the world.* "I'm not here to debate. I tell the facts and stories as I know them and let the audience make their conclusions," Vatis said, trying his best to appease the boys.

"I thought it was amazing," Mia said, interrupting a stuttering Taldor. "But I don't understand why Dinardo didn't become king himself?"

"Good question," Vatis said, itching his chin. Nobody knew the answer; everything Vatis had heard was speculation.

"He never wanted power," Hobb said. Crickets ceased chirping. The fire stopped crackling; for a second, Hobb's raspy breathing was the only noise in the house. The table was stunned, including Vatis. Yes, he had planned to coax a response from Hobb, but those four words were completely unexpected. *Who are you?* Vatis thought, staring at the farmer. He looked haggard, like that secret had been a partly decayed mask, revealing half of his true face. The old man didn't react to the revelation; he watched the others as his hazy gray eyes bounced from person to person. Vatis's mind went blank; he couldn't think of anything. Those four simple words had burnt all his flowering thoughts like wildfire through a prairie. The smoke clouding his mind thickened until Ev stood up and stomped his foot, breaking the spell.

"You knew of Dinardo?" Ev asked, biting his lip, eyes glaring fiercely.

"Yes," Hobb said.

"You're a fucking liar," Ev yelled.

"Ev," Taldor pleaded.

"What? I told you he kept secrets from us."

"It's just a story," Taldor said, seeming to struggle to pick a side.

"Maybe we should go," Vidmar said.

Hobb tugged at his ear. "Don't. Yes, I have secrets; most men do when they get to my age. I have taken vows. I was not always a farmer, but as Vatis said, that is a story for another night. I only wanted to protect you, to keep you safe."

Ev spun and kicked his stool. It shot against the wall, cracking one of the legs when it hit. "I don't need your protection." Ev grabbed Hobb's mug of ale, threw the door open, and disappeared into the darkness. Taldor tried to call after him, but his childish whimpers died in the cornfields.

"Why, Pa?" Taldor said with tears welling up in the corner of his eye.

"We really should go," Vidmar said, tapping Mia on the shoulder. She nodded and stood. Kamet was already out the door.

Vatis stood to follow, but Hobbs's rough, vice-like hand grabbed his forearm. "Vatis, stay. Taldor, find your brother. Make sure he doesn't do anything reckless." Taldor sniffed, nodded, grabbed a lantern, and ran into the dark fields.

Once Taldor left, Hobb turned to Vidmar. "I can help you, but not tonight. Meet me at the tower tomorrow morning." At the mention of the tower, Vatis began to hear whispers of his name in that windy, haunting voice. *Vatis, Vatis, Vatis.* He rubbed his temples, trying to focus on anything except the bone-chilling voice.

Hobb's gruff speech interrupted the whisper. "In exchange, grant me this favor: see that the boys come home tonight. I fear I have pushed Evanor too far. Vatis, I'd like a word with you about that story—*alone.*"

Vidmar narrowed his eyes at Vatis. *What?* Vatis had never felt more dissected by a look in his life. He almost said something. He wanted to say something; however, Vidmar left before he had the chance. That left Hobb and Vatis alone in the shrinking, darkening room. The old man stood, put a log on the fire, and poured himself a new mug of ale. Vatis put aside his thoughts of the tower but didn't know what to say. *What do you want, Hobb?* He searched his mind for stories with the name Hobb, but the dusty shelves in the back of his memories revealed no answers.

After a long drink, Hobb raised his eyes to meet Vatis's. "Why were you in the tower?" The tower's voice returned louder and more persistent. *Vatis. Vatis. Come Vatis.* He didn't know how to answer. He didn't know which voice to answer. "Why were you in *my* tower?" Hobb repeated sternly.

If Hobb was going to help Vidmar, if Vatis was going to get his story, he needed to be honest. The question was how honest did he *need* to be. "It called to me," he said finally.

Hobb's bushy eyebrows furrowed into a frightening yet intriguing look. "What do you mean it called to you?"

"I was exploring your farm when I heard my name. I followed that voice into the tower, up the staircase until I lost my footing, then you know the rest," Vatis said, stretching his injured arm.

"It *called* to you," Hobb said, his tongue poking out of the side of his mouth.

"Yes. It said Vatis, Vatis, Vatis, over and over again. I was travel-weary, so my mind could have been playing tricks on me, but that is why I was in the tower." *It wasn't a trick of the mind. There's something strange about that tower, something connected to the Kokor Forest. What are you hiding, Hobb? I need to ask him.*

Hobb stroked his mustache and refilled his ale. "Travel-weary?" he said, tapping his cane on the table. He slurped his drink but never took his eyes off Vatis. "I know what you are," he said at last.

Vatis felt his heart pound in his chest; his stomach sank to his knees. The edges of his vision darkened as the enclosing room blurred. "Excuse me," he said, biting his lip to stop it from quivering.

"I know what you are."

Just five words, five terrifying words that Vatis had dreaded for over a decade. Hobb's delivery was almost more frightening than the words themself. His stoic demeanor portrayed a man who was three moves ahead. Vatis wasn't even playing the game.

Through the haze, Vatis's tavern response escaped habitually. "I'm a simple traveling bard, looking for new stories and interesting people."

"More like a wandering bard looking for lives to destroy." Again, the farmer's demeanor horrified Vatis. It was so calm, so measured. *If I escape here with my life, I might have to incorporate that into a new character. He won't kill me, though. Will he?* Vatis thought, diverting his gaze from Hobb's inquisitor's glare.

Sweat dripped down the sides of his face. His cheeks were magma as he wiped the sweat away. "What do you mean?"

"You're one of the cursed."

A momentary sense of relief washed over him, followed by stomach-vacuuming dread. Hobb was the first person who'd discovered him, at least the first to accuse him. *I didn't stick around to find out, but Kytia knows; I'm sure of it. I'm getting too reckless.* Hobb didn't seem like the type of man to spread it around the world. *Do I kill him?* Vatis had never killed anyone before, not intentionally. There had been some unlucky individuals when he had lingered somewhere too long, but he had never murdered anyone. For the moment, he decided to play dumb. "One of the what?"

"Don't pretend with me, Vatis. It won't end well. You are one of the cursed," Hobb said, almost yelling.

"Why do you think I am cursed?"

"You have The Wandering Curse, Montalvo's curse."

Vatis's jaw tightened. "How could I have a curse that died hundreds of years ago?"

"We both know it didn't die, and I won't debate history. You need to leave and never come back," Hobb said.

"I'm not leaving. My companions won't follow me until you give them answers about your relationship with The Pact. You're a member or, at the very least, a descendant of a member," Vatis said, matching Hobb's ferocity.

"I will share no secrets with you. You're a deceitful liar, and you've put my family in danger for the last time. Leave now," Hobb commanded, using his cane to stand.

"What evidence do you have? What makes you think I'm cursed?" Vatis had played out his discovery in his mind a hundred times. Kings had confronted him in palaces; his guild accused him at the college, and even Vidmar berated him in their travels. All these reveries seemed possible. Vatis practiced his responses for each situation and more, but he never expected a secret member of The Pact to find out and interrogate him in his dining room. His mind scrambled to make up for its unpreparedness.

"My cherries returning to health, the wolf attack, and my cow getting better. These could all be a coincidence, but you confirmed my suspicions when you said the tower spoke to you. It wasn't the tower. It was the invading vines from the Kokor Forest."

Vatis stiffened at the mention of the forest. He remembered the shadow offering him rest—he *needed* rest. *This oaf has ruined everything. What do I say?*

"Stop scheming," Hobb said, straightening his arched back. He seemed to double in size, giving a glimpse of what was once an imposing figure. "There is no more debate. Leave now." The top of his cane suddenly glowed a bright iridescent yellow.

Vatis stood too quickly. Stars danced around the room, gently shooting toward his head as if attempting to knock him over. "What are you? Who are you?"

"Someone who can see the damage you will do to this world, the damage you *have* done to this world. Leave now. This is my final warning." The cane glowed brighter, illuminating the room.

Vatis wanted to call his bluff. He wanted to see what sort of jester's trick Hobb was using to light his cane. "You won't kill me."

"I don't have to kill you," he said. The light now pulsed as if it were alive. "There are other ways to make you leave. I could wipe your memory, erase all those stories you have worked so hard to cultivate."

"You're bluffing," Vatis said. His arms shook, his knees wobbled, he wanted to collapse, but something held him in place. His head felt even lighter than before; then his feet left the floor, and he was paralyzed in the air. He felt a pain in his mind like a rodent burrowing deeper and deeper, carving holes in his cherished memories. "I'll leave. I promise. Don't take my stories." Tears ran down his cheeks. His stories were all he had left. If he didn't have them, what was the point of living? He felt a familiar hard surface beneath his feet. *The floor, oh, thank the gods—the floor.* The pain in his head dissipated.

Hobb slunk back into his seat. The wrinkles in his face deepened like a creek after a brutal storm; he seemed ancient. *Maybe he is a member of The Pact?* Vatis thought. "Go," Hobb said powerfully as if his magic were lightning and his voice was thunder.

Vatis quickly grabbed his pack and jogged out the door with his boots untied. He heard heavy footsteps follow him onto the porch. *You've ruined everything,* he thought, bending down in the dirt to tie his laces. He looked over his shoulder. Hobb hovered like a storm cloud; his eyes seemed to flash in the darkness. Vatis mustered what little courage he had left. "Please help Vidmar. His story deserves a proper ending."

Hobb's mustache twitched after a long sigh escaped like a ray of sunlight through a cloudy sky. He nodded once, then pointed to the road. "Leave."

Vatis hoped that nod meant yes. "Goodbye, Hobb," he said with a stiff bow and wandered into the cold night.

ANSWERS

Vidmar

What do you mean he left?" Vidmar said, running up the steps of the porch. The farmer sat in his rocking chair, casually drinking tea.

Hobb blew a wisp of steam away. "Exactly that, he left."

"Why would he leave now? He's followed me halfway around Emre, and when I get close to the end of the story he's chasing, he leaves. It doesn't make sense. What did you say to him?"

"I told you I would answer your questions at the watchtower. Now it's time for tea." Hobb took a slow, aggravating sip of tea and rocked in his chair.

Ev kicked the front door open. "Would you quit the bullshit and tell them where their friend went?"

Hobb stopped rocking. "Watch it, Evanor."

"Ev, just let it go," Taldor said from the doorway.

"I've had it with this farm, this family, and all the damn lies. I don't know why I came home last night," Ev said, marching down the road into town.

"Where are you going?" Hobb called. "There is work to be done."

"Do it yourself."

Taldor jogged after Evanor. "Ev, come back. Sorry, Pa. I'll get him."

Hobb sipped his tea. "Leave him, Taldor. Take Mia and feed the chickens, gather the eggs; if any of the hens have stopped producing, well, hopefully, there won't be any surprises today."

Taldor started to protest. "But..."

"Don't you start, boy." Hobb favored the younger brother, or at least he was gentler; his menacing tone softened when he spoke. Kindness glimmered behind his gray eyes and bushy eyebrows.

Vidmar bent to be at eye level with Mia. "I'll tell you everything," he whispered.

Mia didn't make eye contact. Instead, she shuffled her feet in the dirt. "I just don't understand why he left."

"Me neither, but I'll find out. Go with Taldor. Besides, feeding chickens seems fun," Vidmar said, tussling her hair.

Mia shuffled toward Taldor. "Fine." *She deserves the truth,* Vidmar thought, watching them drift toward the chickens.

"Where's the mercenary?" Hobb asked once the children were out of earshot.

Vidmar didn't want to answer. *Why should I? You won't tell me about Vatis.* But he had to play the old man's game. He needed answers, and Hobb was probably his last chance. "Trying to sleep off the mead from last night."

Hobb snorted. "I expected a man of his stature to handle his mead better."

"He's out of practice."

Hobb's laugh surprised Vidmar. *He seems more relaxed.* "I'll meet you at the watchtower in an hour. I have some work to do first."

Vidmar nodded and took the signal to leave. *What am I supposed to do for an hour?* He occupied himself by waking Kamet, sharpening his knives, and practicing his aim with his left hand. He was getting better, though, nowhere as accurate as he used to be with his right, but serviceable. Kamet sat on the ground next to a tree stump. Vidmar aimed at a smaller log he had placed atop the stump. Between vomiting sessions, Kamet picked up or straightened the log, pulled the knife out, and tossed it underhanded to the right of Vidmar.

"What happened to you," Vidmar said, picking up his knife.

Kamet retched. "It must have been the cherries or the beef. Mead wouldn't do this to me."

"Hobb's brew is particularly strong. I learned that last time we were here." He threw his knife. It whirled through the air, sticking a finger's length away from the small nook he had been targeting. "Shit."

"What's wrong? You hit the log," Kamet said, wobbling as he tried to pull the knife out.

"I missed my target."

"Were you aiming at me?"

"No - that nook."

Kamet examined the log. "You barely missed," he said, running a finger along the indent the knife had left.

"A miss is a miss. It's the difference between life and death. What good will I be in a fight if I can't hit my target from a few paces away?"

"We already," Kamet began. He stopped and pointed behind Vidmar. "The old man is heading for the tower."

They hustled to meet Hobb, who arrived moments before them. "You're late," he said, leaning on his cane.

Vidmar forced a smile. "Sorry." *I'm done playing games. Now tell me what you know.*

Hobb exhaled, tilted his head, and grabbed one of the dark green vines that wound up the face of the tower. "You recognize these?"

"The vines. No. I mean, I've seen vines before," Vidmar said, rubbing the strangely heavy plant. The surface was oily; brown and yellow freckles covered the small diamond-shaped leaves.

"It's an invasive species. There is only one other spot in Emre where you'll find these – the Kokor Forest."

Vidmar looked at Kamet. Chills spidered up his back and onto his neck.

"Tell me exactly what happened. I can help you–I will help you, but you need to help me first. What happened in the Kokor Forest?" the old man said, blue veins bulging in his neck beneath his clenched jaw.

Fine. "There is a path that we found as scouts years ago. It avoids the heart of the forest. I heard some strange noises but nothing too frightening and made it through unscathed. Twice, actually. So, after hearing the stories, I considered them to be exaggerations. We used the path again, but this time was different. The air felt heavier than before like we were walking through fog, but there was no fog. I was still recovering and adjusting from our unfortunate trip to Haran, so I fiddled dumbly with my knife as we walked. It helped calm my nerves. Anyway, this figure appeared out of nowhere. A shadow; I couldn't see its face. It seemed human, though it was no larger than Taldor. It just stood there, blocking our path. Vatis said it spoke to him, but we didn't hear anything. He told us to sheathe our blades, and then Vatis started to wander off the path like he was under a spell. Kamet pulled him back, and the creature screeched. Then it charged at us, whatever it was. The pain was immense like my blood boiled inside my body."

"It felt like I was being suffocated, like an anvil was sitting on my chest," Kamet said.

Hobb winced as he cracked his neck. Vidmar continued. "After it attacked us, it screeched like nothing I've heard. The sound seemed to wrap around us. I felt pressed to the ground, frozen in place. I couldn't move—couldn't think. Then Vatis stood and yelled 'stop,' and the monster obeyed. Once I came to my senses, I ran. The air still felt thick and odd, but we ran and made it through. I'm never going back there again."

The cane Hobb leaned on appeared to glow. Vidmar couldn't tell if his eyes were playing tricks on him or if the sunlight had struck the wood at the right angle. Hobb's gaze shifted slightly from Vidmar to the tower. Then, Vidmar heard movement behind him, like a stone door grinding open. When the illusion ended, Hobb looked older. His wrinkles deepened. The circles under his eyes transitioned from a cheery red to a dark purple. It was as if life had been sucked from him as Vidmar talked. *What happened?* "You've passed through the Kokor three times?" Hobb asked. His voice was weak.

"Yes. Kamet has, too."

"Were you with him every time?" Hobb said, his voice regaining a bit of its accustomed strength.

"Yes, why does that matter?" Vidmar said. This whole line of questioning seemed odd. Hobb was supposed to tell him about the crown, the Pact, and what happened to Vatis.

"Patience. Follow me," Hobb said, walking into the tower.

Fallen stones and rubble crowded the entrance. A shallow dust-covered nook held an empty lantern mount. It appeared to be engraved with symbols of The Pact, at least the triangular markings with which Vidmar had become familiar. Hobb stopped in front of the winding staircase. His tongue moved behind his mustache, making it appear like a hairy gray caterpillar crawled under his bulbous nose. "Tell me again, why did you leave Kandrian Ambita's service?"

"Why?"

"Trust me."

Vidmar rubbed his eyes. When he opened them, golden specs appeared like stars emerging on a cloudy night. "You are burning my trust to ashes, old man. I left because I couldn't follow him any longer. If a man can order the death of women and innocent children, he isn't capable of being king."

"There are many who would say the opposite," Hobb said, placing a second hand atop his cane. He stood like a gargoyle defending the stairs. "It is a burden to be king. There are tough choices to make."

"When a man's actions lead to countless innocent deaths, he is no longer fit to bear that burden," Vidmar said, trying to restrain his squirming anger.

"I agree," Hobb said as he turned to walk up the stairs. The cane tapped on the stones as he climbed. Vidmar looked at Kamet, who shrugged, then followed Hobb to the top of the tower. The view was breathtaking; Vidmar inhaled the clean air as he surveyed the land. Tactically speaking, the tower was in an ideal location. Fertile farmlands painted the flat ground with rows of corn, beans, and other vegetables to the south and east. To the north, a thick forest stretched for miles. A jagged, angular stone poked through the trees near the middle of the woods. And to the west, peaks of mountains were visible behind the thin grove of apple and cherry trees. The old man sat on a stone stool once they reached the top. It took a few moments for him to catch his breath. "I apologize. I'm not as spry as I once was."

"It's a long way up," Kamet said, leaning over the side. A stone slid, and he leaped back almost onto Hobb's lap.

Under normal circumstances, Vidmar would have found Kamet's reaction hilarious, but he was sore, tired, and confused. So, he ignored Kamet and continued to survey the land; Taldor and Mia spread seeds for the chickens. He couldn't see if she was smiling, but she appeared happy as she skipped back to the hen house. "Why is this tower here?" he asked as he watched the kids chase each other around. Chickens scattered about as they ran.

"It was a lookout," Hobb said.

Vidmar's teeth ground together. *Don't start that bullshit, Hobb. It's a fucking tower. I knew it was a lookout at some point.* All he managed to say was, "Hobb."

Hobb cracked his neck, exhaled, and rubbed his nose. "You have been patient enough. It is time for answers. What would you like to know first?"

What do I want to know first? Where is the crown? Who are you? What is the purpose of this tower? Then, after a second's thought, he asked, "Where's Vatis?" He surprised himself with the question; there were much more pressing matters than the whereabouts of a bard.

"I sent him away," Hobb said frankly.

"You sent him away. Why?"

"Every extra second he stayed here put my family in danger. What do you know about him?"

Vidmar furrowed his brow. "He's a bard; he wanted my story. He's harmless. How did he put your family in danger?"

Fury coursed from Hobb's clenched fist to his narrow, wrinkled eyes. "He's a wanted man."

"What? Vatis, Vatis-of-the-road is a wanted man, for what? How do you know this? He can't be more wanted than me. The King and his only rival both consider me an enemy." Vidmar didn't believe him. Yes, part of him knew that Vatis had secrets, but this didn't make sense.

"True, you are a wanted man, but there are few more sought-after than you; Vatis is one of them. Has he ever forced you to leave somewhere abruptly? Why do you think he's a traveling bard?"

Vidmar scratched his chin while he thought. *We did leave Dartmore in a hurry, but that's a coincidence. Perhaps he told Hobb as much, and now the old man is using it against me.*

"I knew there was something off about him," Kamet said, pacing along the eastern half of the tower.

"Yes, he's strange, but I find it hard to believe that there is another human in Emre more wanted than me, other than Anaar."

"You know Anaar?" Hobb said quietly.

Vidmar answered with a question of his own. "How do you know Anaar? Who are you, Hobb? If you tell me you're a simple farmer, Kamet will throw you off this tower."

"I'm a well-informed relic," Hobb said with a hint of a smile beneath his mustache.

"How long did it take you to come up with that answer? How many people have asked you that question before?" Vidmar was tired of Hobb's games. It was time for a direct approach.

"Three."

Vidmar bit the only remaining knuckle of his right index finger as he brought a misshapen fist to his mouth. "How many have you answered truthfully?"

"One."

Is he lying? Vidmar couldn't tell. "So, who are you?"

Hobb looked across the eastern horizon. The sun passed its apex, beginning its western descent; a short, crooked shadow crept closer to Vidmar's feet. "A well-informed relic is not far from the truth," he said. His eyes followed a pair of vultures circling in the sky. "I am old, even older than I seem. Taldor and Evanor are not my grandsons by blood. My grandsons died long ago. I am a watcher, a warden, a guardian, if you will. I inform a specific group about threats in the western half of Emre."

"I told you he was mad, Vidmar," Kamet said, sitting with his back against the stone wall.

"Enough, Kamet," Vidmar snapped. *He's finally talking, you damn oaf.* "Let him speak."

Hobb glared at Kamet but continued. "There's not much more to say. That's who I am. That is my assignment. I've lost track of how long it's been. I will say this: I've watched the rise and fall of too many kings to know that we are on the verge of another war."

"So, you are a member of The Pact? It still exists?" Vidmar asked.

"The Pact exists, yes, but I am not a member. I am an impartial observer whose values align closely with that organization."

Vidmar's heart raced. The answers he craved were at his fingertips. "The Pact exists today?"

"If I am going to repeat myself, we will be here all day," Hobb said. "Yes, The Pact is still active today, though not so much on this side of the Kaharn Desert."

Questions blossomed in his mind like flowers in spring; this was too much to comprehend. He needed to focus. *The crown, the stone, Vatis, stay the course.* "You know what's on the other side of the Kaharn?" His first question betrayed him.

"I do, but is that what you want to know?" Hobb asked.

Vidmar rubbed his temples with his ring fingers. "No. Can you help me find the crown?"

Hobb smiled. "Now, that is the first question I thought you would ask. Yes, I can help you. I don't know its exact location, but I can provide the sister stone and help decipher the clue."

"If you are this guardian of Emre, why would you help me find the crown?"

"Another good question," Hobb said. He relaxed onto his stool. "The crown is largely symbolic. It cannot hold power."

"What do you mean it cannot hold power?" Vidmar asked.

"I mean, it's a crown. The men who long for it are mistaken. It is just a symbol – a symbol of failure. But legends are born out of mystery, and I am afraid that the crown's abilities have been wickedly exaggerated. Yes, some part of the commoners would worship the man who wore it as the true King. Honestly, I don't know why Dinardo hid it. He said a true king wins his kingdom through valor, not jewelry. I think the allure of the legend has clouded the minds of those who seek it. What does Alcin want with it?" Hobb didn't break eye contact with Vidmar; the intense stare sent shivers down his spine.

Vidmar flinched, turning his back to Hobb. "I don't know what he wants with it. I think he doesn't want Kandrian to find it. The King had started to obsess over it before I left."

A thick, turtle-shaped cloud passed over the farm. Vidmar watched it glide carelessly, a freedom he envied. Boots clanged against the stone as Kamet paced. Hobb cleared his throat. "I'd rather have anyone other than Kandrian Ambita possess the crown."

Vidmar could feel Hobb's gaze, but he didn't turn around. Instead, he focused his attention on the clouds. "I used to feel the same." The ghosts of his missing fingers itched. "Alcin is cunning, inspirational, and powerful. But I don't know what he wants. Kandrian hated the world and wanted the power to change it. He achieved that with deadly action. Alcin doesn't support Kandrian. I know that much, yet I don't know why he strives for power."

"Kamet, would you mind giving us a moment alone?" Hobb said.

Vidmar turned around, locking eyes as Kamet nodded. He returned the gesture before Kamet descended the winding staircase. Hobb's cane screeched against stone as he stood. Shaking, he braced himself against the tower wall and pointed to the stone poking out of the forest. "There is your sister stone."

Vidmar spun, striding aside Hobb. "That," he said, pointing at the enormous silver rock.

"Yes," Hobb said, sitting back on his stool but facing Vidmar.

"What does it say?"

"Let me see your stone."

Vidmar grabbed the small stone from the pouch on his belt, reluctantly handing it to Hobb.

The farmer rubbed the markings like a blind man exploring an unfamiliar object. "You believe it says:' It lies near the dead.' That is close. It truly reads, 'It lies *with* The Dead.' The Pact intentionally left incorrect translations in texts they left behind. Scholars and bards will tell you this symbol means 'near' or 'far' depending on which way the arrow points, but it actually means 'with' or 'without.' Also, Vatis was right about the message having a double meaning. Though he had the wrong word, which I believe was intentional – a riddle within a clue, something Dinardo was quite fond of."

Vidmar exhaled, his lips vibrating to create a slight buzzing noise. "I'm becoming deathly aware of that."

Hobb held the stone to the sun. Specs of silver twinkled in the light. "The sister stone is the *only* sister stone. All of The Pact's stones were extracted from it. Find your stone's place, and this line will point you to your destination. However, I don't think that will be necessary. I know where you must go next."

His breath caught in his chest before Vidmar let a whimpering question escape. "Where?"

"The Kokor Forest."

An icy chill rose the hairs on Vidmar's arms. "How do you know this?"

"When 'The Dead' is carved like this," Hobb said, pointing to the triangular marking with a small line through one of the three angles. "Where the line breaks both sides of the second angle, The Dead means The Kokor Forest."

Frost crystallized through his blood until the icicles exploded out of his missing fingers. "You're certain of this? Why would they refer to the Kokor Forest as 'The Dead'?"

Hobb straightened his hunched back. "Dinardo lost half his company when they escaped through the forest. He claimed he could see their ghosts the next time he was forced to go through. After that, he referred to the forest as death or The Dead in writing. So it makes sense that he would hide the crown somewhere in the Kokor. Few go into the forest, and even fewer come out alive. You are the first person I've heard of who has made it through the forest three times, other than Dinardo himself."

"What about Kamet?"

"He was with you."

"I wouldn't have made it through without him."

"You would have."

"Fine, semantics aside, that forest is vast; even if I went back, how would I know where to go?"

Hobb wobbled as he tried to stand. Vidmar helped him to his feet. "I believe the forest will guide you."

Vidmar stepped back. "What kind of nonsense is that? The forest will guide me."

Hobb waved his cane across the horizon like a comet flying through the night sky. "There are others in this world who can translate the stones, others with sinister motivations. If your words are true, it won't be long until Kandrian finds it. I fear that we are headed toward another war, and the last thing this world needs is another battle to determine the true king. That said, I have one request should you succeed in your quest. Do not give the crown to Alcin; destroy it. Throw it in the sea, melt it in a forge, break its jewels; I don't care how you do it."

Hobb's serious tone made Vidmar's joints ache. "Why help me find it in the first place? I thought it was just a crown. Why do you want me to destroy it?"

A crow fluttered by, landing on the railing of the tower. Hobb shooed it away with his cane. "I've waited a long time for someone like you, someone who reminded me of Dinardo. What will happen if you find the crown and give it to Alcin? I don't want you to make the same mistake he did."

Vidmar had thought about that question for a while, and it always ended with the same answer. *Why do you think I'm like Dinardo? How do I answer that?* "He would start a war. With his ability to inspire commoners and a relic that claimed he was the true king, he would start another uprising. If anything, he is like Dinardo, not me."

Hobb's bushy eyebrows furrowed into a menacing stare. "Do not compare Alcin to Dinardo."

The wind whistled through the cracks of the tower. Vidmar struggled to keep his unusually long hair out of his eyes. "I cannot figure out whose side you're on or what your game is or if anything you have told me is true. Show me this sister stone and prove you are who you say," Vidmar said, brushing his dark bangs out of his eyes. Hobb huffed, then staggered to the stairs.

THE SISTER STONE

Vidmar

Hobb's relentlessly pointless questions put Vidmar in a dark mood. He wanted to trust Hobb, but he knew the old man was withholding information. When Vidmar didn't know who to believe, he trusted his gut. He didn't know if it was hunger or nerves, but his ordinarily reliable instincts insisted that Hobb could help. A squirrel scurried across their path from under a bush; suddenly, it stopped as if confused by their presence. Its long, bushy tail twitched. A branch snapped beneath Hobb's foot, and the squirrel sprang up the trunk of a nearby tree.

"The stone is through that clearing," Hobb said, pointing ahead to a narrow gap between two birch trees. The white-barked trees looked out of place amongst the dark oaks and evergreens. "Find its place, and this arrow will point toward the destination."

Vidmar stopped. "You're not coming?"

Hobb sat on a fallen tree that looked somewhat like a bench. "I've taken you this far. The rest you will have to discover for yourself. But, as far as the stone goes, it will know where it came from."

Vidmar looked at the carved stone, finding the small notch that supposedly would point him in the right direction. *This is ridiculous.* "Fine," he said, stepping between the birch trees.

The Sister Stone was broader than he expected. It was more of a boulder than a stone, sitting in the clearing, illuminated by a ray of sunlight through the canopy. *It will know where it came from, sure. I'm a fucking idiot.* He circled the Sister Stone, holding his smaller rock against it like a whetstone sharpening a massive ax. There were no notches like he had expected, no holes for the stone to fit in, just a simple stone. Only one feature separated it from a standard rock; rivulets of bright silver flowed here and there through the fields of gray.

He circled again.

And again.

A white lily growing happily from the stone's base was an unfortunate victim of his foot's fury. White petals burst into the air, trailing behind Vidmar like falling snow. A feathery dandelion met the same fate as the lily on the other side of the stone. He thought about dragging Hobb into the clearing and demanding answers when he felt something – a strange pull like his stone was being inhaled by the larger stone. The silver rivulets near his hand shined brighter. A peculiar light darted through the stream, moving faster as Vidmar brought the stone close.

Vidmar released the stone. It snapped into place, the Sister Stone absorbing it into its surface. For one gut-wrenching moment, he thought he had lost his clue. Then, the silver light appeared. It lit the engravings on the stone before flowing into the arrow pointing north, slightly northwest – the direction of the Kokor Forest. *Shit.*

His gut was right. Hobb had been honest, though he didn't know if it was the whole truth. He sighed as he tried to pull the stone out, but it wouldn't move. He yanked the stone harder. Gripping was difficult with his left hand; his four good fingers slipped constantly. Finally, the silver light faded, followed by the engravings. Vidmar's throat tightened as if he'd swallowed an uncracked walnut. "No, no, no." He pulled out his cooking knife. Even in his panicked state, the thought of using one of his throwing knives to pry a stone loose sent shivers down his spine.

"You don't need it anymore," Hobb said from the mouth of the clearing. Standing in the shadows, the old man looked ancient. His gray eyes looked like rocks, while his fingers snaked atop his jagged cane.

Vidmar sheathed his knife. "How do you know that? What if it's a key or another clue?"

Hobb stepped into the light. The darkness that surrounded him dissipated. "It served its purpose. Which way did it point?"

"To the Kokor Forest. What is this stone? Magic or something?"

Hobb gently placed a hand on the Sister Stone. The silver light returned, dancing around his hand. "It's the Sister Stone."

Vidmar rolled his eyes. "Is it magic?"

"Magic is such a…." Hobb seemed to search for words as he ran his fingers along the stone. The light followed wherever his fingers led. "Is such a strange term. A catch-all for anything people don't understand. Cicadas were sent by the gods, bringing famine in their wake, until people realized they came every seventeen years. To this day, people think rainbows are created by dwarves when they bury their treasure, but they are simply refracted light and water. There is power in the world, yes, and a few of us can wield it. There are a few who wield it without knowing."

Vidmar's head pounded. *Magic.* "Are you saying I can use it?"

Hobb laughed. "No, you can't wield it. This isn't a story. The hero doesn't discover he had magical gifts his whole life and then triumphs over the adversity he faced. You are a good man with incredible talents and the rare ability to do what's right, but you still have a long way to go."

Disappointment burrowed down his throat into his stomach, where it scratched at the lining like a mole digging a tunnel. Vidmar didn't know why he was disappointed. He felt like a poor child who had just been told their dreams of becoming a knight were frivolous. "You think you know me so well," he said. His emotions continued their child-like behavior. "I've done horrible things. I've killed ten times as many people as I've saved. I've helped two blood-thirsty tyrants rise to power," Vidmar paused. The weight of his task never felt heavier. *I'm tired. I hoped that by finding the crown, I could finally escape, let the kings battle for control, and spend the rest of my days in peace. I know now that I'll never have peace. That was a foolish dream.* "How do I know I can trust you?"

"You can't," Hobb said, scratching his chin.

"Tell me why you sent Vatis away. The truth."

"He's one of The Cursed," Hobb said, bluntly like Vidmar should know what he meant by 'The Cursed.'

"What do you mean he's one of The Cursed?" Vidmar said as his anger clawed its way to the tips of his ears.

"He is The Wanderer. Montalvo was the most famous Wanderer, but there have been others. Curses never leave the world; they find new hosts," Hobb's unwavering eyes and posture showed no hint of dishonesty; even his usually shaky hands were steady atop the cane. "He's why my cherry trees are thriving, why the wolves attacked. He saved my cow, and I feared what would follow, so I sent him away. You must have noticed strange things happen wherever he goes."

Vidmar couldn't believe he had been so blind. The night he met Vatis, he told the story of Montalvo-The-Wise. *How did he fool me, the arrogant little shit?* His quest for the crown had hindered his usual astuteness. "So, Vatis is Montalvo-The-Wise?"

The light from the stone faded as Hobb pulled his hand away. "Yes and no. He has the same curse, but he's not the same person. After discovering his curse, Montalvo wanted to help the people of Emre. I fear Vatis only wants to help himself. I don't know how long he has been cursed. We had lost track of The Wanderer for decades." *We?* Vidmar thought as Hobb continued. "But his good fortune in Yimser could be the start of something horrible. A young woman died because he lingered. He does not care for the people like Montalvo. He cares about himself, being remembered, and his damn stories. One other Wanderer tried to use his curse selfishly. The world nearly ended because of it. Now that we have located him, I will not allow Vatis to go down that same path."

Vidmar's head spun as questions circled his mind. "Why did you send him away then? Why risk losing this *Wanderer?*"

"We won't lose him. We have ways of locating him now that he has been identified. I do fear his recklessness, though. Emre cannot withstand another Awakening," Hobb said, looking upward through the narrow canopy.

What is an Awakening? Vidmar thought as he wrestled with his emotions. It felt like ants were crawling up his legs. He couldn't stand still. Instead, he paced back and forth between the birch trees, shaking his itching limbs. "Are you going to kill Vatis?" *Why do I care about him? He's done nothing but lie to me and hinder my quest.*

"I don't intend to. We can't risk cursing someone else."

A strange weight lifted off Vidmar's shoulders. Hobb limped toward the clearing. "So that's it," Vidmar said. "Vatis is cursed. I have to go to the Kokor Forest *again*, and you're a guardian of Emre." It was too much. How could he have more questions as his search finally neared its end? His thoughts raced from the crown to Vatis to Hobb, then to Mia and Kamet. He couldn't bring Mia into the forest. It was too dangerous, and Kamet wouldn't let him go alone. "I can't take Mia with me."

The sun shined on Hobb's face as he answered, somehow showcasing the kindness behind his gray eyes and bushy brows. "She can stay with us."

Tears tried to escape the corners of his eyes, but Vidmar sniffed them back. "Take care of her. She's a better person than I'll ever be. With a little guidance, she could change the world, but I'd settle for her finding a good home and happiness."

"Aye," Hobb said, nodding. That was all he needed to say. Vicus was a good home, a safe place with some kind of guardian watching over her, much better than Yimser, the road, or the Kokor Forest. There were other children to learn and play with; she would have a chance. He would miss her, though.

"I should say goodbye," Vidmar said as they walked back to the farm.

They found Mia and Taldor on the side of the barn, throwing the blade Vidmar had given the boy a few weeks ago. Taldor threw the knife, and it bounced off the barn into the wispy fescue. "What are you doing, boy?" Hobb said as they approached.

Taldor jumped. "We were just practicing, Pa," he said, rushing toward the barn to retrieve the blade.

A low growl escaped Hobb's lips but nothing more. Mia smiled as she gently swayed with her hands behind her back. Her mischievous grin widened when Taldor stuttered an apology. *She has a chance here.* Vidmar ignored the boy's rambling summary about his chores. Instead, he pulled Mia aside. "Let's talk," he said, leading her away.

They walked to the southern edge of Hobb's property as Vidmar told Mia everything he had learned from the farmer. The only detail he left out was Hobb's true identity. He feared Mia would tell Taldor or Evanor and that the rift between Hobb and the boys would widen. *Hobb can figure that out on his own.* Mia listened without interrupting, twirling a knot into her hair with a finger. Vidmar stopped and leaned against a wooden fence overlooking a pasture filled with sheep and goats.

Finally, Mia spoke. "Vatis is cursed?" she said softly like she was still trying to comprehend all the information Vidmar had given her.

"I didn't believe it either," Vidmar said, watching a black sheep graze on a patch of green grass amidst a sea of tan. "But it *does* make sense when I think about it."

Mia shook her head. "He rambled about needing to leave Yimser the night I found him, but I thought he was just drunk. I trusted him," Mia said, looking down.

"Me too. I don't believe he is a monster like Hobb thinks, but he'll have difficulty regaining my trust," Vidmar said, watching Mia struggle with the revelation. Vidmar exhaled, itching his scalp while he mustered the courage for his goodbye. "There's something else."

Mia's big brown eyes amplified her curious gaze. "What?" she said innocently.

"I have to go," Vidmar said, forcing the words out.

"Alright, when are we leaving?"

"You can't come with me, Mia."

Mia took a hesitant step backward, whisking an ill-timed fly away with her hand. "I won't get in the way, I promise."

Vidmar choked down a lump in his throat. "It's too dangerous."

"More dangerous than what we have already faced? I saved your life. Please take me with you. You know I can help," Mia said as she stepped closer. She gently grabbed Vidmar's wrist. "Please."

Vidmar pulled back and turned away. He stared at the weeds around a wooden fence post. "I'm sorry, Mia. I won't risk your life for this foolish quest."

Mia pulled Vidmar back by his elbow, glaring at him with pleading eyes. She bit her lower lip, crossing her arms in front of her chest. "It's my life. I should be able to decide when and where to risk it. If this *quest* is so foolish, why continue? Why risk *your* life? People need you; I need you, Vidmar." Mia exhaled and scratched the back of her neck. Her powerful gaze left Vidmar and flashed back toward Hobb's home.

I wish I knew that answer. Why do I keep chasing this crown? Vidmar placed a hand on Mia's shoulder. "I will come back for you. This is a good home, Mia. It's safe. You won't have to hide anymore." Mia never looked up. Vidmar watched her feet drift through the grass. *I will come back for you.* "Please, Mia. I only want what's best for you."

Mia stomped her foot. "How do you know what's best for me? How do I know you'll come back? You'll probably go off and die, and I'll be alone *again*."

"You won't be alone. You'll have Taldor, Ev, and Hobb. You'll learn things I could never teach you, but most importantly, you'll be safe."

Mia sniffed as she rubbed her eyes. Mia turned away with a final disappointment-filled glance and walked back toward the farmhouse. She dragged her feet as she walked; an orange butterfly swooped and glided around her. Vidmar thought about chasing after her; he didn't want to leave her like this. She stopped, turned, and rushed back to Vidmar, tears streaming down her rosy cheeks. "Promise me you'll come back."

Vidmar wrapped Mia in a tight hug. "I promise."

CURSED CHARACTERS

Vatis

Vatis knew he should have left Vicus the night before, immediately after the confrontation with Hobb. He could have saved that merchant's stock of apples. He could have saved a life.

Leaving would have been the honorable thing to do, the prudent thing to do, but Hobb cost him Vidmar's story. The story that was going to make him known throughout Emre. So, he chose to linger another night in spite of Hobb. Vatis knew the curse would escalate. He didn't care about the consequences. He got drunk, told a lazy tale about Mia-The-Maiden, and passed out under the bar.

Now, Vatis looked through the darkness at the smoldering remains of The Barnyard Cat. Lightning struck the tavern's thatched roof on the abnormally warm autumn night. The flames gobbled up the wooden building like a gluttonous king. It seemed like a cruel punishment, but Vatis didn't believe in signs, destiny, or divine intervention. The gods had forgotten about him a long time ago.

Only the fireplace survived, though it wasn't fully intact. A rafter fell as the building collapsed, knocking a few bricks loose. The tavern owner, Kat, sat in the ashes with her back against a charred half-wall. Almost every occupant made it out alive, except an elderly man named Tristan, whose room was unreachable through the flames.

Acer, Hobb's local enemy, stood next to him, covered head to toe in ashes. Apparently, he had been quite the hero during the fire, saving Vatis and three others; he smiled because he knew that Hobb would be furious once he heard who had saved him. Vatis would have made a story about Acer if he could remember what happened, but the night was foggy from the end of his story until he was thrown out of the burning building.

"I can't believe it. The Cat–it's gone," Acer said more to himself than Vatis.

Vatis tapped the bulky farmer's shoulder. His finger left a trail of white, revealing the cotton tunic beneath the ashes. "Thank you."

Acer looked down at Vatis. A jagged scar was visible through the soot on his left cheek. It concaved like a dimple when he spoke. "Hmph," he said as ash blew out of his nose. "What was so important in that bag that you had to run back in for it?"

My pack, he thought as panic punched him in the gut. Relief was instant when he saw the bag by his feet. Kneeling over, he opened the pocket with the letter. The edges were charred, and the remains of the wax seal had melted down in streaks, sealing the letter closed. He carefully ran a burnt finger through the opening, rebreaking the wax. The message, as well as the King's signature, were intact. "This," Vatis said briefly, flashing the letter to Acer before he tucked it back into its pouch.

"I risked my life two fucking times for a letter," Acer yelled. Vatis could see a hint of red beaming beneath the soot on his cheeks.

Memories resurfaced above the smoke-filled haze that clouded his mind when he looked at the smoldering husk of a tavern. He *did* go back in after it. He could feel the flames on his face, the smoke in the air, and the burns on his hands; he charged in, thinking of nothing but his pack. It had everything: his secret thoughts, money, clothes, stories, and the invitation. He remembered the front door collapsing seconds after he ran into the building. Luckily, he knew where to find his pack. He liked to use it as a pillow when ale got the best of him. Visions of flames burned to the front of his memory. After he grabbed his pack, he recalled feeling a strange sense of euphoria amongst the fire and falling timbers. *What was I thinking?* He could hear Acer's voice over the cracking of wood beams, crawled to stay below the smoke, and found Acer in the back of the kitchen. Vatis gripped his pack tight, and the big man threw him out the window. Pain shot through his arm right before the world went black again. Here he was alive, with a raging headache, sore arm, burnt fingers, and all his possessions. He also had Hobb's rival to thank for it. *I've had worse nights.*

Vatis dug into his bag and pulled out a coin purse. He placed a rare 100 Kan piece in Acer's palm. "This bag is my livelihood. I have no home, no friends, nothing but an extra pair of clothes, some gold, and a few stories. Thank you for saving me; I plan to repay you tenfold someday."

Acer's mouth hung open as he examined the coin. Then, untrusting, he bit it; ashes fell from his mustache onto the coin. "I didn't know bards were paid so well."

"We aren't, but I've had my share of wealthy audiences, some of whom were generous. Thank you again, Acer. I am in your debt." The big man looked at the coin, then at Vatis, then back at the coin, and stood wide-eyed and soot-covered as Vatis slung his pack over his shoulder and walked away.

Dawn approached. Vatis knew he needed to leave before Hobb heard about the fire. It was a miracle that he hadn't seen it, and he had no intention of confronting that wizard again. Nor did he want to answer any questions when the guards made their rounds. *If only I had a horse,* he thought. Which morphed into, *I could buy a horse, but no one would sell one at this hour, and half the city is in front of the remains of that sorry excuse of a tavern.* Then, his thoughts darkened. *Half the people are in the square. I could* borrow *a horse, though I've no plans to return to this damn town. Let's say it's for the greater good. These simple farmers wouldn't want me here another hour, let alone another night. Now, where can I find a horse?*

The answer was easy – the stables. They had passed them on their way from Dartmore, and they were relatively unguarded as far as stables go. Kamet said as much when they walked by, "They are just asking for the horses to be stolen," he joked. To which Vidmar replied, "I find it assuring that these people trust each other enough to leave their stables unguarded. Also, we'd have an easy escape if things go south." He clenched his fist, thinking of his missed opportunity. *I could try to find Vidmar.* But he had no idea where he was headed next. The only course of action was to head to Barna for the King's tourney. He could decide what story to tell on the way.

Two low-burning torches illuminated the barn. A black cat paced in front, waiting to get in. Vatis hated cats. He leered behind a stack of rancid-smelling barrels, looking for guards. None patrolled. The longer he waited, the more likely he would be caught. However, the fire seemed to have captured the attention of everyone near the town square. He advanced cautiously, moving heel to toe as Vidmar taught him. The cat stared at him but didn't move. Its big green eyes judged his unstealthy approach.

"Get," he hissed. "Get out of here." But, again, the cat didn't move. Vatis kicked some dust; the damn cat twitched its scarred ears and licked the dust off its front paw. It rubbed against Vatis's shins, arching its back as he slid the heavy door open. The smell of hay and horse shit was unbearable. The last two months in Vicus had been sweltering, doing this barn no favors. Flies as big as his thumbnail buzzed in the stalls, mating, biting, and doing whatever it was that flies did in their limited time. Vatis tried to swat them away. One still managed to bite him on the forearm.

"I need to get out of this damn town," he hissed, rubbing the bite.

Vatis didn't know much about horses; however, he knew the four he found in the stable were no palfreys. They looked closer to pack horses. *No wonder they keep them unguarded. They might as well be donkeys,* he thought. The tall gray stallion near the exit was the only horse that showed any signs of life. His head bobbed up and down as he neighed. Vatis approached cautiously. Nevertheless, he seemed friendly, friendly enough to ride at least. Luckily, the tack was in the stall with the horse. Unluckily, Vatis had no idea how to fit them to the horse. It seemed simple enough: blanket, saddle, stirrups, bridle, bit, reins. *How hard could it be?*

It turned out to be quite tricky. Almost an hour passed, during which Vatis had another run-in with the cat and a moment of panic when he thought he heard footsteps outside the barn, but it was only a horse thrashing about as the pesky flies attacked. Finally, he fit the tack to the horse, reopened the barn door, and tried to make the horse move. It wouldn't. He kicked his heels into the animal's ribs. Nothing. The horse looked backward, slightly annoyed, then dug its hooves into the ground.

"Come on," Vatis said, whipping the reins. The horse shook its black mane; dirt and flies sprang into the air. "Please go." His frustration with the horse was reaching its apex. He could have been miles away by now if he had walked. It took all the patience he had left, but he urged the horse forward with a slight tug on the reins and a gentle kick with his heels. It started walking. "Good boy," he said, scratching the horse behind the ears. After a few minutes of maneuvering, they were out of the barn. Orange light began to appear over the eastern horizon. Dawn. He needed to move. The stable connected directly to the road north. Vatis tried to appear casual as the horse cantered out of town. He looked back once. Smoke rose from the ashes of the tavern. No one stopped him.

It was still dark when Vatis woke. He had made good time throughout the day. The old mare wouldn't win any races, but it kept a consistent pace. He needed to find somewhere to practice a new story. *Hobb cost me everything,* Vatis thought. *What would Kandrian Ambita want to hear? Maybe I could tell his story; a little flattery goes a long way with kings, but I'm confident that's been done before. He needs something new.* A few hours before dusk, exhaustion overcame him. He thought about pulling off the road and making a fire, but he needed to put distance between himself and Hobb. So, he trusted the horse and slept in the saddle. He didn't know how far he had ridden, only that it was night, and they were still on the road. Hopefully, traveling north.

A short time later, soon after saddle sores emerged on Vatis's legs, lights flickered in the distance. *A village?* He wriggled in the saddle, trying to find a comfortable position. The golden lights glowed brighter the closer he came. The full moon illuminated the tops of straw-thatched roofs. A young, lantern-wielding man met him on the road.

"What brings you to Flathill at this hour?" he said, shining the light on Vatis but keeping his other hand close to the ax strapped to the horse's side.

Without thinking, his rehearsed answer escaped his lips, "I'm but a simple bard seeking an audience and shelter."

"It's far too late for an audience. But, as far as shelter goes, I can offer you and your horse a stall in the barn, though dawn is only a few hours away."

Vatis faked excitement. "Oh, we would be most grateful, wouldn't we, Kamet." The horse didn't respond.

"That's a strange name for a horse," the man said, relaxing his tense posture.

"True, it's more fitting of a donkey," Vatis smiled, holding back laughter. He especially enjoyed incorporating small personal jests into his stories, specifically for himself; watching an audience try to figure out a joke was more satisfying than when a room erupted with laughter. The young man looked hilariously confused.

"The barn is down the road. Follow me."

Vatis awoke to shouts from somewhere outside the barn. He ran his fingers through his unusually long hair; pieces of straw fell alongside dirt and dandruff. *Gods, I need to find a barber before I perform in front of the King,* he thought, cracking his neck. The commotion continued. *What in Emre is going on?* Kamet, the horse, munched on hay, then nonchalantly relieved his bowels inches away from Vatis's feet. "That's how you treat me after I helped you escape that sorry excuse of a town." The horse neighed, swishing its tail around. Vatis scrambled away from the awful-smelling animal.

He hadn't decided which character he would play in Flathill. Would he be Vatis-of-the-Road? Would he try something new? Would one of his old characters surface in his hour of need? He'd been stuck in Vatis-of-the-Road for so long that it felt odd to abandon him. He tried singing, humming, and whistling, but none of his musical characters felt like making an appearance. It was tough to shake his somber mood. His thoughts always returned to his missed opportunity with Vidmar. *I'll never find a story with that much potential again.* His thoughts darkened until sunlight attacked his eyes when he stepped out of the barn. Vatis tried to squint the stars away, but it only made him sneeze, which in turn caused his sore back to spasm. The ridiculous attack ended with him on his back, rolling and sneezing like a capsized tortoise with allergies.

Gentle hands helped him to his feet. "Are you alright?" a kind, feminine voice asked. Vatis blinked as a stunning red-haired woman came into focus. Her gentle, fawn-like eyes kindly examined him through cascading bangs.

Oddly, Vatis couldn't think of a response. He just nodded and tried to rub his back until a cramp tore into his shoulder. He ground his teeth to keep himself from screaming. Finally, he managed a short, hissed thank you. She smiled and then walked toward a group gathered in the village. Vatis rubbed his eyes. The woman's backside was almost as pleasant to look at as her front; her hips swayed underneath a flowing yellow skirt. Vatis unconsciously followed the woman, partly because he wanted to see her rosy, freckled face again, partly to see what the commotion was, and partly because his charismatic yet troublesome character of Dainius emerged. Dainius hadn't appeared in years; the fraternizing character was a staple in his twenties, but he had long been lost in the dusty cobwebs of Vatis's mind as he pursued more intellectual goals. His anxiety, exhaustion, and temptations were playing strange games with his mind.

He inhaled deeply, tapping the woman on the shoulder. "What's going on?" He said in a smooth, baritone voice.

She smiled as she turned around. Her white teeth gleamed behind thin pink lips. "A miracle. The well is full." He watched her tongue glide invitingly along her bottom lip.

Vatis acted surprised. "Impossible. Thank the gods."

The woman raised onto her toes to see over the crowd gathered in front of the stone well. Her skirt lifted, revealing slender calves. She dropped down. "It's been so long since the gods showed us any favor." She hugged Vatis in excitement. Vatis returned her enthusiasm but backed away to conceal parts of himself that were *too* excited. It had been too long since he'd hugged a woman. "The gods have finally answered our prayers," she said, bouncing up and down. Vatis strained himself to focus on her eyes and not the parts of her that were bouncing pleasingly. "It's been dry for nearly two years. We've had to haul barrels to the river, fill them, and bring them back. I can't believe it—a miracle."

"Unbelievable," Vatis whispered in feigned astonishment. The truth was that this wasn't the first well his curse had refilled. Years ago, shortly after realizing his condition, in a small village near Wayland, a well, much like this one, had incredibly replenished itself.

"I'm sorry. I haven't even introduced myself. I'm Jana," she said, flashing a bright smile punctuated by dimples on her rosy cheeks.

Vatis bowed. "I'm Dainius, a traveling bard who just happened to use your lovely barn as an inn last night."

Jana grasped Vatis's forearm. His palms began to sweat. "A bard. Truly. Oh, you must entertain us tonight."

"I should leave," Vatis said, genuinely disappointed. "I have an appointment to keep in Barna." However, her large emerald eyes begged him to stay along with a particular, unused part of his body.

"Surely, one night won't delay you," she said. Her fingers gently traced their way up his forearm to his shoulder.

Vatis had forgotten how influential his miracles could be after hiking through forests, mountains, and dark alleys for almost a year, unable to witness the magic at work. He knew he would stay, but he didn't want to sleep in the barn again. "I don't know if my back can handle another night in the barn."

Jana smirked. "There's room in my cottage, a comfortable straw mattress with cotton sheets. It's been so long since a bard performed in Flathill. Please stay."

Vatis choked back his guilt, surrendering to more pressing urges. "One night."

"Oh, wonderful," Jana said, wrapping Vatis in another hug. This time, he did not back away. Her eyes glanced downward slightly as she bit her bottom lip. She turned and pulled him into the crowd. "Everyone, this is Dainius, a bard. He will perform for us tonight." The crowd cheered as Vatis tried to adjust his trousers.

An overly enthusiastic rooster welcomed the new day. Vatis stretched his aching limbs as quietly as possible in Jana's creaky bed. She stirred, exposing her bare shoulder and neck resting on her soft strawberry hair; purple-green marks trailed from her collarbone to the bottom of her ear. *I could stay another night,* he thought, looking at Jana. *I could stay here forever.* His thoughts trailed off as Jana opened her eyes. "Good morning," she said, smiling through squinted eyes.

Vatis kissed her. "Good morning, my sweet. How did you sleep?"

"I've never slept better," Jana said, pulling Vatis closer.

As he leaned in for another kiss, a scream came from somewhere in the town square. "What was that?" Jana said. Her eyes widened as she tried to look out her small window.

"Probably just the children playing," Vatis said, pulling her back to him.

Jana resisted. "They never play like that." The breeze brought another scream through the window, followed by a wailing, sorrowful moan like thunder after lightning. Jana rolled over Vatis, threw on a gray cotton dress, slipped into her shoes, and bolted out the door before Vatis could so much as button his tunic. *That's my cue,* he thought, gathering his things.

A few moments later, he found Jana and three other townsfolk gathered at the fence surrounding the cabbage field. Jana was rubbing the back of an old man whose name Vatis could not remember. Jealousy sprouted in his throat. "What happened?" he asked Jana, gently touching her shoulder. Then he noticed. The entire field of cabbage had wilted. The violet heads were just days away from picking when he toured Flathill yesterday; now, they were brown and wilted.

Jana stepped away from Vatis to comfort the simple farmer who'd lost a season's worth of cabbage. "How did this happen? What cruel god made this jest?"

"I've heard the black pod sucker bug can destroy acres of crop in no time," Vatis said, pretending to offer some insight. He knew who was responsible. It wasn't the rare bugs. It was him and whichever god left his curse on the world.

The farmer considered this for a moment, rubbing his nose with his palm. Then, unsatisfied, he bent over to examine his crops. "That's true, but there's no sign of pod suckers, and they prefer tomatoes or cotton. No, this is the work of the gods. The eternal darkness is coming. This is a sign," he said, ripping open the brown husk of a dead cabbage plant. No bugs fell out.

Jana helped the farmer to his feet. "Why would the gods refill our well one day and then destroy our crops the next?"

"The gods are cruel and care little for the lives of peasants," the farmer said.

Vatis tried to comfort Jana, but she brushed him away in favor of the feeble farmer. His jealousy grew.

"The gods are trying to send us a message. Brother Coen could help, "Jana said, pointing to the narrow building with a decaying steeple atop its roof.

The farmer snorted.

Vatis used the distracted bantering to drift back toward the barn. *I'll miss you, Jana,* Vatis thought. She deserved better than Flathill; she deserved better than a farmer. Who knew what would happen if he stayed longer – the curse usually brought progressively worse side effects the longer he stayed in one place. The longest he'd ever tested it was three days, and by the end of the third day, nearly a quarter of the people of Wayland were dead or dying. He watched the group saunter toward the chapel. No one knew he left. No one cared, not even Jana. Even his happiest nights ended with him alone on the road, exhausted.

INTERLUDE

Zidane

I'm going to kill you, Vidmar," Zidane whispered into the bottom of his empty waterskin. He needed an ale. If it weren't for Vidmar, he wouldn't be thirsty in the miserable Overpass Inn on the shore of the Camil River. *Bridgeway,* he thought. *What a dumb name for a town.* Instead, he'd be whispering secrets into Alcin's ear, sipping fine wine, and living the luxurious life he deserved. But no. Here he sat, broke, exhausted, and hungry, watching a blind man struggle to spoon some soup into his mouth.

"Can I get you anything, sir," a haggard waitress asked. Her lip quivered beneath a dark mole. She wiped her hands on her tattered apron, swaying side to side while she waited for a reply. *What can you give me? You common wench. Do you know who I am, who I will be?* Zidane refrained from voicing his opinion. Instead, he watched her sway. Her dark green skirt brushed dust into a neat line under the table.

"Ale. I need ale, but what do you have to eat?" Zidane asked, fishing in his coin purse.

The waitress stopped swaying. "Tonight, we have roast perch, caught fresh this morning, fried catfish, and a fish stew."

Zidane rolled his eyes. He hated fish. "Do you have anything other than fish?"

"Um," the waitress began. "Bread."

"Then, I'll take a loaf of your freshest bread and two ales to wash it down." Zidane dug out a few coins. "How much?"

The waitress did some not-so-quick math, counting on her pox-scarred fingers. "Ah, seven Kan."

Zidane felt his eyeballs nearly pop out of his head. "Seven, fucking Kan. You're joking."

The waitress stepped back. "Grain is hard to come by with the drought in Flathill." She held up her hands defensively.

"Fucking drought. I'll give you six."

The waitress stepped back again, wringing her hands together like she was washing dishes. "Del said it's three for a loaf of bread and two for ale and that I'm not to take anything less, and if someone doesn't want to pay, they can talk to him on the dock."

I can't believe I'm bartering with a tavern wench over bread and ale. Zidane's face felt hot. He reached into his purse for another coin. Luckily, he found one. "Tell Del, whoever the fuck that is, that I don't appreciate being robbed, much less being fucked, but I'm tired and starving and don't feel like walking to the docks."

"I prefer the company of women like Ilyana here," a deep voice called from Zidane's right. Wet boots squished against the floor as they strode next to the waitress. He put a muscular arm around Ilyana's waist and rested the other hand atop a fierce-looking ax. "No need to walk to the docks. I'm Del. This is my Inn. Is something wrong?"

Zidane's throat tightened as he searched for words. The hair on the back of his neck stood. "No, sir, no problem," he said, trying not to whimper.

"No, you were saying something about being robbed. The last thing I want is for my patrons to feel threatened," Del said. His voice lowered an octave, emphasizing the last word while his hand moved onto his ax's handle.

Zidane brushed the hair on his neck down as he tried to weasel out of the hole he dug for himself. *You're an idiot.* He thought—*a goddamn idiot.* "I apologize, sir. I meant no harm. It's been a long few weeks, and the road has gotten the best of me. I apologize. Here," he said, pulling out another coin. "A little something extra."

Del took the coin and handed it to Ilyana. A darkly sinister expression morphed into a smile as he faced Zidane again. "I hope you enjoy your stay at the Overpass, though I would steer clear of the docks tonight. They are extra slippery, and I wouldn't want anyone falling in."

Zidane forced himself to say, "Thank you."

"You're welcome. If you ever find yourself in Bridgeway again, find another place to sleep," Del said, rubbing Ilyana's arm.

If I'm ever in Bridgeway again, I'll burn this Inn to the ground. Zidane sat at his lonely table for quite some time, gnawing on the stale bread and drinking the sour ale. *The worst eight Kan I've ever spent.*

Ilyana approached cautiously. "Would you like another ale? The bard is expected to perform any minute now."

Zidane hadn't noticed the Overpass slowly filling with occupants while he stewed on his confrontation with Del, thinking of various means of revenge. "Do you have any wine or mead? Something less *sour* than this ale."

Ilyana picked up Zidane's dishes. "We have a Numerian wine, but it's five Kan a glass or goat's milk."

He thought about protesting but then noticed Del watching from behind the bar. "I'll have the wine," Zidane said, reaching into his purse. He only had seven Kan left. Reluctantly, he handed out five coins, leaving him with two Kan for the rest of his journey to Haran. *This won't be enough.* He wiggled his unpracticed pickpocket's fingers like the air around him was somehow ticklish.

Ilyana returned with the wine a few moments later. Zidane took a long drink. The dry red featured delicious notes of citrus and walnut – an incredible improvement over his first drink. "Ah. Did you say a bard was performing soon?" Zidane asked, licking a few stray drops of wine off his lips.

The waitress stopped. "Yes, he's taking a bath but should be down soon."

"Who is the bard?"

"Dainius. He's quite charming—came in a couple of hours before you," Ilyana said. Her eyes fluttered like a handmaid watching a handsome prince parade through a city.

Zidane slunk into his seat. *Of course, it isn't Vatis.*

Ilyana stepped backward, obviously trying to distance herself from Zidane. "Let me know if you need anything else," she said in a tone that hoped Zidane wanted nothing more from her.

"Damnit," Zidane yelled before he realized how close to Ilyana he was. Del rushed to her side. Zidane looked up with his hands held high. "I apologize. I traveled with a bard a few months ago and hoped to see him again. Was this bard alone?" He finished, fidgeting on the wobbly stool.

Del sent Ilyana into the kitchen with a quick gesture and a pat on the back. "Unless you count a horse."

"Thank you, Del. I meant no harm," he said, adjusting the brim of his hat.

Del snorted and returned to the bar. A short time later, the bard appeared. *That's Vatis,* he thought, nearly jumping out of his seat. The Vatis-of-the-Road – Vidmar's companion. The bard was thinner and cleaner than the last time he saw him, but it *was* Vatis. The bard introduced himself as he walked between two tables. His voice was different than Zidane remembered, deeper, more exaggerated. Why were his eyes and ears trying to deceive him as his luck finally turned? *That must be him.*

The bard stepped onto a small stage that could also have been described as a large crate. Vatis looked older, too, despite the fresh shave and bath. His clothes were tattered. The bags under his eyes were so large one could smuggle coins in them, and the wrinkles on his forehead seemed to deepen like a creek after a brutal storm. *Where's Vidmar? What happened?* Zidane needed answers but decided to wait until after the story ended, so he took off his hat and tried to blend into the crowd. *There's no harm in a bit of entertainment first.*

As much as Zidane hated to admit it, Vatis or Dainius was a splendid bard. He had never heard someone tell such a captivating tale. The tale he performed tonight was a classic known throughout Emre – The Knight of Seven Lives. Most people heard this story from their mothers at bedtime. Zidane was no exception. He could hear his mother's voice as Vatis described the Knight's first death. He could smell his childhood home as Vatis portrayed the fifth and most gruesome death.

Zidane had barely touched his wine as Vatis reached the climax. He almost felt bad that he had to interrogate Vatis after this performance. Then he remembered the night in the woods, Vidmar's brutality, spending a night tied to a tree, and the massacre on the docks in Yimser. Who cares that he meant to rob or kill them in the first place? Or that he planned on letting them be tortured? Not Zidane. He was done caring about the thoughts of others. Well, except for Alcin and his mother, of course. No sane person wanted Alcin as their enemy, and even Alcin would fear Zidane's mother.

Vatis finished with a dramatic bow, basking in the applause from the small audience. *He wasn't that good,* Zidane thought as a table of women began whistling. *Give me a few months of practice, and I could be twice the bard he is.* Zidane lied to himself. He watched Vatis mingle with patrons at the table nearest the stage. Their laughter infuriated him. Ilyana clearly admired Vatis. She lingered near every table he greeted. Finally, he threw an arm around her, singing a song Zidane was vaguely familiar with but couldn't place.

Zidane threw his hat on as Vatis approached his table. The bard froze.

"Wonderful performance," Zidane said, smiling.

After a second's hesitation, Vatis began another performance. "Why, thank you, kind sir," he said more enthusiastically than any man had a right to be. "Have a *wonderful* night," he finished, perfectly emulating Zidane's greeting.

Vatis started to turn towards the final table when Zidane called out. "Have we met before," he said playfully.

"No, I don't think so, but I have met many people in my travels. Excuse me, sir, may your feet find the road," Vatis said, greeting the final table.

Zidane waited patiently, sipping his expensive wine and watching Vatis mingle merrily with the dull-witted guests. The bard never even glanced at Zidane. *That arrogant fool will remember me after tonight.* The casualness Vatis displayed boiled Zidane's blood. His fingers ached as he released his unconsciously clenched fists. Finally, Vatis broke the tediously long conversation and gathered his belongings from the stage. *Why doesn't he keep his pack in his room like a normal person?* Everything about the bard annoyed Zidane, his blatant acting, his stupid whistling, and that dumb smirk that seemed etched into his face.

Vatis slung his pack over his shoulder, waved goodbye to the few remaining patrons, and bowed to Del behind the bar. Zidane had to act now. "Excuses me, Vatis, sir," he called. The bard turned around slowly. "Could I have a word with you outside?" Zidane had to pressure him in front of the crowd to ensure that Vatis kept up his act.

"It is rather late; perhaps we could meet in the morning," Vatis said, adjusting his pack.

"It will only take a second," Zidane said, performing his best impression of a child begging for a sweet.

Vatis looked at Del, nodded to Ilyana, then stepped toward Zidane. "Who am I to turn down such a well-dressed fan?" he said. *You motherfucker,* Zidane thought, holding the door open. *I'm going to enjoy killing you.*

The bard took a deep breath as they stepped outside and sprinted into the darkness. "Why do they always run?" Zidane sighed.

GRECO'S CROWN

Vidmar

Vidmar found an opening. All he needed to do was squeeze through the narrow passageway, and Greco's crown would be his, or so he hoped. Unfortunately, the cave had other ideas. His forearm caught on a sharp rock as he pushed himself deeper into the tight, dark cavity; a jagged mineral dug into his arm as he tried to pull free. After a few choice words and a firm yank, the cave relinquished, yielding a jacket sleeve torn to the cuff and a deep finger-length gash in his forearm.

Blood poured from the wound like water from a spring. His arm throbbed with pain, his rough, tanned skin turning a deep shade of crimson. Vidmar tried to tear his ruined sleeve from his wounded arm but couldn't grip the slippery fabric with his crippled hand.

"Kamet, I need a little help," he said, running up to the big mercenary, who absently examined a stalactite with a lantern.

"Gods, what happened?" Kamet said, looking at the wound.

"Does it matter? Just rip the sleeve off and apply a tourniquet," Vidmar said, pointing above his elbow.

"You're getting clumsy in your old age," Kamet said. After some effort, Kamet fastened a makeshift tourniquet. The bleeding slowed. He cleaned the wound with a generous pour of wine from his waterskin; any pour of wine, not into his mouth, was a generous pour for Kamet.

Vidmar hissed as the alcohol cleansed the tender laceration.

Kamet laughed. "I have to say. You look pretty dumb with one sleeve and half your fingers."

"Still good enough for your mother."

Kamet scowled, then poked Vidmar's wound. "What did I tell you about my mother?"

Vidmar laughed, but the vibrations stabbed at his cut. "Do you have a bandage?"

"No."

"You brought enough wine to start a tavern, but you didn't bring a bandage," Vidmar said, gesturing for a drink of the wine. Kamet obliged.

"You didn't bring one either."

Vidmar exhaled. "I had other things on my mind. Use this." He pointed to his other jacket sleeve. *What good is a jacket with one sleeve?* Kamet didn't hesitate; he ripped the sleeve off in one smooth swipe. It was a sloppy bandage, but eventually, the bleeding stopped.

Vidmar needed to focus. He didn't know how long they had been searching in the mysterious woods: an hour, a day, a week. Time seemed to move strangely in the thick air of the Kokor. It didn't matter. Whatever the length was, it was too long. He didn't remember why they entered the cave, only that it felt right. He felt pulled toward it. *The forest will guide you,* Hobb's words echoed in his head. Vidmar thought the farmer was full of shit, but he hadn't been wrong yet. Whenever he felt lost, an opening would appear, or a breeze would push him from behind. *I'm going crazy*, Vidmar thought, rubbing his arm.

He almost hit his head on a long, serrated stalactite. A reflexive dodge jerked his whole body sideways, his head tilting as the rock almost trimmed his unusually long beard. His feet crossed and danced to keep himself from falling, a nearly flawless evasive maneuver that ended with his left foot in a shallow puddle, splashing cool water up to his knees.

Kamet laughed. "Graceful." His laughter was energizing in the cold cave.

"Great," Vidmar said, wiping water beads off his damp pants. "We should have kept our heads down and stayed in the army."

"Where's the adventure in that?" Kamet said almost seriously. "I'd rather follow you than that washed-up king any day. Even if it means dying in this forest searching for a crown that probably doesn't exist."

Vidmar nudged Kamet. "Beats guard duty."

"Aye. It does."

Despite the gash in his arm, his ruined jacket, and wet pants, Vidmar smirked; he would find the crown. *The forest will guide me. Fucking Hobb. Well, here I am, cut, damp, and lost, dreading leaving this cave for the forest that lurks outside. Now, where do I go?*

They walked further into the cave, crouching as its ceiling gradually lowered. A shoulder-width pathway revealed itself to Vidmar's right. He numbly ran his bloody hand over the smooth rock, creating a ruby-colored handprint to mark his way in case they needed to backtrack. He slid sideways as he ventured deeper into the passageway. The tunnel became tighter and tighter. Vidmar sucked in his already thin stomach for extra room.

"I'm not going to fit through there," Kamet said.

"Alright, then you're on guard duty," Vidmar said.

Kamet kicked Vidmar in the shin. "Don't get yourself killed."

"I'll try my best." Vidmar moved deeper into the crevasse, carefully moving the lamp in his hand up and down. Mercifully, the light protruded deeper into the cave, signaling that the narrow passage had opened.

Soon, he found himself in a chamber as tall as a cathedral. It was unlike any other cavern he had been in. It looked like an ancient dining hall, or an artificial dome, or *perhaps* a burial chamber of a once-powerful king's crown. *Please.* Water dripped steadily in the chamber, filling the room with a soothing echo. The air smelled different, unlike the thick, stale air that hung throughout the cave's entrance, but a rotten egg-like scent from nearby groundwater.

Vidmar tiptoed around the chamber, carefully watching his steps to avoid further damage to his boots. He surveyed the walls. Columns of minerals sat like the giant pillars of a palace throne room. He looked for another route deeper into the cave. He circled the chamber ten times, shining his lantern up and down almost every inch of the chamber walls; the light could not reach the darkness of the domed ceiling. *Dead end.*

"Damnit," Vidmar yelled. "Damnit, damnit, damnit. There's nothing here."

"What's going on?" Kamet's concerned voice echoed through the chamber.

"Nothing," Vidmar yelled back. "I'm just a fucking idiot who trusted a crazy old man. There's nothing here. I'm going to take one more look."

Kamet didn't respond.

Vidmar continued to berate himself with a slew of insults that would have mortified Kamet's mother. After one final chastising, he took a deep breath and collected his thoughts. He put his lantern on the chamber floor, running his fingers through his dusty hair. Then, he buried his face in his hands and collapsed onto his knees. The craggy floor stabbed his shins, but he didn't think about the pain. His whole body hurt. What was one more injury? Vidmar inhaled deeply, the cool, moist air soothing his twitching limbs. *There has to be something here.*

Vidmar placed his left hand on the cavern wall, feeling for markings or anything that signaled there was more to this room. He knocked every few feet, hoping to find a hollow spot, but that tactic only made his knuckles bleed. The flame in his lantern burned low; he didn't have much more time, and Kamet had the extra oil. *Why is this chamber here?* His hand continued its desperate search until it slid into a small crack. *Please.* The lantern shook as Vidmar tried to examine the crevasse. It looked like a standard crack. He put his ear to it, listening for noise on the other side. There was nothing. Vidmar blew into the small fissure to clear away any lingering debris, then reexamined it.

It's just a crack. "Fuck," he yelled.

"Vidmar," Kamet called from outside the chamber. "Are you alright?"

"I'm fine, Kamet. It's just another dead end."

"Damn. Well, hurry up. I forgot how boring guard duty was," Kamet said. His voice echoed in the chamber.

"One more pass. There has to be something here."

Vidmar continued his thorough search of the chamber. He was halfway through his final pass when the tip of his left middle finger dipped into a small hole. *Please,* he thought, silently begging every god he knew. Vidmar brought his lantern up to the spot. Upon closer inspection, it wasn't a hole but a triangular carving. *The Pact's Symbol.* His heart pounded in his chest. His fingers quivered as he traced the engraving. It was unnatural; something or someone had carved this into the stone. Instinctually, he pressed the center, but nothing happened.

"What does this mean? Why is it here?" Vidmar whispered into the symbol. He rubbed his eyes and pressed the triangle again; the rock didn't respond. He bit the insides of his cheeks to keep himself from screaming. He brought the lantern closer, examining every inch of the shape. It *was* The Pact's symbol; Vidmar was sure of that. He felt relief that there was another clue, but he didn't know if he could decipher it.

Vidmar walked around the chamber. This time, looking for similar engravings, but the rest of the chamber walls were frustratingly bare. He returned to his clue. *What am I missing?* He thought as he pressed each of the three points of the triangle. Again, nothing happened. He punched the shape. His knuckles cracked on the stone wall, but the triangle remained unchanged, mocking his frivolous attempts to reveal its secret.

"Vidmar," Kamet called.

"I found something. Give me a few more minutes," Vidmar said.

"Hurry. This cave is playing games with me," Kamet said, his voice fading into the darkness.

Vidmar's eyes felt heavy; he struggled to keep them open. The weight of his task anchored him in place. He rested his head above the engraving. "What's the secret? Everlasting darkness, I'm going to die before I find this damn crown. It lies with the dead, and Vid...." Suddenly, Vidmar heard a sharp crack like a stone breaking. He stepped back and watched the triangular engraving disappear into the wall. A silver-blue light emanated from the hole where The Pact's symbol used to be, leaving a tiny, glowing tunnel into the cave. More cracking and crunching made Vidmar feel like the cave was collapsing. "Shit," he yelled, stepping further back.

Bright silver lines flowed from the center of the engraving across the cracks in the rock like granite. These lights spidered from floor to ceiling, projecting a faint glow throughout the chamber. Vidmar felt his jaw hang open as he stood. Debris fell; small stones dropped onto his shoulders. A loud, sharp snap near his feet forced him to jump. Underneath the engraving, ribbons of light formed a rectangle, and then a stone emerged from the wall like a drawer opening. The only difference was this drawer was a solid slab of silver stone.

Once it finished moving, a smaller cube rose from its center in the same fashion but vertically. *What's happening?* Vidmar thought, in awe. For a moment, he forgot about his injuries, the forest, Kamet, and even Elisa.

Three bands of light appeared from the bottom of the cube and danced around the larger stone. They circled the cube, then dove into the shape before reemerging as gold engravings–The Pact's symbols. He couldn't translate them, nor did he have any material to create an etching. The triangular mark was etched into the center of each side of the cube. Vidmar's throat tightened in anticipation. He clenched his jaw and pressed the center of the golden marking on top of the cube. A dull grinding sound escaped the cube as the engraving sank into the box. Then, it turned clockwise until the top half created a star shape with the bottom half.

Finally, the grinding stopped, and Vidmar lifted the top half off. The air that escaped was clean, refreshing, and citrus-scented. *Hopefully, that's not poison.* Dust covered the crown inside the box. "Gods," Vidmar whispered before biting his lip to contain his excitement.

He examined the gold, jeweled crown in the box before lifting it. Three rubies were affixed in gold adjacent to three emeralds on the opposite side. Between the six jewels sat the largest diamond Vidmar had ever seen – almost as large as his fist. This *was* the crown of Slavanes Greco – the crown of Emre. Vidmar's palms grew sweaty, his throat swelled, his eyes watered, and he struggled to control his trembling limbs. Finally, after years of searching and losing almost every person he cared about, Vidmar found the crown. He didn't know how to feel. When he dreamt of this day, he thought he would feel joy, euphoria, or, at the very least, closure. But he only felt confusion and sorrow.

He lifted the crown from the box and realized it sat on something – another stone similar to his original clue. He couldn't read the markings in the dark but could feel The Pact's etchings as he ran his fingers across the slab. He quickly slipped it into his pocket. *I have to get this to Hobb. He will know what the message is*, Vidmar thought before returning his attention to the crown. *What do I do now? Do I give it to Alcin? I have a contract, and he will find me eventually. I could give it to Elisa; she would make a good queen, but she'd probably give it to her psychotic brother. Maybe Hobb would take it? Or I could leave the crown, rip the jewels off, and finally escape.*

Vidmar had no idea what to do with the crown now that he finally had it. He put the top back on the cube, the golden light turned green, then disappeared, and it sealed itself shut. The grinding noise returned, along with a glowing red marking on top of the box. He tried to pry it open, but it wouldn't budge. *I guess I'm not putting it back.*

The chartreuse lights on the cube turned azure. More ribbons of light appeared throughout the chamber, now a deeper shade of blue. They circled the room as Vidmar wrapped and carefully placed the crown in his pack. He checked that the crown was secure and that his bag had no crown-sized holes; satisfied, he slung the leather bag over his shoulder. The azure lights flew around the room like trapped birds. They circled Vidmar once, then blinked, then disappeared, leaving only a faint glow from his lantern to light the room.

"Kamet, we're going home," he called.

His friend didn't respond. Vidmar only heard a faint drumming noise above him, like hundreds of pebbles falling onto the cave's ceiling. The drumming stopped. Something hard and heavy fell behind him.

OUT OF LUCK

Vidmar

The cavern dimmed as Vidmar's lantern flickered in the darkness. The drumming started again, this time from the floor. He saw a swiftly moving shadow in the faint light, but it disappeared before he could identify the creature.

He reached for a weapon, Acer's knife, the blade that brought him to Hobb. Vidmar usually stored it in a sheathe beneath his jacket sleeve, but he no longer had any sleeves, so he had moved it to his waist. His highly conditioned brain wasn't accustomed to change. He grabbed his forearm but no knife. He cursed at himself silently. He fumbled at his waist, trying to remember where he stored the blade. He found the brown, leather-wrapped handle near the top of his buttocks. The drumming quickened as the creature circled its prey.

A giant arthropod scrambled into the light, the biggest Vidmar had ever seen. A black-scaled beast with at least one hundred legs supporting a segmented body as large as a horse, two antennae probed the air, vibrating with an audible hum. It left the light before he could react. A moment of hesitation evaluating his predator had cost him a chance to kill the brute while he could see it. Vidmar wasn't sure if his knife would puncture the skin or if he could muster enough power with his unsteady grip. If its feet sounded like an avalanche of rocks, its scales would be almost indestructible. The avalanche grew louder as it approached from the dark. *Think.*

Vidmar turned, using his hearing to track the monster. Even if his knife could pierce its skin, he wouldn't be able to see where he was stabbing. He took a calculated step back to the lantern. He bent down painfully, searching the ground with his left hand, trying to locate his only source of light while keeping his eyes, ears, and knife focused on defending his life. The blade nearly slipped from his hands. Vidmar inched backward carefully and silently, moving in the direction of the light. His hand crashed into the rectangular iron lantern. The light flickered to the right while a long screeching sound echoed through the chamber. The monster made a gargling, hissing noise like a snake warding off a predator with half a mouse in its jaws. The drumming charged towards Vidmar. He tried to grab the lantern's handle, but his two fingers kept slipping. He burnt the knuckles of his missing fingers, tracing them up the hot glass until he finally found the lantern's handle and swung the light toward the clamor. He crouched, barely hanging on to the lantern in one hand and trying to find a decent grip on the knife. Vidmar squinted and pushed both weapons toward the charging creature's snapping jaws.

The creature stopped as if blinded by the light. Terror coursed through Vidmar's veins, briefly paralyzing him. Finally able to see the monster, his jaw opened. It was larger than a horse, nearly ten feet long; the first handful of its segments rose into the air—each segment accompanied by numerous sword-like legs. Four black eyes glared in the light. Its pincer-shaped mouth snapped back and forth. Vidmar aimed the light closer to the monster's eyes. It backed away.

"So, you're afraid of the light," Vidmar said. *I might survive this yet.* A smile crept onto his face.

The creature retreated into the blackness. Vidmar spun, trying to locate it.

"Where did you go? You ugly bastard. I just want to chat," Vidmar continued his nervous rambling as he sheathed his blade and switched the lantern into his left hand.

He saw the tight crack of an entrance he used to enter the chamber and ran. "I hope you're slower than you look."

Behind him, he heard the familiar marching of the monster's legs. He turned around quickly, shining the lantern at his pursuer. It screeched, not like the hiss it made before, but like a painful scream of frustration. The monster backed away again as if catching its breath. Vidmar stepped backward, feeling for the cavern's exit with his free hand and tightly gripping the lantern with the other. The drumming began again, moving up the wall to his left. He adjusted the lantern accordingly. Hundreds of legs moved higher onto the slick, jagged ceiling above him. Vidmar was unsure if the creature was retreating or positioning itself for a lethal strike. Unfortunately, it was the latter. The creature hissed as it dove for the kill.

All Vidmar could do was spin and duck. The monster landed on his back, forcing him to drop his lantern. Light flashed, then faded away into deathly darkness. He could hear jaws snapping and crunching on top of him, but he didn't feel any pain until one of its rock-like legs scraped his calf. Luckily, the creature's killing blow landed on his pack. The crown provided enough depth to stop the monster's teeth before they reached Vidmar's back. He struggled to stay on his feet. He crept toward his escape; his fingertips swiped against cold stone. The monster writhed and wrestled with the pack while its legs continued to tear into

Vidmar's flesh. Then, his fingers found air. He jumped sideways. *I'm not dying here,* he thought, unstrapping his pack. The monster fell backward, and Vidmar slipped into the tight exit. The loss of his bag and the crown sucked the air from his lungs. Vidmar was frozen in place as the creature tore the bag apart. A metallic clang rang through the crevasse as the crown bounced against the stone floor. Vidmar breathed heavily. He thought about returning for the crown, but with no light source, he stood no chance against the monster. "Kamet," he called as he pushed through the narrow tunnel. He was unsure if the creature could fit through the passageway. Vidmar methodically slid backward toward freedom, listening for the terrifying marching sound, fighting the urge to go back for the crown.

His knees trembled as he emerged from the tunnel. Each breath felt forced, like the air in his lungs was afraid to leave his body. He inhaled through his nose, smelling the faint rotten egg odor from the chamber. "Kamet," he repeated, searching the darkness for his friend. "Where are you?"

Vidmar couldn't see the light from Kamet's lantern anywhere but continued moving forward. "Kamet," He called again. "Kamet." He stepped carefully, moving from heel to toe with practiced grace. Slowly, he began to see. Light from the cave's entrance reached lazily into the abyss. Vidmar's eyes adjusted as shadows became shapes. Glass shattered beneath his boot. The remains of Kamet's broken lantern lay scattered on the cave floor. *No, no, no.* "Kamet." His voice cracked as he called for him. The monster's drumming began again from somewhere behind him. Then, he heard a faint frog-like croak. The croak deepened into a cough. "Vidmar," Kamet called through the darkness.

Vidmar found Kamet kneeling with a hand on his mace, covered in black ooze. Blood dripped from a deep gash in his neck. "Vidmar," he choked.

Vidmar tried to make a joke, but he couldn't find the words. He wanted to greet his friend like they always had. He wanted to assure Kamet that he would be alright, but he knew he couldn't. The cut on his neck trailed onto his shoulder, revealing a part of his clavicle. Steam rose from the black ooze that must have been poison or acid as it burned Kamet's leather armor. "I'll get you out of here." That was all Vidmar could muster; even those words were coughed out.

Kamet shook his head. "No." He tried to stand but collapsed onto one knee. The monster's drumming grew louder. Kamet's eyes widened. "Go," he coughed. Blood splattered onto his lips.

Vidmar helped Kamet stand. "I'm not leaving without you," he said, feeling the terrifying heat from the monster's poison.

Stones fell from the cave's ceiling, followed by a deafening crash as rocks collapsed behind them. Hissing, the creature emerged from the rubble. Kamet's mace connected with the monster's jaw and sent the beast tumbling backward. "Go, Vidmar."

"You can't die on guard duty," Vidmar said, trying to pull Kamet with him. Instead, his friend pushed him away toward the mouth of the cave.

The monster charged. Again, Kamet repelled it with a mighty swing. "I can die for you," Kamet said. Each word was forced out slowly, painfully. Kamet nodded, exhaled, and turned back to the assaulting monster. "Go," he called without looking.

Vidmar forced his feet to move, each step growing heavier as he watched Kamet become the attacker. The cave rumbled. The old mercenary screamed as he charged, tackling the beast into the stones. Vidmar felt the floor shake. Sunlight poked through the darkness, beckoning him back to the forest. Vidmar bit his lip, clenched his fists, and ran to the light.

Behind Vidmar, Kamet bellowed. His roar was muffled, then enveloped by leather, blood, steel, and rock, morphing into one bone-chilling squishing sound. Vidmar did not stop running. He followed the faint glow emanating from the cave's opening.

Vidmar smelled crisp, evergreen trees and open air. Tremors reverberated beneath his unsteady feet. He stopped running. *Kamet. I can't do this without you.* A true hero wouldn't abandon his friend, but Vidmar had never considered himself a hero. He took a step back toward his friend. He took another step; his eyes strained as they adjusted to the darkness again. The tremors worsened. A rock almost fell on Vidmar's head, but instinctively, he jumped to safety. Vidmar winced as he looked up and saw the cave collapse on the monster, his fruitless quest, and his last friend. *I'm so sorry, Kamet*, Vidmar thought, backing away from the cave. *Why do I always live?* A beam of sunlight poked through the dense canopy, illuminating a patch of lush green grass, but regret yanked Vidmar back to the cave.

Once the rubble settled, Vidmar frantically searched for openings. "Kamet," he yelled. "Kamet." He pulled rocks away until his fingers bled. He circled the pile of stones until his legs couldn't move. Then, exhausted, Vidmar drifted into the glade, collapsed, rolled onto his back, took a deep breath, and cried.

Vidmar inhaled grass and mud, waking up face down in the small glade. Something poked his back. He rolled onto his stomach, unsheathed a blade, and prepared for a fight. No attack came. A deer-like creature stepped back, neighing like a horse. It had a body similar to a common deer, but its hair was longer, and its antlers curved around its head like a helm. A white streak ran down its spine onto its tail. Vidmar couldn't decide if it was frightening or pleasing to look at. It wasn't trying to attack him now, so he settled for pleasant. *How long have I been out?* Vidmar thought. He scratched his chin; his beard hadn't grown much, but he felt like he had been asleep for a month. Then he remembered Kamet.

It had been years since he'd lost anyone he truly cared about. Not since he abandoned Elisa to her evil, selfish brother, though she was still alive, at least to Vidmar's knowledge. He felt empty without Kamet; they had always been there for each other. Even when they pretended to be enemies, Vidmar knew Kamet would be by his side when he needed him. Now, he had no one. *Maybe that's what I deserve.*

He sheathed his blade, pushed himself to his knees, and watched the strange creature stomp its hooves as if annoyed. "What?" Vidmar said after it nudged him with its wet black nose for a second time. It let out a weak whine and urged Vidmar again.

He heard a strange cackling noise outside the glade. The deer paced around the clearing as if checking for signs of danger. It poked Vidmar again. "You want me to stand up?" Vidmar said. His tender muscles throbbed as he pushed himself onto his feet. The creature stopped pacing.

He heard another cackle through the trees, this time to his right but much louder. "What is it?" he asked the deer, hoping it could respond. The commotion grew louder. Vidmar saw shapes moving behind the branches and leaves surrounding him. Suddenly, the deer darted away, leaping over the rubble that used to be the cave's entrance. *Alone again,* Vidmar thought, returning his attention to the shapes.

Three shadow figures floated between the trees. Two more shadows joined the assailants in front of him. *Think, Vidmar.* He had no idea how to evade these creatures, let alone kill them. They had barely escaped when one attacked, but five, now seven. They seemed to multiply at will. As he evaluated the potential of his escape, the deer crept into his vision on top of the rubble. It stomped as if it were trying to communicate something. "What?" Vidmar screamed.

The shadows closed in.

The deer kicked dirt into the air as it sprang down the other side of the rocks. Vidmar followed; he didn't have any other options. He could feel the shadows chasing him. They didn't breathe or talk but made a haunting, hissing, laughing sound. More creatures blackened the edges of his vision. He crested the top of the rubble, searching for the deer, but it had disappeared. Vidmar turned to see an army of shadows charging toward him. One black cloud hand reached for him. Its icy fingertips stung Vidmar's spine before he slid down the muddy hill. He somersaulted before crashing into a tree. Pain coursed through his shoulder. He felt it pop out of its socket. Vidmar winced as he tried to move it back in place, but he didn't have the strength. Grunting, he forced himself to stand. The deer was gone. *Fuck.* Shadows surrounded him. The army shifted atop the hill as more shadows crept from the trees. Their laughing deepened.

Vidmar grabbed a throwing knife with his left hand, adjusted his grip, and balanced it as best as possible in his only functioning arm. A shadow charged from his right. Vidmar threw the blade. It found its mark, spinning through what he had assumed was the creature's head. The shadow separated momentarily but then sewed itself back together. The shadows closed in collectively, laughing as they carried their icy darkness. Vidmar threw another knife; it also found the mark, but again, the creature mended itself without stopping. The air around him froze. Vidmar could no longer see the trees, only growing shadows. He had two knives left; he couldn't afford to throw another. He bent down, grabbed a handful of mud and grass, and flung it at the shadows, hoping that something could hurt them. They shrieked collectively as the grass sizzled through them. They paused, and Vidmar darted to an opening on his right.

He jumped between two trees. A cramp tore at his left side, and his breath stung his throat, but Vidmar pressed forward. He ducked under a low-hanging branch. The creatures cackled behind him; they sounded close, but Vidmar refused to look back. The ground was slick and muddy. He dreaded falling; a mistake meant death. Each step was carefully placed until a deafening shriek caused him to lose concentration and trip over a root directly on his injured shoulder. *I'm dead.*

Hot knives stabbed his entire right side. He tasted blood as he crawled onto his feet. Then, a shadow grabbed Vidmar's calf. His whole leg froze from the icy touch. The creature's laughing muddled his mind; he couldn't think. Desperately, he grabbed a dead branch off the ground and swung it at the shadow. It connected. The creature screamed as it released its grasp. Feeling slowly came back into Vidmar's legs. The other shadows stopped cackling and appeared to observe their comrade. Collectively, they hissed. Vidmar thought he saw red eyes open on the one he struck, but he didn't let his gaze linger. He pushed himself onto his feet and started running.

Vidmar's legs burned with each step. He scoured the forest for sunlight, thinning trees, a pathway, anything that signaled the edge. The shadows closed in. Vidmar quickly spun, swinging the branch with desperate ferocity. The creatures backed away, hissing like scared cats. To his left, a small window of light appeared. *Thank the gods*, Vidmar thought, planting a foot in the mud and charging toward the light. The shadows' cackling lowered into a beastly growl. Still, Vidmar ran as fast as his legs would carry him. The light brightened, and the window widened. Vidmar screamed and jumped through the white opening. He landed softly in the high fescue outside the Kokor Forest.

Pollen fell from his tattered clothing as he pushed himself to his feet. He looked over his low-hanging, dislocated shoulder and saw the shadows looming on the other side of his escape window. The creature in the center of the pack opened its eyes. Two fiery ovals of red stared at Vidmar. The look alone sent shivers down his spine, but somehow, he managed to smile and turn the other way. The sight of open land in front of him gave him more joy than finding the crown. It had never been *his* quest anyway. He brushed himself off, found his bearings, and forced his aching body to move through the tall grass. Vidmar didn't need glory or recognition.

What do I do now? Vidmar thought as he approached the road. Almost every answer he had led back to Hobb's farm. The only answer that didn't was Elisa, and he didn't have the physical or emotional strength to face her, not yet.

A merchant strolled down the road, whistling a tune. He jumped back when he saw Vidmar and moved to the other side of the road before picking up his pace. Vidmar smiled. He took an inventory of his possessions. He still held the stick that kept the shadows at bay. He had two knives. His waterskin was still attached to his belt, but it was empty. In his right pocket, he found two Kan. In his left, he found the stone from under Greco's crown.

Vidmar looked at it briefly, then carefully tucked it away. He had forgotten about the stone, but it answered his question. Besides, he had a promise to keep.

A PUPPET'S STORY

Vatis

The rope on Vatis's wrist burnt his tender skin. It had been a long, uncomfortable journey to Haran. Hogtied in the back of Emre's ricketiest wagon, Vatis's lips were chapped and crusted with dried blood. His eyes were nearly swollen shut, and he feared his nose was now more jagged than the Cemil River. Vatis couldn't see much in Alcin's underground hideout. He only knew they were there because of the unmistakable smokey aroma burnt into his memory. He scooted across the stone floor with his ankles tied together; someone kicked him, his kidneys taking most of the damage. He could only see two pairs of boots, one under a table, the other to his right.

The rhythmic commotion in the hideout ended abruptly.

"Zidane," Alcin's diabolical voice said. His feet crossed under the table. "I didn't think we'd see you so soon without a certain crippled treasure hunter. What's that?"

The boots to his right shuffled. "That is our ticket to finding Vidmar – Vatis, or Dainius, whatever he calls himself these days," a high-pitched voice said. He wasn't sure if the voice belonged to the boots to his right, but as they came into focus with their ornate purple laces, Vatis realized it was Zidane. Vatis's breath fogged the cold stone floor.

"Who?" Alcin asked, uncrossing his feet and picking his heels off the floor.

Vatis was lifted off the ground by his binding. The rope seared deeper into his skin.

"Vatis, the bard that had been traveling with Vidmar," Zidane said, stepping to the side and gesturing over Vatis like a merchant selling a rug.

The table skidded into Vatis's thighs as Alcin stood to inspect him. "So it is," he said, sitting back down. "I didn't recognize him with all the bruises. You should treat your companions better, Zidane."

"It was the cart that did most of the damage, but I'll take credit for that hideously crooked hole he calls a nose," Zidane said. Vatis could feel Zidane's club pummel him outside Bridgeway. *I should never have left the bar.* He'd done some stupid things in his life, but that might have been the dumbest so far.

Vatis had grown overconfident and reckless and didn't think Zidane, with no guards, posed a threat. He was wrong. Even with a head start in the cover of night, Zidane caught him quickly. Vatis barely made it a mile down the road before the eccentric bandit chased him down. Zidane was much quicker and stronger than he anticipated. After numerous strikes from some sort of club, Vatis gave up. A few hours later, he woke up with his hands tied behind his back as he was being dragged, face-down, across the road.

"And the men call you weak," Alcin said. Vatis detected a hint of sarcasm in his voice. He felt a small smile creep onto his face, despite knowing this was most likely his last night on

Emre. *At least my curse will go to one of these degenerates,* Vatis hoped, though he wasn't entirely sure how the curse found a new host when and if he died. *Does it matter?*

"I suppose you're expecting a reward?" Alcin finished.

Whoever held Vatis up released their grip, and he crashed onto the floor. His head bounced with a hollow thud next to Zidane's boots. Vatis wasn't sure if it was from another blow to the head or if Zidane was nervous, but his shins trembled like he was standing barefoot in the snow. "Well," Zidane started. The shaking intensified. "I wouldn't object."

"Why do they all want rewards, Tycar? What happened to being pleased with a job well done? Fine, if you want a reward–a reward you shall have."

Zidane's legs stopped shaking. Vatis rolled onto his back to see Zidane's face, but he was kicked in the gut as soon as he glanced at the bandit's sinister smile.

"You may live," Alcin said plainly.

Zidane's legs quivered so rapidly that his heels tapped against the floor. "Alcin, Sir, I," Zidane stuttered.

"As a man from the slums of Haran, I thought you would seize whatever opportunity I gave you. But maybe I'm wrong to give you this chance. You may live and continue your task of finding Vidmar. Bringing me some worthless bard does not erase the debt you owe me," Alcin said. Vatis could feel the weight of the threat from beneath the table. Zidane's feet inched together as he rubbed the back of his calf with the opposite foot like a shy child.

"Sir," Zidane's voice cracked.

Alcin slammed something on the table. The wooden legs rattled against the floor. "Find Vidmar or find whichever god you worship."

"Yes, sir. I will not fail you," Zidane said softly.

"Good," Alcin said. "Now, do me a favor before you leave. Drop the bard in my study. I'd like to have a few words with him."

Zidane yanked Vatis to his feet. "Yes, sir."

Alcin stood from his table. "Do not disappoint me again."

Vatis watched Alcin limp toward the bar as one of Zidane's men dragged him through the parlor to an all-too-familiar room. The heavy door creaked open, and they threw Vatis into the desk. Blood stained the gray stone floor. He wondered if that was Vidmar's blood or if it belonged to a collection of unfortunate associates of Alcin. He wondered if his blood would be added to the cluster of stains.

"Let's see you talk your way out of this," Zidane said with much more confidence than he had in front of Alcin.

Vatis moaned as he rolled to face Zidane. "Something tells me your story will end more tragically than mine," Vatis said, spitting out blood.

Zidane laughed. "Something tells me that your story will end *sooner.*"

"I hope that you're wrong."

Zidane furrowed his eyebrows, adjusted his hat, and scratched the black stubble on his chin. "We will see. Have fun, Vatis," Zidane's laughter penetrated the iron door that slammed shut behind him. *We will see,* Vatis thought.

"Get up," an unfamiliar voice said.

Vatis only replied with a moan, shaking his long bangs out of his eyes.

"I said get up," the voice said. Vatis struggled to crawl onto his knees. The new guard was shorter and thinner than the brutes usually accompanying Alcin. He looked like Vidmar with longer hair. *It can't be,* Vatis thought. The guard deftly cut his bonds with a knife. *It can't be.* As he cut Vatis's feet free, he noticed the guard had all ten fingers. His moment of relief dissipated instantly, followed by a feeling of regret that he would never be able to know how the treasure hunter's story ended. *I wish I were there to see more of your story, Vidmar.*

"On your feet," the Vidmar-looking guard said, cutting the last of his bonds.

The air stung his chafed skin, hurting worse than when Vatis was tied up. "Thank you," he hissed through the pain.

"Don't thank me yet," the guard said almost sympathetically before knocking twice on the door.

A few seconds later, Alcin limped in, followed by two more guards. He sat down at the desk opposite Vatis. The guard Vatis was pretty sure was called Tycar threw his pack onto the desk.

Vatis wanted to call out. *My stories.* Everything he had was in that pack; somehow, he restrained himself.

Alcin tore through the two small compartments on the front of the bag, pulling out a small coin purse and the invitation to the King's Tourney.

"I guess congratulations are in order," Alcin said. "Though my sources told me Feya couldn't lose."

Vatis wasn't sure how to answer, but he was confident that Alcin knew Feya had died. "The organizer found me the day after the tourney and awarded me with an invitation." There was no need to divulge all the details. The half-truth seemed plausible enough.

"We aren't going to get very far if you're going to lie to me, Vatis," Alcin said, skimming through Vatis's copy of *The Lost Forest.*

Vatis's throat tightened, making breathing extremely difficult. "The crowd hated me," he admitted. "I didn't receive applause. Instead, they awarded me with fruit, stones, and bruises. But the organizer was a man of the arts; he appreciated my story. Unfortunately, Feya died tragically the night of the tourney. The next morning, the organizer found me and handed me the invitation. I don't know how she died, but he wished me better luck in a city that doesn't hate foreigners."

Alcin clapped. "Was that so hard?"

Vatis shook his head.

"Now, for the rest of our," Alcin paused. "Meeting ... I'd like complete honesty. I want every *single* detail. If you shit in the evening instead of the morning, I want to know. Do you understand?"

Vatis nodded again.

Alcin closed the book. "Good. Let's begin."

Vatis tasted blood. He sucked the thick metallic liquid through the cracks in his teeth, realizing he had lost a tooth somewhere between Bridgeway and Haran.

"Where's Vidmar?" Alcin asked.

Vatis coughed on his blood, spitting specs onto his dirt-covered pants. He looked up. "We parted ways in Vicus."

Alcin's smirk quickly faded into a scowl as he rubbed his eyes. "I assume you know what he's hunting?"

"Yes, the crown of Slavanes Greco. The crown of the true king of Emre."

Alcin looked satisfied. "Why did you part ways?"

"I wanted to go to Barna, and he was trying to decipher a new clue," Vatis said.

Alcin moved his fingers to his temples, pulling his eyes into narrow slits before he pounded the table with both fists. "He found another clue. Where? What is it?"

Vatis forced himself to take a deep breath. "It wasn't so much a new clue as it was a new lead that could translate an old clue."

"I knew that shopkeeper in Yimser was useless," Alcin grunted. "Continue."

"Yes. The shopkeeper didn't help much, but he found a man in Vicus who could help him."

For the first time since Vatis had met him, Alcin looked confused. "A man from *Vicus*. Who?"

What do I say now? Vatis had no love for Hobb, but he didn't want to bring an army to his doorstep. *What if Vidmar is still there? What about Mia?*

"Who," Alcin yelled. His guards stepped closer.

"Hobb," Vatis said, the name spilling out under pressure.

"Hobb," Alcin mimicked, trying to place the name.

Vatis swallowed, still tasting blood on his gums as his tongue played with the hole left by his missing tooth. "Hobbill, he goes by Hobb. He has a farm on the northeastern edge of town."

Alcin ran a fingernail along a ridge in the wooden table. "Why would a farmer know anything about the greatest treasure in the history of Emre?"

Vatis knew he had to be careful here. He didn't know what Alcin would do if he knew how powerful Hobb was. What would be believable? Suddenly, his face smashed into the table. He felt the hole in his gum widen as more blood gushed down his throat. Dark clouds crept onto the edge of his vision, but, unfortunately, he didn't pass out. He felt the guard behind him punch his kidney. The pain was worse than having his head thrown against the table. His foot slipped, and he tumbled onto the floor. Vatis no longer wondered if his blood would join Vidmar's amongst the crimson stains.

"I told you I want honesty, and I want it quickly. I will not wait here while you conjure up some story in that simple mind of yours," Alcin said. "Pick him up."

The room spun as one of the guards threw Vatis back into the chair.

"Now, I'll ask again, why does a farmer know anything about the crown of Slavanes Greco?"

Vatis coughed. Blood splattered onto the desk. "He's more than a farmer," Vatis said weakly.

"Get this fool some ale. I can't understand him," Alcin said. One of the guards handed Vatis a flask. It was potent but smelled sweet, too, like apples on a fall day. Vatis coughed the first sip down. The alcohol felt like bees stinging his mouth as he swallowed, but he kept drinking. He needed something to numb the pain. The subsequent sips warmed his belly pleasantly.

"Thank you," Vatis said, wiping his mouth.

Alcin glared at Vatis. "Now, who is Hobb?"

Vatis had to answer. If he lost any more teeth, no crowd would respect him. "Hobbill or Hobb runs the farm on the northeastern edge of Vicus, but he's more than that," Vatis paused, trying to think of what to say next. A quick-moving guard ended his thinking sooner than he would have liked. "He's a member of The Pact. He calls himself a guardian."

The joints in Alcin's neck cracked as he rolled his head around his shoulders. "I told you I didn't want a story." Alcin nodded ever-so-slightly. A fist to Vatis's other kidney followed the nod. Vatis wanted to collapse onto the floor and curl into a ball, but the guard held him by the collar to keep him from falling. The rough homespun choked him as he tried to balance himself. "Hobbill of Vicus is much more than a farmer. He is one of the last remaining members of The Pact. He protects their secrets."

"Give him another drink," Alcin said.

The ale was not easy to swallow, but Vatis got more down. His throat burnt as stomach acid, ale, and blood forced their way back into his mouth. Vomit covered the gray floor.

"Gods," Alcin said, sliding backward in his chair. Vatis couldn't see what was happening as he continued to get sick, but he could vaguely hear shuffling behind him. Then, a freezing bucket of water splashed over him, trailing down his spine into his pants. A guard forced Vatis to lift his head. "The Pact disappeared centuries ago. How did Vidmar discover this *guardian*?"

Vatis tried to speak through his convulsions and shivers, but only a croaking sound came out. A guard grabbed his collar roughly.

"Give him a moment," Alcin said.

Vatis wiped a combination of water, ale, blood, and vomit off his face. "Thank you," he whispered. Each word felt like a knife in his throat. Vatis let the blades continue their butchery as he worked through a new story. "We had a revelation after Yimser. The shopkeeper confirmed that Vidmar's stone contained The Pact's symbols. I remembered seeing similar symbols inside a tower near Hobb's farm and on the cane he used. We thought through all the possibilities and returned to Vicus. I was there when Hobb revealed his identity, but I don't know more. Vidmar and I had an *altercation* about where to go next. It escalated, and he forced me to leave. So, I made my way toward Barna for the tourney." It was the best performance he could muster under the circumstances. Vatis tried to swallow saliva to ease the fire at the back of his mouth.

Alcin didn't look at Vatis. Instead, he stood and washed his hands in a basin at the back of the room. "A member of The Pact in Vicus, this all sounds like tales from a children's story, but fortunately, I believe you. You are a fantastic performer; however, I have another question. Why should I let you live?"

The guard lifted Vatis from the chair and slammed him on the desk. Alcin returned from the basin with a black dagger in hand. "No, please. I'll do anything," Vatis said, struggling beneath the guard's grip. The chandelier cast haunting shadows on the walls as Alcin stepped closer.

"That's your best effort? I thought we'd get a better plea from a bard," Alcin said, smiling. "Though there might be worse fates than death for you." Alcin licked his lips.

Vatis realized what Alcin meant. He meant to cut out his tongue, his livelihood, the only thing that separated him from a homeless wanderer, the only thing that kept him sane. If he couldn't tell stories, there was no point in living. Sure, he could write them, but only a fourth of the population knew how to read. His stories would be lost in dusty libraries. *Just kill me.* Alcin stepped closer with his glistening dagger. Vatis's whole body convulsed. He tried to speak; words wouldn't form in his aching throat.

A voice in his head whispered to him. "Vatis," it hissed. "Death offers no rest. Use your gift; give him what he wants most." It was the voice from Hobb's Tower, the Kokor Forest, and the Emerald Isles, the voice he thought he'd beaten. It was the voice of the only unoriginal character inside him—the voice of his curse. Vatis struggled against Tycar's grip, but the guard was formidable. Darkness crept into the edge of his vision; he tried to escape the encroaching abyss, but he couldn't. He wasn't strong enough. Vatis gave in to his captor, the voice in his head, and his curse.

"Let me tell your story," Vatis mumbled as Alcin pressed the dagger onto his tongue.

Alcin pulled back.

Vatis exhaled. "Let me tell *your* story—the story of Alcin, the people's champion. I could make you a hero known throughout Emre. I can make you more than a whisper on the tongues of thieves. By the new moon, you'd be on the mind of half the world. By year's end, the people would beg for their hero to take power. Let me tell the story of Alcin – the story of Emre's salvation."

Alcin placed the dagger on the table. "Now, that is a plea worthy of consideration." He nodded and smirked as he paced back and forth.

"I could tell your story at the King's Tourney. I could put fear in the heart of your biggest rival. Alcin, you have a story that *needs* to be told. I beg you to let me tell it. My words could garner more support than a lost crown ever would," Vatis said, letting the cursed character take more control.

"Let him up, Tycar," Alcin said. "We have a lot to discuss."

Vatis sat up; a smile slithered onto his lips. He clenched his fists to stop his disobeying extremities. Vatis-of-the-Road, Dainius, and others screamed in the back of his mind. The curse pushed them away, close to obscurity. A new voice hissed through his teeth. "Where should we begin?"

ACKNOWLEDGEMENTS

I can't believe it. Tales & Treasure is published. It took over five years to get here–five grueling, incredible, painful, fantastic years. This never would have been possible without a bunch of people who mean the world to me.

Remy, Mason, and Charlie, you're the reason I keep going.

Lindsey, I shouldn't have kept my secret project secret for so long, but thank you for being my partner and best friend and for your incredible support. I love you.

Of course, thank you Mom and Dad. Mom your encouragement and support has never wavered. Dad thank you for introducing me to Lord of the Ring and other fantastical worlds; we probably wouldn't be here if you didn't let a 10-year-old tag along with you and your friends to the theater.

Thank you to the Substack community for reading and sharing each chapter of my story.

I can't forget about my beta readers who helped make this story, well, a story. Thank you, Ryan, Aditya, MV, Luna, and Tyler; Tales & Treasure would be stuck on a flash drive in my backpack if it weren't for your feedback and encouragement.

Time to write the next story.

MORE STORIES

Milton Keynes UK
Ingram Content Group UK Ltd.
UKHW042339121024
449589UK00001B/73